"LOUISA?"

"Yes," she said. She didn't know if she was responding to her name, or giving him permission.

She was Lady Irving's niece, wasn't she? She didn't need to grant permission for him to take what he wanted. *She* could take what *she* wanted.

So she chose to reach for his hand. She chose to intertwine her gloved fingers in his. She watched as his eyes widened, as his other hand dropped its weight of mistletoe and reached for hers. His expression was like that of Michelangelo's *David*: wary, coiled, determined.

The failing light made him look ruthless, slicing every slope of his face into a sharp angle of shadow. Surely such a man would allow nothing to be taken from him that he did not wish to give.

She wanted to kiss him, to give this gift to herself. Boldness. Pleasure for its own sake.

Books by Theresa Romain

Season for Temptation

Season for Surrender

Published by Kensington Publishing Corporation

SEASON *for* SURRENDER

THERESA ROMAIN

ZEBRA BOOKS
KENSINGTON PUBLISHING CORP.
http://www.kensingtonbooks.com

ZEBRA BOOKS are published by

Kensington Publishing Corp.
119 West 40th Street
New York, NY 10018

All Kensington titles, imprints, and distributed lines are
available at special quantity discounts for bulk purchases for
sales promotion, premiums, fund-raising, educational, or
institutional use.

Special book excerpts or customized printings can also be
created to fit specific needs. For details, write or phone the
office of the Kensington Special Sales Manager: Attn. Special
Sales Department. Kensington Publishing Corp., 119 West
40th Street, New York, NY 10018. Phone: 1-800-221-2647.

Zebra and the Z logo Reg. U.S. Pat. & TM Off.

ISBN-13: 978-1-4201-2886-4
ISBN-10: 1-4201-2886-8

First Printing: October 2012

10 9 8 7 6 5 4 3 2 1

Printed in the United States of America

ACKNOWLEDGMENTS

Above all, thanks to my husband for his infinite patience as our family entered the new world of "writing to deadline."

Many thanks to my agent, Paige Wheeler, who is both honest and encouraging, and my editor, Alicia Condon, whose enthusiasm inspires me. And to Amanda, beta reader extraordinaire, and my ever-supportive family and friends.

Over the past year, I've had the honor of meeting many romance authors, bloggers, and readers online. The romance community loves books and loves love—and knows that books about love are the best imaginable. It has been a pleasure to laugh with and learn from these wonderful people.

Last and certainly not least, thanks to my readers. Many of you who read my debut, SEASON FOR TEMPTATION, wanted Louisa to get her own happily-ever-after. I'm so glad to share her story with you.

Chapter 1

Containing
Several Damned Nuisances

December 1, 1818
London

A man determined to play a role in polite society must accept the fact that he can never take a day's rest from it. And Alexander Edgware, the ninth Earl of Xavier, had played a leading role among the *haut ton* for years.

Today, though, he had a rheumy cold. To one known more for sin than sickness, this was an irritating development.

He'd greeted the day with bloodshot eyes, his head uncomfortably full and sensitive to sound and light. When the day greeted him in return with the inevitable gray drizzle of early winter, he decided to bypass the bow window of White's—his habitual seat of prominence—for the quieter warmth of the coffee room on the club's first floor.

As he sat in a leather wing chair before the marble fireplace, toying with a snifter of brandy, Xavier's feeling of well-being began to return. White's was a bell jar of wealth and influence, a haven of dark wood and costly carpets, attentive waiters, and fires built high enough to banish the wintry chill entirely.

Oh yes. And White's had the famed betting book. Sometimes he thought his life centered on that fat, worn leather folio. Which was all right with him, for there centered society.

He turned a page of his newspaper and scanned the column of *on-dit*s through his quizzing glass. More gossip surrounding the recent death of the queen. Her many children couldn't stop squabbling, even with grief to unite them. Xavier was not displeased that he was unblessed— or uncursed—by siblings.

He skimmed over the accounts of royal misbehavior and found the next item. He could guess the identity of Lady S——; the Viscountess Shelton had recently been found in a state of undress with two footmen and a maid. Rather ambitious of her.

Ha. Here was another tidbit of scandal he understood.

Lord L—— has parted with his ladybird under mysterious circumstances. The unfortunate female must have failed to give pleasure . . . or failed to give pain?

"It was the pleasure, of course," said a voice at Xavier's shoulder. A moment later, his distant cousin, the Marquess of Lockwood, dropped into the leather armchair next to Xavier's. "Damned nuisance, keeping a mistress."

Xavier folded his newspaper and regarded his cousin. They bore the same dark hair and olive-toned complexions, thanks to a shared Italian ancestor. Lockwood's eyes were pale blue to Xavier's gray, though, and just now the marquess wore a smug smile that Xavier would have considered beneath his own dignity.

"You look very pleased with yourself," Xavier remarked.

"Damned nuisance, being mentioned in the scandal sheets." Lockwood preened.

Xavier couldn't resist. "Quite a tragic day for you, if everything has become a damned nuisance. Well, don't trouble yourself, Lockwood. I believe Lord Lowbrough recently turned off his mistress, too, and likely everyone will assume the item refers to him."

Lockwood's grin fell. Brows knit, he snapped for a waiter. "Coffee. Sugar with it." He noted Xavier's snifter and added, "A brandy, too."

The marquess settled back in his chair and slung a booted foot across his other knee. "I'm better off quit of her. A man of the world has no need to buy such an arrangement, eh?"

"It depends on the tastes of the man," Xavier replied. "I always thought Melissande an elegant sort for a mistress, though her pug was grotesque. At my last year's house party, it soiled half the carpets in the east wing."

Lockwood raised his eyebrows. "How foul. Though it might as easily have been the woman as the dog, for she wasn't as elegant as you presume. I assure you, I'm through with her."

He took his brandy and coffee from the waiter and drained the snifter in one swallow. "Ah. That's the thing for an abysmal day like today."

He set the coffee cup down on a spindly table next to his chair, then shot a look at Xavier. "I say, Coz, you look as though you'd got the devil of a head. Late night?"

Xavier blinked, then realized: his reddened eyes could just as well be a legacy of drink as his cold. He seized the excuse, offering his most maddeningly secretive expression. "I'm not one to tell what I've been up to."

"No, the scandal sheets are eager enough to do that for you. Where were you last night? Didn't see you out on the Town."

Probably because he'd plummeted into bed before midnight. This cold had made him miserable all out of proportion to its severity.

"It wasn't one of the usual places," Xavier said with a slow, curling smile. "It was a private encounter."

Very private. Involving only himself and a headache powder.

Lockwood slapped his knee, bumping the spindly table with his boot. His coffee cup rattled a warning in its saucer. "Private, was it? Who was she?"

Xavier grinned, the sudden flash of mischief that made women swoon and call him wicked. "What makes you think there was a woman involved? Perhaps I simply stayed home and turned in early with a good book."

Lockwood hooted. "If you've read anything besides the *on-dit*s lately, I'll eat one of your boots."

"If you so much as touch one, you'll find it planted in your arse."

Lockwood laughed again, as he was meant to. Ah, the ever entertaining role of Xavier: parrying, puckishness, and a touch of profanity.

The role certainly did not include any pastime so quiet as reading. So he didn't mention that, as a matter of fact, he'd read a little Dante before his bleary eyes closed the night before. He'd never claimed to be a scholar, but he had a knack for languages and a fondness for poetry.

He slid his feet closer to the fire, allowing its warmth to saturate the thick leather of his boots, then turned the subject. "We must set our wager soon for my house party,

Lockwood, since it's less than three weeks away. We can enter it in the betting book before we leave."

Surely half of the White's betting book was filled with wagers between Xavier and Lockwood. The last had been only two days ago, when they'd bet two bottles of Armagnac brandy on who could drink his bottle quicker.

Xavier had won. Xavier always won. It was part of being Xavier. And when he had to go to the washroom soon afterward and cast up his accounts, no one noticed, because he talked his way into the wine cellar and returned with a bottle of still better brandy, which he shared among all the spectators to the bet.

That was part of being Xavier, too.

"I was thinking," he said, "of something to do with that opera singer. Signora . . . what is it? Frittarelli?"

"Frittata," Lockwood snorted, and snapped his fingers for another brandy.

"Fondant."

"Fellatio." The snort became a guffaw.

Xavier raised his eyebrows. "Language, language. You can only hope." He grinned to remove the sting. "I do think it's Frittarelli. She's singing tonight at Lady Alleyneham's musicale."

"I've heard she's quite a prime piece. I'll go and get a look at her. Will you come?"

Xavier didn't have to feign his shudder. "God, no. I'd rather have my fingers chewed off by a dog." His aching head couldn't bear a crowded room, a musical cacophony. Not today.

"No need for mutilation. I'll go alone and check out the wares." Lockwood raised his refilled snifter and inhaled deeply. "I've got a taste for that Grande Champagne brandy you ferreted out a few days ago. Excellent. Makes the Armagnac taste like horse piss."

Xavier regarded his own snifter of Armagnac. "It does well enough for everyday. But you're celebrating your freedom from your pug-loving mistress, aren't you? You ought to have the finest *cru* today. Let me stand you the bottle."

"Much appreciated, Coz. Indeed. I'll have another." Lockwood's eyes were a bit red-rimmed, and Xavier wondered if he was as pleased to be free of Melissande as he professed.

The parting of ways could have been due to lack of funds, not lack of pleasure. Xavier and Lockwood had grown up together, the last remnants of two illustrious titles. But where Xavier's had grown richer over the passing generations, the Lockwood marquessate's fortunes had dwindled.

The mistress's departure, whatever the reason, provided an excuse for Xavier to bear the cost of Lockwood's brandy. When the two men wagered, they never staked more than a token sum. As often as they bet against one another, Lockwood would have been ruined otherwise.

"The wager, then, now that you're fortified," Xavier said. "If not *la signora*, would you care for a match race? I've a new gelding that's at least as fast as your Tarantella."

"Not fast enough," Lockwood said with a slight hiccup. "The wager, I mean, not the horse. No, much better to bet on the party itself, if it's to be the usual sort of raucous affair."

"I'm not inviting Prinny again, if that's what you have in mind." The dissolute Prince Regent had ruined as many carpets as Melissande's pug the previous year.

"No no." Lockwood batted the suggestion away like a cobweb, wobbling in his chair. "It's no kind of a challenge to get Prinny to a house party, and a challenge is what we want." He rotated his snifter slowly, then rapped it down onto the table at his side. "I have the very thing. I'll wager that you can't get a respectable young woman to attend. Ten pounds on it."

Xavier never declined a bet, but that didn't mean he never remolded it to suit his preference. He shook his head. "I won't risk an unmarried lady's reputation, Lockwood. Much better that we bet on *la signora* or someone of her kind."

"But we need a *challenge*. Naturally, the young woman would be permitted a chaperone."

"No, it won't do." Xavier stared down the length of his stretched-out legs. The sheen on his boots was mirror bright despite the drizzle and puddles outside. He had to watch his every step in order to keep them looking just so.

Lockwood tried again. "Your house party's always a roosting place for the birds of paradise with no place to go for Christmas. Just give it a festive air to appeal to the sparrows, too. Mistletoe in the corners, punch every night— revelry will be expected. If you're as charming as all the world says, you should have no trouble in persuading a respectable young lady to attend."

Xavier adopted Expression Number Three, Amused Tolerance. "You said it, Lockwood, not I. I've never professed many virtues."

"The best way to gain virtue," Lockwood replied with his own attempt at Expression Number Three, "is to employ your well-tried methods of seduction. Yes?"

"I'll hardly gain virtue for myself by stealing it from a young lady," Xavier said smoothly. "Though as I said, I have no high aspirations for myself in that area."

"No debauchery need be involved. All you need do is invite the young lady. If she attends, and stays for the full two weeks, then you win the bet. All very proper." Lockwood smirked. "Unless the lady proves otherwise."

Xavier mirrored Lockwood's smirk but hesitated. His

annual house party wasn't exactly the type of party a young lady of quality ought to attend. And he'd never wagered on anyone's reputation but his own.

At his hesitation, the marquess pounced. "If you're afraid you can't do it, you could forfeit the bet. Here, I'll enter the wager in the betting book, and then we'll forget the whole thing."

He held out his hand. "Ten pounds on it?" His expression was guileless, but his eyes were not.

Xavier's fingers flexed, and he clenched them into a fist.

He couldn't decline the bet. He had a reputation to uphold: this creation, Lord Xavier, whose exploits were as much figments of others' imaginations as they were of his own doing. One of Lord Xavier's best-known qualities was that he never turned down a wager. And he never lost.

"No tenner for you," he said in his breeziest voice. "Enter the bet, and name the young lady. *N'importe qui.*"

Lockwood's smile turned feral. He motioned for a servant and demanded writing implements and the betting book, a leather-bound affair of seeming ancientness.

He deliberated over the entry, writing down his name and Xavier's first, then the stake of ten pounds. "It wouldn't do to write the lady's name in the book. But I've hit upon the very one, as you've given me the choice. You shall invite Miss Oliver."

The name was a gut-punch.

Xavier dropped his eyelids, slow and sleepy, to cover his surprise. Louisa Oliver. Damnation.

If there was any young lady in London who was certain to decline an invitation from Xavier, it was she—that quiet bluestocking with uncommonly wary eyes. He knew Miss Oliver blamed him for the scandal that had swirled about her sister's engagement earlier that year.

But he couldn't back out now. And he couldn't allow himself to lose.

"Very well; I'll wager that Miss Oliver will be in attendance," he said with an incline of his head. "For the full two weeks."

"Excellent." Lockwood shut the betting book and handed it back to the waiting servant. "This will be amusing, watching you try to behave yourself for two weeks."

"Amusing for others," Xavier muttered.

His mind was tumbling over his memories of the dark-eyed Miss Oliver, who had already gauged and dismissed him. The only woman ever to do so.

She *had* been lovely, though. Lockwood might be right: this house party could be exactly the challenge his life was missing. Xavier had a way of finding pleasure in unexpected situations.

And he'd finish by taking another ten pounds from his cousin. His Christmas gift to himself.

"If you'll excuse me, Lockwood," he said, rising to his feet. "It seems I have some invitations to dispatch." But they wouldn't be the invitations Lockwood expected.

Already, Xavier's head cold seemed less bothersome.

Chapter 2

Containing All the Ingredients for a Scandal Broth

Three weeks later
Surrey

"Brewing a scandal broth is vulgar, my girl," Estella, Lady Irving, commented as her carriage turned onto the long, shaded drive to Clifton Hall. "I won't have it said that I attended for that reason."

Louisa Oliver suppressed a smile. "No one would dare say such a thing of you, Aunt. They would be far too frightened."

Her aunt harrumphed. "It's not as though this house party will match the scandals of past years. Xavier's tidied up the guest list."

"Much to your dismay?"

"To my delight, my girl." She gave Louisa's cheek a pinch. "If it promised to be any more scandalous, I couldn't have brought you along. And if it promised to be any *less* scandalous, there wouldn't have been any point in coming myself."

The countess loved tittle-tattle with a passion that not even a recent family scandal had cooled. She had jumped at the chance to chaperone Louisa to Lord Xavier's house party, certain that it would involve enough intrigue to curl her still-bright auburn hair without the use of tongs.

For the first time in years, Lady Irving traveled without the comfort of her French lady's maid, who had recently married and been allowed a holiday. Thus far, Louisa had observed that this privation had decreased her aunt's never-plentiful patience.

The countess frowned at Louisa. "Not fretting about missing the family Christmas, are you?"

"I'll answer that with the heartiest 'no' you can possibly imagine," Louisa said.

Her aunt shot her a sharp look. "Yes, I suppose you would."

In recent months, "family" had meant Louisa's stepsister, Julia, and brother-in-law James, at whose country house she'd been living. Kind and protective, they hadn't wanted Louisa to accept the unexpected invitation to Lord Xavier's house party. Though Xavier and James had been friends for years, Xavier had handed the shocking news of James's and Julia's first assignation to one of London's tawdriest scandal rags. Terribly unkind of him, though Julia and James had soon married. They enjoyed life in the country and were now expecting their first child.

Whereas Louisa had spent the preceding months cataloguing their library. And as quiet weeks stacked up, she'd catalogued herself along with the books, and she wasn't at all satisfied with the entry:

> *Oliver, the Honorable Louisa Catherine.*
> *Twenty-one years of age. Spinster. Tallish. Dark*
> *hair and eyes. Shy of strangers. Inclined to be*
> *sharp-tongued. Over-fond of books.*

At least she was broad-minded. No one could deny that, considering her family's scandal had involved the end of Louisa's own engagement to James.

As it hadn't been a love match, she hadn't been deeply hurt when James turned instead to Julia. Still, there was no sense in ending the year as a hanger-on to their wedded bliss. At this house party, she hoped to add a few lines to her Louisa catalogue.

> *Got kissed.*
> *Found some interesting new books.*
> *Made peace between James and Xavier and*
> *convinced the polite world of my charm.*
> *Got kissed some more.*

That would be her Christmas gift to herself. With the holiday only four days away, and the New Year approaching, it was time for a change. Past time.

"You're blushing, my girl," Lady Irving said. "Not thinking of something you shouldn't, are you?"

"I'm so pure-minded that I can't imagine what you're talking about," Louisa lied. "It's warm in this carriage, that's all."

"Hmph." Lady Irving darted a sidelong glance at Louisa as their carriage rolled to a halt. "Already thinking about the books, are you?"

"How well you know me, Aunt," Louisa said, though the blush remained on her tattletale cheeks.

When Xavier had sent his invitation, he had offered her

full access to his country house's library. Clifton Hall was known to have a magnificent collection, from incunables to block-printed books, and Xavier had written that he would be honored if Louisa amused herself with it, since he had heard of her valuable work in James's library. As though tugging James's three thousand books into order had been of interest to anyone but Louisa.

Still, she accepted the polite fiction, for it gave her what she needed: an excuse to escape the worried eyes of her sister and brother-in-law. An excuse to leave them alone in their cozy nest for Christmas. An excuse to go somewhere new, if only to a new library.

But she was determined to see more than that.

She accepted a footman's hand and hopped out of the carriage after her aunt. Her feet landed on bright white gravel, and the faint scent of hothouse orchids wafted from a series of pots lining the stately Tudor home's facade. Clifton Hall was a patchwork of gray and brown trimmed stone, tall and wide and ostentatiously battlemented, with back-flung wings of half-timbering and red brick.

Louisa joined her aunt among the swarm of people in front of the Hall. Faces, familiar and strange, eddied around her, and her legs wobbled as she recognized gentlemen of the *haut ton* who had been witness to her disastrous London season, her engagement-that-wasn't.

There was Lord Lockwood, some sort of cousin of Xavier's; a dark-haired man with a wolfish grin. Lord Kirkpatrick, a Byronic-looking baron who was inclined to toss himself into swooning but brief love affairs. Freddie Pellington, a cherub-faced wastrel whose good humor far outstripped his good sense. Lord Weatherwax, a gentleman in early middle age with hair like candy floss and the loud voice of the constantly inebriated.

A few less reputable sorts were roaming around, too.

Louisa spotted Mrs. Lillian Protheroe, a toothy blond widow who wavered along the edge of propriety. Nearby was an olive-skinned woman whom Louisa recognized as a notable operatic star—and, if rumor was right, the mistress of one of the royal dukes. Though the singer's fur-lined pelisse looked warm, she had unfastened the frogs to display a gown of rich claret-colored velvet, of which very little fabric had been allocated to cover her bosom.

Lady Irving gasped. "I confess I'm shocked," she muttered. "Absolutely shocked."

"I'm sure we needn't consort with anyone improper," Louisa said, though that was exactly what she'd been hoping to do.

Her aunt shot her a withering look. "Don't worry your head about me, young miss. I'll consort with whomever I like. But I'm shocked to see Sylvia Alleyneham here with only two of her daughters." She tutted. "Sense of a sheep, has poor Sylvia. Why stop with two? She's got five daughters to marry off, you know."

"Yes, I know," Louisa said drily. She'd met Lady Alleyneham's endless supply of offspring the previous year. They tended to be more concerned with fashion than friendliness, which hadn't endeared Louisa to them or they to her.

Louisa and her aunt threaded between sculpted topiary across the close-clipped lawn in front of Clifton Hall. Graying grass, dried out and dormant for the winter, crunched underfoot.

Lady Irving waved at her acquaintances as she muttered instructions to Louisa. "Stand up straight. Bite your lips to make them pinker. Nod and smile at the other guests. We are to be spending a lot of time with them over the next two weeks, you know, whether they're matchmakers or light-skirts. *Smile*, girl."

But far from putting Louisa at ease, the familiar faces unsettled her. Surely anyone who'd met her would already have catalogued her, based on her awkward Season: Wallflower. Lacking in conversation. Paltry fortune. A triple failure for a marriageable young woman.

Of course, she wasn't really in attendance as a marriageable young woman. She was here for a new start. She smiled at no one in particular.

"Good God, don't smile like *that*," hissed Lady Irving. "I can see every one of your teeth. You look mentally defective."

A laugh popped from Louisa's mouth before she realized it. "Ah, that's better," said Lady Irving. "You've got a spark in you, for all you try to hide it. Now tug down the bodice of your dress and let's go find our host. This is your chance to catch yourself an earl for Christmas."

They spotted Xavier on the front steps of his home, surveying the chaos on his drive with an expression of bemused tolerance. If Louisa could have translated the expression into words, it would read something like, "Lord, what fools these mortals be."

She trailed after Lady Irving, taking in every detail of her host. He played upon the darkness of his hair and skin, the lightness of his eyes, with crisp white linens, gray waistcoat, black coat. He stood nearly a head taller than Louisa, she knew, and his near-black hair was cropped short, accentuating the clean line of his jaw and the height of his strong cheekbones.

He looked as though he had calculated the effect of his appearance very carefully, and he expected everyone who crossed his path to agree with his conclusion. *Good God, what a sinfully striking man. Let us bow before his majesty. Let us give him whatever he wants.*

Louisa was seized with a sudden, sharp urge to be contrary.

But after her aunt greeted the earl, Louisa scraped a few manners together and offered him a proper curtsy. "I bring you the best wishes of my whole family, Lord Xavier."

The earl's cool eyes brightened at Louisa's words. "Do you really? Are they all well?"

"They are," she replied. "But my sister and brother are unable to travel at this time, as my sister is in a delicate condition."

"I see." He appeared to be reasoning something out. "Naturally, I am delighted for them."

"Xavier," barked Lady Irving, removing the need for Louisa to think of something appropriate to say. "I do hope you'll be behaving yourself."

"No more than is strictly necessary."

"Good man. That's the perfect amount," Lady Irving said. "I trust I can count on you to arrange an interesting card game tonight?"

"If by 'interesting' you mean 'for stakes that are likely to horrify small children and puppies,' then the answer is yes."

The countess nodded her approval. "It wouldn't be worthwhile if we weren't horrifying someone."

"Words to live by, my dear lady." Xavier turned his attention to Louisa. "Do you play cards, Miss Oliver?"

"I do, though I'm hardly the player my aunt is."

"I'm relieved to hear it," Xavier said. "The world would be bankrupted if there were many such players as Lady Irving."

The countess nodded her agreement. "Very true. That's settled, then; we shall all skin each other tonight."

A thump from the drive caught their notice; two footmen had lost their grip on a particularly large trunk. The great wooden affair had split along one corner, and servants swarmed over it like ants assessing damage to their hill.

Xavier turned away, toward the great doors of his home. "Organizing the *beau monde* is more difficult than herding cats, and as little amusing. Despite the tumult on the drive, a fair number of guests have already arrived, and they are taking refreshment in the east parlor. May I show you to it?"

"Please do," said Lady Irving. "Can you manage something a bit stronger than tea, though?"

Their host grinned and extended an arm to each woman. "My lady, I believe I have a brandy exactly the shade of brewed tea. I'll have my man root it out for you."

He turned his head to Louisa. "And you, Miss Oliver?"

"No need for brandy, but after our carriage ride, I'd give my bonnet for a cup of tea."

Xavier studied Louisa's face with elaborate attention. "I've never been one for crimson, though it looks well on you. You'd best keep the bonnet, but I'm sure we can still find you some tea."

Louisa's mouth bent into a small smile, and she allowed her hand to slip into the crook of his arm.

Oh, it was solid. His coat was beautifully cut; even through her gloves, she could tell how fine the dark blue wool was. Beneath it, the form of the man was better still, all solid muscle and long, strong bone.

He flirted with you, Lady Irving mouthed broadly behind Xavier's back. She looked pleased.

Louisa's cheeks heated again as she walked next to him, her aunt now chattering about the Great Brandy Subterfuge she was planning. It was no surprise that Louisa should find Lord Xavier attractive. No one had ever denied his physical appeal. It was also no surprise that he should flirt a bit; in fact, it would be more notable did he *not* flirt with a young woman.

Let us bow before his majesty. Wasn't that what she was expected to feel now?

Ha. Spending time with Lord Xavier was like juggling wax tapers: if one wasn't very careful, one would get burned, or at the very least, wind up with dirtied hands.

Louisa was always very careful. Always had been.

So perhaps it was time she learned to juggle.

"Would you care for lemon in your tea? Or milk?" A young woman bent close to Louisa and added in a softer voice, "Or a splash of brandy, like your aunt?"

At Louisa's side, Lady Irving sat bolt upright with a sniff.

Louisa offered the astute young woman a smile. She was slight, with light brown hair and impish hazel eyes. "Thank you, but I'll leave my tea black. One of our party must remain sober."

"There is such a thing as *too* sober, you know," Lady Irving murmured into Louisa's ear.

They were seated next to one another on a damask-covered rosewood settee of Grecian style. The elegant piece was well suited to the airy room in which a dozen and a half of London's respectable and notorious were now fortifying themselves. The room was papered in the delicate green of a new leaf. Overhead hung a Wedgwood chandelier, its dishes and fonts of black basalt ornamented with graceful figures of the Muses. Evergreen was wound through its metalwork, suffusing the room with a faint, crisp scent.

This carefully tasteful room was, to say the least, not what Louisa had expected in the home of Lord Xavier. Nor was the young woman with the prim pink muslin gown and rebellious face, who had now turned her attention to Lady

Irving. "Do you enjoy an afternoon brandy, then, my lady? I would be pleased to join you in a cupful. I am Miss Tindall. Jane."

Louisa crowded over on the settee to make room. Her aunt harrumphed, and Louisa covered a grin with her teacup, inhaling the bracing aroma. It was warm and fragrant, as if the leaves held the summer sun under which they'd been picked and dried. Surely not even brandy had so much power to soothe.

"Strong spirits are not suitable for unmarried ladies." Lady Irving took a dainty sip.

"Drat," Miss Tindall said. "I am constantly being told that the most entertaining experiences are unsuitable for unmarried ladies. My mother's serving as hostess, you see."

With a crook of her finger, she indicated a round, ruddy-faced woman in a stiff, glazed-cotton gown who sat across the room. As Louisa watched, Mrs. Tindall stuffed an entire ginger biscuit into her mouth and chewed with an expression of transported delight.

"That's how I came to recognize you," Miss Tindall explained. "You are the Countess of Irving and Miss Oliver, yes? I've been poring over Xavier's guest list since he created it, hoping something truly dreadful will happen this year."

She spoke the words with such relish that Louisa smiled. "I'll hazard a guess, Miss Tindall, that you have a liking for Gothic novels."

The young woman shrugged. "I have a liking for anything interesting. For the last three days, I've had the choice of only two activities: sewing or writing letters. Since I cannot embroider without stabbing myself with the needle, I have instead been forced to stab myself with a quill. Lord knows there's been nothing worth writing about so far."

Lady Irving clicked her tongue. "I'll wager there will be plenty to fill your letters before the first week's out."

"Do you think so?" The slight young woman perked up visibly.

"I've been told there will be cards tonight," Louisa offered.

"Oh." Miss Tindall's shoulders sank again. "I hate playing cards with Xavier. He is so repulsively competent."

Before either Louisa or her aunt could respond to this puzzling statement, the man himself stood before them. "Jane, you rapscallion. I should have you locked in the dungeon."

Louisa blinked, surprised, but the subject of his threat only raised a contemptuous eyebrow. "You don't have a dungeon. Empty threats will avail you nothing, Xavier."

He cocked his head at Louisa. "Miss Oliver. I'm glad you have met Miss Tindall. I'd like to ask you to serve as a steadying influence on my cousin, though that would be unfairly burdensome to one of my guests."

"Second cousin once removed," added Miss Tindall. "You shouldn't assume I wish to own you as a closer relative. Especially not of my own generation, because you are much older than I."

Xavier grimaced. "There is only eight years' difference in our ages," he explained. "However, it is enough that I did help teach Jane to walk. She was remarkably backward. I believe she was three years old before she could cross a room without falling down."

"That's a shameful lie," Jane said calmly to Louisa. "He loves to tell people that I took forever to learn to walk. What he doesn't tell them is that it was because he broke my leg."

"Pure accident," Xavier sallied, and Louisa had the feeling they had had this conversation many times before.

"How was I to know you would try to follow me up the apple tree after you had been forbidden?"

Jane rolled her eyes. "It has been nearly two decades, yet the lies continue. He is my only cousin, which is why I tolerate this nonsense." She flicked a hand airily. "I am a positive slave to my own better nature."

Louisa grinned at her new acquaintance. "Don't worry yourself, Miss Tindall. Ancient history matters little to the *ton*; it's fresh blood they love."

Miss Tindall smiled back. "How marvelous. You simply must call me Jane."

Lady Irving smothered a hiccup. "And you must call me in time for dinner, Xavier. Very good *tea*, young fellow. But now I find myself in need of a rest."

"Of course, my lady." Xavier assisted the countess to her feet. "You'd best muster your strength so you can lose to me at cards tonight."

"I never lose," she sniffed.

"I'm not in the habit of it, either." He turned to Louisa, his expression expectant. "And you, Miss Oliver? Do you require a rest before dinner, so that you can astound us all at the card table?"

She shook her head, a rueful smile tugging at her lips. "I fear no amount of repose will affect my game, my lord. I've never had much luck with cards."

"You never know." His mouth curved, sudden and wicked as a saber cut. "Perhaps this is the day your luck will change."

Chapter 3

Containing Speculation and Secrets

Xavier's unusually polite house party was off to an unusually quiet start.

He'd been pleased when he hit on this scheme. He had flirted with respectability instead of the demimonde, mixing a few of his favorite impolite guests with permissive members of polite society.

It wasn't the party he'd have convened if he could have consulted his own preference, which ran more hedonistic. But he couldn't expect to have everything as he liked it while in pursuit of his lofty goal: winning a wager by keeping a respectable maiden at Clifton Hall for two weeks under semi-false pretenses.

Well, that was as lofty as his goals usually were.

Still, the polite babble of conversation at dinner seemed flat. All the women remained fully clothed, no one danced on the table, and only once did Lord Weatherwax slide drunkenly from his seat. Miss Oliver sat far down the table from Xavier, glossed by candlelight, conversing with the pea-brained Freddie Pellington and seeming perfectly at ease.

She damn well ought to be. He'd changed everything for her sake. For the sake of the wager. Which came to the same thing.

The lone disturbance during the sumptuous dinner was created by Signora Frittarelli, who used one of the candles on the table to light a tiny Spanish cigar during the first course. When Lady Alleyneham huffed her disapproval, *la signora* extinguished the cigarillo in her ladyship's soup.

That had brightened Xavier's mood considerably.

After the meal, he shepherded the men through port and cigars, then brought them together with the ladies for the inevitable game of cards in the drawing room.

Lockwood drew him aside before he could join the card players. "I hope you are pleased with how the wager's going, Coz," he hissed. "You certainly went to great lengths to accommodate it."

Xavier shook Lockwood's hand off his arm. "I'm pleased enough. As you see, Miss Oliver is here. And here she'll stay for the next two weeks, through Christmas and the New Year."

His eyes caught on the subject of their conversation. She was standing at her aunt's side, tall and cool in primrose silk, looking around the drawing room with as much curiosity as though she were at a zoological garden. Likely she'd never seen the polite world's edges roughened by the likes of *la signora*. Well, he'd smoothed the way as much as he could.

Too much for Lockwood's tastes, for the marquess narrowed his eyes and clamped fingers onto Xavier's arm again.

"If you weren't my relation, Coz, I'd say you had cheated. Inviting dull sticks like Lady Alleyneham, and watery little maidens like Jane, just so Miss Oliver will feel more at her ease."

Deliberately, Xavier peeled Lockwood's fingers from his arm once more. "If you weren't my relation, I'd call you out for your accusation. As this is *my* house party, I can invite whomever I like. Our wager stipulated only that I invite Miss Oliver. You made no restrictions on the rest of the guests. Besides, I invited *la signora*, as you wished."

The singer had already proved amusing. She might yet provide a more intimate amusement, too. He hadn't decided yet. Lockwood seemed interested in her, and as Xavier was annoyed with Lockwood for forcing their wager, he was inclined to thwart his cousin, out of pique.

"This isn't over," Lockwood said in a low voice. His eyes were now fixed on Miss Oliver, and his jaw set. "You needn't think you've got this victory in your pocket."

"Yet I always do," Xavier said smoothly, to annoy Lockwood. The marquess glared at him before stalking toward Miss Oliver.

Xavier had collected a deck of cards and seated himself at a round table by the time Lockwood returned with Miss Oliver and Jane in tow.

Lockwood rolled his shoulders, limbering himself for hours of play. "What'll we play tonight, Coz? Whist?"

"Speculation," said Jane. "Whist is for old biddies, Lockwood."

Xavier savored the look of shock on Lockwood's face for a second; diminutive Jane made an unlikely but effective markswoman. "Speculation will do admirably."

"And I'll be the dealer," Jane added brightly.

"You will not," Xavier said. "You'll gamble away your entire trust. I will be the dealer."

Jane looked mutinous. "I wouldn't gamble away *all* of it. Besides, you're not considering the possibility that I might win."

"You won't win," Xavier said, helping the ladies into

seats. He knew he wore his most insufferable version of Expression Number Four, Condescension, and was surprised when Miss Oliver only chuckled.

"I don't know why you won't let me gamble, Xavier. It's not as though the trust would help me," Jane muttered, slumping in her chair. "Look at this horrible thing my mother made me wear. She thinks I'll behave better if I look like a complete frump."

The dress in question was a stiff, fussy apricot organdy, unfashionably high at the neckline. Xavier couldn't deny that she looked dreadful, so overwhelmed by fabric.

"It's not the dress that matters, Jane," Miss Oliver said with a determined shake of her head. "It is the woman within it."

"How well you have worded the matter, Miss Oliver," Lockwood said. He shifted his chair closer to her and ran his eyes over her body, from face to chest. "The woman within your dress appears to be finely formed indeed."

Xavier blinked, his blood running a little hotter. *What?* Lockwood never flirted with the marriageable.

Miss Oliver's head snapped back, and she folded her arms with decisive force. "You have begun the game of speculation early, my lord. But some things are not to be wagered on."

"Most things are for wager, if the stakes are high enough," Lockwood said, studying the creamy skin above the fitted bodice of her gown. "I only wish your . . . *stakes* . . . ran a little lower."

Xavier frowned. Lockwood met his gaze and winked broadly.

Oh. In an instant, it made sense: Lockwood was taunting Miss Oliver. He meant to scandalize her, to chase her from the house party early.

That was as devious as Xavier's own tinkering with

the guest list. If he had not been serving as host, he would have invented a new expression on the spot. Number Six: Blatantly Annoyed. He would have to keep Lockwood in line if he meant Miss Oliver to stay.

He might as well be a governess, for all the amusement this house party would yield.

"Suppose we speculate only on our cards," he said. "As you know, for this game, you must all provide a stake and compensate me as dealer."

Miss Oliver relaxed a bit. "For what stakes do we play?"

Xavier considered. "I assume none of you has a purse full of guineas, so I am happy to permit other methods of payment."

"My sister, Julia, and I used to play for hairpins," Miss Oliver suggested with a wry smile. "Though I doubt your lordships can match that stake."

Lockwood looked horrified. "Lord, no. We need a much more adult wager than that. What about sips of brandy? All drink save for the winner."

"I'd love to see you explain to Mrs. Tindall why her daughter has a bad head tomorrow," Xavier said, ignoring Jane's protest. "No, that won't do for a mixed game."

Miss Oliver broke in. "What about time?"

The others turned to look at her. "What do you mean?" Xavier asked.

"Let us wager time." Her dark eyes lit as she explained. "We all have an equal and finite measure of it to promise. So in that sense, none of us has an advantage." She gave a little smile to Jane. "Surely not even your mother would mind that."

Lockwood looked skeptical. "I never heard of wagering time. Sounds a bit flat."

Xavier had never heard of such a stake, either, but he

mulled it over. It was proper on the surface, yet fraught with possibility.

"It will do admirably," he decided, and was rewarded with a startlingly lovely smile from Miss Oliver. Not a tight little polite affair, but a joyful grin. Like a crescent moon coming out from behind a cloud, caressing the ground with its soft glow.

His skin prickled, and he shook himself. Poetic nonsense. He'd been reading too much Dante lately.

"Fine, fine," Jane grumbled as reluctantly as if Miss Oliver had suggested she clean out fireplace grates. "I don't have anything else to wager. Since *someone* won't let me touch my money until I'm of age."

Xavier ignored his cousin. "Shall we begin with a stake of fifteen minutes?" He slid three cards to each of the others, then took three for himself. "As dealer, I must contribute ninety minutes, and you would each then begin by risking one hour of your time."

"If I win, I am going to have you wear a dress," Jane said. "Not you, Louisa. You, Xavier."

Miss Oliver smiled, though Xavier noticed a pucker between her brows as she shifted her face-down cards into a neat line before her. "That would be a sight worth capturing in oils, if only I were an artist. But what would I be required to wear, Jane?"

"I can suggest something, I'm sure," Lockwood said in an oily voice. Xavier glared at him; Lockwood returned a smug smile.

"You can wear Xavier's clothes," Jane suggested, her expression pleased. "It will be like a pantomime."

"Could we defer this discussion of clothes-swapping until you actually win, Jane?" Xavier said, hiding the rough edges of his thoughts under a smooth voice. "Which, I might add, you will not."

He flipped over the top card from the deck and sat back in his chair. "Seven of diamonds. There's our trump."

Jane looked disgusted and slapped her hand on her own cards. "A seven? That's the worst card possible to decide on. Do you cheat, Xavier?"

"How suspicious you are," Xavier replied. "You wound my honor. Or you would, if I thought you knew what you were talking about at all."

Jane put out her tongue like a child, and Miss Oliver laughed. "I feel like I'm home with my four young siblings, trying to keep them from fighting over puzzle pieces."

"It was an excellent retort," Xavier agreed. "I am a noted wit. All the world concurs." He noticed with some pleasure that Lockwood looked annoyed.

Miss Oliver bit her lip. Her fingers danced over the cards that lay before her. The slight taps seemed loud and fraught, and Xavier felt his skin wake again.

"I'll buy the seven from you, my lord," she decided. "Will you sell it for fifteen minutes?"

"Thirty," he said. "A mere half hour of your time."

She looked up at him with those great dark eyes. "That's a great deal of time for such a small card. One can do much, you know, with half an hour."

Didn't he know it. In half an hour, he had once eaten breakfast and then fought a duel.

He had once spent twice that arranging his neckcloth for a ball he didn't even attend, having picked up an opera dancer for an evening's entertainment instead.

He had stared at *Purgatorio* for "the hour that turneth back desire," and wondered how the devil he was going to maintain everyone's reputations—whether proper or improper—for two entire weeks.

"That's my price," he said. "A half hour of your time."

"I'll buy it," Miss Oliver decided. "Show your cards, please, everyone."

Lockwood turned over a three of diamonds into the center of the table with a muttered curse. Jane flipped over her top card and groaned. "The five of clubs. I hate this game."

"You are the one who suggested it," Xavier reminded her. "And you will never win, Jane, if you don't risk anything." At arm's length, he turned over his own card.

Ten of diamonds. Well, well. "Miss Oliver, I own a half hour of your time."

Her cheeks colored at his words, but she raised a corner of her mouth in a half smile, looking almost feline. "The game is not over yet, my lord. We shall see who owns whom by the time we are finished."

He choked.

He covered the sound by clearing his throat, but his head spun as though his rheumy cold had returned. Had the bluestocking flirted with him?

He smiled back, but forgot to tame it into Expression Three, Amused Tolerance. Instead, a real smile slipped its leash, and her eyes widened a fraction.

Again he cleared his throat. "Shall we move on with the game? I hold the highest trump. Does anyone wish to offer for it?"

Miss Oliver bit her bottom lip.

He suddenly became envious of her teeth.

Get hold of yourself, man.

"I don't suppose you'll take a half hour for it, and that's all the time I have left to stake," she replied at last.

He thought quickly. "As you said earlier, time is something which we all hold in equal measure. So you need not feel limited by the amount left in the pot. You can raise the stakes however you like."

"However I like? I'll buy it for an hour, then."

"A ridiculous price. It's worth far more."

"I bid two hours for your next card, Miss Oliver," Lockwood said. He leaned back in his chair and drummed his fingertips on the felt tabletop. "You would own me for two hours. What do you say to that? Will you take the bid?"

"I'll sell for two and a half," interrupted Xavier, ignoring Lockwood's glower. "A beautiful trump. Ten of diamonds. Will you make it yours, Miss Oliver?"

She nodded. "Unless you care to bid, Jane?"

"No," Jane said. "I'm not buying anything at that price. That's highway robbery."

"Not if it means you win," Xavier replied, sliding the ten toward Miss Oliver. "Shall we turn another card?"

He flipped the queen of diamonds. Miss Oliver looked surprised, but shrugged off her swift loss and turned over the queen of hearts. "Nothing," she said.

Jane had a two of clubs, which she tossed onto the table. Lockwood had a knave, and he looked stormy as he threw an extra fifteen minutes into the pot.

"Fortunate that we're not playing for brandy," Xavier said.

The marquess's brows knit in a mulish manner, and Xavier relented. "That doesn't mean we need go without brandy entirely, though. Armagnac for you? No, it's the Grande Champagne you like." He motioned a footman over and requested a bottle.

Lockwood looked mollified. "A little eau-de-vie is always welcome. Especially when the play is not in one's favor."

"Evidently I need a snifter, then," Miss Oliver said. "I owe you three hours, my lord. Clearly I am not made for speculation."

"I'll wager you're made for more than you know," murmured Lockwood, drawing a finger over the back of her hand. She regarded it with mild distaste, as one would a worm crawling out of an apple, until Lockwood pulled his hand back with a peevish expression.

They all sat, fraught, until Jane snapped the tension. "I haven't won a thing yet, and I can't abide it. I'll pay each of you twelve hours for all your cards."

Miss Oliver laughed, but before she could reply, the footman returned. "Beg pardon, my lord," he murmured in Xavier's ear, "but I cannot locate the Grande Champagne in your cellars. Is it possible that the stock has been completely depleted?"

"No, I'm certain it's there. It's near the amontillados in the second chamber, beneath the—" The footman wore a desperate look, and Xavier sighed. "Never mind, I'll come find it."

He turned back to the table. "I must interrupt our game. I do apologize."

Unholy glee spread across Lockwood's face. Ready for more mischief, no doubt. Xavier added hastily, "Lockwood, do come with me and see which *cru* you'd prefer."

The marquess tensed, no doubt torn between the desire to look through the stores of spirits and the urge to unsettle Miss Oliver a bit more.

After a few seconds, the love of fine brandy won out. "Very well. We have nearly two weeks to finish our game, after all."

"I know it." Xavier gave his cousin a chilly smile as they stood.

"Must we pay out now?" Miss Oliver asked. "Except that I find myself deeply in debt, so perhaps I shouldn't have said anything."

"You owe me three hours," said Xavier. "I am shocked by your recklessness." This time, his smile was teasing. If he made an ally of her, she would be less vulnerable to Lockwood. He hoped.

"How shall you claim it? Am I to wear a dress, as Jane suggested?"

Ah, she could tease, too. Excellent. "I assume you shall, but that isn't the limit of my claim." He considered for an instant, then hit on the perfect idea. "Instead, I shall show you the library."

She looked as delighted as one could wish; there was that crescent-moon smile again. Very good. She'd be pleased to see the books, and Lockwood would have no opportunity to cause trouble for that window of time.

He laid a guiding hand between Lockwood's shoulders. "After luncheon tomorrow, then, Miss Oliver. Your time is mine for three hours. Mind you don't forget."

"I won't," she said, still looking a bit starry, and Xavier nodded his farewell and walked with Lockwood to the door.

"Mind *you*, Lockwood," he said when they stepped into the corridor, his hand pressing hard against the marquess's spine. "We may wager against one another, but I shan't have you risking Miss Oliver's good name."

Lockwood raised an eyebrow. "What an old woman you are. I was only having a bit of fun."

"At her expense." Xavier shook his head. "It won't do. Miss Oliver's presence is at stake, but not her reputation. That's worth far more than ten pounds."

"Gracious, Xavier. You act as though you own the place," Lockwood said with a yawn. "See? A little wit never hurt anyone."

"Be sure it doesn't," Xavier said, feeling exactly as prosy as Lockwood had accused him of being.

If he hadn't been so cotton-headed from his cold three

weeks ago, he would never have agreed to this wager. At best, he would finish the house party with raw nerves and an uncharacteristic temper. At worst, far more than his peace of mind would be sacrificed.

"Come, let's find the brandy," he said. "I'll wager we can both use a snifter."

"Ten pounds on it?" Lockwood smirked.

"No bet," Xavier said, chuckling. "Not this time."

Louisa had followed the men, intending to ask Lord Xavier whether she might look in the library tonight. As she reached the doorway of the drawing room, though, she overheard her name, and she stilled.

Eavesdropping is vulgar, her aunt would have said. But not even a saint could have torn herself away from such a conversation.

When the men's exchange ended and Louisa heard their footsteps echoing down the corridor, she slipped out after them and stood in the passage, considering.

So. She was the subject of a wager between a marquess and an earl. And she had been deemed to be worth all of ten pounds. How gratifying.

This explained her invitation to the house party, then. But it didn't explain *why*.

She smoothed the primrose silk of her gown, wondering what about her—neither wealthy nor popular—had drawn their attention. She was unused to much notice from aristocrats; still less to being wagered upon.

The old Louisa would have shrunk from both noblemen, keeping her distance. But she no longer wanted to be the timid woman who lived such a circumscribed life.

As Sir Francis Bacon had once said, "Knowledge is

power." Louisa knew about the wager, and the men didn't know she knew.

Which gave her the power, didn't it? This would be enjoyable.

She smiled as she stepped back into the drawing room, already plotting for the following day.

Chapter 4

Containing . . . Potential

After returning to the drawing room the previous evening, full of her secret knowledge about the wager, Louisa had debated how best to torture the earl and his cousin for presuming to wager on her. Two wastrels who thought they knew the limits of her courage.

As though a few taunts would test anything like *real* courage. As though ten pounds could capture the worth of a human being, even for only two weeks.

At first, Louisa had thought to adopt the persona of a shrinking violet: spooking at every noise, growing faint when teased, scandalized by too much sugar in her tea. She would let the proud earl sweat, wondering which of his words or actions would send her away shrieking from the house party.

But such a role had the undeniable drawback of allowing Lord Lockwood—decidedly the more repellent of the two nobles—to triumph over Louisa herself, as well as Xavier. And it wouldn't allow her any adventures.

So instead she decided to do the unexpected.

And the unexpected began now, in the slow hours after luncheon, with her arm in the crook of Lord Xavier's elbow, standing before the high, carved double doors to the library. The doors would open upon more than a room; they would open to a new Louisa. A bold Louisa, who toyed with secrets and whose self-catalogue was already richer than it had been a few days earlier.

Yes. This new plan would be . . . exciting.

A sudden shiver ran down her spine, made her flex her shoulders and wiggle her fingers within the crook of his arm. Xavier cast her a knowing look. "The anticipation is almost unbearable, is it not?"

Likely he thought she'd have the vapors from the delight of standing at his side. Ha. Handsome devil though he was, his face was nothing but a mask.

She granted him a wafer-thin smile. "*Something* is unbearable."

His eyes narrowed in surprise. Inside, Louisa cheered with triumph; then she pushed open the library door.

As soon as she stepped inside, she forgot to shoot verbal arrows at his puffery. She forgot his presence. She almost forgot to breathe.

"Oh my." She wrenched her arm free from the nuisance of the earl's clasp so she could turn in place, drinking in every detail like a woman parched for learning.

Crested bookshelves of rich wood lined the walls, crammed with thousands of books, while red-patterned draperies swaddled the room in diffuse light. Ancient oil portraits spanned the walls from the tops of the bookshelves to the tray ceiling, which was painted with sinuous characters from mythology. Comfortable-looking chairs and sofas—even a chaise longue—were arranged invitingly. A heavy russet carpet, woven in squares and medallions, cushioned Louisa's feet as she crept around the room, breaths shallow in the exquisite hush.

"It's marvelous, isn't it?" Xavier sounded bored, as though reciting from a script he'd read thousands of times.

Louisa recalled her scheme. In an instant, she'd stilled her feet, straightened her posture, and schooled her expression into one of disdain.

"It's very nice, I'm sure." She turned to the earl, standing a few yards away, and granted him a pitying smile.

"How you flatter me," he said drily. Good, he'd dropped that insufferable I'm-too-marvelous-to-live-among-mere-mortals voice.

"I would never want to flatter you." She walked to the nearest bookshelf and scanned it, top to bottom. "To be honest, your library is a terrible mess. But it has potential."

"You believe this library has *potential*?" With a measured *ruff* of boots over thick carpet, he came to stand beside her. "I am agog, Miss Oliver. Please, explain to me what you mean."

He seemed to be looming over her unconsciously, as though he could box her in with the clean angles and lines of his long body. The scent of him, sweet and smoky like vetiver and spices, made her belly clench in a sudden hunger. She breathed in deeply, just once. *Oh.*

Her voice remained bland and dismissive. "We have only three hours, my lord. I can't begin to set this room aright in that amount of time."

He folded his arms. For an instant, his careful mask slipped and she saw surprise in his face; then he was a polite, polished cipher again.

Some unholy imp within Louisa smothered a laugh.

"Look here," she said. "At the top shelf of this bookcase. What do you see?"

"A row of small books."

"Exactly. Not only are they all small, they're arranged by color. Someone has arranged your collection according to appearance instead of subject. Look at the bookcase by the door." She waved her arm, and Lord Xavier turned.

"They're all leather bound."

"Morocco, actually. See, those have been sorted by color, too. The other shades of leather or kid binding are grouped on the next shelf."

He pivoted to look around the room. "For some reason, this method of organization affronts you deeply."

"A library with books no one can find and read? Yes, it affronts me. It's a waste, my lord. It serves no purpose but that of a striking visual effect."

"That's generally all my visitors are conscious of," he muttered. He rubbed a hand over his face, then dragged it through his hair in an oddly youthful gesture. His fingers strayed to the pocket of his waistcoat as though fumbling for a watch.

They'd scarcely begun their three hours, and he was chafing to leave. It wasn't exactly flattering, but an interlude with unwanted company was no more than he deserved.

"My lord, if you'll pardon my saying so"—which she knew he would, since he needed to keep her here for two weeks—"this is a sad waste of what *could* be a marvelous library. For now, it has potential. Nothing more than that."

She saw it again—that odd little slip of his blank expression, that sudden flash of something much warmer than silver in his eyes. Then he clipped it off. "I am sure you are right."

Enough of this false politeness. "Bollocks," Louisa said.

Xavier's lips parted; his chin drew back. "Miss Oliver?"

"That's right, my lord," Louisa said. "I'm Lady Irving's niece, and therefore I probably know as many horrid words as you. And I say *bollocks*. You were sure I'd fall all over myself praising your library." *Just as women usually fall all over you.*

His mouth curved. "It's a more common reaction than yours."

"You'd be unwise to expect me to react in the common way." She turned her back on him, letting him stew as she skimmed another bookshelf. "Petrarch next to a collection of sermons. Aphra Behn. John Donne. Something in German that looks ghastly."

"It's an anatomical book. The engraver had a comical notion of men's innards. Would you like me to show you?" He stepped around her and made to take the book down.

"Yes, please. Do show me, my lord. I have a particular fondness for illustrations of the heart. Are you familiar with that organ?"

Xavier paused with the book half drawn out. "I've heard of it, yes, Miss Oliver. But I'm not in possession of one myself."

With a quick flick of long fingers, he shoved the book back into its place.

"As it so happens," he continued, "I know where many things are in this library. Since my guests aren't generally of an intellectual bent, I haven't worried about arranging it to suit anyone's pleasure but my own."

"If you mean to compliment me by comparison to your usual guests, I thank you. If you mean to insult me, you ought to be a little more obvious about it. Either way, I'm not surprised that you would consult your pleasure above good sense."

Now the polite mask was gone, and the earl's expression wavered between disbelief and humor. "No, that's only what's to be expected of me, isn't it?"

He paused, fingers drumming on the edge of the shelf,

then seemed to reach a decision. "Please allow me to show you something, Miss Oliver."

He glanced up and down the nearest set of shelves. "These books are all dross. My grandfather collected them in large lots at auction. But here"—he strode to the next crested bookcase and snatched a volume in a plain binding— "is a fine old edition of the *Inferno*. If you should like to walk through *Purgatorio* and *Paradiso* next, the other volumes of Dante are on the bookcase to the right of the windows. Third shelf from the bottom."

He strolled back to her and stuffed the small volume into her hands. Her fingers closed on the worn black leather reflexively. "Anything else you'd like to know, Miss Oliver?"

Louisa stared at him, then looked down at the book in her hands. "Yes. Why isn't this with the other two volumes of Dante?"

"It's a spare copy. Never mind." He tugged it from her hands and tossed it onto the shelf at the level of his elbow. Louisa pretended not to notice as he nudged it straight, then gave the old binding a gentle pat.

"I don't understand your method, my lord." Her voice sounded strained to her own ears. Seeing him treat an old book with care made her feel off-kilter.

"There *is* no method besides that created by my late grandfather," Xavier said. "But I've learned the things I want to know."

His eyelids lowered as he spoke, veiling his expression, and Louisa wondered what he wanted to know, and whether it was as limited as she'd thought.

"I'd like to learn from this library, too," Louisa mused. "But there's no way to know what's here."

"You created a catalogue for Matheson's library, didn't you?"

At this mention of her brother-in-law, James, Louisa caught a quick breath. Her former betrothed, once such good friends with Xavier until the rakish earl had spread scandal about their family. James, Lord Matheson, was now married to Louisa's stepsister, Julia. "Yes, I suppose my dealings with Lord Matheson are all public knowledge now."

Her host waved a hand. "Hardly, Miss Oliver. But you can't think I'd let you in my home without knowing a bit about you. What if you were the worst sort of libertine?"

"Then I'd fit right—" Louisa pressed her lips together when she saw the wicked gleam in his eye. "Well. You know that I'm not, whether that worked in my favor or no. And you know that I did create a catalogue of the library for James. Matheson, I mean. So you must see why I'd hoped for more order in yours, since it's rumored to be such a jewel."

"Don't credit all the rumors you hear about me, Miss Oliver." His lips curved, the expression rueful.

Then he was all distant refinement again. "At least not the rumors related to my library. I'd consider it a great honor if you'd make a beginning at order. Maybe look over the titles and jot a few suggestions for their rearrangement."

This was such an uncharacteristic offer from the *beau monde*'s most dissolute darling that Louisa could only stare. Then the puzzle pieces snapped into place: he was trying to keep her away from the house party. Keep her preoccupied and away from scandal, so she wouldn't leave and he could win his precious ten pounds.

It was too, too bad, because his suggestion sounded heaven-sent.

"I'm here as your guest, my lord. I don't intend to work amidst stacks of old books when I could be frolicking with scandal." Her hand strayed to the edge of the shelf and stroked the beautiful bindings. The faint odor of old leather seemed to tug at her, and she took a step closer to the shelter of the shelf.

"Please consider it, Miss Oliver. You'd gain my everlasting good opinion." The smile he offered was probably meant to be seductive. His vowels were liquid, the consonants crisp as celery, an elocutionist's dream.

Something dark within her rebelled. "You presume that I care for your good opinion, then?" She paused, a beat too long, then added, "My lord."

He didn't even flinch at this rudeness. "A natural assumption, since you agreed to become a guest in my house."

"An unwise assumption. Considering your treatment of my family, you are unlikely ever to receive my good opinion."

There was the core of it. She folded her arms and waited for his withering insult, or his condescending reply. Either way, she was glad she'd said the words.

But Xavier surprised her: he only took her arm in a grasp both strong and gentle. "Please, Miss Oliver, have a seat."

Before she could protest, he'd guided her to an armchair covered in red velvet, drawn up before a preposterously large fireplace. Xavier sat across from her in the twin of her chair.

"I deserved that, Miss Oliver—or I can see why you think I did. It's best we uncover the truth now, don't you agree?"

Louisa blinked. Her arm still retained the feeling of his fingers; her ears were full of his voice, all politeness after her insult. "What is the truth, then?"

"I do not pretend," he said, "to misunderstand your reference. Your sister and Lord Matheson began their romance under shocking circumstances, which I accidentally stumbled upon. You believe I then informed the London scandal sheets."

Louisa looked at her hands, clenched white-knuckled in her lap. "I see no need to discuss it."

"You are the one who introduced the subject." His voice was low and smooth, yet in her peripheral vision, she could see his long form held taut and still. "And you ought to know what I've done. I can't bear to be scorned for an outcome that's none of my doing, when there's reason enough to hate me on my own merits."

"Or lack thereof."

He let this pass. "I did, indeed, tell a friend what I'd seen at Matheson's house, but that was the end of my involvement. A vulgar joke between bachelor friends as they shared a brandy at White's. I can only assume a servant overheard and sold the story."

His fingers reached out to brush her clenched hands, forcing her to look at him. "I am sorry, Miss Oliver. I never intended for anyone to be hurt."

Swiftly, Louisa drew her hands out of his reach, but her eyes fixed on his face. Lord Xavier's eyes were troubled; his hair was mussed from when he'd dragged a hand through it. His urbane mask had been cast aside, his sculpted perfection crumbled.

The air before the extravagant fire felt over-warm and heavy, and she struggled to fill her lungs. Could she believe him? For months, she'd disdained him and resented him. It was better than turning such feelings on herself as her family crumpled under the weight of scandal.

They had recovered, though, through daring and determination. James and Julia were happily married. And Louisa was . . . well, she was here, hoping to start anew.

And Xavier hoped for the same. With an apology, he had turned himself from a pasteboard villain into a human.

"Thank you for telling me," she managed.

"Thank you for listening," he said. "I wished to tell Matheson the same, but he never responded to my letters."

"Likely he was too angry before his marriage, then too happy afterward." Louisa gave a little shrug, as though a cast-off friendship meant nothing to her good-natured brother-in-law.

She wanted Xavier to leave, to let her be alone with the comfort of books and the mystery of her troubled thoughts. She had to revise her catalogue of him, yet she wasn't sure of the final result. Should she strike from it *heedless of friends* and *eager for scandal*, and substitute *careless*? *Determined to be shallow*? *Blessed with a library and a mind for books, and content to let both molder*?

Careless covered it all. It was less wicked than being intentionally unkind, though no more admirable.

Louisa schooled her own expression into a sweet blank. "You need not stay with me if you don't wish to, my lord. I know you're only here because of the wager."

His eye twitched, and she added with false innocence, "From our game of speculation. Our wager of time."

"Naturally." Again, Xavier gave his too-wide smile, which he apparently thought was charming. "But I would consider it shameful to give up on a wager early."

"You have an unusual concept of shame," Louisa muttered.

His smile widened. "Some would express surprise that I have any sense of shame at all."

"I imagine you're proud of that." Louisa felt suddenly as though scraping together her sentences was a pointless exhaustion.

"You've taken a harsh measure of me, haven't you, Miss

Oliver? It's a blow to be criticized in my own home, but I daresay I can tolerate it. Your honesty's rather refreshing."

"I can offer you a bit more, if you like it so much."

"As you'll be here for two weeks, let us parcel it out." He stood, rolling his shoulders, then settled on the arm of his chair and braced himself with long, hard-muscled legs. Clad as they were in snug trousers and high-glossed top boots, it was impossible to overlook their form.

"Mmm." Louisa squeezed her eyes shut for a long moment. The treachery of her own body was sudden and hot.

Xavier evidently took her noise as a noncommittal reply rather than a wish to trail a hand up the length of his thigh. "Each day, you may tell me one thing you hate about me. It will be like the twelve days of Christmas, only I'll receive my gifts early."

"I wouldn't say I feel hatred, exactly."

"No? What is it then?" His gray eyes flicked over her face, pulling apart every thought in her mind.

Except one: *this is what he does*. This interplay, this baiting. Such thoughtlessness, to gossip about a friend; to wager ten pounds on a virtual stranger.

Louisa would not allow him to toy with her and toss her away like a too-small fish. He would not be permitted to be thoughtless of her anymore. If he wanted to win ten pounds for keeping her at his house, he would have to earn them with his own pound of flesh.

"I'll tell you tomorrow, my lord, if you'll meet me here at the same time."

"My dear Miss Oliver, are you setting up an assignation with me?"

"There's no need," she said. "With a man of your reputation, a woman can simply leap when she wants something."

"Yet you are willing to be alone with me. Aren't you afraid I'll leap upon *you*?"

He was stubbornly devoted to his role, but he'd given her a clue he might not have intended. Despite his determined outrageousness, he liked books—or one book in particular.

She stood, then walked away from him to the slim volume of Dante he'd cast onto a shelf. The old leather binding was soft as cloth under her fingertips. From memory, she translated the opening verses. "'Midway through our life's journey, I found myself within a shadowy forest, for I had lost the straightforward path.'"

Behind her, his voice picked up the thread. "'It is hard to speak of it, that savage, rough forest. Even to think of it renews my fear.'"

She turned to face him again.

"You know Dante," he said. He tilted his head, looking as suspicious as if he'd caught her paging through his household accounts.

"I know a great many things, my lord. Including this: A woman of my reputation—an *intellectual type*, I mean—has nothing to fear from men who walk your path. Our destinations lie in wholly opposite directions."

His booted feet swung, kicking against the cabriole leg of his armchair. "I'm sure you are a very intelligent woman. But you don't know as much as you think."

Those cool gray eyes held tight to hers, and she was captured as though the old Italian verses had been a bewitchment. Her skin felt warm, her gown's bodice too tight. It was banded around her breasts, their tips sensitive and eager. She was trapped, and she wanted to slip free from her old self and flee it. Even to think of it renewed her fear.

Her voice came out throaty. "I know more than enough, my lord."

His brows knitted. "Are you well, Miss Oliver? You sound a bit hoarse. Shall I ring for some tea?"

He rose to his feet and strode away from her to the bell pull. Just as his hand reached to tug it, one of the library's tall wooden doors swung open and Lord Lockwood ambled in.

"Here you are, Coz. I *thought* I'd find you amusing yourself with some sort of female." He smirked.

Louisa tugged herself back into mental order, as though plaiting her thoughts and putting a dressing gown on her desires. "I doubt very much that his lordship was amused," she said in a bored tone. "But he was all graciousness in showing me his library."

"Ah. You found the experience pleasurable, then?" The marquess waggled his brows.

Louisa darted a quick look at Xavier, who rolled his eyes in the same God-help-us expression she'd often used toward her young siblings. A smile tugged at her lips, all the sweeter for being a surprise.

"It has . . . potential," she said.

"You gratify me deeply." Xavier seemed all bland condescension, but one eyelid flickered. A wink?

"I am devastated to interrupt such wild debauchery," Lockwood said. "But your opera singer has extinguished one of her damned cigarillos on Lady Alleyneham's embroidery. The women are at each other's throats. Almost literally."

Xavier frowned. "Lockwood, please don't be coarse in front of a lady. I trust we're in no danger of burning the Hall down?"

"Not immediately, no. But do come, man. Make them stop shrieking at one another." The marquess grabbed for Xavier's arm.

Xavier cast a look back at Louisa, whose fingers still rested on the butter-soft leather of the Dante binding. "You needn't worry about me, my lord," she said. "Please, go restore your guests to happiness, or whatever state it was they were trying to attain."

His mouth kicked up on one side. "You are graciousness personified, Miss Oliver. But you owe me more of your time. Don't think I'll forget."

"I would never suspect you of such indifference," she said dryly.

She looked back at the bookcases as the heavy library door closed behind the two noblemen. In the sudden solitude, the shelves seemed endless, the dizzying runs of volumes boxing her in.

She drew a deep breath. She'd already encountered a few surprises in this lovely room. Her host liked Dante. He hadn't been deliberately unkind to James, or to Louisa herself, all those months ago. And he'd dropped his careful, false charm a few times.

There might be a real person under the meticulously designed rake. She hadn't expected that.

Since Xavier had surprised her, she would have to surprise herself, too. This house party was sure to be a fortnight's adventure. If Lord Xavier expected her to adore him, she'd show him: she was not so easily fascinated. If Lord Lockwood thought he could intimidate her, she'd show him: she could not be frightened.

And if neither of those things was precisely true, only she would know. During her awkward, lonely London season, she had perfected the art of impassive expressions and meaningless conversation. No one would take her true measure.

She wondered which of her evening dresses showed the most bosom.

Chapter 5

Containing a Red Blindfold, Used to Great Effect

"We could play sardines," suggested Lockwood, smiling with all the oiliness of one of those tiny fish.

"That's a child's game, Lockwood," Jane countered with a sniff of her little nose. "Blind-man's buff would be much better."

"I am adore the game with *porco*." Signora Frittarelli lowered her heavy eyelids and blew a cloud of smoke from her cigarillo, ignoring Lady Alleyneham's theatrical fit of coughing.

"Ah. You mean you wish to make the beast with two backs?" Lockwood smiled at the singer, who looked at him blankly and dragged on her cigarillo once more.

"She's referring to 'squeak piggy squeak,' you nodcock," Xavier muttered.

After dinner, port, and tobacco—for which *la signora* had remained in the dining room, and which she seemed to enjoy more than any of the men—Xavier had herded his guests into the most formal of Clifton Hall's drawing rooms. A thick Turkey carpet cushioned their feet, while the patterned Chinese wallpaper and the crystals of the ornate chandelier magnified the candlelight and firelight into a soft, forgiving glow.

If only Xavier felt similarly forgiving. But he didn't, because his guests were plaguing the life out of him.

Earlier in the afternoon, Lockwood had dragged him away from a tentative peace with Miss Oliver to make another tentative peace; this time between a fluttery noblewoman with a few singed embroidery silks and a notorious singer with dubious manners. The exchange was not exactly sanguine. More than ever, Xavier felt like a diplomat, overseeing negotiations between two rival factions: the proper and the salacious.

And Lockwood was determined to cause all the trouble he possibly could. "I'd squeak with you, Miss Oliver," he was saying. "If we play that exhilarating game."

Xavier pressed at the bridge of his nose. He had a terrible headache. He hadn't slept well since the house party began. And he'd been sleeping alone. For a long, long while.

Lockwood had arranged the terms of their latest wager quite cleverly. He had nothing to lose except another pittance, while against his trifling sum, Xavier had staked his reputation as the *ton*'s most infallible, most entertaining libertine. The whole debacle hinged on the presence of one sharp-tongued bluestocking. Who half hated him.

Speaking of that creature—Miss Oliver looked luscious tonight in an evening frock of deep pink crepe. Her dark brown hair was coiled tightly, yet looked as soft and rich as velvet, and her cheeks were rosy, probably in response to Lockwood's sallies.

He saw Miss Oliver give Lockwood a sweet smile and lift her chin. "If you reveal all your secrets, my lord, you're certain to lose any game you play. Lord Xavier, wouldn't you agree?"

She turned to face him, her dark eyes bold and bright. The curve of her neck was so graceful, the semicircle of skin above her bodice so softly, touchably pale, that it took Xavier a moment to realize a response was expected of him.

His hand dropped, his headache dissolving. "I'll agree with anything a lady wishes," he said automatically, "and even more that a woman desires."

She gave him a pitying smile, and Xavier's practiced innuendo turned cheap and metallic in his mouth—as though he'd offered a farthing when a guinea was deserved.

He tried again, stumbling back over his words, addressing the roomful of guests. "By all means, let us safeguard our intimate secrets until later in the evening. Those of you who wish to engage in, ah, private amusements may take your leave whenever you wish, but I think a game of blindman's buff will do well for the rest of us."

As several guests scrabbled for the door, and each other, Jane grinned her triumph. "Lockwood, you've as good as lost already, the way you lumber about."

"I don't—" The marquess cut himself off and glared at Jane. "I'll bet ten pounds that I can catch someone quicker than you can."

"Make it fifty," said Lady Irving. The countess was seated in a tall wing chair, which she'd probably chosen for its resemblance to a throne. "A ten-pound note is hardly worth dragging out to blow my nose upon."

Lockwood's jaw went slack.

Xavier settled himself into a chair to enjoy the show. He could use a little respite. In the few minutes since he'd rejoined the women in the drawing room, he'd already dragged his hands through his hair so many times that it probably looked like a dandy brush.

"Why must we bet these pounds?" *La signora* blew a

perfect O of smoke and watched it dissipate. "*Perché non qualcosa di più intimo?*"

"I see no need for us to use a heathen tongue while in England," said Lady Alleyneham, whose manners seemed to be evaporating along with the smoke from the opera singer's cigarillos.

"That's because you've never experienced the proper use of a heathen tongue." Lady Irving cleared her throat. "Though you didn't hear me say that, Louisa, my girl. Nor you, Miss Tindall."

"Nor did my daughters, Estella, I assure you." Lady Alleyneham shot her old acquaintance a frosty look. "I believe we shall retire early tonight. Daughters?"

Lady Irving shrugged. "Suit yourself, Sylvia. But you'll never catch husbands for your girls by herding them off to their bedchambers. Not unless they're cleverer than you know."

As Lady Alleyneham huffed and hustled her protesting daughters from the drawing room, Xavier's shoulders relaxed. Mrs. Tindall, Jane's mother, was snoring in a tapestry armchair near the fire. The warmth, and the sherry she'd consumed, would keep the nominal hostess of this party safely oblivious to the goings-on in the room.

Now all Xavier had to do was make sure Lockwood behaved himself. And Jane, too. And he'd have to keep the others from getting raucous enough to horrify Miss Oliver.

His gaze unfurled over Miss Oliver's fair skin again, stroking its warmth.

Too much; he looked too long. She sensed his scrutiny and turned her head in his direction. Her brows lifted, and he prepared himself for a chilly stare down the length of her nose.

Instead, she gave him a wicked little caught-you smile.

Before he'd drunk in the expression for nearly long enough, she turned back to Jane and made his cousin laugh at something or other, then joined in.

Did Xavier himself ever laugh? He couldn't remember the last time he had. Usually he limited himself to Amused Tolerance; a chuckle at most. To laugh from the belly, as had Jane and Miss Oliver—*Louisa*, Jane called her—was a freedom he hadn't allowed himself in years.

How odd, that watching others laugh should make him feel the opposite of joyful.

He shoved himself to his feet and snapped a fistful of paper spills from the holder on the mantel. Folding one in half and hiding it amongst its fellows in his fist, he said, "Those of you who wish to play blind-man's buff, come draw from my hand. Our first blind man will be the one with the short spill. And our wager . . . *qualcosa di più intimo*."

Something a little more intimate. It would be better than sending Jane or Lockwood into a frenzy of wagering with that gimlet-eyed Lady Irving. Xavier's relatives seemed determined to impoverish themselves.

"A kiss?" This from Mrs. Protheroe, whose wide mouth was already pursed and waiting. "The one who is captured receives a kiss from the blind man."

Lockwood grinned. "From the right person, a kiss could be worth more than ten pounds."

"No kiss is worth fifty pounds," replied Lady Irving. "Which is what I suggested we bet."

"My dear lady," Xavier interjected, "let us save the exchange of cold coin for the card tables. At night, the wagering will be of a warmer sort."

The countess wasn't without humor. She pursed her lips and nodded. "You young rogue."

"Exactly." He flexed his fist so the short spill poked up highest, then approached Lord Weatherwax. The cotton-haired, cotton-headed nobleman was nodding over a snifter he'd procured from God-only-knew where. He could be trusted to stumble around in an entertaining manner, and his inebriation ensured that the young ladies would have better balance than he. A safe choice for a scandalous game. Everyone knew blind-man's buff was only an excuse for public groping.

"Weatherwax?" Xavier cleared his throat when the man didn't respond. "Do you care to choose a spill?"

"Thank you, Coz." With a quick yank, Lockwood caught Xavier's arm and drew the upthrust short spill from his fist. "My, my. What luck."

"You must stop grabbing at my person, Lockwood." Xavier crushed the remaining spills in his fist. "Anyone would think you had a tendre for me."

Lockwood grinned. "Not for you, Coz. Decidedly not for you." He looked around the room. "Ladies? Who wants to blindfold me?"

The silence dragged out a second too long before Lady Irving stood and shook out her heavy skirts. They were a brighter scarlet than the pattern on the Turkey carpet. Xavier had to squint as she approached him and Lockwood.

"I'll see to you, you rapscallion," said the countess. "You needn't think you'll be peeking when I'm done with you."

"Uh." Lockwood shut his eyes and mustered a smile. "Very well."

"While they're occupied, let us shift the furniture." Xavier laid hands on the back of a chair. "Mind you don't wake Mrs. Tindall, or we'll have to behave ourselves properly."

Guests began to move, clearing furniture from the center of the room more quietly than Xavier would have thought possible. "I had no idea the cream of society had such impressive manual skills," he murmured.

Louisa slipped from behind a settee and took a place at his side. "We do your bidding so efficiently out of regard for you, my lord."

"Am I so well-loved?"

"I've no idea," she said. "But I'm convinced, and I'd wager the others are, too, that if you were forced to behave properly, you would die on the spot. And it would be *such* an inconvenience to the servants to deal with a death at this hour."

For an excruciating moment, he could only blink down at her.

It would be undignified, unmanly, to ask, *If you hate me so much, why did you come?*

But she didn't hate him; she'd given him that meager assurance. And she was smiling again, right at him, that sweetly bright and wicked crescent-moon smile, and his neckcloth was over-tight around his throat.

"You are all courtesy, Miss Oliver," he said. "Well, not *all* courtesy. There's something distinctly different from courtesy in your manner."

"So you noticed." God, her lips were the exact shade of a raspberry. "I didn't think practiced rakes ever paid the slightest attention to bluestockings such as myself."

"Will you please cease referring to yourself as a bluestocking? I find it tedious in the extreme."

"So the dog barks, despite all the petting he receives."

"Miss Oliver, your tongue is sharp enough to shave with." Now he *was* barking at her. He folded his arms, reminding himself that he was an earl, and this was his home, and his party, and . . . and none of that mattered to her, did it?

Maybe she hadn't forgiven him. Or maybe she was just a shrew. A shrew who stood at the perfect height for him to breathe in the scent of her hair. *Lilies.*

"Better sharp than heathen? Some would say so." She turned away. "Ah, it looks as though the floor has been cleared. We must put an end to our delightful conversation and join the others. I'm bereft, but I'm willing to make the sacrifice."

Without another glance at him, she strode to the center of the far wall and took her place next to his cousin Jane again. They were laughing once more within seconds.

Xavier began to pick his way through the furniture around the edges of the room, moving as silently as he could in the direction of the two young women. A vague sense of responsibility drove him to keep a closer eye on them.

It was like a toothache, this responsibility. A man could never be at ease as long as he had someone to watch over. Why had he agreed to it?

Lockwood shuffled into the center of the room as soon as Lady Irving had tied the last knot in the red scarf about his head. "Let the games begin," he called.

With a shriek, Mrs. Protheroe—a widow of lusty reputation—darted through the center of the room and just missed being clutched by Lockwood's questing hands. This triggered a roil of movement, as men pressed to the edges of the room and women, laughing, pushed their way forward. Voices rose in a clamor, like a flock of parrots screeching as they took flight.

Xavier checked to make sure that Mrs. Tindall still dozed, then caught Jane's arm as she veered toward Lockwood. "Don't even think about it."

Jane shook off his hand. "About being caught?" She rolled her eyes. "Give me a little credit, please, Xavier. I can imagine nothing nastier than being groped by Lockwood."

"Curse you, Tindall," called Lockwood. "I heard that. My ears aren't covered." He lurched in her direction, hands outstretched.

"Nor are mine," she replied. "So don't be rude to ladies." She kicked him in the shin and flounced off to a safe distance.

"Thankless game," Lockwood muttered as he blundered by, smacking against Xavier's shoulder. "I don't want you, Coz, damn it. Send me toward a woman."

Louisa stood poised a few feet away, watching them with narrowed eyes. *Try it*, her expression said. *I dare you*.

Xavier's skin prickled. *No*. Not this time. He turned his cousin in the opposite direction.

"You're facing the fireplace," he said low in Lockwood's ear. "Walk straight ahead and you'll find Mrs. Protheroe. I think she'd like to be caught."

Lockwood nodded and began stumbling forward again. One step, two, with Mrs. Protheroe's shrieks of pretended terror tugging him along.

And then Lockwood spun on his heel and lunged hugely, collapsing against Louisa.

"I've caught someone," he crowed. "Let me guess who it is."

Louisa went stiff as a column as Lockwood draped himself over her shoulder and breathed deeply of the curve of her neck. "Definitely a woman, unless Pellington's changed his scent yet again."

"I say, dash it," that young dandy called from several feet away.

"Not Pellington, then." Lockwood's head began to slide down, until his face was pillowed at the boundary between naked skin and bodice. "Hmm. I'm sure I can get a *feel* for this."

Louisa caught Xavier's eye, and he took a half-step toward her, ready to yank his cousin bodily from her. She only shook her head. With an admirable efficiency of movement, she plucked a U-shaped pin from her hair and jabbed it into the flesh under Lockwood's jaw.

He yelped and sprang away from her at once, yanking off the blindfold. "Damnation, woman, what do you mean by stabbing me?"

"You're alive," she said in a tone so sugary it could have sweetened a dozen cups of tea. "What a relief. You had sunk so much of your weight onto me, I was afraid you'd perished of an apoplexy."

"He's sure to have one now," said Mrs. Protheroe. "Look how you've creased his neckcloth." The blond woman laughed, throaty and long, her prominent teeth framing the sound.

The marquess was still breathing hard, rubbing at the puncture. "I must claim my kiss now. Miss Oliver, you wouldn't want to be a poor sport, would you?"

"Of course not." Looking almost bored, she turned her face up to his and allowed the marquess to plant a kiss on her lips.

A kiss that was surely far too wet, and far too long. Xavier held his breath. This had slipped beyond the boundaries of a game; there was something distasteful in the scene.

At last Lockwood broke away, grinning. Louisa gave him a tight-lipped smile and turned away, her shoulders unnaturally square.

So she hadn't liked the kiss. For some unaccountable reason, this gratified Xavier.

Except that her dislike had been Lockwood's whole intention. Which did *not* gratify Xavier.

La signora descended from a perch atop a little rococo table, inevitable cigarillo in hand. She looked Lockwood up and down. "*Cazzo*," she declared, and blew a cloud of whitish smoke in his face.

Lockwood did not speak Italian, but Xavier did. Well enough to realize that his cousin had been called a cock.

Judging from Louisa's bright eyes, her mouth that curved into a secret smile, his Dante reader knew it, too. When she caught Xavier's eye, her smile widened, and one hand came up to cover it with graceful fingertips.

Wait, wait. She was not *his* Dante reader. And there was nothing so special about possessing five fingers, or using them to brush at a smile that was both wicked and sweet.

Wait *again*. He was doing that fanciful thing, where he thought in poetry and looked in verse. And he'd stared at her too long, letting the rest of the guests roil and tease as he studied this slender, stately alabaster Diana who jabbed men with hairpins and knew what a *cazzo* was.

Outside of his suddenly muddled head, the game continued with much taunting. Lockwood joined in the merriment, showing his hairpin wound and laughing as loudly as Mrs. Protheroe. He twirled the limp red scarf that had served as his blindfold, batting the lusty widow on her splendid bosom as she squealed.

"Louisa, you must be the next blind man," called Jane.

"Haven't we had enough of this game?" Xavier said hurriedly. "We've already experienced a casualty. Perhaps *la signora* would sing for us instead?"

"If we're going to do something as flat as listen to music," huffed Lady Irving, "I might as well summon Sylvia Alleyneham back to the drawing room, and a vicar or two."

Xavier donned his customary bland disdain. "You are being deliberately shocking, my lady. Surely vicars would faint as soon as they stepped inside my house."

Louisa plucked the red scarf from Lockwood's hand. "What would make them faint, my lord? The elegance of your home's décor, or the savoriness of the food? I've encountered nothing to shock the respectable."

She began to wrap the scarf around her head, her arms flexing and her breasts rising as the scarlet band covered her eyes, the top of her straight nose, a span of her forehead.

If only she would cover her mouth as well.

"Nonsense," laughed Mrs. Protheroe after a silent moment. "Everyone knows Lord Xavier is too, too scandalous."

"You're right, ma'am," Louisa said. "I must have forgotten."

"You are right, too, Miss Oliver," Xavier replied, feeling the headache clutch at his temples again. "As I'm hosting the respectable, I don't wish to shock them." He stretched his mouth into his wicked-rogue smile and added, "*Too* much."

Mrs. Protheroe giggled, as she was intended, and the moment passed.

For most people. But Louisa had tossed out a few seeds of doubt, seeds that grew in Xavier's mind. What did she think of him?

She didn't seem to put much store in his reputation as a rake; not anymore. Their moment of honesty in the library had won him a fresh assessment.

Now she stood straight and still, her slim body vibrating with coiled energy. She wanted something, and he didn't think it was safety.

So be it. He'd prove to her that she didn't have his measure.

But he would have hers, and soon. He could already imagine his hands spanning her waist, pulling her close to his body.

* * *

You're not who they think, Xavier, and I know it.

Louisa felt a twinge at having almost said as much to a roomful of people. Twenty-one years of attention to etiquette had sunk deep into her bones, and she owed her host more politeness than she'd shown him.

Yet what evidence was there of his scarlet reputation? It seemed to sustain itself without the food of misbehavior or the drink of scandal. He teased as though it were true, completely taken for granted.

But Louisa didn't take anything for granted.

Her eyes were swaddled in scarlet silk. She ought to take the chance to cast off restraint. A woman blinded could not be held responsible for what she touched, what she grasped for.

She raised her voice, loud and clear, and spread her hands wide. "You had all better scatter, or I shall find you out."

A chaos of rustling, whispers, raps of boots against furniture legs, muffled curses and giggles ensued.

In all the movement, Louisa sensed that someone directly to her right stood very still. "Someone stays by me? Why don't you move away? I told you I'd find you out."

"I don't think you will." It was Xavier. Her body recognized his voice, her belly clenching warm and eager. The pleasure of the game.

She shot a hand out, a desperate grab in his direction.

"Valiant, my dear lady," he said, his low voice drawling over the syllables like syrup over ice. "But you aren't. Even. *Close.*"

This last word was a whisper in her ear, tickling loose strands of hair against her skin. A hand trailed up her bare upper arm. It felt like a claiming, and Louisa shivered. Too late, she remembered to clutch for it, but Xavier had pulled away again.

"Even a maiden swift as you cannot capture me," he said, the sound of his voice growing fainter. He was moving away from her, then.

She would not give him the satisfaction of a pursuit. Instead, she turned in the opposite direction and placed one foot in front of the other. "Come out, my friends. It's lonely in this scarf, and I need a companion."

"Behave yourself, my girl," said the unmistakable voice of Lady Irving.

"As though I could do anything but," Louisa called back over renewed rustlings and laughter. "You can all see me, though I cannot see you. I couldn't possibly misbehave in such a situation. I should be questioning *your* behavior."

"Impertinent," said Lady Irving. In her aunt's parlance, Louisa knew, this was akin to *well said.*

Meanwhile she was still blindfolded, and she was starting to feel ill at ease. Being unable to see her way left her too vulnerable.

She raised her chin and took two more steps forward, recalling the position of the furniture. She was probably about to bump into a chair—yes, there it was. Her hands gripped smooth wood, her nails finding nubby tapestry. All she needed to do was find someone, *anyone*, to pass off this blindfold to.

Jane would do, if Louisa could find her new friend. She shoved her way past the chair, then past a settee that came from nowhere and pressed against her shins for an endless length. Finally, she reached the end of it, stretched out her hand and touched sleek wallpaper.

"I hope no one's hiding on the window seat," she called, "because I shall surely catch you."

Jane was still sitting there, as Louisa had hoped. The younger woman was all too eager to grab her friend's hand, yank off the blindfold, and crow for her own turn at the center of the game. Once Louisa gave her a quick peck on the cheek, another round of blind-man's buff began amid a chorus of laughter and jeers.

While the tumult of shifting furniture and bodies was at its height, Louisa slipped around the edge of the room. Checking to make sure no one was watching her, she escaped through the doorway.

To be honest, this retreat wasn't a brave move. Boldness sat oddly upon her, though, like a mask that had been formed for someone else's face. She wanted to take it off for a while and be herself again.

She strolled down the corridor, trailing her hand over the rich wood paneling and painted plasterwork of the walls.

Long observation from the sides of ballrooms, from chairs in the corners of drawing rooms, had taught Louisa to notice small details of expression and tone. To pick apart the artifice of politeness. And so she knew that Xavier had shown her something real today—real regret, real flashes of humor. And tonight, real annoyance.

It annoyed him when she noticed things. That was very, very interesting.

The skin of her arm prickled, still remembering the touch of his presumptuous hand. She wanted more of his touch, his speech, his time. She wanted more truth from him, until she could solve the puzzle of who he truly was.

Tomorrow, she told herself. Tomorrow she'd snap a few more pieces into place. Before this house party was done, she'd have Lord Xavier laid out bare before her.

A shiver spun through her body, making her limbs tremble.

Chapter 6

Containing a
Theatrical Fantasy

"*The Taming of the Shrew*. Are you familiar with it, Miss Oliver?"

Louisa's head snapped up at the interruption. She squinted into the clear light of early afternoon; a familiar figure was backlit against the tall library windows. "My lord. I'm sorry, I didn't realize I wasn't alone."

She rose from her crouch before a low shelf of tall, slim ledgers. Bobbing a passable little curtsy, she shook her rumpled skirts back into reasonable order.

"Do stop prostrating yourself, Miss Oliver. You're my guest, not a housemaid."

Xavier hitched a slender, fussily tooled volume into the crook of his arm, then strode over to Louisa's side and handed it to her.

"It's a play by Shakespeare. Somehow it was separated from its fellows, and I know you're flustered by that type of disorder. So here you go. Arrange it as you like. Next to *As You Like It*, if you like."

Louisa smiled. "Literary wordplay, my lord. Are you trying to charm me?"

"There's no point. I know you can't be charmed." He gave a lopsided smile, then half turned to drag his fingers along the edge of a shelf. Under the snug charcoal-dark superfine of his coat, his shoulders flexed, the edges of his shoulder blades pressing outward.

To see the lines of his body, just for an instant—Louisa held her breath at the unexpected intimacy of it. He turned back at the sharp sound of her inhalation, his brows raised in a question, and she made a sudden, impulsive decision.

"My lord," she began, tightening her fingers on the Shakespearean binding. "You're right."

His jaw dropped. "I'm *what*?" He rubbed at his ears. "I'm sorry, I must not have heard you properly."

She held up a quelling hand. "My lord, I'm all too familiar with *The Taming of the Shrew*. I've been shrewish to you, and I wish to offer a truce."

"Am I to be your Petruchio, then?"

Petruchio—the man who'd mastered the shrew, who'd tongued and ravished his Kate into submission.

Lord, yes. "Decidedly not. Your friends aren't witty enough to support you as one of Shakespeare's heroes. What I propose is that I shall be a bit less difficult. If you will extend me the same courtesy."

"Are you suggesting I've been difficult?" Again, the expression of elaborate shock.

Louisa mirrored his posture, folding her arms. "Come now, my lord. I've promised not to be shrewish with you, so you can't expect me to pick up that thread of conversation. I'm only asking you to treat me with the same respect you would one of your male associates."

Gray eyes met hers. "They rarely wear such fetching

frocks, Miss Oliver. I would find the pretense difficult to sustain."

She shook her head. "Honesty, please, my lord. You don't have to say things like *fetching* to me. I'm not going to leave if I'm not complimented every two minutes. In fact, I'd much rather receive no compliment at all than an insincere one."

She gestured at her patterned muslin day dress. "This is clothing, my lord. It covers my body. It doesn't have anything to do with my real self."

She wrapped both hands around the edges of the bound play, stilling herself. Drawing her posture up straight. He wouldn't suspect how she'd unsettled herself by saying *my body* to a rake for whom flirtation was as easy as breathing—especially when she wanted him to touch her.

When he studied her without replying, she made an impatient gesture and laid the play on the nearest shelf. "Excuse me, please."

She crouched again, intending to continue her survey of this long-neglected collection of books. Determined to ignore the tall man lurking behind her, she scrutinized the bindings for some clue as to where to begin. The old, cord-banded spines on this shelf were not marked. Anything could be here, waiting to surprise her.

Xavier loomed over her, and the hair at the nape of her neck stirred in the eddy of his slight movements. Then he sank to the floor, leaning against the very shelf she was looking at, and stretched out his long legs.

"You're wrong, Miss Oliver. When you choose your clothing, you do reveal something about yourself."

He looked at her aslant. "Your gown is simple, yet it follows fashion. This shows that you care about practicality but do not wish to do yourself a disservice by appearing a frump. In the same way, your hair is coiled back from your face, yet its twists have been carefully arranged. In your every choice, you balance the demands of the world with the demands of your own self."

Louisa sank from her crouch to a seat on the floor, an arm's length away. "Oh." She stopped; shook her head. "Thank you?"

She smoothed her skirt, wondering at all he'd read into the floral-patterned fabric. One hand reached up to touch her hair, as though it had altered when spoken of. "I'd never thought of it all that way. You surprise me, my lord."

He lifted his chin and looked at her directly. "Likewise. Please, Miss Oliver, don't assume that every compliment I give is insincere. I might candy my words, but they do have real substance." His expression turned wry. "Well, sometimes they do."

A knot of something tense between her shoulders began to relax. "That's more than many in the *ton* could say. Certainly more than most would admit."

She leaned against the shelf next to him, feeling an odd tug of companionship. It came from the informality, maybe; sitting not on furniture with her back straight as a yardstick, but on the floor, her legs folded up like a child's.

There was nothing improper, exactly, about sitting like this, yet she felt as though she'd left propriety behind her at long last. She sat close enough to the infamous Lord Xavier to breathe in his clean scents of starch and spice; close enough to judge the span of his biceps beneath his coat. Would her two hands meet around it? She felt an almost irresistible urge to try, to wrap her fingers around some part of him and clutch this moment close.

His eyes were not wholly gray, she saw at this close distance; there was a rim of warm brown around the edges. The indentation of his upper lip was sharp.

Careful, Louisa. Her hands flexed. She pressed them to

the floor at her sides; then, to cover the gesture, pushed herself to her feet again.

Xavier sprang upright in one sure movement. "So, Miss Oliver. Now that we are all business, fulfilling our wager of time, what shall we look at? I think you were studying something particular when I came in." He began to prowl the shelves, looking up and down one bookcase, then the next.

"You may call me Louisa, if you like."

He stumbled, catching himself on a shelf of dreary-looking historical tomes. "May I? You shock me again."

"How gratifying. But you mustn't expect me to keep this up, my lord. I'm not a shocking person by nature."

Xavier untangled his feet. "I wonder about that."

He brushed off the mussed cuffs of his coat, twisting the trio of buttons trimming the sleeves. "If you honor me with your name, I can do no less. I've already told you not to curtsy. You must stop *my lord*-ing me, too."

"And call you what? Xavier?"

"Yes. Or—well, no, that's not the same as a Christian name, is it?" Twist, twist, twist, went his fingers on the button. "That's my title. But since I've been the earl virtually since birth, that's all I've ever been called." His brows knit, as though the realization surprised him.

"Even by your family?"

He shrugged. "Jane and her mother. That's it. Lockwood more distantly. We're a sparse family tree."

"What of the other young ladies whom you threaten and intimidate with compliments on their clothing?"

Twist, twist, twist. "You are the only such lady. If the subject of clothing entered my conversation with another female, it would have a . . . different nature."

Her hands tingled. She could guess what he meant;

could see it as clearly as though it were painted on a series of magic-lantern slides.

He would come backstage at the opera to find a lush woman like Signora Frittarelli in her dressing room. He might call her by her first name when he entered, or he might merely draw close, fixing her with those mesmerizing eyes. They need not speak at all as he trailed clever fingers over her neck, down her bosom, into her bodice. His mouth would follow his fingers, hot and demanding, and clothes would be loosened, removed, cast aside.

And then . . .

Louisa stopped herself. Between her legs, she'd grown damp. Talk of letting one's imagination run away; she had put herself in the place of that passionate woman, wishing for his touch, no matter how practiced it might be or how little he might care for her.

He was good to look at, good to breathe in. And he was watching her, a little smile on his lips, as though he'd been observing the scene acted out in Louisa's mind.

"It's fine," she said in her crispest voice. "If you like to be called Xavier, I will—"

"Alexander," he interrupted. "That's my Christian name. Or you could call me Alex. I think I had a nurse once who called me that."

He looked puzzled again. "It sounds odd to my own ears. Yet it *is* my name."

"All right," Louisa said. "Alex."

He gave a final twist to a button, then nodded. "That's settled, then. So. What were you looking at, Louisa?"

"Oh dear. That *Louisa* is going to take some getting used to. Alex."

"I could call you something else instead. I'll return to *Miss Oliver*, if you're repenting of our agreement. Or sweeting. Or muffin."

Louisa choked. "Muffin? If you call me that in front of my aunt, I believe she'd die on the spot a happy woman. You'd fulfill her desires for gossip and matchmaking at once."

"A large burden to place on a mere two-syllable word," he murmured. "The idea is tempting. So. Books, muffin. Is there something you'd like to look for, muffin?"

"If you call me that again, *muffin*, I'll be looking for something to throw at you."

He gave her a sidelong glance, a lopsided smile, then crouched to study the shelf she'd been looking over when he entered. "I'm not sure what these are," he said. "They look like ledgers."

He tugged one from the shelf, handling the old binding with such care that Louisa wanted to stroke his rumpled head. "This one seems to be an old book of receipts." He held the book at arm's length. "Do look. Is this a set of instructions on how to make muffins?"

Louisa turned her head away to hide her smile. "You are a wicked man."

"Simply because I tried to decipher an old cookery book, I am deemed wicked? Dear, dear. You are a harsh mistress, muffin."

He closed the book and gingerly slid it back onto the shelf, then pulled out its neighbor. "Let's see if there are any more muffins in this book."

"I warned you, I will throw something at you. Your vocabulary is lamentably small, my lord, if you can only think of—"

"Alex."

"Right, yes. Not *my lord*. Alex."

But he didn't seem to be speaking to her. He was flipping a page back and forth, squinting, his dark brows pulling into a puzzled line. "Alex. It's the only word I can read." Holding the book out to Louisa, he stood again.

She studied the gnarled, handwritten block letters. "Here's an Eleanor . . . another Alex . . . a Cuthbert."

"Cuthbert? Dear God, what a dreadful name."

Between the names, the page was covered in seemingly random strings of consonants and vowels. "I think," Louisa decided, "this book is encoded. The only things in English are the names. If you can call Cuthbert an English word."

"I don't think any other language would wish to claim it."

She looked up at him. "What is this book? Have you seen it before?"

"Never." With a nod toward a table against the far wall, he said, "Come, let's lay it out. No sense in handing Cuthbert back and forth."

"Now you're sharing Christian names with books?"

"Are you envious? Do you want more names for yourself? Muffin?" He held up his hands as he backed toward the sleek mahogany table and chairs by the tall windows. "I'm not calling you a name. I'm only thinking of food."

"My kingdom for a speck of honesty." Louisa rolled her eyes. A good gesture; she'd appear to be exasperated, and a little amused.

Because it was stupid to feel agitated, flushed, and flirted-with when Xavier—*Alex*—called her by the name of a baked-dough circle. Especially when she saw the danger of it. He was charming, yes, but that charm didn't mean a thing.

She seated herself at the table, and once again they were head to head, this time with a book between them. It made a safe little wall: something to talk about, something to distract her.

"I'm not familiar with many codes," she said, "unless it's a simple substitution cipher."

"How do you mean?" He leaned back in his chair to look her full in the face.

"Substitution. Such as, every time I needed to write a letter A, I'd use a Q instead. That's the simplest form, but I don't think that's what we have here."

"How can you tell?" One hand patted his waistcoat. "Deuce take it; I don't have my quizzing glass. The printing's tiny."

"It's not hard to figure out, if you—" Louisa cut herself off. "You find the print hard to read?"

Alex leaned yet farther back. "Not at all. Or, no more than I would any other encoded text."

"Are your eyes weak, my lord? I cannot believe the astounding Lord Xavier has such a pedestrian flaw."

Humor touched his mouth, though he lifted his chin in a haughty way. "You think I won't notice your question is impertinent if you throw another *my lord* at me, muffin?"

She scrabbled for a quill and flicked it at him. "I told you I'd throw something at you if you started that *muffin* nonsense again. And if your eyes are weak, I have an excellent magnifying lens in my bedchamber. I could fetch it the next time we meet."

She caught her error and corrected, "That is, if we meet again. I realize you're only here because the game of speculation required you to be."

Alex shook his head. "I thought you intelligent, Louisa, yet you seem to have forgotten that I *won* that game. It was your debt of time. I intended to put you at your ease by selecting an activity you would favor. I'm in this library, with you, by choice."

When his mouth curved into a half-smile, Louisa's tidy threads of thought snarled. "Oh."

His smile widened. "Is that your only response to my voluntary admission that I did something mildly courteous?

'Oh'? I've given you the power to ruin my reputation, muffin. I should run right out of here and seduce someone."

Louisa shivered a little and rubbed at her upper arms. "If you call me muffin again, you'll probably ruin *my* reputation. And anything else I can think to say by way of reply would be shrewish. Which I've recently vowed not to be, if you'll recall."

With his arms folded across his chest, his long body flung into the Windsor chair, he looked perfectly at ease. Except for his eyes; those eyes she'd thought so cool were studying her closely, warm and speculative. "While we're alone, Louisa, you may say whatever you like."

Ah, he was tempting her. Clever man. It didn't even appear to be flirtation, yet he told her exactly what she wanted to hear. What else should she expect from a master of the seductive arts, though? He could read her desires—read those of any woman—like a book.

Well, not the book that lay open on the table before them.

The question of why he would bother flirting with her was harder to answer. So Louisa ignored it. Likely she was seeing only what she wanted: honesty and an interest in books. Blade-clean features and weak eyes. Surely these formed the world's most seductive combination.

No. There would be no thinking of seduction. No no no. Only honesty. And books. It was nothing to her own credit when he wielded his gifts of charm in her direction.

"If I can say whatever I want, Alex"—her tongue tripped over the unfamiliar name, but he nodded encouragement—"then I'll say, take another look at this book, if your weak eyes can stand it, and I'll show you what I mean about the substitution cipher."

He raised his eyes to the painted ceiling. "Please, muffin, do not call my eyes *weak* or anything so unmanly.

My vision is hardly dreadful; I can make out the pips on a card. I simply find a glass helpful for deciphering mysterious encoded texts, or other close reading."

"That's not common for a young man."

He picked up the quill she'd flicked at him, turned it in his fingers, then set it down again. "I'm blessed with many uncommon gifts. Hadn't you heard?"

"Not of this one." Despite his light tone, she had the idea he was uncomfortable with the revelation. "Thank you for your frankness, Alex."

She returned to the safety of the printed word. With her index finger, she tapped a script-lettered line. "About the text—if it were a simple substitution code, we'd see a lot more of some letters than others. The code letter that represented E, for example. Or A. But this looks perfectly random, except for the names."

Alex tilted his head back to bring the page into focus. "Alex again. Cuthbert. And a Lockwood." A low whistle issued from his lips. "It must be a family history."

"Of Lord Lockwood?"

"Lockwood's family is mine, too, though distantly. The branches of the family trees have repeatedly tangled. But why would it be in code?"

"Your family must have done awful things. Any Roundheads in the family? Papists? Brandy smugglers?"

"All that and more, I daresay." He squinted at the page again. "Do you think it could be a Vigenère cipher? I've only heard of them; I've never seen an encoded text of that type."

"You know about other types of ciphers?" Louisa realized her eyebrows had shot up. "I'm sorry. It's rude of me to sound surprised that you know about something."

"Indeed, it is. You'd better be careful, muffin."

Louisa seized another quill, ready to flick it, but he

wasn't looking at her. He dragged an inkwell from the edge
of the table to a point directly in front of him and began to
nudge it with an index finger, rotating it a few degrees at
a time. "I must have read about the Vigenère once. Ciphers
appeal to males once they reach the age of being interested
in smuggling and pirates, you know."

"And what age is that?"

He tugged his lower lip between his teeth. "From about
age four to death."

Louisa permitted him to see her smile this time. "You
could be right about Vigenère. It uses a key word and alphabet table to encrypt everything. But if we don't know
the key word, we'll never decrypt the book."

We, she'd said. As though the Earl of Xavier would want
to muck about with an old ledger instead of fornicating
with opera singers.

"Alex." She hesitated. "Are you interested in trying to
solve this? Or shall we put it back on the shelf for another
several generations?"

Once more, he gave the inkwell a little nudge. Then with
a quick shove back from the mahogany table, he pushed to
his feet and paced in a short line. The length of the table,
he paced off, booted heel to toe, then back again.

"I don't know if I'll have the time during the house
party." He dragged a hand through his short hair, leaving it
rumpled. "But yes, I'm interested. It's something to do with
my family, I can tell that, and I know precious little about
them."

"Why is that?" Louisa looked blankly at this tall man,
pacing in such controlled agitation.

"Well. Because. Everybody died."

"Yes? That does tend to happen to previous generations,
Alex."

He paused in his movement and shot her a wry look.

"That's not what I mean, *muffin*. I was orphaned as an infant. It'd be . . . nice to learn a bit about who came before me."

The word *nice* seemed to surprise him.

Louisa liked that.

"I'll do what I can," she said. "The key word might be written in the cover somewhere; I haven't looked through the entire book yet."

He nodded. "I'd be very grateful. I'll help you as much as I can."

He extended a hand, and at first Louisa thought he meant to help her to her feet. But no; it was sideways, not palm up. He wanted to seal the bargain with a handshake.

She sucked in a quick breath, gave a quicker nod, and tried to shake his hand in the quickest gesture of all.

Long fingers—slightly rough, a bit warmer than her own skin—clasped hers. Her naked fingers seemed to freeze within his, but when she sought to draw her hand back, he held it in the tender valley between his thumb and palm.

His eyes held her gaze tight again. How odd were those eyes. They made her feel as though she was the only woman in the world, as though they cared to look at nothing else.

And they made her wish very much that were true, and not simply a skill of his.

Before she could soften like butter in July, she yanked her hand away and turned back to study the page. There was no way to ignore the tall form standing behind her, but she pretended to be unaffected. "You needn't toy with me, Alex. I told you I'd study it."

She thought she heard him say "Likewise" as he stepped away, but she couldn't be sure.

Oh, that man. She pushed back her own chair, wanting to

walk after him, to take his hand again and dare him to look her in the eye again, to say something real while he did.

But before she could rise to her feet, there was a perfunctory knock at the door. Lord Lockwood stepped in, closing the door behind him, then looked around the library.

"Ah, Coz. Having an interlude with a lightskirt?"

"Only *Fanny Hill*," Alex said smoothly. "She's ready for her next customer, if you're man enough."

Lockwood snorted his approval. "Ah, *Memoirs of Fanny Hill*. Only book I ever read with anything like real interest. You've got it here?"

Alex lowered his voice and shifted slightly, and Louisa realized he was trying to block the sight of her with his body. "There's a hidden shelf under the window seat. You'll find her there, and more like her."

"You don't say," came the voice of the now-unseen marquess. "Well, time enough for that later. Mrs. Protheroe and I will find inspiration in your hidden stash, if I have my way."

"You have my best wishes," said Alex in a dry voice. From behind, Louisa saw him fidgeting, raking his fingers through his hair again. "Something I can help you with?"

"Yes." The marquess sounded amused. "If you can bear to leave Miss Oliver, you're needed in three places at once. Your guests are in crisis again."

He leaned widely around the pillar of Alex's body and waggled his fingers at her. "How do you do, Miss Oliver? I must say, I'm surprised to see you fully clothed in my cousin's presence. He must be slipping. Or perhaps he's simply not attracted to you."

The bluntness of this statement stung like a physical slap. Louisa counted to five in Italian, then German. When she reached *fünf*, she was able to offer Lockwood a composed smile.

"Since family tastes seem to run toward the ornamental

and promiscuous, I'd be very flattered if Lord Xavier professed not to be attracted to me."

She turned from Lockwood—and from Alex—and stared at the pages of the ledger with as careful attention as she might study the mysteries of the Rosetta Stone.

"Miss Oliver," said Alex in a stiff, unfamiliar voice, "I've been honored by your time. I regret that responsibilities demand my presence elsewhere."

She picked up the book and held it closer to her face. "I find no fault with your manners, my lord. Please, don't worry about a thing."

As Lockwood snorted again, Louisa cast Alex a sidelong glance. He looked troubled. So she shot him a wink.

He sucked in a deep breath, startled, like a man who saw a tame horse rear up in front of him. Then with a small smile, he took his leave.

So, he wanted it all to be a secret. His interest in the book; his time with her. The use of their first names, and their wobbly newfound truce.

Louisa had never been expected to bear so many secrets before. And she found she liked the unexpected very much. To have a secret with Lord Xavier—Alex—was a wicked little pleasure.

And it was not one that would endanger her, was it? Not her body, mind, or heart. Surely not, if she was careful.

Left alone with the coded book, her eyes scanned the lines of text. But they found no clues, because her thoughts followed Alex out of the library, trying to decode the man himself.

Chapter 7

Containing Balsamic Injections

"What's the crisis this time?" Xavier couldn't keep the impatience out of his voice as he matched strides with his cousin away from the library. "Don't tell me there's another fire. It would be distressingly uncreative of our *cara signora*."

Lockwood caught Xavier's arm and brought him to a halt in the center of the corridor. He looked around, checking that they were alone, then hissed, "*You* are the crisis. It's two days till Christmas, man, and we've got nothing like the proper sense of festivity. You're allowing your own house party to disintegrate, just for the sake of ten pounds bet on some tedious little chit."

Xavier wrenched his arm free and folded his hands behind his back. Expression Number Three, Amused Tolerance, would probably work best right now. He wouldn't dignify Lockwood's accusations; he'd dismiss them.

"There are several inaccuracies in what you say, Lockwood. First, I'm allowing no such thing. In fact, I have something marvelous planned for tomorrow that will bring together the whole house party."

This was a complete lie, but he would figure out a way to make it true.

"Second, the wager was your idea. Third, it's my business how I choose to win it."

He was all ready with *Fourth, she is far from tedious*, but trapped the tip of his tongue between his teeth. Best to let Lockwood assume that Louisa was an investment he sought to protect. If the marquess knew Xavier was beginning to like her, he'd increase his efforts to unsettle the young woman.

Not that Lockwood had been able to succeed at upsetting her so far, either with words or with gropings of her person. The marquess had slid his face over Louisa's bosom; he'd given her a kiss. Wasted opportunities, for he had treated Louisa's body as a chess pawn.

Half-bare breasts and silk-sleek skin. Wry lips that spoke the unexpected. If Xavier were permitted to touch her, he would give her pleasure. Their swift, everyday contact had shot sparks through him, and he didn't think she'd been unaffected. Something burned between them; something livid and eager.

Yet she seemed to resent that, or him. And he owed her more than pleasure. He owed her respect.

Lockwood looked disgruntled. "Well, it's a damned dull business you're making of it."

"Don't pout, dear fellow. We'll find you a woman of your own. Surely *someone* wants something to do with you," Xavier said in a soothing voice.

As he'd expected, Lockwood bristled. "I'll do for myself, *dear fellow*. Don't trouble your empty head about me. See to yourself, why don't you? And see to your other guests. You don't have this party under your usual control."

The marquess's blue eyes narrowed, and his mouth curved into an unpleasant little smile. "Something's different, isn't it? It's not only the *ton* poking its high-bridged noses where they aren't wanted. You're different, too. You haven't even bedded *la signora*, have you?" He chuckled. "I'd thought better of you."

"Maybe," Xavier said in his chilliest voice, "what you've been thinking of as better is actually worse."

He and Lockwood blinked at each other, equally surprised by these words. In his chest, Xavier's heart thudded painfully hard. *Maybe. Maybe.*

Lockwood's mouth opened, then shut again. He looked confused.

Xavier recovered first. With a carefree grin, he said, "Well, why need we consider philosophy? Much better to find a good port. Care to come to the cellars with me? We'll pick an exceptional vintage for tonight's festivities."

Lockwood was willing enough to go along with this return to the familiar, and to return to the cellars. But Xavier's empty head, as the marquess had called it, was filling with questions.

Maybe.

It would be easy to drink them away, to drown his troublesome thoughts in liquor and flirtation, or the simple seduction of a round-heeled woman. But maybe . . .

Maybe he didn't want to do that anymore.

The eyes of the transported youth sparkled with more joyous fires, and all his looks and motions acknowledged excess of pleasure, which I now began to share, for I felt him in my very vitals! I was quite sick with delight! . . . Thus I lay, gasping, panting under him . . .

Good God. Xavier had not been exaggerating the lewdness of *Fanny Hill*.

Soon after the two noblemen had left her, Louisa had retrieved the old novel from the hidden shelf beneath the window seat. Then she scurried off to her bedchamber and stretched out on the dark red damask counterpane of the bed, eager to read Fanny's scandalous tale in the hours before dinner.

Why not? As a scholar, she ought to learn as much as she could on all subjects.

Even so, she hadn't expected young Fanny's transformation from country girl to favored whore to be quite so informative. And the vocabulary was as colorful as the behavior. Why, Louisa had never heard of "balsamic injections"—though considering the part of the body that emitted the fluid, she could guess well enough what was meant.

Good heavens. There were a great many injections and emissions in this book. And Louisa wasn't at all scandalized; she wanted to know more.

Did Alex . . . emit?

Stupid question. If rumors were to be believed, he'd *emitted* with every courtesan and widow in London, as well as a great number of married ladies and supposed maidens.

But were rumors to be believed, where he was concerned?

She only had to recall the way he'd squinted at the coded ledger, willing his indistinct vision to resolve the words, to suspect that he wasn't who he pretended to be. Or who others pretended he was?

The dissonance was intriguing. Any man who could talk of a Vigenère cipher one moment and a whore-book the next was . . . all right, Louisa was interested in him, and not just on a scholarly level. And these ruminations were doing nothing to ease the tight, sharp ache of desire, or to douse the hot color that had flooded her cheeks while she read.

Unfortunate, because the door to her bedchamber was suddenly flung open without so much as an introductory knock.

Without looking up from the thankfully plain binding of her book, Louisa knew who had entered.

"Good afternoon, Aunt Estella." She laid aside the novel with a calm that belied her still-pounding heart, then assembled a blank expression before facing Lady Irving. "May I help you with something? Do you need assistance dressing for dinner?"

The countess paced across the room, then back, then dropped into a chair next to the fireplace. "I've got a maid for that, my girl, though it's thoughtful of you to offer." She extended her feet toward the hearth. "Thoughtful, and completely unbefitting your station."

"You've entered to give me some advice, then." Louisa didn't bother framing the sentence as a question. It was a certainty.

Lady Irving eased her scarlet slippers free from her heels, sighing with contentment. "That's a fine coal fire you've got here. I will say, Xavier takes care of his guests well. He never knows which bedchambers are going to be needed from day to day. Eh?"

"I suppose." Louisa rubbed at her arms, not feeling the same warmth. "But that's surely not what you wanted to advise me on."

Her aunt shot a sharp look. "Give me a moment to settle, young miss. I'm not as young as I used to be, though if I hear you repeat that, I'll have your tongue for it."

"No one is as young as she or he used to be. That's the way time works."

Time, which she'd wagered. In a flash she remembered

the card game, and the wager Lockwood and Alex had placed on her.

The stakes of that hand of speculation had been higher than she knew. But she'd made good use of her three hours, hadn't she? Especially considering the time had been her loss, not her win.

"More of your scholarly roundaboutation," grumbled Lady Irving. "Gentlemen don't want to hear about *time*, my girl. That's the quickest way to run them off."

"The quickest?" Louisa couldn't resist. "Surely there are quicker ways. Such as spilling punch on a favorite waistcoat. Or informing them of a desire for permanent chastity after marriage."

The countess's auburn head snapped up. "What's this nonsense about chastity?" She coughed. "Not that it's nonsense for an unmarried woman."

"You needn't worry about me, Aunt. I'm as chaste as . . ." *As Fanny Hill was not*, she finished in her head, but her aunt had already shaken off the topic and moved on.

"Come sit, my girl." She patted the arm of her chair. "I do have something to tell you, at that."

Louisa ignored the spindly arm of the chair, which looked as though it wouldn't support a cat. Instead, she tugged a pillow off of the bed and plumped it onto the floor, then sat on it at her aunt's feet. "I'm abject before you, dear Aunt."

"Saucy," said the countess, stifling a smile. "Well. Don't think I didn't notice your early departure from the game last night. Mighty unsociable of you, my girl, to leave the party as though you were a dull stick."

That stung more than it ought. "But I'd already had my turn as the blind man," she protested. "And I'd been kissed and groped by Lord Lockwood." Somehow she kept her expression serene as she said this.

"Nothing wrong with that, in the course of a game," sniffed her aunt. "Everyone knows that's the purpose of blind-man's buff. But when you take your turn, then leave, it looks like an escape, my girl. It looks—well, as though you didn't want to be there. And the men noticed, believe me."

"Now I know you're teasing." Louisa kept her voice light. "Men never notice what I do."

"You're talking a great deal of rot for such a smart girl. A woman can't stab a marquess with a hairpin and not expect men to notice what she does after that. Mind you, I won't say you were indispensable to the festivities."

"No, never that."

The countess ignored this interjection. "Your friend Jane had Lord Kirkpatrick up against the wall before a minute was past. That Cornish fellow, you know; the one who doesn't look nearly as much like Byron as he thinks he does."

"How delightful for them both," Louisa said. "Jane's been craving a bit of fun."

"Speaking of fun, my girl." Lady Irving turned a shrewd eye upon Louisa, who wished she were sitting at a more dignified height. "I was absolutely shocked—yes, *shocked*—by the behavior of our host last night."

Louisa's face went hot again. She folded herself up and leaned closer to the fire, hoping her aunt would credit the color to the glowing coals. "He seemed perfectly proper while I was there."

"Indeed, indeed." Heavily beringed hands drummed on the arms of the chair. "That's what was so shocking about it. I must say, I'd never have expected the infamous Lord Xavier to stand aside during a game of blind-man's buff. Especially when that hussy of an opera singer, or dancer, or whatever she is, was displaying her whole bosom for him."

"It's a biological imperative," Louisa said in a wooden voice. "She wants to mate with him."

"Yes, well, she's not the only one," Lady Irving sniffed. "I couldn't get through a day in London without hearing him simpered over in every ballroom and parlor. For a while after that messy business with your sister—all the gossip about her, and Matheson, and your broken engagement—I couldn't stand to so much as hear Xavier's name."

"It *was* a messy business." Louisa swallowed, her throat too dry. "But it wasn't really his fault. So he says, and I believe him."

"Yes, yes. Now we know he wasn't malicious toward your sister. He was only an idiot, and if women start faulting men for that, we'll all have to do without bed-sport indefinitely."

"*Aunt*." Not even coals glowed hotter than Louisa's face now.

"Well, not you. I know *you* could never forgive idiocy. And before you're married, you shouldn't be thinking about bed-sport, either."

"Um." This was the extent of the reply Louisa could muster.

Fortunately, Lady Irving was perfectly capable of carrying on a conversation by herself. "All I'm saying is, you oughtn't to go so hard on the fellow. He's tried to keep this house party proper. If he's looking for a wife, you could do a lot worse than be that lady."

"Um."

This time Lady Irving noticed Louisa's tongue-tied response. "Don't be missish, my girl. You've got to get married eventually, unless you intend to be an intolerable burden on some branch of your family for the rest of your life."

"I rather thought I'd be a widow like you," Louisa said.

"That way I can give the world my opinion and tell everyone else to shove their own."

"It's an excellent plan, with one flaw." The countess stretched, her stays creaking audibly beneath the puce satin of her gown. "You've got to marry first. I planned on being a young widow, too, but I still had to put up with Lord Irving for several years. It'd be best to marry someone you can tolerate."

"And you think I can tolerate Lord Xavier." Louisa stood, turning away from her aunt, and stepped over to the dressing table on which she'd arranged her comb, brush, and a few little bottles of unguents and scents.

"I think you can do more than that." Her aunt's voice was sharp, knowing. "I've seen the way you look at him."

"I can't imagine what you mean, Aunt." She arranged and rearranged the dainty little objects. They could form a hexagon. A pentagon. A border on either side of the dressing table.

"You look at him as though he's a fox and you're a hound. And he looks at you as though he thinks the same."

"That he's a hound? He's *some* sort of dog." A rectangle, this time. The comb and brush made the short sides.

"No. He looks at you as though *you're* the hound and he's the fox. He's fascinated by you, my girl, and a bit afraid, too, I wouldn't wonder. All in all, that's not a bad foundation for a marriage."

Louisa's hand slipped and knocked over a bottle of perfumed oil. The stopper popped out, spilling lily-scented oil on the sleek wood of the table. "Drat. I'm sorry, Aunt Estella, but I've just—I need a cloth."

Lady Irving tutted, then whisked forth her lime-colored fichu. "Here, here. It'll do as well as a handkerchief. No, I don't want it back; I'd smell like I'd vomited up flowers."

As Louisa wiped up the scented oil with her aunt's

gaudy lace, Lady Irving pressed on. "How is your work with the books going, my girl? Are you happy now that you've got your hands on one of the finest old libraries in Surrey?"

"The library is everything I hoped it would be." Louisa knew her voice sounded flat, but at least she wasn't blushing the color of a poppy.

"And is it all you want?" Her aunt was far too perceptive.

"It's all I want in a library," Louisa said.

"That's a weasel of an answer."

"I know. But it's all I'm sure of right now."

Lady Irving shifted again, trailing a ringed finger over the arm of the chair, then reaching for the carved edge of the fireplace. "Marble," she commented. "Nothing but the finest."

She looked up, her eyes the clear russet of brandy in the fire's glow. "My girl, I believe that's the first time you've ever admitted you were unsure of something."

"Nonsense. I—" Louisa stopped when her aunt raised penciled eyebrows. "I probably have admitted that before."

"Hmm." Lady Irving shoved her feet back into her slippers, then stood with another creak of stays. "I'm glad you're trying something new, my girl. Leaving a place doesn't do you any good if you take all your problems with you."

Louisa shuffled her foot, not sure what to say. And then her eye caught the plain, worn binding of *Fanny Hill*.

At home, she helped her stepmother take care of her young half-siblings. With her sister, Julia, and Julia's husband, James, she was the odd one out, useless as a third wheel on a curricle. And as a third wheel on a curricle would, she sapped the excitement from their journey. No one needed her at either place.

Here, her role was not set. Not yet. She could be anyone.

"I don't think I've brought my problems with me." She offered a wry little smile, a carefully composed expression that combined humor and mischief and a touch of secret. It was good work. She'd practiced it many times during her dreadful London season.

Her aunt's eyes were sharp and bright. Her mouth quivered, and she drew Louisa into a quick hug.

"That's my girl," said Lady Irving. "Now, mind you wear something dashing for dinner. I want Lord Xavier to be salivating over your chest."

"Um."

"Exactly." With a pat on Louisa's cheek, Lady Irving strode out of the room as abruptly as she'd come in.

Louisa blew out a deep breath, sinking onto the edge of the bed's rich red counterpane. No, she hadn't brought her family problems with her.

But she had a new set of problems now. She had two wagering-mad noblemen to best, and a most inconvenient desire to master. Or not to master at all.

It felt like the beginnings of a life of her own.

The novelty was sweet, in its way.

Chapter 8

Containing a Dreadful Imitation of a Stag

Considering he'd had no plans for "something marvelous" when he'd talked with Lockwood the afternoon before, Xavier thought he had put together a decent activity for his guests.

"But what *is* it?" Jane persisted, half running to keep up with Xavier's long strides. "I don't want to walk halfway across your estate if you've got something dreadful in store. I can be bored indoors without freezing off my—"

"*Jane*," he warned.

"—toes," she finished. "Good Lord. How suspicious you are, Xavier. Does that come with querulous old age?"

Xavier made no reply; he just lengthened his stride a bit more. It was an effective revenge, because Jane was forced to drop back from his side.

He enjoyed a few minutes of blessed quiet then, as he led his house party to the seldom-used folly on his estate. It was about a half mile southeast of the house, a small building in a clearing. He hoped the servants had carried everything out according to his instruction.

This wasn't an unpleasant day to be outside, no matter how Jane complained. The weather was mild for late December, though the breeze did have a sharp nip. A few ridges of pitted, soggy snow remained against tree trunks, and the ground was spongy from fog and rain, pleasantly soft underfoot. The last of autumn's dry, curled leaves crunched beneath his boots. Behind him, he heard bubbling voices and an occasional peal of laughter.

There was a peace in the bracing wind, the heedlessness of the leaves that danced toward him and away. Xavier's head was still full of *maybes* which not even page after page of Dante had been able to chase away the night before. Today his eyes felt dry and gritty.

But he had a role to play. They all would, once they reached their destination. That was the brilliance of his plan.

Ah, there was the folly. The walk hadn't been at all strenuous, especially after he got away from Jane's yawping.

The small building was a delicately wrought eight-sided Gothic temple atop a gentle hill, a stark, bright white against the gray-brown of the trees that surrounded it. The structure was all arch and turret, of no earthly use whatsoever except to look beautiful. Cushioned benches ran around its inside edges between each pointed archway, and in front of it was a giant cauldron hanging over a banked fire.

An enticing smell of spice and sugar, sharpened with the tang of strong spirits, wafted from the cauldron to greet the guests. A tray of copper tankards lay before it.

Good. The scene was set.

"Rum punch," called Lord Weatherwax. "Very festive. Excellent on a cool day like today." Beneath the floppy brim of his hat, the wind had snarled his downy white hair and bitten his nose red. He looked a trifle insane, though harmlessly so.

Behind him, the other guests trailed toward the folly in a long, ragged line.

"It is indeed rum punch," Xavier confirmed. "My butler, Wheeling, mixed it himself. It is a point of pride with him."

"What have you planned for us, my lord?" Lady Charissa Bradleigh demanded. "You said you were going to give us all cause for celebration."

"Ah yes," Xavier replied. "I did."

He paused until all the guests, some huffing with effort, reached the folly. They clustered around the warmth of the cauldron, and Weatherwax, that old inebriate, took it upon himself to begin ladling out punch to anyone who picked up a tankard.

"I told you all a slight untruth," Xavier said. "You are to give *me* a cause for celebration."

Puzzled faces stared back at him, and he continued. "As I'm sure you all know, today is Christmas Eve. I don't intend to ask you to do anything so prosaic as cut greenery or find a Yule log. Tradition is for those who can think of nothing better to do by way of celebration."

"And you've thought of something better?"

This from Louisa, of course.

She was swaddled in a scarlet hood and pelisse, her hands stuffed into a muff the same rich brown as her hair. Against the colorless sky and ground, she seemed the only vivid thing in the world.

"That depends on you," he replied, and his lips silently shaped the word *muffin* for the pleasure of watching her breeze-pinked cheeks turn a deeper shade.

He waved the guests into the folly, toward the benches, and added more loudly, "It depends on all of you. I ask you to share your talents, and if we all find the entertainment more compelling than denuding trees, we'll have ourselves a pleasant Christmas Eve."

Which expression would work best now? He settled on Expression Number Two, Haughty Certainty. That usually convinced the sheep of the *ton* that an idea was worthwhile.

"What talents you say?" *La signora* this time. "You wish I sing?"

She had thrown back her cape, the better to display her undeniably magnificent bosom. With her chin raised and her dark eyes defiant, she looked more like Mozart's Commendatore than his Donna Anna.

Xavier smothered a genuine smile at the thought, then contorted it into Expression Number Three, Amused Tolerance. "Not if you have another talent you wish to display. You must all be at your most innovative. The most talented guest will be permitted to name a favor or set the next wager."

As he spoke, he made his voice calmer, more languid. If he sounded as though he didn't care whether they agreed or not, they'd be more likely to agree. Especially with a little rum punch in them.

It would be more amusing if they weren't so predictable.

"Presumptuous, aren't you, Xavier? We are not all performing monkeys," Lady Irving barked. "I don't have any talents that I wish to trot out for the group."

All right, they weren't *all* predictable.

More of Expression Number Three. "My dear lady, knowing your incisive wit, I should never dream of asking anything of you but to drink and be merry. Your own talent can be demonstrated by sitting aside and passing judgment upon others."

Lady Irving's eyebrows shot up. "You want me to get tipsy and criticize everyone."

"I knew you'd put the right words to it."

She choked. "It seems Christmas has come a day early this year. That's the best gift I've ever been given."

"I want a gift, too," pouted Lady Audrina Bradleigh. "What will you give me?"

The youngest of Lady Alleyneham's numerous daughters, and the boldest, sat at the side of her skittish mother. The countess looked as though she was poised on the balls of her feet, ready to sit or bolt as his reply dictated.

Maybe. Maybe he didn't want to give the usual sort of reply, as maidens and chaperones stared at him, as *la signora* wielded her bosom like a deadly weapon. He was particularly aware of Louisa's gaze, like prickling heat at the nape of his neck.

Yet Lockwood had been right; Xavier bore the responsibility for the success or failure of this house party.

So be it: he would create a diversion. A diversion so diverting that they would all be delighted, and he would disarm any disastrous designs.

He rubbed at the back of his neck, as though his mental alliteration was Louisa's fault.

"My gift," he said, looking over the heads of all his seated guests, "is to perform first."

He *had* to stop saying things without having a clue what he intended to do.

Expression Two, then: Haughty Certainty. His mind reeled, and he stalled. "I will require the assistance of Mrs. Tindall. If you don't mind, Cousin?"

His hostess had just settled herself with a tankard of punch, and her ruddy face bore an expression of great contentment. Her small eyes blinked wide with surprise.

"No no, dear," she said. "You can't want me. Have Janie help you instead."

Xavier pivoted slowly to face Jane. "Yes," he said. "Miss Tindall will serve the purpose."

Jane stood, her jaw set. "What fool thing are you going to ask me to do?"

At last, Xavier had an idea. "We shall perform a charade together."

When she blanched, he whispered his plan in her ear, battering her with words until she gave in. "You're a madman, Xavier."

"Careful, my dear cousin. Insanity runs in the family," he said cheerfully. He looked at Louisa for a reaction and was please to note a suppressed laugh behind her glove.

He turned back to Jane. "Goddess, to your bath. Would you care to use the cauldron? I can have it emptied."

"You're mad," Jane said again in a resigned voice. She plopped down at the center of the patterned stone floor. "Mercy, it's cold." She sighed. "I'll have a bath to warm up."

With dispirited gestures, she began to mime taking a bath. "Dum de dum dum, I am a goddess. Dum de dum, I hope no one watches me in the bath. Dum de dum dum. I'm soaping my arms. Dum de dum dum. I love to hunt. I hope no one walks by. I would hate to get up off of this cold floor—I mean, out of my warm bath. Dum de dum dum."

"That's the worst singing I've ever heard," Lady Irving commented loudly. "I hope she's portraying Jean-Paul Marat, so Xavier will come and kill her."

"Aunt, how can you say so?" Louisa sounded shocked. "That's a dreadful guess. She said she was a goddess, which Marat decidedly was not."

"Helen of Troy!" Lady Alleyneham squealed, patting plump hands together.

"She wasn't a goddess, either," muttered Jane. "Which I am. Dum de dum dum."

"She was a goddess of beauty," said Lord Kirkpatrick. He turned his head to the side, displaying his sharp profile. Good Lord. The man really did want everyone to think he was Byron.

Still, the guests were interested enough. Which meant it was time for Xavier to play his own part. He took a deep breath and prepared to make an idiot of himself.

"Strictly speaking, you ought not to make a sound during our charade, Jane," he said, then darted out through one of the folly's Gothic archways and stood half hidden behind a delicate column.

Jane rolled her eyes and continued to mouth words as she acted out her bath. If he was reading her lips aright, she had an impressive vocabulary of swear words.

Idiot-making time.

He strolled halfway across the span of one archway, one hand up to his shoulder as though supporting a quiver of arrows. When he saw Jane, he stopped walking. He let his jaw sag open and his eyes bug out. He turned to face her, his arms limp at his sides, standing rooted, staring.

"Xavier, there's no future for you on the stage," Lady Irving called. "You look more like a half-wit than a man in love."

"There is no difference, my lady," Lord Lockwood replied.

Xavier shot his cousin a quick Look, then returned to gaping at Jane. She continued to scrub at her arm with an invisible sponge for a few more seconds, then turned her head. Her face froze, and her eyes narrowed as she saw him. Unfolding her small frame with such majesty that she seemed much taller, she stood, pivoted on the balls of her feet, and pointed an imperious finger at him.

Well. She was quite good.

He clutched at his throat, indicating his silence, and Jane nodded haughtily and began to turn away. Xavier stamped his feet, holding a hand up to his mouth as if calling for help.

Jane whipped her head back and pointed at him again.

So white-angry was her face that her small gloved hand seemed to carry a current. She was a goddess disobeyed; her expression was terrible and majestic.

"Now *that*'s an actress," Lady Irving said. "And I mean that in the most complimentary of terms."

"Well done, Janie," echoed Mrs. Tindall over the edge of her tankard. "You look ever so fearsome."

No compliments for him? Ah, well. The charade was almost played out.

He clutched at his chest, scrabbling at his clothing, sending his hat scudding across the floor of the folly. *What would it feel like to suffocate, with everyone staring at him?* He twisted back and forth in feigned agony, shuddering and crumpling down, down, until he touched the earth with his hands.

That was that. As soon as all fours touched the earth, he lifted his head, all pain gone. His eyes blinked wide, and he turned his head in all directions with short movements.

"He's a sheep," guessed Lady Alleyneham.

"Who can tell?" Lady Irving replied. "He's dreadful."

"Aunt," Louisa said again. "He's a stag, don't you see? Actaeon, interrupting the goddess Diana in the bath. Diana turned him into a stag as punishment for watching her."

Xavier shot to his feet. "Excellent, Miss Oliver. Which means you shall offer the next perf—"

"Wait," Jane interrupted. She lowered her hand to her side, and she was simply Jane again. "We forgot to choose people to act as the hunting dogs. Who is to tear apart our Actaeon? After he became a stag, he was destroyed by his own dogs. So sorry for your fate, Cousin."

"Death by dogs?" Xavier sighed. In for a penny . . .

Before he could think about all the reasons why not to do this, from the tailoring of his coat to the demise of his dignity, he flung himself to the ground again. Prone, he writhed and shuddered and kicked.

After several seconds of this, he stopped and stood again. Expression Number Three: Amused Tolerance. "There you go, Jane," he said, breaking the stunned silence. "Death by dogs."

He brushed at his clothes, then walked into the folly, caught hands with Jane, and bowed.

A second later, she bowed, too, and the guests began to applaud and catcall.

"Was that your idea of being torn apart by dogs?" Jane shouted to him over the noise. "It looked like an apoplexy."

"I've never been torn apart by dogs before, so I made my best guess at the experience."

"I've never transformed anyone into an animal before, but you didn't see me making a fool of myself," Jane replied.

He folded his arms and stared at her until she relented. "All right, I did make a fool of myself." She dipped into a brief curtsy. "Happy Christmas, Xavier. I know you could ask for no better gift than my humiliation."

He gripped her shoulder for a second and gave her a smile. When she pulled a horrid face at him, he knew she'd understood his message: *thank you*.

He snapped up his fallen hat and pounded it back into shape. "More rum punch for everyone before our next performer? Miss Oliver, it's to be you."

She took a deep draught from her tankard, then shuddered. "I'm to be punished for knowing something of mythology?"

"Temper, temper," he chided. "You are *rewarded*. Please, feel free to astound us all. Remember, the stakes are high."

"Not high enough," said Lockwood. "What have we wagered?"

"That depends on the winner," Xavier replied.

"How democratic," said Lady Irving. "I think I could retch."

"Drink it away, Aunt," said Louisa, thrusting her tankard into the countess's hand.

"More punch," called Lord Weatherwax, and Mrs. Tindall scurried to fill his request.

More punch. Yes, that was a good idea. Xavier fetched a tankard for himself and found a place near Lockwood. He remained standing, undecided. Had it been unkind to single out Louisa? Should he go to her rescue? Help her, as Jane had him?

No, she didn't want safety. Here, then, was her chance to be bold.

She glanced at him—glared, actually—as she took her position at the center of the folly.

Good luck, muffin, he mouthed, and she shook her head at him, but he could see a smile trying to fight its way free. It rounded her cheeks, brightened her wood-brown eyes. In the breeze, the fur collar of her pelisse ruffled up around her face; fine curls tugged free from her hairpins. She looked a little wilder, flung into the outdoors. A little taller as she stood at the center of attention.

"I ought to thank Lord Xavier for choosing me to follow his performance, and Miss Tindall's," she began.

"Then do so," Jane called, and everyone laughed.

Louisa smiled. "But I won't. I *cannot* thank him. My own talents can't possibly compete with such theatrics as yours, Jane, or with a stag shot to the heart."

"The stag wasn't much to look at," commented Lady Irving, "though the actor himself wasn't half-bad."

Louisa only shook her head, a faint smile still on her lips. Slowly, she began to turn in a circle, taking in the faces upturned toward her own. Xavier knew every one of those faces: not unkind, but difficult to impress.

"Lady Audrina," she said at last. "Is there a Christmas gift you would like to receive?"

Lady Alleyneham's youngest was all titters and fidgets at being singled out. "Oh. Um. Jewelry?"

Louisa nodded. "In particular, a black pearl necklace with a heavy gold clasp. Yes?"

Lady Audrina's mouth fell open. "Yes, I mentioned that to my mother only yesterday. Did you overhear?"

"No." Louisa's arms folded more tightly inside her muff. "I simply made a guess."

"How on earth did you guess such a thing?" Lady Alleyneham laid a protective hand on her daughter's arm. "It's not possible. You must have overheard us. Though . . . we were in my daughter's bedchamber."

Her brow furrowed with confusion, and she looked around the circled benches at the other guests.

Xavier leaned against one of the folly's slim columns and crossed his arms. This was an intriguing start. "Come now, Miss Oliver. Either you possess the hearing of a bat, or you've some mysterious talent for divination. Which is it?"

"Neither, my lord." She hunched her shoulders, but her voice rang out strong. "It was a matter of observation. Lady Audrina, I've noticed that you prefer to wear dark colors. At this moment, you've matched your deep-green gown with black pearl earrings, but you wear a cameo at your neck that—if you'll forgive me—does not seem in your usual dashing style. I assumed, then, that the pearls were your own choice and the cameo a family piece, and I further assumed that you didn't yet own a necklace to match the earrings you like so well.

"Because I know you to enjoy walking and games and other active pursuits, any jewelry you wear would require a heavy clasp. And what lady with your rich coloring would choose any adornment but gold?"

When she finished, there was silence for five endless seconds. Then Lady Audrina, looking dazed, began to applaud. "I—Miss Oliver, you are a wonder. You noticed—you think I am dashing?" Her cheeks looked pink, and she raised a gloved hand to one of the black pearl drops at her ears. The smile she gave Louisa was wide and sincere.

Xavier had nothing like Louisa's talent for observation, but he could guess one thing: this was more friendliness than Lady Audrina had ever demonstrated before in Louisa's company. The Alleyneham family generally saved their smiles for those with the bluest blood.

"Choose someone else," called Jane. "What do I want?"

Louisa turned her way and regarded Jane with close interest. "A scandal."

Jane hooted. "Everyone knows that. What else?"

Louisa grinned. "A bigger scandal."

Xavier raised his eyebrows. "She's got you there, Jane."

As everyone else laughed, he gave Louisa a little smile. Lovely work. She noticed a startling amount, and he would enjoy the entertainment. As long as she didn't turn her deep eyes his way.

"And I?" Lockwood this time. "What do I want for Christmas, Miss Oliver?"

God, Xavier had taught him nothing. The way Lockwood was waggling his brows, he looked like some old roué from a comic opera.

Louisa looked him up and down, cool as ever. "A scandal for you, too. But you want it to be someone else's."

"Dash it," called Freddie Pellington, "they can't *all* want a scandal." Pellington had impeccably styled curly hair, which covered a completely empty head.

"Naturally we all want to see some scandal, Pellington,"

confirmed Lady Irving in a carrying voice. "That's why we've come to spend Christmas with Xavier, you ninny."

Pellington's pleasant face sagged, and Louisa chimed in, "You're right, Mr. Pellington. I was distressingly uncreative. I would guess that his lordship would also like . . ." She tapped a gloved finger on her cheek, her muff balanced on her other arm. Seated on the bench at Xavier's right, Lockwood tensed.

Ha. Xavier knew many answers, none of which Lockwood would care to have repeated to the party as a whole. Miss Oliver's departure and the resulting ten pounds? Any winning wager in the betting book at White's? A mistress who wouldn't leave him for a richer man? The respect of his peers?

"A lavender cravat," Louisa decided.

"Nonsense," Lockwood replied, visibly relaxing. "I've never thought of such a thing." He huffed, booted feet sliding out before him in an obnoxious pose.

Xavier did not roll his eyes. He simply asked, "Why do you suggest that?"

With her free hand, Louisa indicated Lockwood's high-crowned hat. "His lordship enjoys being at the forefront of fashion. His friends can count on him to wear unique pieces, many of which set new styles."

Lockwood's chin drew back, and he blinked several times in quick succession.

"And so," Louisa concluded, "while you might not have considered a lavender cravat in particular, my lord, it seems like the kind of thing you would enjoy owning."

This was Spanish coin rendered into speech: beautifully gilt, totally worthless. Lockwood dressed like a cit, all flash and dash. It did draw notice, though, which Xavier guessed was all Lockwood wanted.

Yes. He was preening now. Again, Xavier did not roll his eyes.

Lockwood gave his own version of Expression Number Three, Amused Tolerance. "Excellent guesswork, Miss Oliver. I've always suspected you were a woman of *unusual talents*."

To hell with it. Xavier rolled his eyes.

If anyone else noticed Lockwood's lewd little dig, they ignored it. Louisa had impressed these jaded folk at last.

Xavier realized he had folded his arms so tightly that he was starting to lose feeling in his hands. He forced himself to loosen the talon-grip he'd been keeping on his own arms.

It was not as though Louisa was *his*, after all. Just because they'd shared a few confidences, permitted each other the familiarity of Christian names—why, he'd scarcely touched the woman. She wasn't his . . . anything.

The cold seemed to hit him suddenly, the breeze reaching for his face, slapping a chill through his body. She noticed so much, and the only assurance he had from her was: she didn't hate him.

If that was the best she could say, then she might leave. And he'd miss—

No. And he'd have to pay ten pounds to Lockwood.

It wouldn't happen. Lord Xavier never lost. And he *was* Xavier, damn it. Not the *Alex* she called him; not the sentimental being who cared what Louisa Oliver thought and whether she stayed, and who told her he needed a glass to read and . . . and met her in the library because he wanted to.

That was *not* how Lord Xavier spent his house parties.

He turned his gaze to Signora Frittarelli. The singer had garbed herself in white and scarlet today, like the berries of mistletoe and holly. She was the Christmas present he'd thought to give himself: lush and merry, her ripe bosom bobbing as she laughed.

Xavier didn't feel like so much as stealing a kiss from her.

"Xavier." Jane's voice cut through the clamor of voices like a chime.

At first he thought she was addressing him, but when others started repeating his name, he realized that his dear cousin, whom he would probably be killing before the New Year, had suggested Louisa turn her gimlet eye upon him.

There was only one possible response: Expression Number Four, Condescension. "By all means. Let Miss Oliver divine my deepest desires, if she's so inclined."

Louisa was meant to look intimidated at this head-on acceptance. But she never did what she ought. She only smiled—not at him, but at Jane—and shook her head. "It wouldn't be right. He'd be far too embarrassed."

Xavier made his most Xavier-ish face. A little lift of the brows; a droop of the lids. His mouth curled. "How kind you are to seek to spare my feelings. You make me curious, though."

Beneath his thick superfine coat, the sleek gray of his waistcoat, the linen of his shirt, his heart thudded quick and restless. But it was hidden deep; no one would know.

"'I would by no means suspend any pleasure of yours.'" Louisa's mouth kicked up on one side. Likely she thought no one would recognize the quotation. *Pride and Prejudice*.

Xavier narrowed his eyes. Never mind. He wasn't expected to know about books. "Then what have you to say?" He tilted his head back ever so slightly, lifting his chin. Expression Number One: Veiled Disdain.

Louisa's smile widened. "I ask you to trust me, my lord. It would not be a pleasure for you to hear what I have to say."

So they were back where they'd started at the beginning of the house party—except her eyes seemed lit with hot mischief instead of cold contempt.

"Perhaps I'll persuade you later," he said in a voice of utter boredom. "We ought to return to the house before our fingers all fall off in this breeze."

"Rather warm, m'self," said Lord Weatherwax, tipping back yet another gulp of the hot spiced punch.

"But we must choose a winner, must we not?" Jane stood, stuffing her little hands into a red-fox muff and jutting out her chin. "I think Louisa's performance was the best."

"Miss Oliver. Yes, that was most entertaining." Lady Alleyneham granted a tight smile.

"Not bad, though it lacked theatricality," said Lady Irving. "With a fair sight more punch in me, it'd seem more impressive to hear a young lady talk about gewgaws."

"Aunt, be fair. I talked about scandals, too." Louisa slipped from the center of the folly to stand at her aunt's side.

"Unless anyone protests—or wishes to offer another performance—then it seems we have a winner." Xavier spoke quickly, not wanting to allow anyone else to break in. He was done with this farce, done with performing. Done with Numbered Expressions. Just for a little while.

"How delightful." Louisa appeared everything that was sweet and placid. Xavier wondered if anyone else noticed the furious workings of her fingers, teasing through the soft fur at her pelisse cuffs. "I get to pick a forfeit of my choice, then?"

"A favor," said Xavier, as Jane said, "A wager," and Lockwood said, "Of *my* choice."

Xavier did not roll his eyes. He adjusted his expression to one of unhurried patience. "As you like it."

Louisa shot him a sharp look. "Yes," she said. "I wish to do something festive, if none of you object. This evening, we could pair up, then see which couple can collect the most greenery."

"Pairing off?" Xavier shook his head as Lady Irving nodded.

"Excellent notion," said that lady. "We'll all get a bit of Christmas cheer about us, and I'm sure the pairs will be—hmm."

"But it'll be dark later," said Jane. "How could we see when we're off alone in the—*oh*. Never mind. I like it." She shot an assessing look at Kirkpatrick. God help the man if she got him alone.

"We'll hunt for greenery," Xavier decided, "before the daylight's entirely gone. If dinner's set back a bit, there will be time for an hour of searching. And at dinner, we can set the prize for the winners."

"I already have a prize in mind," Louisa said. "The winning pair shall claim kisses from the people of their choosing. As many as there are berries on a branch of mistletoe or holly."

Xavier's throat felt dry; he wished Lord Weatherwax hadn't tossed back the last of the rum punch. "Which branch?"

"That depends on what the winners gather." Her smile looked a little wild.

How much punch had she had? He wasn't sure. But in case she wasn't perfectly sober, it would be wise to talk this planned wager over with her. Catch her before the whole party went tramping around in the twilight, half-drunk and ready for kisses.

He could groan at the very thought of it.

He'd have to make sure he was paired with Louisa—no, he probably ought to watch over Jane. But Jane would never consent to accompany her own cousin. And who knew what might happen to Louisa under the influence of mistletoe and dusk, if someone like Lockwood got her alone?

This cursed responsibility. *He* wanted to slip into the woods, lose himself with her.

But maybe he was already lost.

He permitted himself to roll his eyes at his own mental fumblings, then—with a passable version of some Numbered Expression—led the way back to the house.

Chapter 9

Containing a Well-Timed Muffin

Once the flurry of return was over, once women had exchanged their boots for slippers and men had handed off their greatcoats, once guests had melted off for rest or bed-sport or whatever they pleased, Xavier went hunting for Louisa.

It was not much of a hunt. He knew where she was always to be found.

As soon as he pushed open the library door, he saw her: standing before the inevitable great fire, studying the pages of a small book in the warm light. The draperies had been drawn, and the room seemed to vanish into cold gray at the edges. With Louisa's slim body outlined by the light, and her pale gown splashed flame-orange, she looked other-worldly; some angelic vision born from wishes and coals and too much to drink.

That was only an observation. It was not one of those unnecessarily poetic thoughts.

At the low *thump* of the heavy door finding its frame,

she looked up from her book. "My lord," she said. "I mean, Alex. Happy Christmas Eve to you."

"And to you." He paused an arm's length away from her. "So. What is it that you think I want for Christmas?"

She shut the small volume and tucked it under her arm, then turned to face him. "That bothered you, didn't it?"

"That you played coy and didn't come up with so much as a lavender cravat for me? Yes. After our—" His hands flexed, as though he could grab the right word from the firelit air.

"Conversations about Cuthbert and the cipher?" She gave a maddening little half-smile, as if she was thinking of a secret that amused her. "You thought you deserved better."

"It's not important. Never mind." This conversation was foolish; beneath the dignity of a grown man. An earl. Xavier.

"Please." She caught his wrist with her free hand before he could turn away. "I gave you the best reply I could before the group. Lord Xavier likes a little mystery, doesn't he?"

"You needn't talk as though I'm not present." Her hand felt like a manacle around his wrist, and his stomach squeezed a protest. *Get away, before it's too late.*

It was already too late.

"But you're not." She dropped his wrist and folded her other arm across her chest, hugging the book to her. "At least, that creation the world knows as Lord Xavier is not."

She turned her head away, her profile clean and traced by light, as she stabbed him with low, mellifluous words. "I see you differently, Alex. And what I see is that you don't know what you want. Not for Christmas; not for any day."

"You are mistaken," he said with a passable attempt at coolness. "My wants are both simple and well-known. Wine, women, and song, to be pithy about the matter."

She always smiled at the most unaccountable times. "You needn't be pithy on my account, Alex. But you also needn't hide behind your reputation. If there's one thing I do believe about Lord Xavier, it's that he holds surprises."

Xavier's jaw worked, his back teeth grinding against each other.

"You don't want seduction or debauchery, or you'd have those things," she said. "You don't want any of the sins you're so often credited with. But you have nothing with which to replace them."

Her voice had dropped low and quiet by the end; the sinking sound of pity. No. She could *not* pity him.

"I know what I want," he said. The words sounded clumsy and harsh, the denial weak.

For a second, she turned her face toward him, and her dark gaze seemed to peel away the lie. "Then I apologize for being wrong," she said in a colorless voice, and turned to look at the fire again.

Untouchable. Unreachable. Unfathomable. And he had nothing to say to her by way of reply. He was still too full of *maybe*, and void of any certainty.

"Why are you here?"

Her shoulders hunched. "Because I don't know what *I* want."

Ah. There was a world of secret, unbearable pride in that one small sentence. His hand lifted. To touch her? Comfort her? Draw her close?

Push her away again?

He studied his fingers, splayed and waiting, debating. Never had he hesitated so long over a simple gesture. But answers didn't come easily where this woman was concerned. She was as deep-caught in mystery as that encoded family history.

Finally, he laid his hand at the curve of her neck. Just

laid it down, soft and slow, where the tender skin of her neck sloped into shoulder. Her skin was cooler than he'd expected, as though the fire had licked her with color but denied her its warmth. She trembled beneath his touch.

She drew in a deep breath, and her shoulder muscles knotted under the light pressure of his fingers. "I don't want that," she said in a rush.

Slow and gentle, he trailed his fingers up her neck, along the straight line of her jaw, until they found the point of her chin and turned her face to him.

His own breath seemed to come with an effort; the air was too thin, and too hot, and his hand trembled to slip the leash of his control and go skating over her curves.

"Come out with me," he said. "This evening, for the mistletoe. Be with me."

Her eyes were fathomless. "Is that wise?"

He dropped his hand to his side. "Not particularly." He laughed, a short, sharp rasp. "But it's wiser than letting Lockwood get his hands on you."

"Oh, yes." That mysterious half smile again. "You and Lockwood. Always competing."

"It's not a competition." Stung, he added, "Besides, I find your company tolerable."

"Tolerable, you say. How could I fail to be complimented by such an offer?" She turned to the fire again, dismissing the subject with her whole body, and Xavier was left with the feeling of having bungled without knowing how.

His mind spun for words—the practiced, candied words that served him so well with so many others.

You will light the evening with your smile.

Your very presence is better than any compliment.

You play the game so well, my dear; any man would crave you for a partner.

None of them was right; all over-dramatic and false.

"Muffin," he said.

Disaster. He squeezed his eyes shut, waiting for the blow.

No, she only laughed, a quiet, bubbling sound.

"You ridiculous man," she said, and Xavier knew the danger had passed, but so had some opportunity. A fragile bridge between them had snapped, and they were back to whatever they had been. Sparring partners, kept at a safe distance by the length of their bladed words.

Yet now he knew how she saw him: Alex, not Xavier. There was no going back from that truth.

"What is this book you're holding?" he asked. It was the kind of thing she would expect Alex to notice, probably.

Her expression altered. If Xavier had to put it into his own terms, it was the face he would make if he expected to breathe in the woodsy, buttery richness of Armagnac, and instead inhaled vinegar.

In a flash, that look was gone, and her face was a sweet cipher. "I believe I've found the word that will unlock the Vigenère. This"—she indicated the small book in her grip—"is an old commonplace book that I found stuffed behind that row of ledgers on your bookshelf."

Xavier leaned one shoulder against the mantel, ignoring the dig of marble into his upper arm. A little discomfort was a fair price for a pose he knew to look elegant and languid, all unconcern. A Numbered Expression, performed with his whole body. "A commonplace book full of what? Favorite quotations and such?"

"Yes." She held the book out to him, but he only looked at it as though it were covered in soot. To move from his determined slouch would spoil the line of his coat, and would undermine the effect he sought: *it matters little to me whether you think I'm the finest vintage, or whether you think I've gone sour.*

She studied him for a few seconds, then shrugged and

clasped the book in her hands again, pulling it against her chest. The stillness of her body was like a third person in the room, the chaperone that made sure they'd keep a proper distance from one another.

"It seems," she said, "your ancestors shared your love of Dante. The *Purgatorio*, in particular, is so often quoted that I believe it to be the key we seek. I'm only looking for a few more clues before I make the alphabet tables and try deciphering the ledger."

"*Purgatorio*. That does seem fitting, considering what I know of my family."

Louisa nodded, her expression still bland politeness. "Very wealthy. Titled. Admired. I can see how such circumstances would feel like a living purgatory. I only admire their fortitude in not thinking of it as hell."

Xavier snapped upright before he could suppress the urge. "Careful, muffin. You're growing a long nose and tail." When she stared at him, he added, "Turning into a shrew. All right, you're not in the mood for humor."

"Was that humor? My apologies."

"Listen." He squared his shoulders, keeping his arms carefully still at his sides. "I don't know much of my predecessors, but if they were anything like the *ton* today, they wouldn't be grateful for anything given to them in this world. They'd only look at those higher up and rave at the unfairness of being set lower."

Her brows had puckered. Good. She was listening, the prickly creature.

"I'm not saying it's right or wrong," he added. "I'm simply saying that you'll rarely find a person in this world who would call his own life *paradiso*."

Not that Dante's tale of paradise was all celestial light and ambrosia. But then, they weren't really talking about Dante anymore.

"If someone dislikes something about his life, he should make changes, if they are within his power," Louisa mused. She looked at the fire, then at the book in her hands. Her fingers tightened on it, a protective gesture.

"Maybe changes are not," Xavier replied.

Maybe again.

Maybe they weren't. Maybe they were. Maybe he didn't want to change after all.

Or maybe he already had, just a little.

For one thing, he desperately wanted to kiss her, to break her control and make her shatter in his arms. But he hadn't done it. He hadn't done any more than turn her face. And as long as she stood still as a statue, she was no more touchable than one.

"I will meet you on the front steps when it's time to collect greenery," he said at last. "I believe we have about an hour before the pairs set out."

She nodded. "I'll be ready."

He nodded back, feeling as uncertain as a child boosted onto his first pony, a boy handed his first gun. Was this not another rite of passage, to step into a new territory without knowing the lay of the land?

If so, then: "Thank you." Then he added, "Louisa."

She looked up at him, and her smile was like an arrow, clean angled and true. And he was Actaeon, shot and staggering.

"You are welcome. Alex."

He left her then, not knowing whether he was Alex, or Xavier, or some creature that he'd not yet fathomed.

But he had only an hour to wait, and then he'd have her all to himself again. This time, with mistletoe.

Chapter 10

Containing
One Berry Too Few

"You've found mistletoe, Alex? That's excellent. Can you reach it?"

Louisa handed Alex a small knife and watched him stretch up to slice branches from the dainty twining plant. His dark greatcoat swung about his body, the shoulder capes catching bits of breeze and jumping up, as though they wanted to look over his shoulder.

Louisa shouldn't have been surprised that they'd spotted their festive quarry so quickly. Pairs of guests had taken off in all directions, but Alex and Louisa had headed away from the firs and pines. On a hunt for mistletoe, which dropped waxy smooth and evergreen from its host tree, one would notice it most easily amidst bare-branched trees that had lost their leaves for winter.

In a small clearing not far from the folly where they'd sat and drunk that afternoon, the trees were tall, shadowy bones against the evening sky. And the bunch of mistletoe they'd found was huge and riotous; it must have been growing for years.

"Damn." Alex drew his hand back swiftly, then studied it. "Good. Didn't cut through the glove."

Louisa stepped closer. "What happened? Is the knife not sharp enough?"

He shook his hand out, flexing it, and regarded her with a thin-lipped expression. "I don't have my quizzing glass with me."

Louisa understood in an instant: in the low light, with the haziness of his close vision, he wasn't able to cut accurately. "If you'll help raise me up, I could cut the mistletoe."

Alex passed the knife from one hand to the other. "Impossible."

"Impossible because you think yourself insufficiently strong, or because you think me excessively heavy?"

His nostrils flared, but he didn't smile. "Unwise, then."

"Because you think yourself insufficiently careful, or because you think me excessively clumsy?"

"My dear muffin, you will please cease your retorts." He poked the tip of the knife into the pale bark of the silver birch that hosted the bunch of mistletoe they sought. "I'm thinking only of your reputation. It's not wise for you to allow a man to put his hands all over your person."

Louisa shivered and clutched at the edges of her cloak. A chilly mist was beginning to creep around them, smoke-white and damp. "It's not an act of flirtation, Alex. It's an act of ambition. If we're to win the challenge, we need as much mistletoe as possible."

Picking with the knife point, he carved a tiny pit in the birch bark. His dark face was a study in concentration, all hollows and shadows. "You want to win the challenge?"

"Of course I do. It was my challenge."

She wove her gloved fingers together as a sweet tingle shot through her body. If she won, she'd have to claim kisses. It would be dishonorable not to. This was her strategy: forced boldness, forced bravery.

It was easier than taking all the initiative herself. And if she was fortunate, the result would be the same. Triumph. Every pearl-white mistletoe berry was an opportunity.

"If we win"—she swallowed—"whom would you kiss?"

His body went still for one second—two—three. Then with a *scritch*, he dragged the short-bladed knife down, slicing the tree. "Whom would *you* kiss?"

"I've not decided," she lied. Her heart thumped with more than usual force; her fingers went cold from the bones outward.

He began to score thin lines in the bark, like rules on a paper. "Not Lockwood, surely."

"Not Lockwood," she agreed.

"Pellington's a decent fellow. He wouldn't try more than you wished him to."

"Lord Kirkpatrick is very romantic," Louisa said through bloodless lips. "Surely he knows what to do with a kiss."

A sliver of wood the size of a fingernail flipped free. "I wouldn't know," Alex said, studying his work with careful attention. "In any case, we might not win."

Louisa tugged her cloak around her again, shivering as though the mist had suddenly slid through her. "Nonsense. You always win your wagers."

He muttered something, then turned his face away and dropped his hands to his sides, leaving the small knife sticking out of the birch's trunk.

"What was that?" Louisa pressed.

"Xavier always wins," he said, too loudly. "Everyone knows that."

Louisa would have given much to see the expression on his face. Was it closed? Angry? Wistful?

Whatever it was, he didn't want her to see it. So she let him have his distance. With a quick yank, she pulled the small knife free.

"If you want to keep your perfect record," she said in a brisk voice, "you need to raise me up so we can cut this mistletoe."

He didn't respond at once; his shoulders rose and fell. But when he turned his face back to Louisa, his smile flashed bright.

"Here we go, then, muffin." Before she knew what he was about, he'd clasped her on either side of the waist and raised her up from the ground.

Oh, my Lord. Even through the thick layers of her cloak, gown, stays, petticoats, shift—the pressure seemed indecent. His hands were only inches from her breasts, from her untouched parts; he held her up, supporting her, in control of her body.

She shut her eyes, letting the feel of his hands claim her senses.

"Are you intending ever to cut down the mistletoe?"

Her eyes snapped open again. Alex was looking up at her, his eyes shadowed by the brim of his hat. "Do let me know," he said, "if you require a rest. I myself could stand like this forever."

"Hush," she said, thankful for the cover of twilight to hide her blush. With a few slices of the knife, a great mass of mistletoe came free and tumbled to the ground in a rustle of branches.

Alex lowered her at once to the ground and stepped back. Louisa crouched to study their spoils. "A good find," she said. "If we win, we shall be positively kissed raw."

He made a choking sound.

"Let's see if we can find some more." She stood, clutching the bunch of mistletoe in one hand. "Surely we've already used much of our hour, and this won't be enough greenery to secure our victory."

"Wheeling will ring a gong back at the house when the challenge has elapsed," Alex said, referring to his butler. "But I do think the hour is almost up."

A cold sting bit Louisa's cheek; then another. She shielded her face with her free hand. "Sleet?"

Alex held out his hand, palm up, and squinted into it. "I think so."

Louisa held out her own hand; two tiny beads of ice smacked her palm almost at once. "Indeed. We'd better head back to the house at once, then. I've no desire to be caught in sleet."

Alex took the mistletoe from her, then studied it at arm's length. "We might have a chance at winning with this. It's full of berries, and as big as a dog."

"A puppy, at the very least." Sleet slapped her on both sides of the face at once, and she raised the hood of her cloak. "Ouch. Yes, we'd best take our chances with our mistletoe puppy. Would you like your knife back?"

He accepted it, sliding the blade into a leather sheath before pocketing it. Louisa turned one way, then back. "Which way is the Hall? We've gone back and forth so much, I've lost my bearings."

"This way." Alex laid the fingers of the hand not currently gripping a mistletoe puppy under her elbow, guiding her onto a faint path she'd overlooked.

"Though the sleet is driving us back to the Hall early," he said, "you can't deny that it's picturesque."

"It's much more festive than the sight of dead grass," Louisa granted.

"I commissioned it myself," said Alex. "I couldn't let a Christmas pass without some sort of wintry precipitation. What sort of host would I be?"

"A host that doesn't wish his guests to get stuck on the road to church in the morning, and doesn't require his servants and tenants to have the extra work of shoveling their animals free?"

He slanted a sideways glance at her. "What an impossible paragon you describe. Besides, I hardly think most of the guests will be eager to roll out of their beds for a church service tomorrow."

Louisa missed a step; Alex caught her elbow as she stumbled. "Are you all right?"

She shook her arm free. "Yes. I just hadn't realized you didn't plan to go to Christmas services. My family always does."

"Ah. But you chose to spend Christmas away from them, didn't you?"

"Yes, I did." She walked a few more steps, considering her reply. "I thought it was time to go my own way for a while. But that doesn't mean I wish to abandon everything familiar."

"A goose for dinner? Greenery in the hall? We shall have all that."

She walked on, her feet crunching over beaded sleet as it fell more thickly. The hood of her cloak constrained the world to a tunnel, straight ahead and dim. She couldn't see Alex. She couldn't see anyone.

"I think," she decided, "I should like to attend mass all the same. My aunt will likely go with me. What time is your service?"

"I don't know," came Alex's voice. "Wheeling could tell you."

Louisa nodded. They were almost free of the trees now; soon they'd see Clifton Hall on its rise, its windows aglow with lamplight. From ahead, the low note of a gong sounded thin and clear.

"That's the end, then," she murmured.

Even if she and Alex didn't win, she had risen to her own challenge. She'd held her own amidst the other guests earlier, managing occasional wit. She'd organized a wager. And she had enjoyed it, this stolen hour with Alex.

Her belly flipped; his warm hands still seemed to press at her waist. He was close enough to her that she could imagine the swift progression: they'd stop walking, turn to each other. His hands would slide around her again, as natural as turning the next page of a book. And how would the story continue then?

She would draw him close, if he would let her. She'd tell him what it had meant for her to leave her family at Christmas; to join games and make wagers. She was trying to leave fear behind and find her own way.

It was horribly difficult.

She wanted to tell him all that, if he could stand to hear it. If *she* could stand to hear it. She didn't know where this path would lead her, but it had a much more significant destination than Clifton Hall.

Which way do you want to go?

She stopped walking. As if yoked to her, he stopped, too. They turned to face one another.

Sleet stung her face as the wind cut beneath her hood, and she squinted against the chill. Alex set his hand under her elbow and drew her forward, one step, then a quarter turn.

"Louisa?"

"Yes," she said. She didn't know if she was responding to her name, or giving him permission.

She was Lady Irving's niece, wasn't she? She didn't need to grant permission for him to take what he wanted. *She* could take what *she* wanted.

She didn't want to let herself think; "the woman that

deliberates is lost," Joseph Addison had written in *Cato*. Yet the habit of parsing everything was bone deep, and she would feel more lost if she did not deliberate this. If it were not a conscious decision, but a raw impulse, would it mean less?

So she chose to reach for his hand. She chose to intertwine her gloved fingers in his. She watched as his eyes widened, as his other hand dropped its weight of mistletoe and reached for hers. His expression was like that of Michelangelo's *David*: wary, coiled, determined.

The failing light made him look ruthless, slicing every slope of his face into a sharp angle of shadow. Surely such a man would allow nothing to be taken from him that he did not wish to give.

She wanted to kiss him, to give this gift to herself. Boldness. Pleasure for its own sake. With a tug at his hands, she pulled him across the space that separated them. Their clothing snapped and whipped in the wind and sleet, greatcoat and cloak as eager to touch as the people who wore them.

That was all it took: one tug, and some cord of propriety snapped. He lowered his head, and their lips knew how to find each other, pliant and hot and hungry for this touch. This was no gentle promise. Louisa raised herself onto her toes, wrapping her arms around his waist so his hands, still within hers, were pinioned. Oh, he was tall and strong and solid, yet she could mold him with a touch. He let her press his hands behind him, his chest raising, brushing the tips of her breasts. Through layer upon layer of clothing, she felt the pressure of body on body; unmistakable and erotic. *Yes*.

He touched the tip of his tongue to hers, lightly, a caress. A jolt of pleasure shot through her; she pressed her thighs together at the sweet shock of it. Her hands, drifting out of her own control, gripped his fingers yet more tightly and pulled him against her, grinding her needy body like a blade against the stone of his form. He would sharpen her, hone her; there was something sparking in her now, removing her dullness.

She moaned.

No. Too much. She'd revealed too much. As soon as she'd swallowed the sound within her throat, she twisted her hands within his and freed them. When she took a step back, his arms slid free, then dropped to his sides as though boneless.

"Hell of a beginning at going your own way," he said. He sounded a little foggy.

Louisa bent and retrieved the mistletoe, shaking beads of sleet from it. Carefully, then, she selected a mistletoe berry, plucked it between thumb and forefinger, and tossed it away.

"But . . . that berry is worth a kiss."

"Which you gave me. I had to pay, didn't I?" She held the mistletoe puppy out to him, and he took it with a frown.

"There was no need." Even in the dim light, she could read his puzzlement at her daring to toss away any scrap of his attention.

I must. I want it too much.

Her cheeks felt hot, and she fumbled for words. "Why we should make such a fuss over mistletoe, I don't know. It's only a parasite. It'd be nothing without a tree to grow on."

"That has occurred to me," he murmured. He turned back in the direction of the house. "Shall we return to the Hall now, and see how we stack up against the others?"

Only a parasite. Why we should make such a fuss, I don't know. Mistletoe was much like a rake. But he was more than that—though how much more, she wasn't sure. And as long as he kept her guessing, she had to do the same to him.

Louisa was a sensible girl. She always had been. What had she wanted? A kiss. Had it been pleasurable? It had. Had she covered her slip? Yes, she'd done that, too.

She had gotten what she wanted, then, and there was no reason on earth to feel disappointed in herself for tossing it away, a berry on the ground.

They were almost the last pair back to the Hall. Amidst the stamping of feet and shaking of cloaks, stacking of branches and waggling of prized bits of greenery, Xavier could see enough of what had been collected to guess that he and Louisa had a fair chance of winning. Those who had collected holly had far fewer berries to boast of, and no one had found as large a mass of mistletoe as he had.

A parasite. Nothing to be proud of.

He squelched the thought ruthlessly. There was no sense in feeling a little bereft at leaving the woods behind, or having Louisa toss his kiss away like a meaningless trinket. Lord Xavier should expect careless pleasures, and he'd worked for a long time to become Lord Xavier.

Right now, he couldn't think why.

Wheeling, the impassive butler who had served Clifton Hall since the previous earl's time, stood snowy-haired and spare in the corner of the high-ceilinged, marble-tiled entrance hall. His slightest gestures and quietest commands directed footmen and maids to take wraps and sort the gathered greenery. It was a tiny wonder of choreography, and Xavier marveled at it for an instant, wondering why he had never noticed it before.

Or why he had bothered to notice it now. Louisa's habit of observation seemed to be contagious.

He pushed through the sloppy mass of his guests until he reached the butler's side. "Wheeling. Christmas morning services are at what hour?"

"At nine o'clock, my lord." The butler didn't even blink his surprise. His version of a Numbered Expression: a complete cloak over all emotion and thought. He played his role as ably as Xavier did his own.

Xavier nodded and shoved back through the laughing, cloak-shaking group until he reached Louisa. She had slipped to one side of the hall and was standing near a half-round table on which stood a huge majolica vase of hot-house blooms. The ostentatious bouquet nearly hid her from view.

Once he got her attention, he communicated what he'd learned from Wheeling.

Her dark eyes met his, surprised; then she smiled. "Thank you. I'll tell my aunt. Do you think Jane would care to attend, too?"

A slippery urge to keep her smiling must have made him say the next words. "I will make sure she does. I'll accompany her."

Louisa's brows lifted. "Will you."

"You could *try* to make that sound like a question," he grumbled. "And yes, I will. I've said so, and I'll do it. The word of a gentleman is sacred."

She turned her head, tossing a smile to Jane—just entering the hall with Kirkpatrick—then looked at Xavier from the corner of her eye. "So I have heard."

That was all. Nothing else. No praise for Lord Xavier for intending to enter a church. Not even a confirmation that yes, he was a gentleman.

Impatient, he turned away. "I'll see you in the drawing room for our reckoning."

It was a good thing he was so used to playing the role of

Lord Xavier. For the next ten minutes, the sly comments and *bon mot*s came to his lips almost without thought. If Mrs. Protheroe's laughter was any indication, he was as witty as ever. If Lady Irving's sharp looks were any clue, he was just as notorious. And if Louisa's silence meant anything . . .

She regretted kissing him. She had thrown away the mistletoe berry, and a goodly chunk of his pride. Now, he could only show her that it mattered as little to him as it had to her.

"You've all been very industrious," he said with a nod at the neat piles of Christmas greenery that now dotted the formal drawing room.

Lockwood hooted. "Count the berries!"

A chorus of shouts succeeded this, and Xavier held up his hands. "Wheeling has already seen to it. If I might have your full attention, ladies and gentlemen, lovers and fighters, singers and rascals?"

"Rascals?" Jane sounded intrigued. "Do you mean me?"

Xavier ignored her. People began to perch on furniture and nestle on the carpeted floor, all warm and informal. It was as though they'd just had more of the rum punch, and the strong spirits had improved their own.

Or there was something joyful in the air. Anticipation, sweetly crisping every moment.

He unfolded a paper that Wheeling had handed him and held it at arm's length. Penciled scribbles resolved into names and numbers: the quick count the servants had made of all the greenery.

"In last place," he called, and the hubbub quieted at once. "Lord Weatherwax and Lady Irving, who merely collected a few hothouse roses from the vase in the corner."

From her chair near the great fireplace, Lady Irving

grinned wolfishly. "You're lucky you got that, young fellow. I'd much rather enjoy a sherry than go tramping about in the cold. Eh, Weatherwax?"

"Except for the bit about the sherry"—Weatherwax hiccoughed—"I am in complete agreement, my lady." He drained a snifter of something so strong, he shuddered as the drink went down his throat.

Xavier suppressed a smile. "Very well. Next, Lady Charissa Bradleigh and Mr. Channing, who collected sixteen inches of evergreen garland."

That young woman clapped a hand over her mouth as she giggled, and the stuffy Mr. Channing tugged at his cravat and cleared his throat.

"Hmm." Lady Irving said what they were all thinking.

"Lady Audrina Bradleigh and her mother, Lady Alleyneham, made another team"—and so it continued, Xavier naming off pairs until he got to the last few sets of names.

His eyes skimmed the paper, taking in everything. *Oh.*

A Numbered Expression. Any one of them; it didn't matter. Haughty Certainty, Amused Tolerance, Veiled Disdain . . . Insipid . . . Confusion . . . he had to paste something on his face. *Now.*

"In third place," he said, trying to ignore a tic beating at the joint of his jaw, "Lord Lockwood and Signora Frittarelli, who collected holly and mistletoe containing one hundred forty-two berries."

La signora nodded, her heavy-lidded eyes half-closed, and blew a smoke ring in Lockwood's direction. Lockwood attempted to look gratified.

"And in second place, myself"—Xavier attempted to look gratified, too—"and Miss Oliver. With a lucky bunch of mistletoe, we collected one hundred sixty berries."

One hundred sixty-one.

His eyes caught Louisa's over the top of the paper. She gave him a tiny shrug, a tiny smile.

"I won, then!" Jane shrieked. "Kirkpatrick, we won!" She jumped to her feet and grabbed the hands of the baron, who stood with a dazed expression as Jane pumped his hands up and down, shouting her victory.

"One hundred sixty-one berries," Xavier called over Jane's ruckus. Again he met Louisa's eyes.

She looked glassy, frozen. She'd realized that if she hadn't thrown the berry away, they would have tied for the win.

"You mean to say," Lockwood said in an over-loud voice, "Lord Xavier did not win a wager?" He rose to his feet with deliberate sloth, shaking and smoothing his coat, looking around to catch as many eyes as he could.

Amused Tolerance spread over Xavier's face, stiff and false as a mask. He folded up the paper from Wheeling and slipped it into a pocket of his coat. "Indeed not. Miss Tindall and Lord Kirkpatrick are to be congratulated."

Yipping and shouting, Jane was calling, "One hundred sixty-one kisses! Kirkpatrick, think of it!"

The other guests burst into applause and laughter, and Jane started pressing kisses over the face of the dazed-looking baron as Lady Irving began a loud count. Xavier joined in, and others picked up the call, until the whole room was counting and Kirkpatrick was turning as red as a holly berry and Lockwood's comment seemed forgotten.

But it wasn't; not by everyone. Xavier's neck prickled under some scrutiny, and he turned his head to see his cousin watching him with cool blue eyes. Lockwood hadn't failed to notice, and he wouldn't forget. He was more mindful of Xavier's reputation than anyone.

"Snapdragon!" Jane shouted once the flurry of kisses

came to an end. "We must play snapdragon, or it simply won't be Christmas."

"Good game, snapdragon," agreed Lord Weatherwax. Any pastime that involved lighting a bowl of brandy-soaked raisins on fire was sure to appeal to the old drunkard. And Jane had a thirst for blood—or for watching people burn their mouths on flaming raisins.

"As our winner, my dear cousin, you shall have your snapdragon," Xavier decided. He'd keep them all occupied into the late hours; too full of pleasure and punch to think about anything but festive revelry.

Before five minutes were up, servants were bustling in with the ingredients of the game, and a new round of hooting and cheering had begun, with Jane at the fore.

Louisa applauded for her friend, looking as though the evening was going exactly as she wished.

And maybe it was, at that. Maybe there was nothing wrong with losing by one. Single. Berry.

For this way, when he kissed her again, she would know it wasn't because a wager required him to.

Chapter 11

Containing No Room

It had been years since Lord Xavier was up early enough to catch the sunrise, though he'd often gone to bed after bidding the sun good morning. And it had been years since he found anything beautiful about the morning except the curve of a hip, the swell of a breast, as he blinked blearily at his occasional bed partner.

This morning, though, he'd awoken alone. He'd gulped coffee, arranged his cravat with fumbling fingers, and dragged himself down to the entrance hall at twenty of nine.

When he saw the group awaiting him, arranged on the marble floor of the hall like living chess pieces, he suddenly felt more alert. Lady Irving and Louisa were there, as he'd known they would be. The countess looked formidable in blues and purples, a wintry swirl of velvet. Louisa wore red under her dark cloak; it tinted her lips and cheeks as ripe as a holly berry.

Jane was there, as he'd ordered. Smothered in peach satin, she looked tired and miserable.

Especially because she was holding Lord Lockwood's arm.

Lockwood? Going to church? Interesting.

And not precisely welcome. Lockwood hadn't abandoned

his mischief-making, it seemed, though what he thought he'd do in a church, Xavier had no idea.

Xavier pounded down the stairs, noting the limp hand the marquess raised to his temple. After nodding to the ladies, Xavier said in a voice of infinite concern, pitched low for his cousin's ears alone, "Lockwood. You look as though you've a bad head. Not up too late doing something you oughtn't, I hope."

"If I was," muttered Lockwood, "I daresay I wasn't the only one. Please, not so loud on the tiles. Are your boots soled with metal?"

"Your bedchamber is carpeted," Xavier noted. "If my footfalls are too much for your ears, pray retire to your room and sleep away the morning."

"Nonsense." Lockwood's voice gathered a little strength. "I've got scarcely more than a week to send away the blue-stocking, if I'm to win our wager."

"How tedious you are," Xavier said, forcing himself to keep a low tone. If Louisa heard them: disaster.

"*Moi, mon cousin?*" Lockwood's expression of inno-cence would have been more effective had he not clapped a hand to his temple again and groaned. "I'm not the one who organized a party of churchgoers."

I'm not either, Xavier almost replied out of habit, but he bit his tongue. No point in belaboring the significance of the wager with Lockwood.

That wager on Louisa's presence—ah, damn it to hell. That was hardly a thought one ought to be having on Christmas morning, but he'd almost forgotten the wager. He wished he *could* forget it.

Taking the arms of Lady Irving and Louisa, he escorted them outdoors. Jane was welcome to walk with Lockwood. His aggravating cousins deserved one another.

* * *

The church bell rang from the steeple, deep and sonorous, and Lockwood's face went the starchy yellow-white of blancmange at the sound.

The church on Xavier's estate was small and Gothic in style, with a high gable roof and narrow, pointed-arched windows. The building was constructed of the same gray and brown stone that made up the original part of Clifton Hall. A generation later, the back-flung wings had been added to his family's estate, but no one had ever seen the need to enlarge this church for the earldom's tenants.

Probably because the lords and ladies of Clifton Hall had never frequented it much.

When he stepped inside, he was pleased that its structure had remained so untouched. The stone floor was smooth from centuries of wear; a dark and well-worn patterned carpet ran down the nave. The old wood and stone of the walls—arches and buttresses and whatever all these high-reaching sweeps of architectural strength were called—were smoke-dark from candles and tinted faintly red and blue in spots by the lacy stained-glass window over the altar.

It was a chilly building, but a peaceful one. The cold didn't matter as much in here, as though people were warmed by their sense of purpose.

They could have been warmed by their proximity to others, too. People sat shoulder to shoulder and stood wherever there was space. Every pew was crammed full, including the Xavier family pew, high-backed and ornately carved, which stretched across the front of the nave.

Xavier stood uselessly as the rest of his churchgoing party sidled through the doorway and surrounded him. There was nowhere for them to sit, and he wasn't sure what to do next. Which was one of his least favorite feelings in the world.

He countered this with Expression Number Two, Haughty Certainty, and motioned the others from his party to pass him and step away from the cold entrance.

For once, even Jane was silent. Whether from respect or confusion, Xavier wasn't sure.

When they'd come in, the rows of heads had been prayerfully forward-facing. But the party from Clifton Hall was starting to draw notice. Like ripples in a pond, the churchgoers began to turn their heads toward the back of the church with tiny, jerking movements that were probably meant to be unobtrusive.

A cough sounded behind Xavier, and he turned to see a sandy-haired man in early middle age. The man's cassock and surplice proclaimed him the vicar; his sheepish expression proclaimed him in some state of distress.

"My lord. Lord Xavier," he stammered, sketching a little bow and making his greeting to the others. "My lord, what an unexpected pleasure. The . . . party at the Hall . . . we hadn't . . . that is . . . I'll have the family pew cleared at once."

He fiddled with the embroidered collar of his surplice. His ears had turned almost purple.

Wintry chill seemed to slap at Xavier again. "Very good," he said.

The vicar looked relieved at the mildness of his patron's reaction. He looked over Xavier's shoulder, eyebrows raised, eyes bulging, and made a sweeping gesture with his hand.

Xavier turned back to the pews in time to see a gaggle of chastened churchgoers vacate the carved front pew and its environs, threading into any gap they could find in the crowded building.

Damnation. As though he wasn't credited with enough

wrongdoing, now his tenants would blame his caprice for splitting their families during Christmas morning services.

But they'd shouldered him from their church. No—*his* church. His church, on his land. His living to grant, yet they hadn't left room for him.

A dark rebellion shot through him as he studied the people in the church. Plainly curious, though trying not to show it. Dressed in their serviceable best: warm, dark wools and linens. All strangers to him, as he was to them.

It shouldn't be that way, should it?

Suddenly, desperately, he wanted to turn on his heel and leave. But he could not, now that they'd made way for him.

Without looking around, he led the way to the front of the church and slid into the now vacant family pew. The half inch of skin between his cropped hair and the stiff linen of his cravat seemed horribly naked.

So he squared his shoulders and prepared for a long ordeal. No matter the effort, he must keep Expression Number Two, Haughty Certainty, in place. To show that he belonged here; that he had a right to lord it over the people who now looked past him to the modest vicar and raised their voices in festive song.

Chapter 12

Containing a Most Seductive Fiction

When Xavier returned to Clifton Hall after the Christmas morning service, he found himself a drink. After luncheon, he found another. All through dinner, with roast goose and much merriment, he plied himself with wine, and once the meal was over, he changed to brandy.

Truth was never found in the bottom of a bottle, he knew, but he hoped it could be drowned there.

It could not, though. Not today; not this Christmas. By the time his guests had begun to trundle off to various bed-chambers, he'd failed to exorcise the knowledge that had crept into him along with the chill of the church.

That is: he'd become trapped in his role.

Only one person had ever noticed this before. He'd resented her prying eyes, her unanswerable questions. But today, he'd realized she was right to ask them. In courting the London scandal sheets, he'd neglected his tenants. They had abandoned the very notion of a family pew—for better or worse, almost as sacrosanct a space as the altar—as a pointless fiction. They simply never expected to see him.

This was not their fault. It was his. And there weren't enough drinks in the world to dissolve the pain of that thought.

There was one place, though, where it might hurt a bit less. So he gulped water to clear his head, straightened his neckcloth, and turned his feet in the direction of the library.

The oiled hinges moved silently as Xavier opened the library door a sliver. Good. Louisa was here, just as he'd hoped. She had spread out the encoded ledger on the mahogany table by the windows. In the pool of light shed by a Carcel lamp, she was trailing her finger over some scrawled-upon piece of paper, referring to the ledger, jotting letters down.

She didn't look up from her papers when he entered.

He cleared his throat.

He nudged the door shut and gave it a *thwack* with his boot heel.

She *still* didn't look up.

So he gave way to annoyance. "Good God, Louisa. What's so fascinating?"

She lifted her head, squinting into the dimmer light by the door. "Alex? You sound as though you're in a charming mood."

He scrubbed a hand over his face. "I'm always in a charming mood," he muttered.

"And I'm the most popular woman of the *ton*." She shrugged a shoulder, her bronze silk gown whispering against the mahogany desk. "What good storytellers we are. Now, do come and take a look at what I've deciphered."

She hooked the chair next to her with an ankle and shoved it back.

So easily, she dismissed his irritation. He strode over to the table but pointedly remained standing.

She looked up, her expression puzzled, and then she

smiled. "Of course. With your weak close vision, you can see the pages better while you stand."

Xavier sat.

Louisa gave him an odd, narrow-eyed look, then turned her attention back to the ledger. "You seem out of sorts, especially for a man who's about to be treated to a scandalous tale about his forebears."

"You mistake the matter, I assure you." He shifted his weight in the spindly Windsor chair, drawing back his chin until the ledger and her scrawled papers came into focus. "What have you found, then?"

She studied him for a long moment, and he began to feel as though she was poking at a bruise. When she spoke, though, she was all business. "*Purgatorio* was indeed the key to the early part of the ledger. Once I created the Vigenère tables, I could begin uncovering your family's dramatic history of misdeeds."

She slid a loose sheet of handwritten paper over to him. Crossed and blotted and block-lettered, it was almost impossible to interpret. "What is this? It's as obscure as a cipher itself."

She grinned. "Impressive, no? It's my sheet of notes. Since the cipher doesn't have any breaks between the words, the answer takes a bit of figuring, even with the key."

"That seems an ungodly amount of trouble. Have you learned anything that's made it worthwhile?"

"I should say so." She pulled back her blotched, scribbled-on paper and scanned it with knit brows. Lamplight gilded her face and shadowed her lashes.

Xavier's stomach gave a painful twist. Too much brandy today, and too many disappointments. He made a fist and shoved it against his abdomen as Louisa began to speak.

"The history begins in Tudor times, though it appears to have been written down much more recently than that. If

I'm reading it correctly, your ancestor was originally given a viscountcy for a very, ah, *personal* service granted to one of Good Queen Bess's favored ladies-in-waiting."

"A persuasive service, was it?"

"More persuasive than any foreign tongue could be. I can hardly wait to discover how the viscountcy became an earldom some few generations later."

"Hmm." Xavier pressed his knuckles more tightly against his rebellious body. She wasn't trying to tantalize him. There was no need for these tumbling insides.

"What I'm not sure of yet," Louisa continued, "is why it was necessary to encode the whole book. Can it matter at this distance in history whether a family became noble because of lovemaking skills as opposed to, say, lining the queen's purse?"

He wished she would not keep using words like *lovemaking* and *tongue*. This late in the day, his manners were ragged, his whole body in a rebellion of sensation. "It always matters," he ground out. "The *ton* has a terribly long memory, especially for scandal."

The *ton* didn't even have to rely on its memory where Xavier himself was concerned. The betting book at White's had recorded a full and complete history of his indiscretions—some real, many false—from the time he'd reached his majority.

Now it seemed his family's peccadilloes had been treated the same way from the very beginning. *What is bred in the bone will come out in the flesh.* Wasn't that the saying? It ought to be a family motto.

He let his hands drop to his sides. Suddenly he felt very still inside, and rather cold.

"Yes." Louisa looked at him with those big cocoa-brown eyes, half her face bright and half in shadow. "I had not much to do during my London season but stand at the fringes of ballrooms, noticing things. And I certainly noticed that."

Louisa furrowed her brows, and she tapped the ledger with the barb of the quill. "What I can't figure out is the *why* of this ledger. Why bother to encode ancient escapades? Alternatively, why write them down at all, if there was so much fear of their discovery that a cipher had to be applied?"

Xavier tried to don a Numbered Expression, but it simply slid off. "Some kinds of scandal are tolerated, and some are not. A single gentleman of good fortune can engage in scandalous behavior without detriment to his name, but women cannot. And, in truth, married men ought not either. It reflects poorly on the children."

"Such a stringent moral code from the Earl of Xavier?" Louisa looked back at the papers scattered over the table and began neatening them, lining up corners, wiping pens, capping the bronze inkwell. "I suppose I ought to be surprised."

"Never mind," Xavier said. He was wishing he hadn't come into the library to talk about codes and scandals with a woman who noticed everything. What did it matter if he was trapped by his reputation? Why should he start regretting that now? Soon enough he would return to London, and he'd slip back into his old, riotous circles like a hand into a glove.

The idea seemed tepid, at best. But at least it would be familiar.

"But I'm *not* surprised." Her hands stilled on a row of quills. She spread out her fingers as though checking for flecks of ink in the lamplight. "I've noticed things about you, too, Alex. You don't enjoy scandal as much as your reputation would suggest."

He shrugged, a tolerable simulacrum of unconcern. "Rumors. One can never credit them."

"Indeed not. Rumor would have me believe that you betrayed a friend intentionally, yet you told me you did not. Rumor would have me believe you've bedded Signora Frittarelli, but I've never seen you look at her with any particular warmth."

His spine went stiff. "You've heard rumors about *la signora* and—" He cut himself off, shaking his head. He hadn't known this. The fires of gossip were now blazing without any fuel, and he—yes, he was trapped indeed.

She gave a little shrug, still not looking at him. "I hear a lot of things. I don't believe anything without evidence."

Her slim arms slid out, stretched forward on the table; then she folded them and laid her head down upon them. The lamp turned her skin golden, her hair the dark of ebony. The expanse of uncovered skin above the bronze silk back of her gown seemed endless and defenseless.

He wanted to run his hand over that skin, to test it and protect it and understand it. How could a woman with a knife-sharp mind have such satin-fine skin? The combination was devastating. There was no possible armor against it.

He watched the movement of her lips as she spoke.

"Alex, you trusted me with the truth when I first came to your house. I'll do the same for you now. You come from wicked stock, perhaps, but that's no matter. You have a—well, I needn't describe your reputation to you. But it doesn't matter, either. Nothing matters but the choices you make. Rumor and reputation will follow."

His reputation. It felt like a manacle. "It's not so easy as you seem to think. When I attended this morning's service, no one could stop fidgeting and staring at me."

She shut her eyes. "The effect of novelty, that's all. The

first time I saw a lion in the Royal Menagerie, it seemed wondrous and frightening. The second time, it was nothing more than an imposing creature tugged from its rightful element."

Was this how she saw him—an imposing creature, caged?

Then . . . what was his rightful element?

"I see," he said. But she was the one who saw. When her eyes opened, sweet and slow, her face like a sculpture on her folded arms, he felt as though she'd read his every thought.

And still, she'd pulled out a chair for him to sit at her side. That was a Christmas gift in itself.

He wanted to understand *how* she knew these things. How had she seen what he had just realized himself?

"Did you . . ." He trailed off. Shook his head. Began again. "The lion. You visited it twice, you said. Would there be any point to your seeing it again?"

Her mouth softened at the corners; the lamplight gilded the fine hairs that had pulled loose from her coiffure. "The lion wouldn't know or care if I saw it again. My opinion of the lion does not matter to it. It simply *is*, itself."

Xavier mulled this over. "You think it does not notice if the crowds thin around it? Or if the exclamations turn to jeers?"

"It might. But does that matter? It exists in the best way it can. There's very little anyone can do—be they animal, vegetable, or mineral—to influence a crowd."

No. That wasn't so. He'd gambled his entire adult life on the idea of influence. "I disagree with you."

Louisa unfolded herself. Lamplight played over the bronze sheen of her gown as she shifted, as her curves flexed into brightness and dark.

Xavier's mouth went dry. He did not permit himself to shift and squirm in his seat.

She leaned back in her chair, her face passing into shadow. "You have the right. But I'm the one who saw the lion."

He shook his head. "The *ton*. I know you're talking of them. Do you truly believe they cannot be led?"

"Of course they can be led. You lead them every day, don't you?"

Before his quick squeeze of relief had time to spin through his body, she continued, "But their passing attention is all they can give. The polite world as a group— you'll hold its notice only as long as you fill the scandal sheets."

Her fingers played on the arm of her chair. "A person is different from a group, though. Only make a connection with a person, and he or she will gladly look beyond the surface."

"You assume I want that?" He folded his arms to cover the thud of his heart. Yes, he wanted that, and desperately. He was a bottomless pit of need, unable to stay away from the fleeting regard of the world. Powerless to deny the harsh seduction of her honesty.

An honesty that came wrapped in sleek curves, a wry mouth, and the high, serene brow of a Botticelli beauty.

He could have groaned. But he did not permit that, either. Instead, he jammed his hands tighter into the vise of his folded arms, hoping the pressure of his own limbs would remind him not to reach out for her. Or anything else that was foolish.

"I'm only talking to you, Alex," she said. "It's up to you to decide whether my words bear any relation to your life."

He was glad that he was seated, that this chair could give shape to his disintegrating form. "Tell me more, if you wish."

"A question for you, then." She paused. "What have you received in return for all you've given up?"

"I've given up nothing."

"Are you certain of that?"

He frowned. "What could I possibly have given up? I've an earldom to oversee. A house in London. I have servants to care for and, right now, a houseful of guests to keep happy, though certain among them seem determined to hate each other."

As he spoke the words, he felt their hollowness. His servants cared for his estate and home in London. His guests cared for themselves. And he—he had no one to care for but himself, and no one to care much for him.

It had always been that way. Orphaned as an infant, he'd been used to fending for himself in his gilded cradle. As a boy, he formulated the cleverest pranks; as a man, the betting book at White's served the same purpose: to win and hoard notoriety like others collected coin. He had learned early in life that truth didn't matter; only reputation. If one never confirmed nor denied rumor, the *beau monde*'s fascination would increase.

But what was the purpose of such fascination? It had left him isolated, always mustering one Numbered Expression or another. His life was a performance, with little truth in it.

Except from the woman sitting next to him.

Louisa had leaned forward, her face light-limned again, breaking into gilded curves at the edge of his vision. To him, she looked like hope: warm and shifting and impossible to pin down. And completely desirable.

The thought was a jolt of heat, of desperate longing that loosened the binding of his own arms around his rebellious body. Because she was right: he'd given up much, including the right to pursue a respectable woman such as herself.

He propped an elbow on the arm of his chair and shaded his eyes with his hand. As if that could erase her from his mind.

"Indeed you do have great gifts," she said. "A man could do much with such gifts of birth and fortune."

What she did not say, but what flashed through his thoughts, was, *but you have not*. Another truth that could not be suppressed any longer.

In a burst of movement, he rose from his chair, strode to the fireplace, and gripped the mantel in both hands. "Why do you say this? What do you want from me?"

Her voice was quiet behind him. "I ask only for what you're willing to give. You're the one who decides what that is."

"And why do you ask anything of me at all?" Something was making his heart beat wildly, his voice ragged. Was this anger, frustration, unbearable desire? He didn't know; he only knew that it filled him brimful, and he wanted to be emptied of it.

"Because no one ever has."

He clenched his fingertips on the marble edge of the mantel so tightly that he could feel stone pressing against bone. She was wrong, yet she was terribly correct.

Oh, he'd made himself essential, but only in the most inconsequential ways. He was a paste necklace of a person: suitable for parties and masquerades, but not appropriate for occasions of genuine significance.

Part of him wanted to deny this, yet part of him knew that only trickery had brought her here, kept her close. He'd bribed her here with his books, tied her here with a mystery. Counted on her intellectual curiosity to win him ten pounds and sustain his reputation.

A reputation he didn't even want anymore. Maybe.

Was he Xavier, or Alex? He was all knotted up, all confusion. Yet no matter who he was, he *wanted*. He wanted to convince her of his value. She, who was the first to suspect he had a hidden stash of it.

He wanted her eyes on him; her thoughts turned his way. And if he kissed her—*when* he kissed her—by God, he'd make sure it was a kiss she wanted to hold fast to.

Her hand slipped around his tense forearm, and he flinched. He hadn't heard her approach. She rested her hand on his sleeve—one second, two. Gently, then, she pressed down on his arm. *Let go.*

He dropped his hands from the mantel, his shoulders sagging, and turned to face her. Tried for a smile.

She must have seen something dreadful in his face, because she took a step backward. Her hands lifted, palms out, the silk of her gown shushing over the carpet. "You look like you could use some privacy. I'd best bid you good night now, and happy Christmas. Do excuse me."

Before he could unlock his tongue, she had already backed up several more steps.

"Wait, please." He raked a hand through his hair. "Please. Louisa. Don't leave. Not like this."

He didn't want her to ask him any more terrible questions. But he couldn't let her leave; not before he had an answer for her. Or himself.

She stopped. "How should I leave, then? Shall I recommend a book to you first? *Purgatorio* was good enough for your ancestors, and they were good enough for the queen."

"No." He pulled in a sharp breath. "Yes. Louisa. We don't have to be only about books, do we?"

She looked away, into the dark depths of the library. "You and I? We don't have to be anything. I'm just here for your house party, to entertain myself in a safely scandalous way, then retreat to the library whenever real life gets too overwhelming."

"I see," he replied. His hands felt blocky and numb at his sides. "Yes. I—I shouldn't have expected anything else from you."

He stammered under a wave of mortification. It welled up from within; it washed over him with every flicker of her dark eyes.

She didn't leave, though. And she didn't stop looking at him. With a tilt of her head, she said, "I've told you not to expect me to react in the common way."

She sank to the floor before the fire and extended her hands. The burning coals cast their warm light through the wavy glass of the fireplace screen, burnishing her skin to flame gold as her bronze gown pooled around her.

"In a novel," she commented, turning her hands before the flames as though toasting them, "someone would surely interrupt our conversation at the decisive moment."

Xavier stood by the fireplace like an andiron. "Can it be possible that this conversation hasn't yet reached the decisive moment? I think we've had twelve decisive moments already. I'll have to go directly to bed and pull the coverlet over my head."

A trick he'd often used with Lockwood: stating the truth so baldly that it sounded like a lie. Lockwood always laughed.

Louisa didn't, though. She only watched the flicker of flame behind glass. "That's not much of a way to spend Christmas night, is it?"

His jaw flexed. What on earth was there to say by way of reply? There was no point in denying anything to her. At best, she'd shrug it off; at worst, leave.

He didn't like the idea of her leaving—and not because of the wager with Lockwood.

"No," he said. "It isn't. But then, not much about this Christmas has gone as I wished."

She rose to her feet, graceful as a *danseuse*. "And what

did you wish for?" Her eyes were focused above his left shoulder, in the direction of the desk where they'd been sitting.

Aha. She was nervous, then? Or expectant?

Whatever she was, she was not indifferent to him. He'd read the language of desire often enough to interpret it now: the breath that came quick and shallow, the flush on her cheek that not even firelight could disguise.

"I hardly know," he said. "I suppose the best gifts are those we don't know we need."

"Like brutal honesty?" She smiled, a sweet sliver of mirth.

"Yes. Like that. I'll get around to being grateful to you eventually."

At this, she laughed, her hands fluttering up to her breasts.

He could let it pass over them, this light moment. They could bid each other happy Christmas and go their separate ways again, moving on as friends.

Or he could do it differently this time.

His eyes traced the movement of her hands, long fingered and slim. An artist's hands, or a musician's—only her art was observation, and the song she played was the clear chime of truth.

Her hands stilled, laced together. They lowered to her waist, smoothed the warm sheen of her silk skirts, then rose up and folded beneath her chin.

No. She was not indifferent.

"What do you want for Christmas?" he asked. "Ought I to guess? Surely there must be something I could do for you."

Her eyes met his. Her hands pressed tightly against one another, as if they could protect her throat, her heart.

"What does *something* mean in your parlance, Alex? I'm already a guest in your home. Since I'm working on decoding your book, that seems instead to be a present from me to you."

He lifted his brows. "You are admirably concise. You neglected only to mention that I am not permitted to compliment your appearance, either. Unless you've changed your mind about that?"

She shook her head. "No, please. No. I don't want anything false from you."

Her hands dropped to her sides. "Please," she said, so quietly it was not much more than a breath. "Please, nothing false."

In the firelight, her eyes were shadows, her mouth all mobile softness.

"Just because it's a compliment," Xavier said, "doesn't mean it's false."

But it was Alex who moved forward, slowly and cautiously. Alex closed the distance between them and reached for her hands, hardly daring to breathe as he laced his fingers with hers and pulled their bodies close.

"Nothing false," he whispered again.

Her shadowed eyes looked deep into him. "Then what will you give me?"

"Whatever I may." Only a breath apart now, their bodies so close to touching that he could feel the slight heat of her on his front, the fire on his back. He wrapped her closer, drawing her slim form against his. *Ah.* She was all curves against his angles, yet a perfect fit.

He slid his hands up her arms, the skin smooth over long, fine bones. "Whatever you'll permit."

Please, permit it. She'd seen deeper into him than anyone ever had. She was the only one who had thought to look. And so—she couldn't dismiss him now, or he'd be gone again, and there would be nothing left but his bright, empty shell.

His fingertip drew over the cap of her sleeve, down the curve of her dress's bodice. Not touching her breasts; nothing so intimate. Only the very edge of the fabric.

She permitted it.

His hand trailed down the curve of her neck, the swell of her chest, dipping under the cloth of her bodice. So much cloth in the way of her skin. He slid his fingers deeper, under the hemmed edge of corset and shift, and she drew in a swift breath.

But she permitted that, too.

"In a novel"—he echoed her earlier words—"someone would indeed interrupt us. A gift to us both, so we need not place a limit on our own control."

Her mouth twitched. She held herself still, as though his hands might spook.

His eyes closed, he bent his head, breathed in the lily scent of her hair. "Because we are afraid we won't stop once we start, and we don't know if we want to stop."

We need. We are. We don't . . . The words flowed from him like a spell, murmured between light kisses at the fragile skin of her ears, her jaw, her neck. Did they come from some deep understanding, or from wishful thinking? Would she let him consume her, standing proud and pliant and warm?

Or was she consuming him? Heat from the fire; heat from her body; a heat that bubbled within. So much heat he felt he was crumbling to ash.

"You're right," she said. With his lips at the juncture between jaw and neck, he could feel the vibration of her voice. "I won't want to stop. If you keep kissing me with that talented mouth, I'll let you go on indefinitely."

"Yet you said I didn't want a seduction," he reminded her.

"You don't." Her throat worked, and her voice sounded ragged when she added, "If you did, you'd have it."

He drew back, staring. "With you?" His fingertip stroked her collarbone, and she tilted her head, her eyes closing.

"I'm sure you can be very persuasive," she murmured. "And you're not a complete fright. I'm generally able to look at you without feeling nauseated."

She caught him off guard with that comment. It took him a full three seconds to process it, and then—

He laughed.

A real laugh; a laugh that used up all of his breath and wouldn't stop; a laugh that tugged his hands from her body so he could brace them on his thighs, heaving for air. An unfettered, free, graceless, genuine laugh.

God, it felt good to laugh without the strictures of a Numbered Expression. Just as he'd imagined.

He gulped in a breath and pulled himself up straight. Louisa was looking at him with an expression of great curiosity. "I assume something I said amused you?"

"That was—" He was still wheezing for breath. "Marvelous. I can't remember the last time I laughed like that. If ever."

"Then you haven't been holding the right sorts of conversations."

He shook his head, drinking in the sight of her, and she folded her arms around the body he'd been touching moments before. "You are very—" He broke off. No. Neither of them was ready for him to complete that sentence.

More lightly, he finished, "You have a unique way with words."

"Not really." She smiled, that tight little crescent moon of brilliance. "I'm merely curious about you. Alex."

With a swoop of limbs and a swift rustle of fabric, she pressed herself against him. Lips crushed against his; fingers wound through his hair. His eyes flew open for a startled instant, then closed again. *Mmm.* Another brush of his lips over hers; he couldn't pull away from their soft welcome.

A flicker of conscience intruded. Made him think for an instant. *This is not a novel. She is not a lady of scandal.*

He lifted his mouth from hers and tried to speak. "We needn't—"

She pulled his face down again. *Mmm.*

There ensued a foggy interval, during which he learned the shape of her waist and hips.

Oh. Conscience. Yes. "Louisa. This—we—anything we do will have consequences."

She gripped his shoulders as though he was worthy of holding fast to. "I only want to know more of you." She whispered in his ear. "Alex."

His name sounded like a secret, precious and intimate.

"Besides," she added, "who's to say this isn't your imagination? Who's to know, besides us, what happens in this room?"

"That makes no sense."

"It doesn't have to," she said. "It's our story, isn't it? We can twist the plot however we wish." Her hot tongue found the rim of his ear, and he shuddered, his hands tightening on the gentle curve of her waist.

When she put the matter like that, how could he resist her? She had brought tidings of comfort and joy on this unsteady night.

With his hands on her body and his heart in her hands, they toppled away from the fireplace toward a chaise longue, to write the next scene in his remaking.

Chapter 13

Containing a Most Seductive Reality

This is not like you, Louisa told herself as her calves hit the gold velvet seat of the chaise and she collapsed onto it, Alex's waistcoat fisted in her hands.

Yes, it is, she argued back.

Yes, she was decidedly herself: holding an internal argument even as Alex nudged a knee onto the chaise at her side, crushing the bronze silk of her gown beneath his weight. She'd always been a creature of imagination and observation; now she dared to knit those wisps of fevered longing into reality.

She scooted on the chaise until she reached the sloping back; her full skirts *whished* over the velvet as she moved. Then she reclined, holding out her arms. "More of you, please."

He laughed, and lust shot through her like a lightning bolt. He settled his long body next to her.

"I'm going to crush your skirts," he commented.

"I doubt it'll be the first time such a thing has happened."

He propped himself on his forearms and looked down at

her with a dire expression. "Louisa, this has nothing to do with anyone else."

"Come now," she said lightly over the swift beat of her heart. "I was only guessing that someone, somewhere, at some time in this house party, has had rumpled skirts."

He looked wary. "Yes. Well."

She wound her fingers around the back of his neck, holding him fast. "You didn't think I would refer to your past experiences with women, did you? How terribly unappealing."

He narrowed his eyes. "Are you getting at something?"

"Your bare skin, I hope."

The look of shock on his face was most gratifying, as was the speed with which he unknotted his cravat. Without its starched prison, the collar of his linen shirt stretched to expose the hollow of his throat, the sleek lines of his collarbones.

"That's all I wanted," she murmured. She shut her eyes and *noticed*: the long, solid weight of Alex's body; the cradle of his arms on either side of hers. The scent of his skin was a revelation—spice and soap and something indefinable that made her want to breathe him in until she knew it by heart.

So she did. She lifted her head and kissed the angle of his neck and shoulder, the spot where one solid muscle met another. She inhaled, deeply, just there. *Yes*.

He bent his head, his lips finding her jaw, her ear, the curve of her neck. The pressure was gentle, like the tickle of petals. All she had to do was breathe, soak in the scent and the sensation and let her body melt. Already, her intimate parts had become slippery with desire. And as Alex kept up his kisses, as his long body nudged her legs apart, she felt emptier. Wetter. Greedy for more.

"Stop messing about with my jawline, please," she said

roughly. She'd learned this trick from her aunt, Lady Irving: brusqueness as a cover for vulnerability.

At once, he pulled back, then dropped his forehead to her bosom. "Yes. We should stop. You're right."

Louisa allowed herself a secret smile, unseen by the proud earl. In a small way, she'd mastered him. It was a pleasure to know such a thing was possible.

"Don't stop," she whispered. "Move on, please. I have so many parts you haven't kissed yet."

She felt a bit hot at these bold words; words that could have been spoken by Fanny Hill, or someone like Signora Frittarelli. Women who were used to mastering men with their own desires, while she was beginning to feel that her desires were mastering her.

As he groaned and nipped the edge of her bodice with his teeth, she almost cried out at the abrasion, gentle but sharp against her skin.

"In a novel," he said, "I should lick you everywhere the firelight touched your body. And then I'd slide my hands beneath your clothing and shift it so the firelight touched some more."

A tremor ran through her, and her eyes fell closed. "I should like to read that novel."

She *wanted*, so desperately; a want that made her press her legs against his hips, that made her tug up her skirts when they bound her legs too tightly. Yards of bronze silk were wadded and crushed as he settled himself above her, hips on hips, and through his breeches she could feel his hot length against her gartered thigh.

Her whole body went tense. This want—what should she do with it? If she unleashed it, it would devour her. Consume her present; destroy her future. She could not succumb to it.

Not entirely.

"Is there something we can do," she managed, as his hand began to slide over her breasts, down her ribs, over the swell of her hips, "that would not be . . . irrevocable?"

He paused. Looked down at his hand, as though he wasn't sure what it was doing on her body. "Yes. Many things."

"Shall we proceed?"

His eyes met hers. Now she wished for more light; a lamp at the side of the chaise that would reveal every nuance of his expression. Was he as eager as she? Obliging? Like she, did he have a blessed nuisance of common sense that would not allow him to shut thought off?

"As you like it, muffin," he said, and even in the dim light, she could see his smile. Not the too-wide one that was meant to be charming. This one was a bit wistful.

But there was nothing wistful about his hands. They slid down her legs, swift and sure, tossing aside folds of skirt, of petticoat. A wall of fabric rose above Louisa from hip to thigh: a fashionable evening dress reduced to a crushed barrier. She lifted her head to see what the hands were going to do next, behind the fabric wall.

"Lie down," Alex said. "Let me surprise you, if such a thing is possible." His straight dark brows yanked down in an expression of great concentration.

"You look like an archaeologist uncovering a fascinating old relic," Louisa said.

"What a dreadful comparison," Alex said without looking up. "Why, I haven't found anything fascinating yet under all this cursed fabric—ah, there we go."

Fingers fumbled against the thin linen of her shift and peeled it back so nothing lay over her skin except the fine knit of her silk stockings. The ribboned garter. And above . . . she sucked in a sharp breath. Her upper thighs were bare, and his hand was dancing over her skin, hot and strong and startling.

"Now this," he said, "*is* fascinating. But it's hardly archaeology. Perhaps it's anatomy?" His fingers slid down the curve of her thigh, then up again. "Perhaps it's poetry." One finger tickled through her private hair. "Or theology. Philosophy. Something no one fully understands."

His fingertip slid downward, and Louisa shuddered. "I . . . I don't know," she stammered. "This is a new field of study for me. With a bit more research, I could identify it properly."

He shot her a skeptical look, and then he shook his head, laughing low under his breath.

He didn't laugh often enough. That was for the best, for when he did, she felt a little squeeze in her chest. A tenderness that was almost unbearable, and though it was too, too late for her body, she could not abandon anything else to him. Why, he ought to—*oh*.

He ought to do that thing with his finger again.

"Do that thing with your finger again," Louisa said. "Please."

He obeyed. It was a slow glide through her folds, a flick on the sensitive nub. A stroke of sheer pleasure—a pleasure that kindled greater want. *More.* With every brush of his fingertips the need flared, fueled by his touch, hot and demanding, and she ground her hips up into his caress so he would not stop, never stop that intoxicating sweep of sensation.

"Alex," she moaned. "Please . . ."

"You become most polite when there's something you want desperately," he commented. He bent over her body, pressed a hard kiss onto her collarbone, and plunged a finger inside her.

He was *in her* and *over her* and his fingers were doing

those wondrous things and there was his mouth moving over her skin in a hot trail of need, and it was too much, all of a sudden, and she split into pieces, quivering and gasping.

He must have felt her shatter, because his hand stilled at once. He sat up straight.

For an instant, it was a relief to have it over, the on-slaught of overwhelming, indescribable sensation.

And then she felt boneless and hot, and a little ashamed.

She pushed herself up onto her elbows, then up to a sitting position. Now they faced each other on the chaise, and if her skirts weren't rucked up to an alarming height, she could almost pretend that nothing had happened. But between her legs, she throbbed. Never had such a desire wakened in her; never had she imagined how pleasurable it would be to sate it.

Had she forgotten herself, or found herself?

She could ask the same question of Lord Xavier. For all that she called him Alex, he was owned by the world. This burst of passion—this was no more real or lasting than the pages of a novel.

She must show him she placed no more significance on it than that.

"Thank you very much." She stood, smoothing and shaking the layers of her clothing back into place. Not a wall anymore, but a different type of barrier. "That was a very pleasant Christmas gift."

Alex stared at her. His left hand hovered an inch above the fabric of the chaise, still wet from her excitement.

She looked away as he stood, a protracted unfolding of his long limbs. But when he remained silent for far too long, she glanced back at him.

Alex stood with his back to the fire. Hands at his sides. Shoulders square. Simply stood, his posture unreadable, his expression in shadow.

"Please turn so I can see your face," Louisa said. She crossed her arms over her heart, wishing she had worn a gown with long sleeves. There was a distinct chill in the air.

He made a precise quarter turn. His face—so perfect, like the profile on a Roman coin—was as much a cipher as the ledger they'd studied together.

She blundered on. "I admit, this isn't how I expected to celebrate a breakthrough in cryptography. But it's not inapt, wouldn't you agree? I breach a code, you breach my skirts."

His head dipped; an unwilling smile scuttled over his features.

"And I asked you for nothing false. That felt quite real, indeed," she finished. "So—thank you."

If he'd let out a breath that long and slow through his mouth, it would have been a sigh. Instead, his exhale sounded like an unburdening, as though he released tension along with air.

Oh. Of course he was tense. He hadn't . . . emitted.

Should she offer to help him—no, her mind shied from the idea. She'd had enough new experiences for one day. She had to sift through these and sort them out into her Louisa catalogue before she could accept any more.

Finally he spoke. "Was it everything you wanted, Louisa?"

There was no air to say anything more; his lungs simply heaved fruitlessly.

She studied him with those dark witch-eyes. "For now." She looked wary. Her fingers played with the lace at the edge of her bodice.

He hadn't even seen her breasts. He'd barely removed any of her clothes before stroking her to life, to the little death.

He sagged against the mantel, letting the fire toast him from back to calf. "For any other woman, I'd say that you didn't know what you were talking about. But since you always know what you're talking about, then I must ask you what you want next."

She gave him a tight smile. "Don't worry that I shall make demands upon you. We haven't done anything irrevocable, so I assure you, I don't require anything more from you."

He couldn't have felt cheaper if she'd handed him a fistful of guineas and told him to return at the same time next week. "I assure *you* that I am completely uninterested in being *required* to make any gesture of regard."

She drew back a half-step, almost out of the fireplace's nimbus of light. "Oh."

"I said *required*, Louisa."

She turned her head, looking at him aslant. "Oh?"

"I don't want to be used," he muttered. "And I don't want to use anyone."

"Oh," she said again. This time it was soft and wondering. "Yes. I see."

"Do you? I don't know about that." He turned to face the fire, wishing its heat would slice through the chilly numbness that seemed to freeze him from the inside.

His hand felt sticky. She had trusted him, and he'd stuck his hand up her skirts. It didn't matter that she liked it. He shouldn't have done it. He would never prove that he was more than Lord Xavier, child of scandal and lust, as long as he gave in to either one.

"I *do* see, Alex," she said, quiet as a lullaby. "Since you first quoted Dante to me, I've known you were more than a shallow rake. And . . . I like that."

"And what am I instead?" He felt as though his ribs would crack from the effort of speaking calmly.

"I can't answer that if you can't."

He turned to look at her, suspicious, and she smiled again. "But I'll help you figure it out. For a start, decode the family ledger. Fabricate a magnificent entertainment for Twelfth Night. Keep Jane under observation."

"And *we* are?"

She bit her lip. "That depends on who you are. For now, I think we are . . ." Her head tilted. "Friends?"

"The idea surprises you?"

"Yes, it does. Not two weeks ago, I held you in the deepest distaste. But how else would you describe what we have become since then? With whom else but a friend could one talk about enciphered scandals, have an invigorating argument, and then come near a quick tumble? And then finish it off with another disagreement. Most stimulating, all of it."

Her voice bubbled clear and cool as any mountain stream. If she hadn't been so near the fire, he wouldn't have been able to tell she was blushing.

But that blush? He could have given her his shallow, worthless heart for that blush, because it meant he wasn't nothing to her. Whatever he was, she called him "friend."

"I've never had a friend like that," he said.

"Nor I," she admitted with a little shiver. "I like it, though. I think."

"I don't detest the idea, either," Xavier said. Oh, to hell with it. With this woman, he was Alex.

The smile that spread over her face was a new, lovely creation: bright as sunlight, welcoming as a warm sea. There was a world in that smile, and the power of it stole his breath, made him dizzy.

She's dangerous, said some small inner voice of self-preservation.

But when had he ever been afraid of danger? When had anyone else been able to create more danger than he could stir up himself?

Louisa swanned over to the mahogany table, just visible at the edges of the firelight, and stacked up the loose papers and the ledger that, apparently, contained his family's secrets. "You can take the alphabet tables with you. You ought to have a look at the text, since it's your family's own story. You might even uncover how your family got that earldom."

She padded back to him and piled the bound volume and papers into his unresisting arms. It was all as though he'd just entered the library, brimful of brandy and bad mood, and the interlude on the chaise longue had never taken place.

Who's to say this isn't your imagination?

If a few locks of her long hair hadn't escaped their pins, he would wonder precisely that.

Who's to know, besides us, what happens in this room?

No one; no one would ever know. It was their secret, locked away like text hidden within a Vigenère cipher. Only the two of them held the key.

"Thank you," he said, inclining his head so she'd know he was referring only to the papers in his arms.

She was impossible to fool. "Don't get all missish with me, Alex, please. I'm sure I'm not the first woman you've diddled in the library."

"I—"

"Don't worry your passably attractive head about it. We're friends. I don't expect anything more of you."

"You should," he muttered before he knew what he was saying. She should; everyone should. An earl shouldn't be absent so long his tenants forgot him; a man shouldn't use women like handkerchiefs, to be soiled and tossed away.

He shouldn't permit himself to gain notoriety for lies. Rumors. Scandals.

Nothing false.

The weight in his arms seemed much heavier than one would expect for a mass of papers and a few leather-covered boards. "I'll see you in the morning," he said, his voice thick.

"You should," he thought he heard her reply faintly, but he was already out the door.

Chapter 14

Containing an Incorrect Tally of Livestock

"Six million head of sheep."

It was a wild guess, and Xavier knew it. Across the paper-cluttered mahogany desk in his private study, his secretary steepled his fingers before his mild-featured face.

Xavier pressed his lips into an impatient line. "What is it, Hoskinson?"

Hoskinson was a young man with thinning fair hair, thick spectacles, and a soothing manner. He replied in a careful voice, as though calming a fractious dog. "What did Mr. Chatterton say the second column represented, my lord?"

Xavier laid down his quizzing glass, then rubbed a hand over his eyes. "A gibbet. I'm going to hang him. I don't need a steward anymore."

In all fairness, it wasn't Chatterton's fault Xavier was having a difficult time. This morning he had looked at the estate accounts for the first time since . . . well, ever. When one had a capable steward like Chatterton, who kept everything running smoothly for year upon year, decade upon decade, there was no need to look over the books. Xavier's own time was much better spent elsewhere.

Or so he'd thought, until recently.

"My lord?" Hoskinson prompted.

"Thousands," Xavier muttered. "Six thousand sheep, and I won't kill Chatterton today."

Hoskinson looked amused. "Mr. Chatterton will no doubt be pleased to survive Boxing Day, my lord."

"Boxing Day. Of course it is." Xavier rubbed at his forehead. "I ought to see to some sort of distribution to the staff today. Little gifts and such?"

"It's already been seen to, my lord," Hoskinson said. "Mr. Chatterton was able to provide a list of servants requiring compensation, and I authorized the expense."

"Did you, now." The afternoon sun slanting through Xavier's study windows reflected off the lenses of the secretary's spectacles, so it was impossible to tell whether his gaze held scorn or simply the bland detachment of a man reporting on his duties.

"Indeed, my lord. Mr. Chatterton also provided an inventory of tenants and the sizes of their families. I recommended a Christmas gift of wheat and beef, proportional to the sizes of the households."

"Did you, now." Xavier was repeating himself.

He dragged a hand through his hair and settled back into the Norman-style chair. Some forebear had decided the massive burled walnut piece, with its carved, arched seat back and worn gilt detailing, was suitably imposing. Unfortunately, the piece was also uncomfortable. Every muscle along Xavier's spine, from skull to hips, seemed knotted and aching. The carved back was so high that it pressed against his head, jutting his neck forward.

"Thank you for your expedient action, Hoskinson," he said. "I am sure the tenants will appreciate it."

Hoskinson's face softened. "Mr. Chatterton and I were pleased to attend to the matter, my lord."

Mr. Chatterton. Hoskinson seemed to roll the sound of the steward's name in his mouth like a boiled sweet. The secretary positively idolized the steward.

Truth be told, the review of the accounts would have gone more smoothly if Xavier had requested the help of the elderly Chatterton himself, instead of Hoskinson. Hoskinson's area of proficiency was the elegant invitation, the diplomatic refusal. He knew little of tenants and crop yields.

But Xavier preferred his secretary's company. Hoskinson was *his* servant, chosen by his own hand; Chatterton was a legacy from his father. Xavier couldn't shake the feeling of his own ignorance when the steward held forth about estate matters.

He dragged a fidgety hand through his hair again before catching himself, folding up his fingers and rapping them against his thigh.

"Hoskinson," he decided, "you must be longing for a half-day off. I believe you've earned it, now that you've taught me not to expect six million head of sheep on my lands."

The secretary stood, looking uncertain. "Do you intend to remain in your study, my lord? That is—might I have some refreshment brought in to you?"

Xavier waved him off. "Go debauch a housemaid under the mistletoe. Write letters to the prime minister. Whatever it is you do for amusement. I won't break the earldom if you leave me with the accounts for a few hours."

Hoskinson's mouth crimped. "I live to serve, my lord." He bowed his way from the room.

As soon as the door snicked closed, Xavier felt that a burden had been lifted. He eyed the sideboard. It was a bit early for brandy, but at the rate the house party was progressing, drinking would soon be the only vice left to him.

Well, drinking and toying with virgins.

One virgin.

Who had toyed with him as well.

He poured himself a brandy. Cupping the snifter in his hands to warm the fiery liquid, he moved to the tall study window and stared out over his grounds.

He tried to fix his mind upon the view. He never saw it at its best, coming to Surrey only in winter. Whenever he saw Clifton Hall, the grass had lost its green, and most of the flowering plants had long since tucked their blooms away. Still, the land around the house was clean of fallen leaves, well-kept thanks to a gardener's vigilant care.

He wondered how many gardeners took care of the place. He ought to know. Louisa would know, if this were her estate. She would know their names, and what they were paid, and who worked best with what type of plant. She would know who all the tenants were, too, and would have seventeen ideas about the proper Christmas gifts for each family.

It was daunting, how much she knew and noticed. Daunting, and fascinating.

He swirled the red-brown Armagnac in its snifter, allowing its buttery-sweet, astringent scent to tickle his nose. All thoughts seemed to lead back to *her*, and he didn't feel so light anymore.

What had they done in the library, with their "in a novel" teasing and their cool-headed goodbye? As quickly as she could stand and shake out her skirts, she had turned the intimacy from a pleasure into a transaction.

He'd done nothing that the world didn't expect him to do. And Louisa had given him permission to walk away.

She'd even walked away herself, as though it all meant nothing.

She ought to be his perfect woman: well-bred, intelligent, witty. And making no demands on him, except—how had she put it? *What you're willing to give.* Something like that.

But she *should* ask more of him. She deserved, and should accept, nothing less than honorable treatment. Honesty. Fidelity.

It was his reputation dragging him down, wasn't it? His damned reputation. Louisa liked him well enough, yes—but she had *used* him and seen nothing wrong with that, and thought they could part as friends. And the hell of it—the nine-circles-of-*Inferno* of it—was that, after he'd had his hands on her, he would have agreed to anything she'd asked of him.

She had a dreadful hold on him. On the best pieces of him.

The gentle swirl of brandy in his snifter became a slosh. Armagnac flopped over the side in a syrupy trickle. Xavier raised the snifter to his lips and licked it away.

Horse piss, Lockwood had so diplomatically called this vintage, though in truth it was a very fine eau-de-vie. But today it didn't appeal to Xavier.

He replaced the snifter on the sideboard and returned to his desk. The estate accounts awaited, mocking him with their long, impenetrable columns of figures. He stuffed himself into the too-tall, too-hard Norman chair, then popped up again at once. If he was to spend a decent amount of time at this desk—or a few more minutes of his life, total—he would have a chair he liked.

The chair across from the desk, recently vacated by Hoskinson, was much smaller; a fussy rococo affair of limed oak, with cabriole legs and a plush red velvet seat. The style seemed designed to undermine the dignity of any man who faced the earl across the wide sweep of the polished wood desk. Especially when the earl sat in that throne-like Norman monstrosity.

Xavier eyed the rococo chair once more, then sat on it gingerly. "Mmm." Heaven in a limed oak frame. He settled his full weight onto it.

No wonder Hoskinson had been better able to concentrate than he. This chair was magnificently comfortable. He shut his eyes and wondered if he ought to try to sleep for a few minutes.

Or if he would just wind up thinking about *her* again.

A fist thudded against the door. The sound of the door being flung open, thwacking against the lead-gray study wall, dragged Xavier upright in an instant. "Lockwood. You look frightful."

The marquess's olive complexion had curdled; circles under his eyes muddied their blue into a bloodshot grayish color. Not even his pale blue linens could give his face a healthy color.

Lockwood yawned. "Late night. Early morning. Both well worth the effort, if you know what I mean."

"I know exactly what you mean," Xavier said drily. "My felicitations. Who is the lady?"

"Oh, she's no lady." The marquess smiled.

Xavier and Lockwood were commonly thought to bear a fair resemblance to one another. If the expression on the marquess's face looked like Xavier's smile, then it was no wonder Louisa had been immune to its supposed charm.

He shrugged off the thought. "Make yourself useful, Lockwood, if you can bear to. Help me swap these chairs."

Lockwood eyed the limed-oak chair. "Is that what you've been up to in here? Playing footman with the furnishings? This chair is ridiculous. It looks like it belongs in a seraglio."

He shuffled around the desk and shook the throne-high back of the Norman chair. "*This* is an earl's chair, Coz."

Xavier folded his arms. "Sit in them, then tell me which one ought to be an earl's chair."

Lockwood obeyed. His haggard face pulled into a grimace as soon as he'd settled into the Norman chair, and he began tugging at it without further comment.

Until his gaze lighted on the sideboard. "Ah. Is that Armagnac?"

"Your favorite horse piss," Xavier confirmed, dragging the seraglio chair against the wall to make way.

Lockwood abandoned his task and sidled over to the sideboard. "For me?" He held up the snifter Xavier had poured for himself a short while before.

Xavier shrugged. "Go ahead. You're welcome to it."

He took Lockwood's place behind his father's chair, pushing at it with all his weight. It was heavy, and its legs had made deep furrows in the faded floral pattern of the antique Aubusson on the floor. It was as though the chair was telling him, *This is where I belong. Here, and nowhere else.*

"To hell with that," Xavier muttered, and with a heave of his shoulder, he shoved the chair from a spot it had not left for a generation or more.

"There you have it, Lockwood," he said, breathing slightly faster than normal. "An earl's chair. Care to repose yourself in it while I move the seraglio chair into place?"

"In an earl's chair? I'd never so disgrace my arse. Do you have a marquess's chair to befit my lofty station?"

"Certainly. You can find it here." Xavier gestured to a rude location, and the marquess laughed, as he'd been intended.

The rococo chair was much easier to move. Xavier had it behind the desk in a minute. It looked much too small behind the polished stretch of mahogany desk; this would be a temporary solution. But a temporary solution was better than none.

Lockwood perched on the corner of the desk, snifter in hand, and Xavier sat in the seraglio chair.

"This appears to be my first order of business in my scandalous new chair," he commented, injecting a touch of ennui into his voice. "What's on your mind, Lockwood?"

The marquess looked down at him sharply, then adjusted his posture. One of his boot heels began drumming a rhythm against the side of the desk.

"It's this wager," he confirmed. "The Oliver chit. The ten pounds. You're determined to win it. But why? You've already proven that you're not infallible. You were bested by Jane, of all people—"

Xavier broke in. "As were you, and there's no shame in that. If I recall correctly, you were also bested by Jane at blind-man's buff. She's a worthy adversary."

"She's a disrespectful little minx, and I'm thankful she's no direct relation of mine. Yet I've never known you to lose even the most insignificant of wagers."

"It *was* insignificant, though, wasn't it?" Xavier replied. Expression Number One this time: Veiled Disdain. "And I am only human, much to my own disappointment. I can't be bothered to devote my utmost energy to every whim thought up by some crack-brained . . ."

Too late, he recalled that the greenery-gathering had been Louisa's idea. He must have stumbled on his words, because Lockwood kicked the desk again and smiled.

That smile was deeply unappealing. Far too wide and showing too many teeth. Xavier resolved to adjust his own future smiles to improve upon the appearance.

"That is," he continued, raising his voice, "I shan't be told when I ought to win, any more than I will permit you to tell me that I can't lose."

That was the crux of it, wasn't it? He'd had enough. He didn't want to be Xavier anymore. Not the Xavier everyone expected him to be.

He didn't know what he wanted instead, but he'd never figure that out while men like Lockwood were cluttering up his time and sapping his ingenuity with their frivolous demands.

"I'd never tell you that," Lockwood said with another of those vulpine smiles. *Kick. Kick.* "After all, your money will line my pocket if you don't triumph over the Oliver chit."

"Please refrain from damaging the furniture." Xavier raked a hand through his hair, only to find it already bristling. Well, this was why he kept it cropped short. "And please refrain from insulting my guests."

"I won't insult anyone who doesn't want to be insulted," Lockwood said. *Kick. Kick.* He tossed back the brandy and smacked his lips. "But little Miss Oliver's got a wild streak, don't you think? I've seen the spark in her eye. I think she wouldn't mind a bit of . . . insult."

The snifter thumped onto the desk. Lockwood had set it on—oh, hell, on the ledger and papers Louisa had given Xavier last night.

After he'd brought her to orgasm on the chaise longue in the library, as though she were a lightskirt. A lightskirt and every inch a lady, who had left him achingly unfulfilled and dreadfully uncertain.

He drew his chair closer to the desk, willing his body not to recall Louisa, the wet silk of her folds, the startled gasp she'd let out when her body shuddered apart.

"Please take the snifter off of my papers, Lockwood," he said harshly. "Have a care."

"Why ought I to start now?" Lockwood slid from the desk and slammed the snifter back onto the sideboard with enough force to make his muddied eyes squeeze shut in pain.

He sauntered back to the desk and turned the stack so it faced him. "What are these papers that you're so infatuated with?" His brows knit. "What is this? Russian? I can't read it."

"It's a history of our families, but it's been ciphered. Miss Oliver has begun to decipher it. Did you know the first viscount won his title from Good Queen Bess for—"

"Is he the one who diddled the maid?" Lockwood looked mildly interested. "My father mentioned it to me once. Had a taste for books. I never did, but scandal's always interesting."

Xavier blinked. "Yes. As a matter of fact, he *did* diddle the maid. Actually, the queen's favorite lady-in-waiting."

"I'd love to know what he did to her," Lockwood mused, flipping the pages of the encoded ledger. "Anything that earns a man a viscountcy must have been a sexual masterpiece. Does it describe the act? This book?"

Xavier was still trying to shake off the wonder of Lockwood's knowing something about their family history that he had not. "Ah . . . no. Not in any greater detail than what we've already mentioned."

"Pity." Lockwood raised one of Louisa's scribbled-on papers to the slanting light from the window. "And this is the key, then? She's a clever one, that Oliver chit."

"Don't insult my guests," Xavier repeated, and Lockwood shot him a *ha-I-got-you* look over his shoulder before returning his attention to the paper.

He wasn't playing his part well enough; Lockwood would grow suspicious. Xavier scrabbled for his usual languid tone, his casual pitch. "The whole book's full of scandal from what I can tell. It's a wonder our lineage survived long enough to create us."

"It didn't." Lockwood turned back to the desk and set the paper down. "Title's in the second creation."

"I was speaking figuratively," Xavier covered. Fortunately, he had spent a little time the previous night with Louisa's tables and the ledger. It wasn't as though he could drop off to sleep in the state she'd left him, and the code tables offered a welcome distraction. "Yes, our families behaved badly following the Restoration. Do you know about the mistress?"

Lockwood frowned. "Melissande?"

"Not *your* mistress. That is, former mistress."

Lockwood's frown deepened, and Xavier explained, "No, the second earl fathered several children by a mistress. The legitimate heirs all died off with suspicious swiftness thereafter."

"Hell of a coincidence."

"I doubt it," Xavier said. "The king granted the title to a distant cousin, who married one of the mistress's children. It's like something the Borgias would have arranged."

Or something in a novel. Anything could happen in a novel.

He dragged his chair still closer to the desk, until the solid mahogany pressed tight against his midsection.

"You don't say." Lockwood looked interested. "Well, I'm not surprised we've got scandal in our blood. After everything we've entered in the betting book at White's—"

"Lockwood, I'm afraid I am rather busy right now," Xavier cut off his cousin. So many times had they talked of scandal, and wagers, and White's, and he had no desire to hold such a conversation again. He drew before himself the account book Hoskinson had left behind, then laid hold of his quizzing glass. "You know how it is. Tedious estate affairs."

"Lord, yes," Lockwood replied at once, filling his snifter once more. "Absolutely dreadful, aren't they? It's a shame you have to deal with all that during a house party. You'll be missing all the fun."

He stood. "Well, I'll leave you to it. Don't forget about tomorrow, though."

"Oh?" Xavier looked up from his steward's crabbed writing. He couldn't remember what was in store.

Lockwood sighed. "Your aunt or cousin or whoever she is—Mrs. Tindall—thinks we all ought to tramp around some cursed ruin at the edge of your property." He drained his glass. "I must say, Xavier, I preferred your parties of past years."

"I'm sorry to hear it," Xavier replied, his voice vague to suggest that he was already concentrating on his account book again. He stared at the page as Lockwood set down his snifter and walked to the door.

In front of Xavier's eyes, numbers swam, and as soon as the door closed behind Lockwood, he pushed back the chair and returned to the window. It was no good, sitting and pretending and chattering about coded scandal. Even his family's old misdeeds reminded him of Louisa, since without her, he'd never even have known of them.

He sucked in a deep breath and clutched at the wooden window frame. Louisa was not the first woman who had made him feel that he was not good enough. But she was the first who made him feel he could be more.

Like everything about her, this was equal parts aggravating and intriguing.

Xavier liked surprising people. And how it would surprise the world if he embarked on the greatest scandal of all: turning over a new leaf.

He turned back to his desk, ready to fold himself into the seraglio chair again and make sense of Chatterton's accounts. Really. He would, this time.

But then he noticed that the ledger, and all Louisa's papers, were gone from his desk.

Chapter 15

Containing the Tale of a Paddling

"Where should this book go?" Jane asked for the six hundred thirty-seventh time.

All right, not that many. But Louisa's morning in the library had been full of questions and chaos, since Alex had bid his young cousin to work off her speculation debt of time by, as he put it, "obeying Miss Oliver's every command in the library, if you can manage such a sensible act."

Louisa wasn't sure if he'd meant this as a kindness to her or Jane, or if he simply wanted both women out of his sight for a while.

Fine. Louisa didn't mind keeping the troublesome man out of her sight for a while, either. She couldn't trust herself to behave wisely around him; she had learned that the previous night.

But she *could* trust *him*. He'd done nothing worse than follow her lead. He'd stopped when she stopped him.

Wait. Why had she stopped him?

She shivered. Never mind. She and Jane had plenty of

books to occupy their time, and Louisa ought to keep her thoughts occupied, too.

"Jane, are you still taking notes on the morocco-bound books?" Louisa called over her shoulder as she heaved a beautifully bound folio from an upper shelf. "You'll have to flip those open and check the pages. The binder didn't mark a single spine. Very unhelpful of him."

"I do like creating chaos," Jane commented. "Is there any point to what we're doing beyond that?"

Louisa stepped back, folio clutched in her arms, and turned to her friend. "Yes."

She laid the folio on the chaise longue—*cover it with books, don't think of what you did here last night*—and knelt before it, stroking the finely tooled and gilded leather with her fingertips.

"Your cousin requested that I learn what I could about the library," she said. "Even make a beginning at a catalogue."

"I knew you were brilliant," Jane commented. "You're doing exactly as he said, but in such a way as to infuriate him."

"Why should he be infuriated by our obedience?" Louisa asked blandly. Jane grinned and dropped another book with a *thump*.

Assisted by a capable housemaid named Ellie, Jane and Louisa had been slamming books around for several hours now: noting the titles, stacking them in tottery towers, and distributing an ungodly amount of dust. It was the first time Louisa had truly looked around the library since finding the encoded family history. The books, and Jane's chatter, were welcome distractions.

"Besides," Louisa added, "it's not as though anyone uses this lovely room. The only times I've ever encountered another guest is when someone entered looking for Lord Xavier."

"You've been spending a lot of time with him, haven't you?" Jane asked. "Ugh, this is geometry. Or calculus. Something dreadful." *Thump*. "Ellie, hand me another book."

As Jane and the housemaid handed off volumes, Louisa flipped the folio open, her eyes dimly noting the fineness of the marbled endpapers. "I suppose I have spent a lot of time with him, yes," she answered.

Jane's chatter was now failing as a distraction. This was not good.

"Well, I pity you," Jane said. "Xavier is dreadfully dull."

This was so surprising that Louisa sat back on her heels. "Dull?" She turned to face her friend. "Isn't he widely supposed to be a rake? A charmer? A scandal in human form?"

The apple-cheeked housemaid, Ellie, looked up, her eyebrows raised with interest. An industrious worker, Ellie had banished most of the dust from the denuded shelves and the much-abused carpet. She was also an entertaining companion, a fount of belowstairs gossip about the other guests and other fascinating but unmaidenly topics.

Jane snorted. "I'll grant you that he's my relative, so his manly appeal escapes me. But surely the polite world can cough up a better example of charm and scandal than Xavier."

"There's many who would call him charming," said Ellie, returning to her dusting. "Though I myself haven't ever seen him do nothing so scandalous. When he'd have his house parties in the past, his guests were a wonder, but he wouldn't take part in much himself."

Jane plumped down onto the chaise, almost sitting on the folio. "I'd agree with that. He likes to shock people, but the better you know him, the duller he is."

The better Louisa knew him—no, he didn't seem dull. He was like those nested Russian dolls; every time she broke through one facade, there was more to discover behind it. Never had she expected to find a rake who read Dante. Who cared for his young cousin Jane's well-being, and for Louisa's. Who took none of his own pleasure; who only gave.

Stupid. She was remembering the chaise again. He'd sat where Jane was sitting now; his long fingers had slid over Louisa's skin, slipping within her.

She turned her head and took a deep breath. Self-control. Yes. One of her polite masks. She assumed an expression of bland curiosity. When it felt like it was molded correctly on her features, she folded her legs and sat on the floor, then looked up at Jane like a child begging a story from a governess. "You think Lord Xavier is boring? Do tell, please."

Jane smiled. "Any interesting qualities he may have, he got from me, which means he must have been a positive cipher for the eight years of his life before I was born."

"For instance . . ."

"For instance," Jane said, warming to her subject, "he used to play cards with me for hours when we were young. I always dealt from the bottom of the deck, and it took him *months* to figure out how a mere girl could beat him so soundly every time. I do believe his notable skill at cards today is due to my ability to cheat over a decade ago."

"Ah," Louisa said. "That's why he kept teasing you during our game of speculation."

"Yes," Jane admitted. "Now that I can't cheat when I play him, he's much harder to defeat. It's hardly any fun playing by the rules."

Ellie laughed, but when Jane and Louisa looked over at her, she simply continued her dusting.

"What about his reputation as a rake?" Louisa's throat felt dry, and she coughed. "Pardon me. It must be the dust we've stirred up."

Jane waved a dismissive hand. "I can't think of a man in the *ton* who hasn't had a bit on the side. Xavier's not married, so he can do what he likes. But he doesn't do all that much, believe me. He flirts, but how often have you seen him touch a woman? Or pursue her?"

"Um." Louisa felt the need to study her cuticles. With great attention.

"Exactly," Jane concluded. "He has these shocking ideas, but it's someone else who always does the dirty deeds. He might squire around a new opera dancer every week, but it's all for show. He had a very sad childhood, you know," she added in a mock-tragic voice. "Death of his parents and all that. The poor man positively thirsts for attention."

Her small slippered feet swung and patted the floor. "The very subject is revolting, considering my relation to him, but I don't believe he knows what to do with a woman half as well as the *ton* thinks he does."

"Hmm," Louisa replied, thinking of a strong hand sliding up her thigh. She was sure her face was as red as a morocco binding. She kept her head bowed, studying her nails, her hands.

"He does tell the most fascinating stories, though," Jane mused. "I've heard bits of a tale about an opera dancer and a pineapple, but I can't get anyone to explain it to me."

"I've never heard a complaint about him from the other maids," Ellie added. "Some of them other gentlemen, now, they're a different story. Pinchy hands, if you know what I mean."

"No, I don't," Jane said. "But I want to. Won't you tell us?"

Louisa looked up at the housemaid, safe now with this change of subject. If she was flushed, it would only be because of the promise of gossip. Yes. Good. She scooted to lean against the long seat of the chaise, and Jane slid onto the floor next to her.

"Well"—Ellie pretended reluctance—"I've seen gentlemen in here many a time in past years. Not for the books on the shelves, but . . . for these." She dropped her dustcloth and trundled over to the window seat, pressing on the wood face of it until it flipped open to display its hidden shelf.

Which Jane had, apparently, not known was there. "Gracious," she breathed, then lunged for the secret shelf, scuttling and crawling across the room.

Louisa followed. Why not? She'd filched the copy of *Fanny Hill*, but there were dozens of other books she'd never opened.

Jane tugged a book in yellow paper covers from the line of naughty works, opened it up at random, then slammed it closed again with a gasp.

"Let me see," Louisa said. Her friend let the book fall open to a most instructive woodcut, and both young women stared at it.

"That can't be accurate," Louisa decided. "Grown gentlemen wanting to be hit upon the bottom, like children being punished?"

As she said it, the slippery heat between her legs reminded her: yes, there was something intoxicating about being pushed down and pleasured. About surrendering one's dignity into someone else's hands.

Even so. Hitting upon the bottom? Ridiculous.

"There's some that do like it, miss, that's for sure," Ellie confirmed. "I've never seen it done myself, but last year one of his lordship's guests brought a mistress that told me about it. I won't say who brought her, for it's more'n my job is worth. But she would put on a special outfit cut down to here"—she drew her hand across her torso just below her bustline—"and then she'd have at his behind with a book."

"These poor books," Louisa murmured. "Does anyone ever *read* them?"

"I don't believe it," Jane said. "The mistress must have been lying."

"Why would she lie about something so embarrassing?" Louisa asked.

"It makes for a good story, doesn't it? Here it is a year later, and we're still talking about it."

"It's true, miss," Ellie insisted. "I swear it. I heard the sound of the paddling myself when I was up in that hallway to lay the fires."

Jane blinked, assimilating this fact. "Well, there aren't going to be any good stories from this year's party, that's certain. Not unless I make them up."

Louisa had to laugh. "What, giving Lord Kirkpatrick one hundred sixty-one kisses wasn't interesting enough?"

Jane was now lying flat on the floor. Her whole head was beneath the window seat, the better to see the books hidden on that shelf. "Not the way I did it," came her muffled voice. "Kirkpatrick would never so much as hold my hand if he wasn't forced to, but the wager was a matter of honor, so he had to agree."

She poked her head out. "Do you think that's because he knew me as a child? Xavier has such dashing friends, but to them I'm like a younger sister. I can never seem to turn these old relationships to my advantage."

Louisa slid forward to lie on her stomach beside her friend. Their dresses were already creased and dusty; there was no sense in worrying about appearances anymore. And there was a delicious freedom in lying flat on a carpet during daytime, without a single chaperone around to protest.

"I wonder, Jane, if Xavier hasn't been protecting you from

his friends," Louisa said. "He does seem to feel responsible for you. And he wouldn't want someone like, say, Lockwood to pursue you."

She disliked even the sound of the marquess's name. Propping herself higher on her elbows, she shrugged as though she could cast him off.

"Lockwood? How vile." Jane rolled onto her back, staring up at the painted ceiling of the library. "I won't learn what I want from a book. I won't learn it at *all*, as long as Xavier holds the purse strings. I did tell you he was dull, didn't I?"

Louisa's cough was almost sufficient to cover her laugh.

"But next year I'll be of age, and I'll have money of my own," Jane concluded. "I might even have a suitor, if I can ever get a man to look at me."

"Remember, it's the woman inside who counts," Louisa said. "Men get distracted by curves and giggles, but those don't last. And the good men will realize that."

"I wish I believed you," Jane said.

"I know. Sometimes I don't believe myself."

Louisa bent her mouth into a reasonable approximation of good cheer, then looked over her shoulder to see whether they had been overheard. No; having concluded the discussion of paddling, Ellie had moved off to straighten the teetering stacks of books they had built that morning.

So Louisa asked, "What type of man would you choose, Jane? If you had the freedom?"

"I don't know," Jane said. "I'd want to marry someone who didn't see me only as Xavier's cousin. As a poor relative of someone they wanted to get close to."

She shut her big hazel eyes. "My life is even duller than Xavier's. I'm sometimes tempted to create a scandal just so people can't look through me anymore."

"I *knew* you wanted a scandal for Christmas." Louisa

took a deep breath. "But please believe me, being gossiped about can be dreadful."

She was thinking of her own broken engagement to James, Viscount Matheson. A matter of convenience, it had been dissolved as logically as it was formed. But a scandal had erupted when James took up with her stepsister, Julia, instead; a humiliation of stares and whispers infinitely worse than being shuttled aside, unnoticed.

It had worked out well in the end, though. Julia and James were happily married, and Louisa . . .

Everyone had forgotten about her again.

"I do understand what you mean, Jane," Louisa added. "Sometimes anything seems better than being ignored. Until something worse happens."

Jane opened her eyes. "You're horribly sensible."

She rolled up to a seated position. "And you, Louisa? What type of man would you choose?"

"Someone with all his hair and teeth."

Jane folded her arms. "Give me a *real* answer."

Louisa laughed. "Let me think. I've never had the power of choice before."

An understatement. She'd never had a single suitor before James had seized on her for convenience's sake. Surely this was why Xavier and Lockwood had bet upon her: she was the most unlikely subject imaginable.

Her eyes roved over the painted ceiling. Sinuous classical gods and goddesses lounged across the span of the room in a swirl of smoky draperies and pale limbs. Apollo was Louisa's favorite, and always easy to spot: youthful and clean-shaven, with a lyre tucked against a narrow hip. The god of knowledge, truth, and the arts. He was interested in everything, that Apollo.

And he stretched his arm across the ceiling, lithe and long-limbed, his hair a ridiculous mop of curls. For the first time, Louisa wished that Apollo had tamed his hair a bit. Cropped it off short, so when he ran his hand through it in an unconscious gesture of frustration, the damage to his coiffure would be minimal.

She squeezed her eyes closed. "I would like to find someone who . . ." She swallowed. "Someone who would want to know what I'm really like," she finished in a rush.

"Well, yes," said Jane. "I took that for granted."

Louisa's eyes flew open, and she stared up at her friend. Jane scrunched up her face. "That's all you want? You don't care if he's, say, wider than a beer barrel?"

But he's not, Louisa thought.

"Not that wide," she said, and Jane's expression unscrunched a bit.

"And you don't even care if he likes you? Only that he really knows you?"

This was easy to answer. "Yes." Louisa shoved herself upright and folded her legs before her. "That is, I'm not interested in a man who thinks he likes me *without* knowing me. I'm not possessed of either curves or giggles in plentiful supply, but if a man could look beyond that, then that would be a foundation for . . ."

She trailed off and raised a hand to her burning cheek. "Something real."

"But if he knows you well and doesn't like you," Jane asked in a small voice, wrapping her arms around her knees, "isn't that the worst thing in the world?"

Louisa considered. "Worse than being forgotten? Or never known at all?"

If no one ever knew her, she could maintain the fiction that someone, someday, would recognize her worth. But if that fiction vanished, she would be alone. And her Louisa catalogue would stretch on, lonely and long and unchanging.

Alex wasn't the answer to this particular prayer. She'd

known that even before she'd rucked up her skirts so he could touch her fervent body.

Oh, he was a puzzle, and Louisa found puzzles irresistible. But resist him she must. As long as he was determined to hide his finest qualities from the world, she should not pin any hopes upon him.

"There are worse things than being alone," she told her friend bracingly.

She wanted to believe that.

Chapter 16

Containing a Lavender Cravat

The following day, certain members of the house party remained abed late, not wishing to walk to a nearby ruin beloved by Mrs. Tindall.

Among the slugabeds were Lord and Lady Weatherby and Mr. and Mrs. Simpkins, whom everyone knew exchanged spouses as often as other couples changed their clothing. Less scandalously, Lady Irving elected to remain behind with Lord Weatherwax, imbibing and gambling in the morning room.

"Xavier's old butler has let slip that he hasn't uncorked the best bottles yet," grumbled the countess. "Can you imagine? Keeping us here over Christmas without fostering inebriation."

Louisa looked over her aunt's shoulder at the dozing Lord Weatherwax. His cottony hair was wildly disarranged, and he'd scattered his hand of cards before him on a felt-topped table that had been set up for the players.

"I don't think your companion needs any help becoming inebriated," Louisa said. "Honestly, Aunt, aren't you ashamed to skin a gentleman who's only half-awake, and much less than half-sober?"

"I'm never ashamed of anything," replied Lady Irving with a sharklike smile that set off the ermine trim on her turban and gown. "Besides, you'll be better off without me. Mrs. Tindall's serving as chaperone, and"—she lowered her voice to a whisper—"that woman doesn't notice half of what goes on around her. Only get her napping, and you'll be able to do what you like. Within reason."

"I'm always reasonable," Louisa sighed, accepting her aunt's pat on the head with better grace than the gesture deserved.

A familiar group marched westward into the cool air toward the ruin at which, Mrs. Tindall confessed, the late Mr. Tindall had first professed his love (her ruddy face reddened still more before she squeaked out the final word). The party included Lady Alleyneham, keeping her daughters on a short leash; Jane; Lockwood and Kirkpatrick; Signora Frittarelli and Mrs. Protheroe; the stolid Mr. Channing, whom Louisa had rarely heard utter more than three words together; and Freddie Pellington, whom Louisa had rarely heard utter fewer than three sentences.

And Alex. Striding at the side of Mrs. Tindall, he was all cool colors, his coat the same gray of his eyes, his boots the coal dark of his hair. His hands were gloved against the cold, but she remembered the hot slide of his bare skin over hers.

This memory was not helping her determination to keep him at a friendly distance.

A distraction, then. "Jane." Louisa pasted a smile across her face and turned back to her newfound friend. "Do come and walk with me."

Jane had been dogging the footsteps of Lord Kirkpatrick, and at Louisa's invitation she trudged away from the oblivious baron.

"Stupid man," she muttered as she reached Louisa's side. "I told you, he never notices me."

Jane was swathed, as usual, in a too-bulky cloak over a too-bright gown. Her cheeks were rosy, as though she was baking in her layers of fabric.

"I'm the last person anyone should consult for romantic advice." Louisa's breath blew frosty from her lips. "Well, possibly second-to-last. If there's a hermit on the grounds somewhere, I could probably do better than he."

Jane shook her head. "I don't think there is. Sorry."

They walked on, both preoccupied, to the boundary of the Great Hall's manicured grounds. When they crossed it, gentle hills and scrubby gorse unrolled in a gray-brown stretch of wintry heath. The tenants farmed to the east, Louisa realized; to the west it was only this wild, untamed land.

"Why are we always having to walk everywhere?" Jane complained. "I'd much prefer to be back with your aunt, drinking myself into a stupor."

Louisa interpreted this statement to mean *This outing is not amusing me, because I hoped for a dramatic change, which has not occurred, in the behavior of the object of my interest.*

Ha. She could hope for that, too, couldn't she? Alex had taken Mrs. Protheroe on one arm and the busty *signora* on the other. Playing the part of Lord Xavier to perfection. Not a flicker to betray that anything the slightest bit special had passed between himself and Louisa.

She hated him for that, just a little. And she hated herself for caring. She'd known it would be this way; she'd expected it. Even encouraged it. So she had no right to hope for anything else.

"I'll tell you what, Jane." She extended a gloved hand to pull her shorter friend up a rise in the heath. "When we get back to the house, we'll get drunk as sailors. Your mother won't notice, and my aunt will call us vulgar and then forget all about the matter."

This brought a small smile to Jane's face. "It *would* be vulgar, wouldn't it?"

"It would be nothing more or less than what the men of the party do every day."

But she knew, and knew Jane did, too, that they would never follow through on this promise to get roaring drunk. Just as Alex had told Louisa, unmarried women couldn't bear much scandal. And Louisa was too grimly sensible to think that an excess of drink would give her anything but a headache.

"In any case," she added in a brisk voice that made Jane squint at her, "it's a lovely day to walk out. I've never seen a ruin. Don't we owe it to ourselves to snap up a few new experiences?"

"I hate it when you're logical," Jane muttered.

"No, you find it intellectually bracing."

"Bracing. Yes. That's what I meant." Jane rolled her hazel eyes, but she smiled.

They walked on, and Mrs. Tindall scurried ahead, her round figure moving with surprising lightness. She called back, motioning for everyone else to hurry. "Almost there!"

The ruins of Finchley Castle reared up suddenly when they rounded a hill. The old bones of the medieval fortress were barely recognizable as such anymore. A few arches remained, and the round base of what had once been the keep, but most of the ancient walls had tumbled into piles of rubble, and the stone was hung with straggling ivy, brown and dry.

"Lovely," Louisa breathed. The place seemed full of hidden knowledge.

Jane looked mildly interested. "It's exactly like something out of a horrid novel. Do you think there's a dungeon?"

Before Louisa could reply, Alex had turned toward them from the edge of the ruin. "Jane, come and see. I've found the steps to the dungeon, and now I can lock you in."

"And there are cellars over this way," cried Mrs. Tindall, waving her arm for the line of puffing guests to follow her. "Ever so private. I'll show you the one where my dear Mr. Tindall and I . . ." She covered her mouth.

"Does my mother," Jane said in a tone of infinite disgust, "honestly think that a cellar is a good place to meet a lov—no, I can't say it. It's too repellent."

"When a woman's in love, I suppose a ruined cellar is as good as a castle," Louisa replied.

Jane shuddered. "I'd rather have Xavier lock me in a dungeon than hear any more of my mother's bizarre romantic past."

Louisa laughed and waved Jane away. The younger woman trudged over to her mother, and Lady Alleyneham followed, herding her daughters before her. They looked as reluctant as if they were going to get teeth drawn.

Alex didn't follow at once, Louisa noticed. He was standing upon a fallen block with arms folded, scanning the sweep of ruined stone, the fallen-in cellars. Posing like the statue-lord he'd played upon Louisa's arrival at the house party: looming on his front steps, trying to impress everyone with his grandeur.

She knew him better now, and she could recognize the cracks in his disdainful mask: the softening of his mouth when he saw his younger cousin safely led around by her mother; the furrow of his brow as Lady Alleyneham shoved her elder daughter into the path of Lord Kirkpatrick, and the younger toward Mr. Channing.

He was watching out for them all, but he didn't want anyone to know it. She could have kissed him and kicked him for that.

Instead, she turned away.

And bumped right into Lord Lockwood.

"Careful, sweeting." He clutched her forearms, though she was in no danger of losing her balance.

She shook her arms free and stepped back. "I'm always careful, my lord. And if you've forgotten my name, you need not be ashamed. I am willing to make allowances for the incompetent." She paused. "And lords."

The marquess was wearing a lavender cravat—evidently she'd been right about his sartorial innovation. The color was pleasant against his deep blue coat and olive skin. But the expression on his face was everything dreadful: a syrupy quirk of the lips; calculating eyes.

"Miss Oliver. Ruined." He rolled the consonants over his tongue.

"Ah, you do remember my name. Good for you, my lord." She gave him a pitying smile; she couldn't be openly rude to a noble. "But you puzzle me. Does it surprise you that a ruin should be in a ruined state?"

He narrowed his eyes and widened his smile. Quite a feat of engineering. "Is the ruin the only thing that's been . . . ruined?"

"I doubt it," she said calmly. She would not think of Alex's fingers trailing over her body. "These are Lord Xavier's guests. Are they not purported to include the scandalous along with the fashionable?"

"Ah, how right you are." He drew a watch from his pocket and began swinging it at the end of its fob, as though they were sitting tête-à-tête in a parlor. "Sometimes the scandalous become fashionable, though the fashionable rarely become scandalous."

Swing, swing, went the watch on its golden chain. Louisa followed it back and forth with her eyes. The case was elaborately chased and inlaid. No doubt expensive. He was fortunate not to have lost it to a creditor, if the rumors of his financial troubles were true.

"And which are you, Miss Oliver? Scandalous or fashionable? Or both?"

Louisa blinked and looked up at Lockwood's face. He was studying her with ill-concealed curiosity.

"I'm neither," she said. "I'm a prosy bluestocking who wanted to see Clifton Hall's library."

"Ah. Is that why you came to the house party?" He flipped his watch and tucked it back into its pocket. "And here I thought you had a more personal interest in someone at the party."

"I am honored, my lord, that you've devoted an iota of thought to me."

"As you should be. It's more than many did during your London season, if I recall correctly."

Ah. Her debut in society, marked by desperate loneliness. Lockwood had scored a direct hit, and he knew it. Louisa struggled to breathe normally. If she showed him he'd drawn blood, he would only strike again.

"You do recall correctly," she said. "Which is why I find myself unwilling to shackle you any longer with the dullness of my presence. Do excuse me, my lord."

She turned and strode over the rough ground, pebbled with stone chips and clotted roots. She had come several yards closer to one of the deep stone pits—a dungeon or a cellar, she couldn't yet tell—before Lockwood caught up with her and seized her arm again.

"I do not require your assistance," she said, tugging free from his grip.

"Very well. How about my company?"

She walked straight ahead, not looking at him again. "You are free to do as you like."

"I know it." His drawl was no more than a passable imitation of Alex's own Bored Voice.

And where was Alex? Not that she needed him herself. But if he could steer Lockwood in another direction—such as into the bosomy path of *la signora*—the diversion would be most welcome.

He had climbed down from his stone perch, and she couldn't locate him at once. A cacophony was issuing from one of the other pits. People were hustling down the steps, and Mrs. Tindall's unmodulated tones were clearly audible.

That must be the Cellar of Love, then, and their hostess was expounding on her long-ago romance. Louisa hoped no souvenirs from that romance were to be found in the cellar. Jane would likely suffer an apoplexy.

Lockwood followed Louisa's gaze. "Xavier's relatives. Poor fellow. I'm thankful to claim no blood relation to Mrs. Tindall, though I'm sure she's a very good sort in her own way."

"In anyone's way, I should say," Louisa corrected. "She's a very kind woman. I've never seen her in an ill humor."

"Because she sleeps more than a cat."

Louisa ignored this slight to their hostess and looked down into the stone pit. About twelve feet deep, a square twenty feet by twenty, it had probably once been used as a root cellar. The light wind that nipped under the edges of her cloak would leave the excavated space unbothered; cool in summer and sheltered in winter.

It wasn't such a terrible place to meet a lover, if one could ignore the danger of being crushed by falling rocks.

The walls looked ancient, their timber bracing long since rotted away.

"Do you know," Lockwood began again, "Xavier has dreadful relatives beyond those that are living."

"That doesn't surprise me," Louisa said. She chose to take his mention of "dreadful living relatives" as a reference to himself, and so she let it pass.

"Yes, I was looking through a coded ledger he found. It's full of the most *interesting* stories. Would you like to hear some?"

He had the ledger? Louisa didn't like the idea of the old book in Lockwood's hands, though she knew he had more of a right to it than she. It was foolish to feel any ownership of it, as though it was her secret. Hers and Alex's.

"I can't stop you from telling me, my lord," she said, and began to pick her way down the wide steps into the cellar.

"Very true. For example, then, after the Restoration, the first earl set up his own company of play actors. He built himself a sizable stable of actresses after sampling their talents."

"That was sensible of him." Louisa feigned obtuseness. She set her half-boots carefully as she descended each step; some of the old stones were roughened and loose.

"Not sensible at all, Miss Oliver." Lockwood sounded annoyed. "Indecent. He sampled their talents in the bed-chamber."

"Why should that be relevant to a career upon the stage?" Louisa reached for the earthen wall of the cellar to aid her balance.

"It wasn't relevant to—good Lord, Miss Oliver, he was a scandal, that's all. The theatrical company was naught but a cover for his harem."

"Well, why should he bother hiding the secret?" Since

she was facing away from Lockwood, leading the way down the stairs, she needn't hide her grin. "Surely an earl can have a harem if he wants to. Earls can do virtually anything they please."

"As can marquesses?"

"That depends on the marquess."

Lockwood jumped down several stairs at once; Louisa heard the thump of his boots, the rattle of pebbles, and then he was at her side on the wide cellar steps. "You are handling this talk of scandal very coolly, Miss Oliver. Have you some secret scandal of your own?"

She offered him her blandest expression. "My lord, I'm simply unbothered by the roistering of nobles who have been dead for centuries. How can their behavior affect me?"

"A fair point." He cut his eyes sideways. "What of new-found scandal, then? Have you heard Xavier's tale of the opera dancer and the pineapple?"

Lockwood stretched his arms, his knuckles grazing the bare stone wall at Louisa's side, and she flinched as a rain of pebbles pattered onto the steps.

"I haven't," she said, "though I've heard *of* it. In fact, Miss Tindall and I were discussing it only yesterday. As a prosy bluestocking, I am greatly interested in the collection of new knowledge. Will you tell it to me?"

Lockwood's boot slipped, and he caught himself roughly on the crumbling stone edge of the cellar. He took a long moment to check the sheen of his boots, then looked at her with a suspicious expression. "It's not my story to tell."

"I didn't realize you had scruples about telling tales that were none of your affair." She set her feet on the most solid-looking flags. "I shouldn't wish to embarrass you. Perhaps I shall simply ask my host to enlighten me."

"I'm sure he'd be willing," Lockwood said. But his

usual sly demeanor had lost its edge. His boot skidded again on pebbles.

"Watch your step, my lord," Louisa said, turning away from him. "The footing isn't as sound as it appears, especially if you overreach yourself."

"You are remarkably sharp of sight."

"It's one of my finest qualities." Louisa sped down the stairs, sliding a little on loose stones. It was a good parting line, and she wanted to end the conversation at that.

Lockwood only played a game; she knew that. His taunts stung, but they didn't truly wound her.

No, what bothered her was his determination. Even if Alex wanted to change, to drop his rakish facade, men like Lockwood would resist his reformation. They liked their performing bear's tricks too much.

Down in the cellar, she regretted descending the steps so quickly. The smell of mildew and damp was strong, and there was not much to see but dirt-crusted stone, gray-brown and pitted. Chunks of rotted wood might have been the remains of timbers or storage barrels. Nothing was holding these old walls up but habit.

The tread of boots rang on the flagged cellar floor. Lockwood had followed her down. A wary prickle raced down her neck, and she spun to face him.

"You must show me more of your finest qualities," he murmured. In an instant, he had wrapped himself around her, his mouth nipping at her neck, his hands sliding beneath her cloak. "You've shown them to Xavier, haven't you? As much time as you spend alone with him. Does your aunt know what you're really like?"

His arms were stiff and forceful, his words like icicles. The scent of lime cologne slapped at her, over-strong and cloying. There was nothing of real desire in his words or movements. No, this was an exercise in power, and he thought to use her as a pawn.

She jabbed him with an elbow, and he heaved a curse at her.

Through gritted teeth, Lockwood spoke on. "I will ignore your impoliteness and assume that you have answered in the negative. Well, you'll soon learn. If you stay, Miss Oliver, the world will discover far more about you than you ever intended."

"I doubt the world cares to discover anything about me," Louisa ground out. "I am quite invisible."

"Much to my pleasure." He squeezed her forearms tight. "It means we are sure to be left alone."

Louisa twisted again. "Hell," she muttered. She had to get away before they were seen.

She swooned against Lockwood's chest. Caught off guard, the marquess relaxed his grasp, and she flung herself backward at that instant. She had enough room now to raise her knee, swift and deliberate, between Lockwood's legs.

She knew where a man was most vulnerable. She had grown up in the country, and she was well aware that men had the same parts as stallions and bulls.

The effect of a blow to those parts was the same, too: it completely ended all interest in rutting. Lockwood wheezed and released her at once, doubling over.

With more grace than Louisa realized she could summon, she stepped out of his reach and crossed to the stairs. "Lord Lockwood, I don't care to know why you seem to delight so in competing with Lord Xavier. It does not and will not involve me."

She pounded up a few stairs, then turned around to face the still-gasping marquess. "Oh, and my lord? If you take hold of my person again, you'll be gelded."

She gave him a sweet smile—it was easy, now that she was free, to smile her triumph—and then darted up the steps.

She almost smacked into Alex at the top. "Steady," he said, catching her forearm.

Reflexively, she snatched it back from him, and he looked at her askance. "Is something amiss?"

"Your cousin is down in the cellar," she said. "I believe he's in some sort of masculine distress. Please excuse me."

And she strode away, as though she had all the confidence in the world.

For a woman who had never won much notice, she was drawing the wrong type in recent days. She'd been correct in what she'd told Jane: there *were* worse things than being alone. Lockwood's pawings, and the foul breath of scandal, could easily take away her good name.

This was the life Lord Xavier had chosen; this was the company he kept.

And this was why she walked away from him now, though she ached to call him by name.

It was self-preservation, in every sense.

Chapter 17

Containing an Entirely New Numbered Expression

Xavier watched Louisa rush away. She stumbled over a loose stone, then called a greeting to Jane as his orange-swaddled cousin emerged from her mother's beloved cellar.

Louisa had shaken off his touch; she'd never done that before. Especially since they'd agreed to be . . . friends . . . and he'd had his hand up her skirts.

All at once, he understood her reaction. "Lockwood," he ground out. Lockwood had done something to her. This would not stand.

He thundered down the stairs. Just as he'd suspected, the marquess was standing on the flagged floor of the cellar. Looking slightly green, and breathing hard.

Xavier drew up short. "Lockwood?"

"Your little bluestocking . . . kneed me," Lockwood panted, bracing his hands on his thighs and pulling in great gulps of air.

"Care to tell me why?"

"Because . . . she's vicious." He shut his eyes and dragged in a hoarse breath. Surely nothing but Lockwood's concern for the gloss of his boots and the cleanliness of his coat was keeping him from collapsing onto the damp, dirty floor of the ancient cellar.

"Try again." Xavier folded his arms and fixed Lockwood with a variant of Expression Number One, Veiled Disdain. He might call this Expression One-Half: Disdain. There was no reason to veil it now. Especially since Lockwood could barely focus his eyes.

"Oh, very . . . well," the marquess heaved. "Because . . . she didn't like . . . being touched."

Yes, she did snapped into his mind. And then: "You *touched* her?"

He closed the gap between himself and Lockwood and caught the end of his cousin's cravat in one hand. "Stand up, damn you. If you touched an unwilling lady, you deserve much worse than what you got."

Lockwood hauled himself upright, still greenish, still blowing like a winded horse. "She's not so unwilling for you, is she?" Somehow, he donned that too-wide smile.

"If you were drunk, I would let that pass. If you weren't family, I'd call you out." Xavier let go of Lockwood and raked a hand through his hair, then caught himself in the gesture and impatiently crossed his arms. "I'm calling you *in* instead. Once we return to the Hall, you will meet me in my study. We have much to discuss privately."

"And who are you to order me about?" Lockwood mimicked his posture, folding his own arms. A little of the marquess's normal olive tint had returned to his face.

Olive tint wrapped in a lavender cravat. Xavier would have laughed if he hadn't been so furious. Louisa had summed Lockwood up in a few seconds.

She noticed the essential core of every person, yet few returned the favor. And she had paid for her perception with a groping in a ruined cellar.

Xavier focused on keeping his expression blank, his posture still.

"Fine, fine. Say what you have to say now." Lockwood scowled. "No sense in transforming a paltry little affair into a huge ordeal."

"This is not a paltry little affair."

Xavier took care to speak calmly, mainly because he knew Lockwood would find it annoying. "I told you when you proposed this wager that a woman's reputation was worth far more than the ten-pound value you placed on it. And now I find you trying to destroy that reputation. This is completely unacceptable."

Lockwood squared his shoulders and began to bluster. "Your reputation is as much at stake as hers, Xavier. You needn't pretend you care only for the young lady, and you needn't pretend you're at all disinterested."

"I'm not disinterested," Xavier replied, sounding just that. He stretched out a hand and straightened the seams of his glove. "I have a conscience, that's all."

"Do you? That's a new development." Lockwood leaned back against the rough stone wall of the cellar, then grimaced. "Damn. That can't be good for my coat's tailoring."

"I am astonished to find you caring equally about the lines of your coat and the harm you've done a lady of quality."

"I'm astonished *not* to find you doing the same," Lockwood replied. "What happened to the Xavier who couldn't wait to open up the White's betting book when he reached London? What happened to your spirit, Coz? Once upon a time, you'd do anything to win."

"I'd never contribute to anyone's disgrace. Especially not a lady's." God, he sounded like a governess. But Lockwood was acting like a spoiled child.

"Then we have a different idea of disgrace," Lockwood

said. He sidled toward the stairs, and Xavier sidestepped to cut him off.

"We do if you think you have any right to touch Miss Oliver."

Lockwood smiled. It was a familiar expression; Xavier had seen it on his own face in his entrance hall's pier glass every time he returned home from a night's roistering. Smug. Satisfied. Ever so pleased with himself.

Why had he felt that way? What was there to be proud of in dissipation and disgrace?

A look of disdain wasn't strong enough. Time for a new Numbered Expression, incorporating contempt and impatience. He sifted the two and turned the expression on the marquess.

"Don't you pull a face at me, Coz," Lockwood said. "You're as vulnerable as your precious little chit. Your reputation was largely built on my shoulders. Who would you be if I didn't bet against you all the time? Who will you be if I don't bet anymore—or if you start losing all the time?"

His smile spread wider. "What if you should lose Louisa Oliver her reputation, yet end in losing our wager after all? Such a pity." He clicked his tongue. "And the world used to call you infallible. You've fallen, and hard."

"I'm the same man I always was." Xavier felt as though he were scrabbling for words. His instincts were finely honed for sidestepping battle, or for dismissing it with languid tones and careless gestures. But how did one deal with a head-on confrontation?

Head-on.

So be it. "In essentials, I've never altered, Lockwood. I have tried to steer you from your worst excesses. I've never participated in your grossest debaucheries. And I've shielded your name when I could, because you're my relative."

He took a step up the cellar stairs, placing himself

several feet above the marquess. "But know this: I won't shield you now. My guests are my responsibility, and you will not harass them. Not any of them. If you won't agree, you will be required to leave."

Lockwood's eyes narrowed. "Maybe you have changed, at that," he mused. The smile returned. "But I haven't. I'll do anything to win this time, Xavier. And if Miss Oliver gets compromised in the bargain—well, I ought to marry eventually, oughtn't I?"

His expression turned considering. "I wonder what she tastes like. Have you found out yet?"

Xavier clenched his teeth; the muscles of his jaw spasmed. "You may have the assistance of a footman in packing your trunks. I expect you gone by sundown."

Lockwood waved this command off as though it were toothless. "But I don't care to leave yet. Not until this wager's played out. Until the party disbands at the end of two weeks, or until you lose." He stepped up from the cellar floor—one stair, two, until he was nose to nose with Xavier.

Reflexively, Xavier reared back to keep Lockwood in focus. This elicited another smile from the marquess.

Xavier cursed his weak vision. He couldn't see what was right in front of his face.

"You could force me to go," Lockwood continued. "But it would be such an ugly public scandal. Why, Miss Oliver's name might get dragged into it also. And if she had to leave early for some reason, you'd still lose the wager, wouldn't you?"

Xavier could only stare. His sycophantic, coarse-minded cousin had been transformed into something altogether devious. Insidious. And Xavier was completely unprepared to respond, because . . . well, no one had ever defied him like this.

"The wager doesn't matter to me," he bit off.

"Come now, don't look like such an old toad," Lockwood said, with a more familiar grin. Confident; appeasing. "It's all in good fun. We always have fun, don't we?"

He trod up a few stone steps, then looked back. "When we get back to the Hall, we'll share a *cru*. The Armagnac, if you like. What do you say, Coz? A toast to determination."

He continued up the stairs—a bit slower than he normally would have, had Louisa not kneed him in a vulnerable area—then vanished over the edge of the cellar.

And Xavier was left somewhere he'd never been before: behind.

It would be easy enough to smooth things over with Lockwood. Simply ply him with expensive brandy and make a few bawdy jests, and they'd be back to their old ease.

Now he knew, though, that resentment simmered on Lockwood's side—the resentment of a man continually beaten and surpassed.

Xavier felt resentful, too. So he was to be criticized if he didn't provide an endless stream of dirty diversions? He was to be thwarted and mocked when he tried to protect the reputation of a worthy young woman?

Louisa deserved better than that. And he was beginning to think that he did, too.

Swift as that thought, he pounded up the cellar stairs and teetered at the edge of the old ruined pit, searching for Louisa.

There she was, standing safely with Jane and Mrs. Tindall. Laughing, her cheeks nipped pink, her skin pale as cream over the dark wool of her cloak. Joyful. Carefree. Oh, so lovely.

And this slim maiden had had the presence of mind to temporarily neuter Lockwood.

She was as complex as a cipher, was she not? And like

a Vigenère cipher, one would get nowhere with her without the right key.

He shivered, and something within him squeezed tight and didn't let go.

He was responsible for her. For everyone in his house. And if Lockwood meant to continue his game with her, then Xavier would have to keep her all the closer.

Thinking of it that way, he didn't mind at all.

Chapter 18

Containing a Lost Parrot

Louisa had promised to add four entries to her Louisa catalogue at this house party. After eight days, she had done nearly all of them.

First: Get kissed. Indeed. And she'd done the kissing.

Second: Find some interesting new books. This had gone better than she'd hoped. She'd found an ancient, coded ledger and worked out an alphabet table for deciphering it.

Not to mention she'd read *Fanny Hill.* That had been a revelation.

Third: Make peace between James and Xavier and convince the polite world of my charm.

The second part of that resolution was still underway, though she had made a new friend in Jane. And she'd heard enough from Xavier to convince her that, if he ever told his old friend what he'd told her, James would happily forgive him. Her brother-in-law was a pleasant-natured sort.

Fourth: Get kissed some more.

Oh, yes. There was that.

She had vowed not to lock herself away from the house party, but the day after the outing to ruined Finchley Castle, she was doing precisely that. She had spent the morning flipping idly through books from the stacks she and Jane had created, hoping to distract herself with the familiar comforts of silk-fine vellum and sturdy rag paper, leather-covered boards and hasp bindings, block printing and black lettering.

The history of knowledge surrounded her in stacks, but as a distraction, it failed utterly. Her mind kept flitting away from the pages before her to the gold velvet chaise near the fire. Its spindly mahogany legs held up far too many memories. Far too many temptations. It might as well be speaking to her.

Just once more. Surely you could handle one more interlude. One more burst of passion before you leave for . . . whatever comes next.

She sank to the floor, heedless of her sprig-muslin gown. Folding her legs beneath her, she tugged a striking volume from one of the tottering stacks she and Jane had created. Velvet over board binding, with gold-thread embroidery. The binding was a work of art in itself.

Yet as her fingers chased the fine-sewn flowers and leaves, she thought only of the gold velvet of the chaise, and Alex sliding his hand up her thigh as she lay back and let her careful world disintegrate.

"That's not how friends behave with one another," she muttered.

They could be nothing more than friends as long as Alex was determined to play the part of rakish Lord Xavier. Such a role allowed for no leading lady. Eventually she would have to stand aside and let him play the part without her—so how much ought she to risk?

She had already ventured too much. Here she was, sitting amidst stacks of rare and marvelous books, and her mind was too full to devour their secrets.

She laid aside the embroidery-bound book without opening it. Honestly, she ought to beat herself upon the head with it. She was obviously an idiot.

The door was flung open then, thumping against the edge of a bookshelf before swinging shut.

"Good God," said a familiar male voice. "What has happened to the place?"

Louisa stood to face the man who was currently driving her to consider self-head-bashing.

"Good morning to you," she said, wiping her dusty hands on her skirts.

"It's after noon," he replied. "And you may disregard my question. I just recalled that Jane was assisting you a few days ago. Considering that, the level of destruction is no more than moderate."

It was disconcerting how striking he looked. He'd attired himself in his usual stark palette: black coat and gray waistcoat, white linens and buff breeches. As he wound through stacks of books, he looked as elegant as a man performing a country dance.

Ummmm.

No. Friends didn't think *ummmm* when they looked at one another.

His foot knocked against one of the stacks and set it to teetering. "Damn. Ah, sorry."

"Let me guess," Louisa said, attempting to discipline her thoughts. "You've forgotten your quizzing glass."

He frowned at her. "I didn't forget it." He pulled the quizzing glass from a pocket in his waistcoat and spun it in his fingers. The lens was round, the frame of chased silver, with a loop at one end of the thumb-length handle.

"You could string it around your neck," Louisa suggested. "Then it would be readily at hand."

His frown deepened. "I prefer not to use it all the time. Besides, I ought to be able to walk around my own house without knocking into things."

Louisa shrugged. Likely he thought it too unfashionable to peer through a glass all the time, a habit more common in their parents' or grandparents' generations. "I'm afraid the obstacles will be here for a few more days. It will take some time to reorder the books."

"Do you find that they have potential?" His face was all politeness. "These books, I mean. A brilliant young lady once told me I should not expect more praise than that."

He was only teasing, she knew, though she could have held on to the word *brilliant* and petted it like a kitten.

"I've found some lovely items, as a matter of fact," she said. "Since I haven't had the ledger to work on, I've been making some notes on your other holdings."

"Ah. About the ledger." Alex shuffled sideways, bumping another stack of books. "Damn. Sorry. I shouldn't have said—*damn it*."

A tower of morocco-bound volumes had toppled. He took a deep breath, nostrils flaring.

Louisa bit down hard on a laugh. "Don't trouble yourself. My aunt has a wide and colorful vocabulary. Would you like to have a seat?"

"I'd best. I seem to be as destructive as Jane." He sidled to the gold velvet chaise and sat down.

On the chaise. *That chaise.*

"Ohh." The exclamation popped out unbidden, an embarrassing clue to her thoughts.

Alex met her eyes. "Oh?" His mouth was solemn; his

gray eyes burned like heated steel. She was caught, her body all tingles and wishes and quaking desire.

She turned her head away. "You were going to say something about the ledger?"

There was a long pause. Louisa looked determinedly across the width of the room. The windows—she'd look out the windows. At the heavy brocade of the draperies. Anything.

"Yes," he finally said. "I'd been working at the next portion of text, and Lockwood swiped it from my desk, along with the alphabet key. I didn't think much of it, since it's his family, too—for the most part—but I'll try to get it back."

He gave a sigh so deep that she turned back to look at him, curious.

His mouth made a wry shape, like a smile ironed flat. "Lockwood is being . . . obstinate. I'm very sorry he harassed you. It won't happen again."

Gooseflesh broke out on her forearms, but she refused to rub at it. "No. It will not. I was very clear on that point."

The corners of his lips softened; an expression of such empathy that she felt positively enfolded.

"I told him to leave," Alex said quietly. "But he refused. I'm not sure I can do more without creating a great scandal."

"I understand," Louisa said. "As a host, you must respect the needs of all your guests."

This was true: she did understand. Rightly, Alex had told Lockwood to leave. If Lockwood refused a direct order from his host, and she was pulled into the scandal of a feud—no, Louisa didn't want that. The very word *scandal*, with its hissing sibilance and harsh consonants, still evoked a visceral reaction, a swift pang of distaste through her whole body.

"Louisa." He hesitated. "Perhaps you'd better leave instead. For the sake of your reputation."

The suggestion was eminently reasonable. But if she left, he'd lose his wager with Lockwood.

It had been some time since she'd recalled that Alex had virtually slapped a sum across her chest. She didn't mind the wager now that she knew him better; she could guess how it had come about. He'd been deep into his Xavier role, and someone had baited him, and he'd felt he had something to prove.

Fine.

And yet—as little import as it might hold for her, or him, it held much for Lockwood. In order to force Louisa out of the house, he'd harassed her ever since her arrival. In the ruined castle cellar, he had pushed his prank far beyond the pale.

She couldn't let Lockwood win. He wasn't a man who deserved that kind of power, especially over Alex. He would abuse it. He'd already tried.

"I am here under my aunt's protection, and yours," she replied. "My reputation will survive. I assure you, I'm most unobtrusive where the *ton* is concerned."

"Lockwood is determined to bother you, though." He scrubbed a hand over his eyes, then down the line of his jaw, as though checking whether his face still had its accustomed contours. "I don't want this house party to bring you anything but the fondest memories."

Unbidden, her eyes wandered over the chaise longue. Yes, she had made some fond memories indeed. When she'd reread the startlingly intimate bits of *Fanny Hill*, she'd understood them far better than the first time.

"Are you concerned that I won't be able to control myself around you?" She meant it as a jest, but her hands misunderstood. They fluttered at her sides, wanting to follow the path his own hand had taken across the planes of his face.

He gave a harsh laugh. "You? That's hardly what's worrying me. Between Lockwood and myself, there's not a safe place for you in this house."

"I'm not looking for safety."

"You should be." He dragged his hand through his hair again.

She shrugged and tapped at a fallen book with her slippered toes. Judging from his example, diversion was the correct action when the conversation took an awkward turn.

One fat little morocco-bound volume splayed open as she knocked it. And she saw—

"A fore-edge painting."

At any time, a wonder. At this moment, an excuse to snap a thread of talk that was becoming increasingly snarled.

She bent to study the book more closely. She shut the volume and studied the gilt edge, then fanned the pages aslant again. "Alex, do come look. This is remarkable."

He threaded between stacks of books, his long limbs setting towers wobbling as he settled into a crouch at Louisa's side. She ignored his clean scent of vetiver and starch. Mostly. Her treacherous female parts gave a little squeeze, and she breathed harder as she handed him the book.

He shot her a sideways look, then peered at the title page through his quizzing glass.

"*Life on the* Golden Hinde, *or My Adventure Around the Globe. A Fantastic Account of Sir Francis Drake's Explorations in the New World, As Told by His Parrot.*"

He handed the book back to her. "I must be over-tired. I'm afraid its wonders are hidden from me."

Louisa smiled. "You are exactly right." She turned the book so its gilded front faced him, then fanned the pages out into a slant, flexing the paper.

A picture appeared on the angled pages—a small wooden ship, tossed on a stormy sea under moody gray clouds. A winged speck flew about the ship's tallest mast, buffeted by strong winds that lashed waves almost over the deck of the small boat.

Alex ran his fingers over the image. "How did you do that?"

"If you paint on a book while it's held at a slant, just a tiny bit of paint goes on each page. You can't see the painting again unless you hold the pages at the very same angle."

She shut the book, causing the picture to disappear, then fanned the pages so the storm-tossed parrot and the angry sea reappeared. "It's lovely work, isn't it?"

"Indeed. Very stealthy, too." He flexed the pages again as she held the book, his fingers almost touching hers. "I am always pleased to find that something is more than it seems."

"I, too." Their eyes caught. Yes, he understood.

But he didn't look away from her, and those two words rang in the silent room. She'd meant only to show loyalty, but it was twisting now, changing into something much sharper.

She tried to tame the feeling. "Despite his reputation, Lord Xavier possesses a very fine library. It has much more than potential."

"Thank you," he said, and with an awkward smile, he drew back.

He sat on the floor and stuck his legs out before him, his boots knocking into another tower of books. "It's a gem of a painting. Who knows what else we shall find if I keep blundering about? This is what comes from not using my quizzing glass."

He twirled the looped handle on one finger and grinned at her. Faint creases formed at the corners of his eyes when he smiled.

At this close distance, without the glass focusing his sight, his eyes looked cloud-soft. He looked . . . oh, like he ought to be touched a little.

She could sweep a hand through his hair, surely; that was something a friend might do.

So she reached out for him, threading her fingers through his cropped hair. It was coarse, as though it wanted to curl if he'd only allow it, and faintly scratchy, like the tickle of evergreen on bare skin.

When she scraped her nails lightly over his scalp, he shut his eyes, and the hand holding the glass sagged.

Since his eyes were already closed, she let hers fall shut, too, let her fingers twine more roughly in his hair, tugging his face closer until mouth found mouth.

Louisa, you idiot. That one final thought intruded, and then it was all blasted away as his mouth opened, as the soft heat of their tongues touched. She slid closer, dropping the book from her nerveless left hand, then cradling his face between her palms.

Just for now. Just a little more. There was nothing so dangerous about a kiss.

Before she could pull back—not that she wanted to—his arms slid to her waist and tugged her astride his legs. Belly to belly, they faced each other, and Louisa was torn between the contrary demands of her conscience and the startling lust that rushed through her veins.

She was much more used to obeying her mind than her body. She gripped his shoulders, hard, until his eyes blinked open.

"Alex. We seem to be—"

"I know. I'm sorry." The muscles in his thighs felt tense and solid between hers.

He shook his head, sliding his fingers over the carpet until he found the quizzing glass. But he didn't look through it; he only rolled the handle between his fingertips. "With you, I can't seem to do what's wise."

"What would be wise?" Why did she ask? She didn't want to know the answer.

"Sending you away." He gave a hollow laugh. "Or—something more proper."

A betrothal? Her heart stuttered. "Don't be ridiculous. We've done nothing irrevocable."

"We vowed to be friends. So we shouldn't—"

"I chose to begin this." She forced a smile. "And you ought to be used to women being unable to leave you in peace. That's what the world says of you."

His face changed for an instant; a look of revulsion, then a blank. "You certainly do not leave me in peace," he murmured.

The sharp need twisted through her again, and she rocked against his body. A little moan escaped him.

If she'd ever wanted to add more to her Louisa catalogue, there was no better time.

"Alex. Is there more that we can do? Without being . . ."

"Irrevocable," he finished. His right hand tightened on her waist; his left gripped his quizzing glass. "Yes. Yes, there's much more. But—we're friends. You're a gently bred maiden. We shouldn't—it's not Christmas anymore."

So they only needed that excuse to give one another the unaccustomed gift of pleasure? Well, then. "In a way, it's still Christmas until Twelfth Night," she said.

His grip on her waist hadn't slackened. He spanned it, shaping her body, and she waited for his reply.

It seemed to take an age.

With a little shudder, like the shaking off of control, he tossed his quizzing glass away.

"Very well, then." And his mouth was on hers.

Chapter 19

Containing
Unexpected Shadow

It's still Christmas until Twelfth Night.

They had another week, then? Another week of this hidden, sweet suspense. Another week to give one another the gift of something new.

The idea was shatteringly appealing. So much so that Alex could almost forget how she'd tossed his reputation in his face with a *despite*. The "you have potential—*despite*."

Almost. He could *almost* forget.

Louisa pulled back and stroked his lips with a gentle thumb. "Is something wrong?"

"What could be wrong? Is this not what a man of my notoriety wants?"

She looked at him oddly for a moment, as though he'd spoken in a heathen tongue.

And then she laughed.

"I wounded your pride, didn't I?" Her nails found his chin, stroked his jaw. "Dear me. What did I say?"

He tried to ignore the tickling sensation, the intimacy of

such a touch. "I know my character is of no value to you. But I thought, too, that you knew it for a fiction."

Conscience—the conscience that no one thought he had—made him add, "In part."

Her hand stilled against the pulse hammering beneath his jaw. "Yes, just as you know mine is. In part. Do you not?"

Apparently he didn't, because his mouth failed to emit any words.

She smiled at his silence. "It's true that I have an immoderate liking for books. But I also know how to dance and play cards. I string a sentence together once in a while. I can even display a few social graces."

"I am aware of all that." He knew he sounded irritable. "You mustn't snipe at me simply because the *ton* took up some wrong-headed idea of you—oh. Yes. I see what you're getting at."

"You understand me, then." Her hand drifted to toy with his earlobe, and everything that was not her fingertips seemed further away and less important. "I want to be seen for myself, and—and wanted."

"You most definitely are."

"As are you." She patted around on the floor until she grasped his quizzing glass, then held it in front of his eye. "Don't be so worried about fashion. Here, look at me."

She was blushing now, the flush spreading down her chest and reaching beneath the bodice of her gown.

He smiled. "How far down does that blush go?"

"You're welcome to find out." Her thumb traced his lips again. "You. Alex."

Those simple words—they were the best Christmas gift he had ever received. *You are wanted. You. Alex.*

He knew it wasn't right to indulge his desires with a virgin, no matter how much she offered. But she *was* his friend, and—well, he simply needed her. He was already captivated by her newfound promise; her simple statement *you are wanted.*

Not for his title. Not because of his notoriety. Not for anything outrageous he had done, or been thought to do.

His lips captured her thumb, and her eyes widened. Her mouth curved into a slow half smile, and she rubbed her thumb on the soft inside of his lower lip.

"I don't need the glass," he murmured, pressing down the hand that held the circular lens before his face.

At once she became a haze of color: the darkness of her hair, shell-pink for her flushed skin, and a sweep of creamy speckles for her patterned gown.

If she wanted him just as he was, this was it: face-to-face, purblind and overeager. He breathed her in, soap and flowers and intoxicating warmth.

She settled herself more securely across his lap. The pressure was no doubt an accident, but his body immediately responded, swelling to a full erection. Her hands, caressing his face, plucked away his control as effortlessly as he might, once upon a time, have plucked a flirtatious widow's handkerchief from the floor.

He disliked the thought of the past. Here, there was no space for it. Despite everything he had done that was foolish and wrong, Louisa wanted and liked him. The knowledge seeped through him, bone-deep and astounding.

He wanted her to feel more than his body; he wanted her to know his very self.

So he kissed her, slow and gentle, his lips entreating: *trust me.* Tilting her head in the cradle of his hands, he slid his mouth to the hot pulse on her neck, then murmured down its length. Nonsense? Poetry? It didn't matter. She shivered, and he sucked lightly at the fragile skin. Not hard enough to bruise; only enough pressure to mark her memory with pleasure.

You are wanted. You. Louisa.

As though she could hear his thoughts, she chuckled, low and lovely. He could feel the hum of the sound under his lips. He trailed them down her neck, her collarbone, finding the soft hollow between her breasts. Relishing every catch of her breath, every clench of her fingers on his arms.

I am wanted.

It was wondrous.

Lord Xavier would never have stopped here; Lord Xavier—if the cursed man had ever existed—would have taken his partner's willingness and experience for granted.

But Alex *knew* her. And so he stopped.

"What is it?" asked Louisa, and he opened his eyes to the lovely blur of her face. He could make out the dark curves of her brows, slanting down as though furrowed. "Is something wrong?"

"I want your permission before I remove any of your clothes."

She laughed again, a quavery sound. "I'd intended to grant that implicitly, but you're very kind to ask. Need I ask your permission in return?"

"You may assume that you have it. Anytime."

"Anytime?"

He wished he could read the expression on her face. He could guess at it from the way her voice turned wry: a mischievous twinkle, a tight press of her lips that could not keep one corner from curving up.

She continued, "I shall keep that in mind, if I find that the soup at tonight's dinner isn't to my liking. 'My apologies, everyone,' I shall say. 'Since I'm not interested in eating at the moment, I'll remove his lordship's clothes instead.'"

Alex had not thought he could grow any harder, but he did. Nudity . . . a public confession . . .

He realized he'd been holding his breath. When he exhaled, she sank fully against his chest, blanketing him from shoulder to groin. "Mmmm," she said, rubbing herself against him.

"You shock me," he said lightly.

"I read *Fanny Hill*. It was very enlightening."

"You've read *Fanny Hill*." He shook his head. "I don't know why I'm surprised."

"Nor do I. You ought to be aware, I want to learn everything."

She clambered off of his outstretched legs, and her features resolved as she slid farther from him. A dark spiral of hair had fallen across her face, and she tucked it behind one ear. "For instance, I want to see what Fanny called your *machine*."

"My machine." Alex had braced his reclining body on one elbow. He felt suddenly self-conscious.

"Yes. Well, she called it some other things, too. But you know what I mean."

"Yes," he echoed. "Well. I did give you permission to remove my clothing." *God*.

She didn't remove anything, though. She simply went exploring, her flattened palm sliding hard over his body from thigh to waist, then back down. He tried valiantly not to embarrass either of them by rolling into her touch. At last, her fingers raked lightly up his inner thigh, finding the tightening sac, the steel-hard shaft through the fabric of his breeches.

He inhaled, hard, through his teeth—a hiss of pleasure.

"Excellent," Louisa said. "You liked that, I can tell. I'll do it again." And she proceeded to.

Why was he bothering to hold himself up on one elbow? Why not simply collapse?

There was no reason. So he lay down flat on the carpet and surrendered to her touch.

"You look," Louisa commented, "like some sort of feast laid out for my gustatory pleasure. What shall I select next, and what will it taste like?"

"You are shockingly articulate for such a moment," he gasped, and then his eyes rolled back as her hands went wandering again.

Louisa worked open the buttoned fall of his breeches and slipped her hands within. Her fingers were cool as they rubbed and wrapped around his overheated shaft. "I didn't realize your *machine* would feel so soft."

"Soft?" He lifted his head and frowned at her. His cock felt hard enough to club himself into unconsciousness with, if he'd been able to bend that way.

She scrunched her nose. "Just the skin of it. The texture."

Her fingers slid down, then back up, wrapping around the sensitive head. He collapsed back onto the carpet, unable to muster any protest—or any words at all—as she slid her fingertip through the moisture beading the tip.

"Your body works like mine," she observed. "This wetness when you're aroused."

She rubbed it around, testing it between her fingertips. Then she bent her head and *licked the tip of his cock*.

His hips jerked. Every muscle in his body knotted tight.

"I assume you liked that, too," she said. Her mouth was unbearably wicked, mouthing these calm observations as she drew him to the unraveling edge of his control.

"Mmuungh," he replied astutely.

"Well said. That's how you made me feel on the chaise."

His fogged brain managed a flicker of pride. And then his conscience spoke up once more, and he realized he was close to spending himself in the hands of a respectable virgin.

In an instant, he sat bolt upright, tucking his erection back into the placket of his breeches. He owed Louisa better than that, and so he walled off his ragged lust like the beast it was. Never mind. He'd take care of it later in the washroom.

"Now you've felt my machine"—it was hard to say the word with a sober expression—"and it's my turn. From what book shall I take my own inspiration?"

"I couldn't possibly suggest something," Louisa said. Her eyes had gone wide, the dark pupils huge, as though she could swallow the sight of him.

He wished she would.

"*The Tempest*, then." He whisked his fingers over her collarbone, then onto her chest, savoring the peach-fine texture of her skin, the quick rise and fall of her breath.

With a gentle tug at the edge of her bodice—fashionably, delectably low—the frail muslin slipped to reveal low-cut stays. They needed little enticement to release her breasts to his view; a few more twists and tugs of the fabric and she sat before him, half-nude, her upper arms pinned by her pushed-down sleeves.

And he—he simply stared as though he'd never seen a pair of breasts before in his life. For the effect she had on him, that might as well be true.

He reached for her, brushing a hand gently across the delicate points of her nipples. She drew in a sharp breath. He feared, for a second, he'd gone too far.

"Why *The Tempest*?" She held very still. No; she breathed more deeply now, pressing her breast into his cupped hand.

Alex trailed his fingers around the sweet curve. "'Where the bee sucks, there suck I,'" he quoted.

He bent to taste what his hands had touched, palming her in one hand as he nibbled and sucked the rosy nub of the other breast.

She gasped, and the sound was poetry. As he pulled and caressed with his lips, he felt her posture loosen, the press of her legs against one another slackening. She was unwinding under his touch, and he helped her on, gently pushing her backward while supporting her in his embrace. His mouth pulled at one nipple, then the other, drawing them into peaks of desire. Her skin was velvet and honey, soft and sweet.

She was quivering by the time he lifted his head. "Your quotation is inapt. No bee has ever done such a thing to me."

"You can't stop thinking for an instant, can you?"

"Very rarely." She shifted in his arms, sliding her bottom over the carpet. Rucking up her skirts, she slid her legs to either side of his, her inner thighs pressing against his outer ones.

She was embracing him with her whole body, and his heart gave a painful, joyful squeeze.

From *Measure for Measure* this time, then; not *The Tempest*. In the secret curve of her ear, he said, "'Go to your bosom: Knock there, and ask your heart what it doth know.'"

"You would have me believe it's my heart you're interested in? I know that's not so, my rakish lord." She murmured this, laughing, then caught his earlobe between her lips.

Sensation fireworked through his body—her mouth, the tickle of her hair against his cheek, her lily scent turning hot and lustful—but underneath, he went cold.

His hand went still, covering her breast like a cage. "You make a comment about my reputation every time we start removing our clothing."

"Only a joke," she murmured, her mouth trailing to the pulse beneath his jaw. His heartbeat thundered there, desperate.

And she thought it was a joke.

He'd once joked about it himself, saying he had no heart at all. But he hadn't realized Louisa thought so, too.

She had said she wanted him just as he was—but Lord Xavier cast too long a shadow, and even now, they hadn't escaped it. Twice now, she'd twitted him about his reputation. Neither of them could forget it. Neither could leave it behind, even when they were alone.

His chest gave a heave; his eyes prickled.

"Alex, won't you continue your poem from *The Tempest*?"

A poem spoken by the sprite, Ariel, who was forced always to use his abilities as others wished. "There I couch when owls do cry," the song continued.

He almost felt that he could, too.

But Xavier had a Numbered Expression for every occasion. This one was Number Five: Mocking Drollery. He put it on. It fit well on his face; as worn smooth as an old slipper.

He gave Louisa the end of the little poem: "'Merrily, merrily shall I live now, under the blossom that hangs on the bough.'"

That was what the world expected of him, wasn't it? Merrily, merrily, should he live.

"That's what I was waiting for," she murmured.

Her hands slid downward, making his abdomen hitch, then his cock throb. Ah, God, she was stroking him through his clothing, and his thoughts were dissolving into hot need.

"You have the bough," she whispered. "I have the blossom. Should I hang upon you?"

Through his breeches, her thumb rubbed over the swollen

head of his shaft. He craved her touch again; he craved *her*. He wanted to feel her slick heat clenching around him, the heat that he'd worked his fingers in until she woke to her own passion.

He wanted her to hang upon him, rest on him, stay with him and remold him. As the graceful oval of her face filled his weak vision, as her breasts still peeked from her bodice, exposed for this touch, and her hand worked wonders with his needy body—he could so, so easily let himself go, take what she offered him.

And he'd end by debauching her, or marrying her, or both.

Oh. Hell. No. No, he couldn't.

He'd never considered such a thing. Had no *right* to.

He'd once been waylaid by five drunken men in a tavern. He'd shot a highwayman in the arm. He'd wagered a fortune on the turn of a card. But her trust scared him more than any of those things. How could he possibly deserve it?

He couldn't. Not Lord Xavier. Not even she thought so, for she had called the idea of *something proper*—a betrothal— ridiculous, when he'd done no more than hint. Neither of them knew this new Alex creature well enough to rely upon him.

So all he said was, "No."

Her hand stilled at once.

Before he lost his resolve, he scooted back in a frantic untangling of limbs, bumping a stack of books as he moved. He ignored the thump of bindings over carpet and sought to bring his body under control, her face into focus. Just a foot back—there. Now he would be able to read every nuance of her expression and . . .

All right, he was looking at her breasts again. This wasn't helpful at the moment.

He turned his head to one side and gingerly reached out a hand toward her. His fingers found a soft curve of unseen flesh; the edge of her breast. He trailed his fingers downward—*her skin was so warm and soft*—until he found the edge of her stays. With a tug, he drew the snug garment upward, until her fingers closed over his.

"I'll do it," she said.

He darted a glance at her from the corner of his eye. The seductive scholar, the inventive intellectual. She had turned slightly to one side and was pulling her garments back into place.

It was safe to look again, then.

Except it would never be safe, because now he was noticing things he'd never noticed before. The tension in her neck. The stillness of her face as she coaxed her clothing back into order. As though she felt nothing; neither humiliation nor joy.

Like himself, she had Numbered Expressions to hide her true self. No matter how much of her skin he caressed, there were depths to her that he could not touch.

The realization made him watery-kneed, so he could hardly struggle to his feet.

As she stood to face him, she formulated a smile. "Thank you for your restraint. When we've both calmed down, we'll be glad for it."

He could only nod. What was there to say? He wanted to be so much more than Lord Xavier, but also more than simply not-Xavier. And, unwise though it was, he wanted Louisa most of all.

"Louisa." He summoned a few hopeless words. "Please, do consider leaving the house party. For your own sake." *And mine.*

"I understand why you're asking," she said. "But I will not do it."

He didn't understand her. Maybe he never would. Hell, he didn't even understand himself.

Politely as strangers, they finished putting their clothing to rights, and he took his leave of her, and the library.

But he was determined: his leave was the last thing he would take from her, as long as he was trapped in this role he'd so long and so carefully portrayed.

He meant well. He meant to be honorable. Yet when the library door closed behind him, leaving her behind, he felt as though he had sealed off the best part of himself.

Hell and damnation.

For a man who'd always had all the advantages in the world, there was no longer any way to win.

Chapter 20

Containing the Ingenuity of Lady Irving

The long table in the dining room looked wrong to Xavier.

Oh, it was laid as perfectly as ever, sparkling with crystal and china, laden with dishes of succulent food. It was flanked, as always, by two long rows of talkative guests. Some of whom held cigarillos at the table. Some of whom were so deep into their cups that they had nodded off into their plates.

This was not the part that looked wrong.

No, it looked wrong because some of the guests—one of the guests—Lockwood—*of course*—was sitting far too close to Louisa Oliver, murmuring God-only-knew what sort of rubbish into her ear.

Her lovely little pale peach shell of an ear, that had heard Xavier say—

"Cat got your tongue, you young rogue?"

What? No. Not that. He blinked, shaking himself free

of his thoughts, and then turned to the person who had addressed him from his right side.

Lady Irving. Louisa's aunt, though they bore each other little resemblance. Where Louisa was sleek and elegant, showing her claws only when provoked, the countess was everything gaudy: bright fabric and tinted curls, loud speech and sharp tongue.

He flashed his widest smile. "I'm quite well, my lady. And you? Are you finding the dishes to your liking?"

Usually his smile was viewed as charming, though the Oliver women seemed never to receive it in the proper spirit.

"You've got something in your teeth," Lady Irving commented.

"I did that intentionally," he replied. "I get hungry while the other men are drinking port."

The countess snorted and adjusted her vivid yellow turban. "Good for you. I was beginning to think your reputation for wit was all puffed up out of proportion."

A startled sound escaped Xavier, and he gulped wine to force it back down. "Dry throat," he said, trying out his smile again.

Lady Irving looked at him askance, then turned her attention to her fricassee of chicken. "I don't believe all of it, mind." She took a bite, then pointed her fork at Xavier's chest like a sword. "Your reputation. You've treated my niece well, and I thank you for that."

Xavier felt his smile go crooked. His throat seemed entirely blocked by his furtive knowledge of *how* he'd treated her niece. Bringing Louisa to the first orgasm of her life—was that good treatment? Cutting off her request for a seduction—was that? Keeping his distance from her in the hours since then?

It didn't feel as though he'd treated her well. It felt as though he'd bumbled, but he had no notion how to rectify matters.

He stared down at his plate. Somehow most of the food had vanished from it, but he had no idea when, or how, or what the food had been.

"Thank you for sharing your opinion," he finally said.

"I always do." She popped the bite of chicken into her mouth with a flourish.

As Xavier met her gaze again, the resemblance clicked into place. *The eyes*. Louisa's eyes were darker than her aunt's, but both women noticed everything.

The deliberate way Lady Irving regarded him now—it reminded him of the way Louisa had studied him the first time he'd escorted her into the library. While he'd fidgeted about with his beloved old Dante, she'd simply watched, and he'd seen her:

> *Gauging me, her deep eyes pitying—*
> *But pity false or true, I could not tell.*
> *My heart was kindling, ready for a blaze . . .*

No. That was Petrarch, not Dante, and there was no time for poetry now.

"Tell me, then, my lady," he said, "what is your opinion of Lord Lockwood? And what think you of his attentions to your niece?"

He tilted his head back to keep her in focus. He wanted to note every nuance of the countess's expression as she looked on Lockwood.

Who was running one hand down Louisa's arm, and with the other, waggling a spoonful of some creamed vegetable in her face.

Lady Irving considered them for a long moment. When

Louisa nudged Lockwood's outstretched arm, sending creamed vegetables in a splatter down his coat, the countess turned her attention back to Xavier.

"He's a ninny." Her brows were lifted. "But then, you knew that already. My question is—is it a family trait?"

"Knowing things?"

She returned to forking through her chicken. "I see it *is* a family trait. I meant ninny-ness, you ninny."

Xavier's hand went slack, and his own fork clattered to the table. "Damn. Ah—sorry."

"Never you mind, Xavier," said the countess. "I say much worse."

"Yes, so your niece has told me."

"Mmm." She took another bite, then waggled her fork at him. "That's why you're a ninny."

"Because I speak to your niece?"

"No, because you sit here while that cousin of yours drapes himself all over her like a bolt of cheap India-print muslin."

"She's capable of protecting herself."

"Yes, but she doesn't have to like it." Again she brandished her fork in the direction of his throat. "Nor do you."

"I don't."

"Then why don't you do something about it?"

"I have."

"Mmmm." That noncommittal noise again.

"I tried to." He disliked the wheedling tone in his voice.

"Lord Xavier did no more than *try*?"

Now he disliked *her* tone of voice. "Lord Xavier is hardly infallible, ma'am. Sometimes he doesn't get the response he wishes. Sometimes he tries to avoid scandal and winds up creating—well. A bigger mess."

"You talk of yourself in the third person?"

He squeezed his eyes shut. "Sometimes Lord Xavier does that, too. It is one of his many faults."

"Hmmm." The noncommittal noise had a different timbre this time. "You might not be such a ninny after all, young man." She paused, then added, "Whoever you are."

"I hardly know," he said.

She gave her lemon-bright turban a pat, her brusque manner relaxing. "Not a ninny. Well, well. Don't you think you owe my niece and yourself another try?"

He couldn't see what was right before his face, but Xavier's distance vision was painfully sharp. A few yards away—one-third of the length of the table—Lockwood had dribbled wine onto Louisa's arm and put out his tongue, as though he meant to lick it off her.

Good idea. Bad time. Wrong person.

Louisa looked more amused than unsettled. As Xavier watched, Lockwood's face contorted. He smothered a yelp and scooted away.

Louisa's right hand emerged from beneath the table, holding her ivory-handled dinner knife. She aligned it neatly with her other utensils and, coolly as though the incident had never happened, wiped the droplets of wine from her arm and took a sip from her goblet.

Over its rim, she met the eyes of Xavier and her aunt. She gave them a wink, and . . .

And something tight and shameful within his chest unknotted. He felt as though he'd been pardoned for his ungraceful departure earlier. She always saw so clearly; surely, then, she had seen his good intentions?

The answer to that question rested on a quicksand of error. The betting book at White's. Ten pounds. An unexpected invitation. Lockwood's bitterness.

A mistletoe berry, thrown away on the ground.

He hadn't always had good intentions. But he did now.

"Yes," he said to Lady Irving. "I owe your niece a great deal. I'll make sure she knows it."

"And what do you owe your cousin?"

Ten pounds, if I have my way about it. "The way he's behaving? Not a thing."

"Good boy," said Lady Irving, and took another bite of chicken.

How Louisa wished she was sitting by her aunt. Though that would mean also sitting near Alex, around whom she was never able to be wise.

Instead, the guests had shuffled themselves along the dining table, and she'd wound up next to Lockwood, who was acting like a complete ulcer: embarrassing and painful.

"Do keep your beverages off of me, my lord," she hissed when he lunged at her with his wineglass again. Not even a knife poke could keep him in his place. The man was determined to win his ten pounds.

She remembered the sudden darkness of his manner in the ruined cellar, and the nape of her neck prickled with cold. He seemed to want something particular from her that had nothing to do with money.

He would not have it.

She selected a carving fork from a platter of beef and held it lightly in one hand, as though deciding on the slice she wanted. "Lord Lockwood," she commented, "I do wonder if you would prefer to leave the table. You've become remarkably soiled."

A poor choice of words. She'd given him a perfect opening. "Not as soiled as you've become, my dear Miss Oliver," he hissed. He stretched out a hand and took the fork from her. She folded her hands, knotting them tightly in her lap.

"I don't wish to converse with you anymore," she said. At the head of the table, her aunt was chortling over something Alex had said. When he shared in the laugh, he looked painfully handsome.

Louisa looked away from him. For now, she was trapped, but not for much longer. Only until she could leave the table without making a scene.

"Very well," said Lockwood, at whom she was also not looking. "I shall converse with Lady Alleyneham instead."

He raised his voice and committed the social offense of speaking across the table. "My dear lady," he said to the countess, as Louisa studied the pale green of her creamed peas on the bone-white of Alex's china. "Have you heard any good gossip at this house party?"

"Oh my," the countess fluttered. "I've always got my ears open, but you know, it's been a lovely event. Lovely."

Without looking up, Louisa could imagine Lady Alleyneham's expression. Turbaned like Lady Irving, her round face would flush at the attention from a marquess. An *eligible* marquess, whom she might coax to show an interest in one of her daughters.

"No gathering could be as lovely as your daughters," Lockwood said, as he was intended. Lady Alleyneham made a squeal of delight. Louisa peeked across the table and saw the countess's daughters pretending not to have heard, though they shifted in their seats and blushed.

Louisa returned her gaze to her plate and began picking through her peas. The sauce was delicious, buttery yet light. Much more worthy of contemplation than Lockwood's tepid flirtation.

And then he struck.

"It pains me to admit that not all ladies at this party have comported themselves as your daughters have." From the corner of her eye, Louisa saw him tap himself on the nose. The old I've-got-a-secret gesture.

Lady Alleyneham picked up the bait. "Surely not. Why, this party is most respectable. At least, more so than in the past. Some of the guests are positively . . ."

Her words dwindled away. It didn't matter, because Lockwood's loud comment had caught the ears of others. Mrs. Protheroe. The spouse-swapping quartet of Lord and Lady Weatherby, Mr. and Mrs. Simpkins. Louisa abandoned her plate and studied the others with the same dubious expression their faces showed. No one knew to whom Lockwood was referring; each woman wondered if he was speaking about her.

Louisa could guess what he intended to say next.

She was right. "I don't want to say too much. Ladies are entitled to their fun, just as gentlemen are." He gave a very wide smile that made him look like a shark ready to feed. "That is, *married* ladies are. But you know what they say. Once a scandal, always a scandal."

He turned to Louisa with a solicitous expression on his face. "Wouldn't you agree, *Miss* Oliver?"

Louisa felt the weight of stares pressing on her, taking in every detail of her appearance from posture to the placement of the seams on her gown. They must be wondering— *was it she?* Whatever she said next would confirm or deny their suspicions.

"I would never contradict a marquess," she said sweetly. "Unless he had no idea what he was talking about."

She returned her attention to her plate and pretended to dissect her food with great interest. Around her, tension seemed to relax, but whispers swelled nonetheless.

They were wondering, now. Wondering why Lockwood should harass her. Wondering whether his veiled hints had referred to her, and whether she didn't deserve his respect.

And *wondering* was enough. It was tinder for rumor, and rumor was fuel for scandal.

She'd been through this once before, nine months earlier, when she ended her engagement. The gossip had been dreadful.

Unbidden, her eyes searched out Alex at the head of the table. He noticed her glance and raised his wine glass to her. The gesture was simple, yet so thoughtful that she couldn't help smiling back.

Around her, the whispers grew louder.

Chapter 21

Containing Startling Revelations

It had been a mistake to swap the study chairs. Or rather, not to change them back.

Yes, Xavier was comfortable as he faced Lockwood across the desk in his private study—but he sat low in his seraglio chair, as though he were waiting for a harem girl to leap upon him. And Lockwood shifted and huffed in the thronelike Norman chair.

Xavier tried to summon the presence of mind to ignore the chairs. The words were what mattered.

"Lockwood, this can't continue."

"The chair? I know it. Feels like I'm sitting on a bag of rocks. Let's have a brandy." The marquess popped from his seat and moved over to the sideboard, pouring Armagnac into two snifters.

"In truth," Lockwood said over his shoulder, "I'm glad for the chance to speak privately. I've learned something which I believe will be of great interest to you."

Xavier's fingers gripped the edge of the desk. "About Louisa Oliver?"

"No." Lockwood moved back to his chair, settling onto it with a groan, and set a snifter on the desk before Xavier.

Xavier worked on unclamping his fingers as Lockwood added, "However, I'm intrigued to learn that Miss Oliver is the subject foremost on your mind."

"In a conversation with you? Yes. As would be anyone whom you had harassed repeatedly."

"Hmm." Lockwood drained his snifter in one long pull, then made an *ahhh* of satisfaction. "Is this Armagnac? I'm beginning to think it's not so bad."

Wordlessly, Xavier nudged the other snifter across the desk. Lockwood picked it up with a salute, then sent its contents the way of the first.

Fine. He was mellowing. Maybe he'd listen now.

"Here is what I propose, Lockwood." Expression Number One, Veiled Disdain. "I give you ten pounds. When next we're in London, you write your name in the betting book at White's as the winner of this wager that I should never have agreed to. And you leave Miss Oliver in peace for the remainder of the house party."

Xavier leaned back in his chair. "I no longer care about avoiding a family scandal. Lord Xavier is always associated with scandal, is he not? So if you do not agree to my terms, I will have you ejected from my house. Whether you leave with dignity or not is for you to determine."

Lockwood waited for him to finish.

And then he laughed.

It was not the laugh of a drunken man who wishes to appease. It was not simple mirth or joy. It sounded like . . . triumph.

Goose bumps raced down Xavier's arms. He slid one hand to the side, fumbling for something to hold on to. His correspondence seal. Yes. That would do.

Lockwood's laughter subsided as he stood, moved to the

sideboard, and refilled his snifter. With a shrug, he carried the decanter back with him, too.

"Coz, you are such a fool. You think this is as simple as one little line in the White's betting book?"

Well, he *had*. "Of course not, but I fail to see—"

"Exactly." Lockwood nodded emphatically, brandy loosening his gestures. "You don't see. You've gotten besotted with a few things lately, haven't you? Miss Oliver. Propriety. Your precious books." He sneered. "And while you have your head up your arse, you don't see what's changing around you."

Xavier tensed. "Apologize."

Lockwood raised placating hands. "I take it back. But minus the arse, what I'm telling you is true."

Xavier rolled his seal between his fingers. A small block of ivory; proof of his worth. "Explain."

Lockwood rummaged beneath his chair for a moment, then straightened up with a ledger in his hand. "I returned this to the study earlier, while you were out. It's a very interesting book."

He slid the book across the desk to Xavier and leaned forward. "Have you read the end of it?"

"You know I haven't. You filched it from me before I had the chance to decode beyond the Restoration."

Lockwood smiled. "True. Since it told of my family as well, I thought I had a right to know. I was particularly interested in the recent history. Say . . . that of our parents' generation."

"You clearly have something scintillating to say. Please assume that I've begged you to reveal it on bended knee, so we can return to the main point of this conversation."

"Ah, but this *is* the point." Lockwood flipped open the ledger and removed a loose sheet of decoded text that was tucked into the cover. "Do have a look at this, won't you?"

Xavier found his glass, then took the crisp foolscap and read these lines:

The beautiful Lady Anne Wilkes married the eighth Earl of Xavier against her parents' wishes. Ah, marriage—in the immortal words of Richardson, it is "the highest state of friendship: if happy, it lessens our cares, by dividing them, at the same time that it doubles our pleasures by a mutual participation."

Neither her ladyship nor his lordship appeared to have read Richardson, however. Their cares were doubled and their pleasures divided; theirs, and those of their families.

After the eighth countess survived three years of marriage to the unyielding, dissipated earl, she took a base-born lover of her own. In 1790, she presented her lord with a cuckoo in his nest, then died in childbed, released from her woes. When the earl died of drink a few months later, the succession was broken. But who was to know? Perhaps one day . . . the world.

Xavier skimmed the text over and over, more meaning sinking in each time. "This can't be right," he muttered.

The paragraphs implied that his mother had had a lover, and that he—Xavier—was the child of that man. Not of the eighth earl.

He read it again, but the words on the page were ink black and unchanging.

Lockwood watched, a half-smile on his face. Xavier composed his expression and handed the paper back to Lockwood. "Assuming you've decoded correctly, this is a very interesting little anecdote."

"It could be much more than that," said the marquess. "Your parents died in 1790, did they not?"

"Yes, but that's hardly proof of anything more."

"I don't need proof." Lockwood smiled again. "You, of all people, ought to know the power of rumor. You've benefited from it long enough."

His smile twisted, his fingers crumpling the edge of the paper on which he had printed out the text. "You didn't think I believed everything the world said of you, did you, Coz? That I truly thought you won honestly at cards? That you'd coaxed dozens upon dozens of women into bed?"

"No one can control rumors," Xavier said. "I never claimed credit for anything untrue." His fingers fumbled his seal, and it fell with a *clack* on his desk.

Lockwood pressed on. "Ah, but somehow you've still used rumor to your advantage. You entered the polite world with a full purse, and all you've ever had to do is dip into it. Society loves you, and you've never done anything worthwhile to deserve it."

His face contorted as he spoke, but his voice dropped ever quieter. It was smothered by an emotion stronger than annoyance. Or resentment. Or anger, or despair.

Why, this was *hate*.

The world tipped and jarred with a tuneless chord, and Xavier sat stunned.

His own cousin, whom he had always considered a harmless sycophant, *hated* him?

From the cold deliberation of his speech, it seemed Lockwood had bottled and stored his hate for a long time. And Xavier had never suspected its existence.

He rubbed a hand over his too-unseeing eyes, then dragged his fingers through his hair. Stupid gesture. It wasn't as though it could wake up his brain.

He thought of Louisa's eminently organized mind, then

stated, "Lockwood, let's take these problems in turn. First, you're behaving like an ass. Second, you say it's nothing to do with our bet, but because of some resentment you feel. Third, you believe this old book justifies your insulting behavior."

Lockwood's skin looked skull-tight over his features, but he managed a silky voice. "The book doesn't justify anything. The book takes all justification away. Some types of scandal are permissible, as we know, my dear Cousin. The polite world winks at the debauchery of a rake. It laughs at his outrageous behavior. But what if he is a bastard? There is nothing much to like about a rake, if you think about it. A rake is nothing but a parasite. A *bastard* rake is an abomination."

"Words in a book don't make it so." Xavier's heart seemed to stutter, tripping over itself. He knew nothing at all of his parents, who had died in his infancy. This book might tell the truth, at that.

"No, but they needn't. You didn't actually have to seduce the Marchioness of Flitworth for everyone to *believe* you had." Lockwood bared his teeth. "All one needs is the right rumor at the right time to make a reputation . . . or break it."

He leaned back in his chair, a quick spasm of discomfort crossing his face, and crossed one booted foot over his other knee. "You owe me your reputation, you know. I'm your foil, if you want to be literary about it. Which it seems you do. Tell me, how long since you've left the bluestocking's pocket?"

Her stockings aren't blue. They're silk. Naturally, Xavier didn't say that aloud.

Instead, he went on the offensive. "You think you've done me a favor, Lockwood? With your endless bets at White's, you've scripted a very narrow role for me: the

merry, entertaining rogue. No one takes me seriously as
anything else. I don't thank you for that, and I don't care to
have it continue."

Lockwood's eyes glittered ice blue. "You dare com-
plain? Your role in society is the equivalent of—of playing
Hamlet. It might not offer much variety, but it wins you ad-
miration."

Xavier shook his head. He picked up his seal again,
grounding himself with its smooth weight. It was *his*. It
was real.

"I'm more than that, Lockwood," he said, feeling
stronger with each word. "I was *never* the person the world
thought. If they—if *you*—made me into a dumping ground
for rumor, it was no favor to me. I've played that part long
enough."

He set the seal down and held himself straight in his
chair, eyes focused on Lockwood. He wouldn't miss what
was right in front of his face again. "Rumor may paint me
as a rake. But I'm also an earl. Rumor can't touch that."

His own words surprised him. Would they ever have occurred to him, much less been spoken aloud, only a few
weeks before?

Being around Louisa had encouraged him to think.
Since he'd decided to invite her to his house party, he'd
made changes, and more changes. And now . . . *he* had
changed.

A smile must have played over his face, because Lockwood looked stormy.

"Yes, your precious title," he spat. "Even there, you've
gained benefits you never deserved. I outrank you, yet you
were always the one with the money. It's always rankled,
ever since I came of age and discovered that my own dear
father had depleted the estate so much that there was barely
enough to keep me out of dun territory. Everything you

have comes from your title. And maybe it shouldn't be yours. *Bastard*."

His voice rose to a heated pitch, his hands flexing with unrestrained emotion.

Xavier listened to this tirade, arms folded, thoughts humming. A blessed coolness stole over him. "Do control yourself, Lockwood. You've come dangerously close to upsetting my decanter. And please remember that, regardless of rank, you are in *my house*."

He paused, letting this sink in. "You think you can take from me, Lockwood? You might be able to damage my reputation, but I've already told you, I don't care for it. And it's not as though lowering me will help you. Bitterness doesn't sit well with the *ton*. Brutality doesn't appeal to women."

He lifted his brows, knowing calm would infuriate Lockwood further. "If you try your best to destroy me, you will still be yourself, and you'll have no one to blame for your troubles then."

As Lockwood's face reddened, Xavier pressed his advantage. He leaned forward over his desk, letting Lockwood's face swim out of focus. "Tell everyone whatever you like; you'll only make yourself look ridiculous and desperate. You've got nothing on your side except a few scratches in an old book. You can't *touch me*."

With these final words, he jabbed Lockwood in the chest with his forefinger, then sat back down in his chair.

It was well played: the dramatic gesture, the rise of his voice for emphasis. Unfortunately, Lockwood didn't demonstrate the expected reaction.

He simply smiled.

"You think I can't touch you. Well, there's something I *can* do." His smile widened. "This conversation started, if you recall, because you were concerned about Miss Oliver's reputation. How much is it worth to you?"

Xavier narrowed his eyes. "I'd never put a price on a lady's good name. I've told you that since the instant you conceived of this idiotic wager."

"And how much is yours worth?" Lockwood lifted the decanter, studied it, and then poured another inch of brandy into his snifter. "Not to you. To her."

Xavier watched Lockwood swirl and sip his brandy as casually as if they were joking at White's. "I'm not sure what you mean."

"Would it appeal to her to be associated with a rake drowning in scandal? One who might have come by his title dishonorably? What do you think?"

"I think Miss Oliver is too wise to credit rumors, especially when she has seen no evidence for their truth."

"You think so." Lockwood tossed back the rest of his brandy and smacked the snifter down on the desk. "Are you certain? Not so long ago, she blamed you for a scandal that touched her family. Now scandal's starting to swirl about her again—because you and she have been spending a little too much time together. Alone. How would she react upon learning you're as bad for her as she once thought?"

"How did you know she blamed—" Thoughts arced and fizzed, and he realized: "*You* told that scandal sheet last spring. About Matheson and the girl he married. Miss Oliver's sister. You sold their story for all the *ton* to read, after I told it to you in confidence."

"Naturally." Lockwood flicked away the accusation like a gnat. "It was the perfect opportunity to lower your friends' lofty opinion of you. It worked with Matheson until Miss Oliver got it in her lovely little head to play peacemaker."

For as long as that—*months*—Lockwood had been

trying to poison him. Even then, the marquess had used Louisa as a means to his end.

Xavier inhaled deeply. Though his heart pounded, he kept his voice calm. "I don't think we have anything more to say to one another. You may leave in the morning; I'll grant you that much time to collect your possessions and fabricate some sort of family emergency."

Lockwood struck the desk, hard, with the flat of his hand, making the snifter rattle. "You're not *listening*. You can't continue this way, Xavier. You're losing wagers already. Getting soft. You've got nothing to go on with."

He leaned forward, his features fragmenting into planes and shadows as he brought himself nearly nose to nose with Xavier.

"But I can change all that, for a small price." He paused, and Xavier imagined his fuzzy features curving into a smug smile. "A night with Miss Oliver. Nothing you haven't already had, I am sure? It's a more than fair bargain: I get to have her, and you get to keep everything else."

He dropped back into his chair, and Xavier relished his grimace of discomfort as he settled into the thronelike Norman seat.

"Your idea is repulsive," Xavier said. "Miss Oliver is no one's possession to give or receive, but I can promise you that you will never lay a hand on her again."

"I think," Lockwood said, rising to his feet, "she *is* yours to give. She wants you more than she realizes. I think you feel the same about her, too. And therefore, it will be my very great pleasure to take her from you."

Xavier stood, instinctively matching his height against the marquess's, though he knew the time for physical intimidation was past. "You won't have Miss Oliver, no matter how much scandal you try to stir up. I'll let everything else go before I let you touch her."

Lockwood smiled, master of himself again. "Your emphatic words let me know that I have chosen my price well. You simply need a little time to come to your senses. But don't take too long. I've already planted a few seeds of rumor. Her reputation won't last, and she'll never forgive you for its loss."

"And what if I . . ." Xavier trailed off, letting a new idea sink through him. "What if I protect her with my name?"

Lockwood shrugged. "If you propose marriage to her, I'll violate her."

The coldness of the statement froze Xavier.

Lockwood could do it, too. All the time, maids and governesses suffered the unwanted attentions of their employers. The women of polite society were slightly better off, if they had the protection of a male relative. Still, all it took to blight a reputation was a few minutes alone with the wrong man. And what recourse was there, once a woman had been so abused? The best she could hope for was to be married to her abuser. Shackled for life to a bitter, violent man.

No. Xavier had to protect Louisa. It was his responsibility, was it not? He'd made her a target, just by caring.

He shut that thought up tightly. "No need for threats, Lockwood." Xavier still felt icy, and his words came out just as cold. "We shall keep our quarrel between ourselves. There's much you would hate to lose, just as I would."

Lockwood trailed his fingers over the encoded ledger. "Everyone has something to lose, Coz. Especially you. My question is, what will you risk to keep it?"

"You ask me about risk? We've filled half the betting book at White's with our wagers." Xavier seated himself on the corner of his desk. "If I have much to lose, I also have much to gamble with."

A palpable hit; Lockwood grimaced at this reminder of

his own empty pockets. "But you *have* grown soft, Xavier. You're not willing to gamble with Miss Oliver. And I am."

He gave the ledger a shove back toward Xavier. "Go ahead, keep this. Who knows what you'll learn?"

And with that, he left Xavier alone with his thoughts.

With only one thought, really: that just when he realized what was most important, he might lose it.

Oh, Lockwood couldn't threaten his title. Xavier had been born within the bounds of marriage, and in the eyes of the law, that made him his father's son. The rightful earl. A rumor was nothing but a rumor.

Yet a rumor turned against him could topple the house of cards that constituted his reputation. For now, he was notorious, but he was also respected. If he lost that respect, he'd also lose all his respectable associations.

Or he'd take them down with him.

He sank down into his seraglio chair, the soft seat cradling his bones. Creative as he might be when plotting a worthless wager, he had only one idea now.

He'd trade on his reputation once more, for Louisa's good. To keep her safe. To lead her not into temptation, but deliver her from evil. And then . . .

Then she'd be gone, and it didn't matter what became of him after that.

Chapter 22

Containing Some False Statements, and Some True

"Thank you for meeting me, Lady Irving." Xavier faced Louisa's aunt across the desk of his private study. This study had hosted more dramatic scenes in the past few days than it had in the few decades before.

He took a deep breath, then implemented his plan. "I have a confession to make."

"Yes?" The countess lifted her brows. Her melon-colored turban clashed violently with the furbelows of her royal-blue gown, and she, as ever, looked unconscious of the fact.

Expression Number Five, Mocking Drollery, would be the most offensive. Xavier slipped it on. "I have little enough conscience for a great wrong, but enough for a small good. You see, I've attempted to seduce your niece. And while we haven't done anything irrevocable"—his throat caught on the word—"I think it best for the sake of her reputation that you remove her from the house party at once."

He waited, Mocking Drollery firmly affixed, for the

explosion. He hoped it would be huge. He hoped she would shout. Even strike him.

That was what a man deserved if he treated Louisa Oliver poorly.

Lady Irving sat straight-backed in the horrible Norman chair, looking puzzled. "Is this some joke?"

"It's not a joke."

She nodded, then lifted a heavily beringed hand to her temple. "I could use a brandy."

"Allow me." Xavier popped from his chair and walked to the sideboard, filling a snifter for her ladyship.

Lady Irving sipped, then nodded again. "It's good." She set the snifter atop the desk and folded her hands in her lap. "Now. You've been bothering my niece, you say. And you want me to take her away. Can't control yourself?"

Mocking Drollery wavered. "I . . . can't, no."

"Don't intend to marry her?"

Xavier could only stare dumbly. *If you propose marriage to her, I'll violate her*, Lockwood had said.

She apparently took his silence as a negative. "Of course you don't. I ought never to have expected that of you."

He smiled, feeling Mocking Drollery crack at the corners of his mouth and eyes. "No one should expect commitment from Lord Xavier. You and your niece ought to be honored that I scraped together enough restraint not to ruin her."

The countess pressed at her temple again, then scrabbled for the snifter and wrapped her hands around its bowl, rings clicking against the glass. Her shoulders sagged, and she seemed to gain ten years.

"It's my fault," she murmured. "Her parents trusted me. *She* trusted me. Thought I could keep her safe, even here . . ."

Xavier turned his head, looking at her aslant. This was not the reaction he'd hoped for.

Then she speared him with a stare sharp as broken glass. "It's your fault, too."

Ah, *there* was the reaction he'd expected. He threw kindling on the fire. "*My* fault? Nonsense. Everyone knows what these house parties are like. If your niece wished to be a guest here, she should have been prepared for the price of admission."

The countess's face drained of color, leaving only two spots of rouge on her cheekbones. "She was unwilling?"

He smiled, wide and flashing. "Not by the time I was finished with her."

His stomach churned, as nauseated as it had been when he drank an entire bottle of Armagnac on a bet. That foolishness seemed ages ago.

Sick rose into his throat, but he kept the smile fixed on his face: the damned smile, damning him, until the countess began to stand. She stood in stages, the pained movements of someone very old or very tired. Hauling herself forward, grasping the edge of the desk, bearing her weight on her arms. Forcing herself upright, then drawing her shoulders back.

Quick as a whip-crack, she slapped him.

He was almost relieved.

She looked down her nose. "I regret trusting you. I regret allowing you another chance. Not everyone deserves one."

With careful control, she pushed her chair toward the desk, set her soiled glass on the sideboard, and turned to face Xavier again. He held his breath, waiting for the final verdict.

"I thought you were the sort of man Louisa needed. Someone who could bring her out of her shell and care for her just as she is."

Xavier's throat closed again. He couldn't deny it.

"But I see now that you are the sort of man no one needs at all." She turned her back on him and walked to the door with measured steps, then turned once more. "We'll be gone by midday."

He nodded his acceptance. His smile didn't fade until she closed the door behind her.

This was the way things were to be now. He'd made his bed, of rumors and speculation, and it was far too large for anyone to lie close to him. At least he would not allow anyone else to be hurt.

It was a hollow triumph. But it was better than a defeat.

Louisa had not seen her aunt in such a temper since the end of her engagement long months ago, early in the spring. At that time, the countess had reserved most of her wrath for Louisa's stepsister, Julia, and for Louisa's former betrothed, James. Even for Lord Xavier.

Now, as Lady Irving crammed Louisa's gowns into trunks over the clamor of an affronted lady's maid, Louisa realized that she had been fortunate to be spared the brunt of her aunt's anger.

"Foolish girl," said the countess, mercilessly crushing Louisa's favorite primrose silk. "No. *Stupid* girl. Stupid, to dally with a rake. Stupid, to open yourself up to scandal *again*."

Slippers followed the gown, clunking against the lid of the trunk and falling onto the wadded fabric.

"Please, my lady," cried the abigail, waving her hands. "Please, have a care for the gowns!"

"Damn the gowns," said Lady Irving, snatching an armful of undergarments from the wardrobe and heaping them atop the silks in the trunk. "We'll buy new gowns in London. My niece seems to crave something less demure."

Louisa went cold. "Please excuse us," she said to the frantic lady's maid. She escorted the servant to the door of her bedchamber, then shut it and turned back to her aunt.

"What has happened?" she made herself ask. "You came in here like a whirlwind and started ruining my garments. I gather you've heard something from Lord Lockwood?"

Lady Irving stopped shoving at the linens and raised her head, nostrils flaring. "Lockwood? You've been fooling about with him, too?"

"*No.*" Louisa made her way to the armchair by the fireplace and sank into it. "No. I haven't been fooling about with anyone."

"Liar." Lady Irving turned back to the wardrobe and grabbed another armful of petticoats and shifts. "I heard it from the man himself."

She tossed the clothing roughly into the trunk, then sank onto the bed. Her tight, boned stays creaked as they held her body straight. "Louisa, my girl. You foolish girl."

Apprehension made Louisa wobbly-kneed; she couldn't have stood up if she'd wanted to. Again, she asked, "What happened?"

Lady Irving grimaced. "Our host summoned me to his private study for a most revealing interview. Seems he's been toying with you. Doesn't have enough manhood to marry you; only enough to ask me to take you away."

"Oh." Louisa felt as though she'd been deflated. "That was a very ungracious thing for him to do."

The countess adjusted her turban with an impatient huff. "You know, I believe he thought he was doing us a favor. Said we should be grateful nothing irrevocable had happened."

Louisa swallowed heavily. In spite of the tension in the room, her belly gave a quick squirm of heat. It was true, nothing but Alex's restraint had kept them apart.

She understood exactly what he was doing. Somehow, he'd decided her good name depended on her leaving the house party, and he had forced the matter.

But she wished he'd gone about it any other way. He had betrayed her—their—confidence to one of her closest and dearest relatives. Louisa had the good opinion of few enough people, and she hoarded it. Treasured it. He should not have sold her so cheaply. Not even if he meant well.

It was carelessness, just as she'd suspected the first time they'd spoken in the library. It was less wicked than being intentionally unkind, though no more admirable.

"He is trying to help," she said dully. "He wants me to leave for my own safety. He believes Lord Lockwood is a threat to me."

Lady Irving inhaled deeply, like a hound scenting a new prey. "Then why wouldn't you simply leave? You're a sensible girl. Unless there's more to the story than that."

Louisa gave a dry laugh. "There's much more. Yes." She rolled her shoulders against the upholstered back of the chair, forcing herself to sit up. *Don't be spineless.*

Even now, she had a little too much pride to tell her aunt about the wager. That she knew Alex and Lockwood had invited her to the house party for the sake of ten pounds. That she'd tried to protect Alex from the consequences of losing that bet to his vindictive cousin.

Her aunt was right: it sounded foolish.

"I lost my head over him," she admitted. "He made me feel as though he wanted to know me, just the way I am." The words nearly choked her.

"Any man should want that," Lady Irving said. Though her posture was still tense, her voice had softened.

"But they don't, Aunt." Louisa hated the way her voice grew thick. "They never have. The one man who ever paid me attention was only interested in a marriage of convenience; then he fell in love with my sister." James and Julia. Louisa had thought it didn't hurt anymore, but she was wrong.

Lady Irving patted the counterpane next to her, and Louisa forced herself up from the chair to sit on the bed next to her aunt.

The countess took one of Louisa's hands between hers. "It's terrible, isn't it? It *is*. It's terrible that you should be unappreciated."

She gave Louisa's hand a pat, then released it. Louisa clasped it tightly in her lap with her other hand and tried to feel nothing.

Lady Irving wasn't through with her, though. "I understand why you were charmed by the earl, my girl. Charm is his stock-in-trade. But you still did wrong."

She tugged a bolster to her, resting her elbows on it. "Not as wrong as he. He should never have dishonored you with his touch. But Louisa, I brought you here for two reasons. First, to get away from Julia and James, so you could start making your own path. Second, to open yourself to new experiences."

She took off her melon-colored turban and scrubbed at her disarranged auburn curls. "I hoped you would find love. With Lord Xavier, even. The man has . . . potential."

Louisa gave a choked laugh. "I thought so, too."

Lady Irving patted her hand again. "I know you didn't mean to break faith with me."

So her aunt's anger had subsided into disappointment. Louisa felt lower than a worm. She didn't even have her own anger at Alex to buoy her; only a numb, dull feeling as though she'd been kicked.

"You were right," Louisa said. "I did need something new."

"I didn't intend for you to have as many new experiences as you've apparently had." Lady Irving gave her a wry look, then slid from the bed. "Gad, look at this mess. Disgraceful; your gowns will be ruined. Where's that maid of yours? We need to finish collecting your things. I told Xavier we'd depart by midday."

Louisa let this pass; she simply trudged to the door and summoned the waiting abigail to return, to try to salvage her clothing.

As the maid and Lady Irving began a spirited discussion on how best to pack a trunk, garments flying in a froth, Louisa again seated herself in the chair by the fireplace. She let her eyes grow unfocused, and she required herself to think.

So. They were leaving, but scandal was still only a threat. Alex—Xavier—had contained it to her family circle. He thought he'd done her a kindness.

And then there was Lockwood, shallowly ruthless. Ruthlessly shallow.

She gripped the spindly wooden arms of the chair.

She'd come here shy and afraid, though determined to change. And she had. She'd taken her pleasure with a rake and left him unsatisfied. She'd jabbed a marquess with a hairpin, a knee, and a blunt-bladed dinner knife.

The memory brought an unwilling smile to her face. If she had courage enough to geld an assailant, she certainly had enough to hold her own in a conversation with a starchy matron. If she had sufficient pride to leave this house with dignity, she had more than enough to spend an evening at a ball without a dance partner.

The polite world would never terrify her again. That was some consolation for all she had lost.

* * *

Xavier remained in his study for the next few hours. There was no reason to leave until it was time to dress for dinner.

Smothering himself in work, he realized that the account books were beginning to make sense to him. The columns of neat figures, totting up his holdings—this was proof that there was something of substance to his title. Lord Xavier was more than a scandal sheet, if only he could convince the *ton*.

While he worked, he could almost forget that he'd betrayed Louisa in order to chase her away. He'd meant well, so there was no earthly reason for him to feel so low and dismal.

All right, maybe he wasn't forgetting anything.

A knock sounded at the door, and Xavier set down his quizzing glass. He rubbed a hand over his eyes and tried to smooth his mussed hair. "Who's there?"

"Wheeling, my lord. I have a letter of particular interest for you."

Xavier bade his butler enter and received a folded and sealed note. "This didn't come through the post," he observed.

"No, my lord." The butler hesitated, though his expression, as ever, betrayed no emotion. "It was left for you by one of your guests."

Xavier knew, then; Louisa had left him with some parting words. Would they be bitter or sweet? "Thank you, Wheeling, that will be all."

He could hardly wait for the butler to bow himself out before he cracked the seal.

The paper contained only one sentence, written in a copperplate-clear hand.

We made a lovely novel.

Xavier subsided into his seraglio chair. Their time together had been lovely, yes, but had it been no more than a fiction?

Then he noticed another paper on his desk. It had apparently been folded within the first, and in his eagerness, he hadn't seen it flutter out.

It took him a long moment to assimilate what his eyes told him: it was a ten-pound note, written on a London bank.

Ten pounds. The wager. She'd *known*.

She'd known? For how long? And she left him with this note—this brief and poignant reminder of their time together. *In a novel*, they'd told each other in the firelight, then explored the limits of their own control.

What had been real? How did she see him?

He would never know, because he'd sent her away.

For a man so fond of poetry as Lord Xavier, there were suddenly no words.

Chapter 23

Containing Advice
from a Variety of Italians

True to her word, Lady Irving had removed Louisa from Clifton Hall by the time Xavier emerged from his study.

He handed the ten-pound note to Lockwood before dinner, trusting that the presence of the party in the drawing room would confine Lockwood's triumph to a non-deafening level.

This was a vain hope.

"What's this?" Lockwood asked in a tone of shock. "Dear me. Lord Xavier has handed me *ten pounds*. Do look, Pellington. Channing. Weatherwax. Gather round!"

Xavier adopted Expression Number Three, Amused Tolerance. In truth, he felt neither amused nor tolerant as Lockwood stepped onto a striped Chippendale chair and waved Louisa's banknote in the air like a flag.

"Lord Xavier has lost a bet, and to me. Has day turned to night? Does the earth spin around the sun?"

"Of course it does, you bacon-brain," Xavier muttered.

Lockwood's tomfoolery was drawing interest, as a grown man standing atop furniture inevitably does.

"What has happened? Something entertaining?" Mrs. Protheroe had stepped closer to her precious Lockwood, her fair hair a cloud around an avid face.

"It's simple," Jane said. "Lockwood has won a bet, and he has felt the urge to climb onto a chair."

Lockwood shot her a poisonous look. "There's nothing simple about this, *Jane*, because Xavier lost. To me. After all the times we've bet, this is surely worth celebrating. How the mighty have fallen!"

Xavier deserved some sort of award for not rolling his eyes. "If you mean to gratify yourself, Lockwood, you ought not to stress the rarity of your triumph."

"Don't be a poor sport, Coz." A sly smile crossed the marquess's face, and he jumped down from the chair. "Shall I tell them what this wager was for?"

There was no hope for Amused Tolerance; not as Xavier went cold within all the layers of his clothing. He affixed Expression Number One, Veiled Disdain. "When men of honor make a wager made in confidence, it ought to remain so."

He gripped a sliver of hope that this would quash Lockwood's boasting. If the marquess started bandying Louisa's name around as the subject of a frivolous wager, she'd become a laughingstock. A *scorned* laughingstock.

Lockwood's blue eyes narrowed; Xavier saw his own tension reflected in his cousin's face. He'd hung the wager on the question of honor—and there was only one possible response for men who wanted the respect of their peers.

"You are right," Lockwood said at last. "It was a confidential bet." His flashing smile returned, and he cut his eyes sideways at Xavier as he added loudly, "Confidential because it was a bet upon a woman! I cannot say who. But Xavier was to keep her here for two weeks, by means fair or foul, and he has not."

The guests looked around. They realized at once who was missing and began to mutter.

"Estella never kept a firm enough hand on her niece," Lady Alleyneham was saying in a voice clearly intended to be overheard. "This is the natural consequence. The subject of a wager—can you imagine? Why, I should be horrified if my girls . . ."

Xavier turned away, wishing he could stop hearing the terrible words.

He had made the bet—he and Lockwood. Yet Louisa's reputation was the one that would suffer. He'd sent her away for nothing. Hurt her with his good intentions the first time he'd really tried to act on them. The realization was repugnant.

His fingers felt like frozen sticks, but he caught his cousin's sleeve. "Damn you, Lockwood," he said below the tumult of speculation that now filled the room. "You're a cheat."

"Only if you are, my dear Coz." Lockwood smiled, and Xavier felt a strong urge to disarrange those rows of teeth. "Who was the one who accepted the bet? Who arranged matters to secure his own victory, or so he thought?"

Lockwood turned to a laughing Mrs. Protheroe. "Shocking, is it not? To learn that our host is only human?"

"We all have feet of clay, my lord." She grasped the lapels of Lockwood's coat and murmured something in his ear, then cast a smile over her shoulder. "Don't worry yourself about it, my dear Xavier. Other women will come along. They always do."

"Not exactly good *ton*, though." Dandified Freddie Pellington looked worried under his cherub-cloud of curly hair. "Betting on a lady and whatnot. Seems dashed . . . well. You know. Not the thing."

He trailed off when his eyes met Xavier's, then turned

away to speak loudly to Mrs. Tindall about snipping a sprig of mistletoe for his buttonhole.

And Xavier realized, with the clarity of a slap, that he'd been given the cut direct. For the first time in his life, his behavior had been judged publicly unacceptable.

And it *had* been unacceptable. Lockwood had not even had to lie.

If Xavier had declined the bet in the first place, the blow to his precious reputation would have been far less, and Louisa would never have been implicated at all.

If he hadn't manipulated the house party to appeal to the respectable along with the disreputable, then she would never have come.

If he hadn't spent time with her—gotten to know her so well—he would never have been linked to her.

In so many ways, he could have put a stop to this. But rumor was a runaway carriage, and one way or another, he was overdue for a crash. Unless he acted with the swiftest of reflexes, as though he wasn't aware of the shifting danger until his feet were steady again.

He began at once; managed bits of conversation, offered liquors and sherries as his guests waited to be summoned into the dining room. The Smile served him well; he could summon it by rote.

First: Expression Number Five, Mocking Drollery. He broke off some mistletoe (not from the bush he'd collected with Louisa; *not from that one*) and handed it to Pellington with a flourish, which coaxed a smile from that fellow. With a bit more spoon-fed attention, he'd have Pellington back in his pocket.

Next: Expression Number Two, Haughty Certainty. He told Lord Weatherwax that they would enjoy the finest *cru* in his cellar that night. That was enough to recapture the goodwill of the old inebriate.

And for Lockwood—nothing. He ignored Lockwood's crowing as unutterably vulgar. He could only hope the others would follow his example, as they'd been used, by habit, to do.

When Wheeling announced dinner, Xavier trudged along with the floating chatter of his houseguests, wishing it would drown out his thoughts.

Because he'd made the most dishonorable discovery of all: though he ought to wish Louisa hadn't been pushed into the river of gossip, there was a deep and sullen part of him that was glad these people knew he'd been tied to her, just for a while.

After the endless, empty round of gustatory pleasures—dinner and port and tobacco—everyone gathered in the drawing room for games. With the New Year only two days away, the weather had turned gray, with an endless cold drizzle that suited Xavier's glum mood.

But he knew better than to betray that, especially with Lockwood scrutinizing him. So he had the fire built up roaringly high and had mulled wine circulated among the guests as they organized for a game of squeak piggy squeak. This flirtatious amusement involved much lying atop one another's laps and shrieking. All in all, a most pleasant evening.

Well, it should have been. Xavier had thought himself a hedonist, once. But the pursuit of pleasure was neither *pursuit* nor *pleasure* when it was handed to one, pointlessly, on the lap of a near-stranger.

"Lord Xavier!" A hail from the double couple—Lord and Lady Weatherby, and Mr. and Mrs. Simpkins. "Do think of a new game for us."

Lady Weatherby gave him a feline smile and twined a

forefinger through one of her long, dark ringlets. "We have great faith in your . . . talents. Perhaps you could wager on . . . us?"

Could the woman not speak a sentence without pausing for ten minutes? Doubtless it was intended to be seductive, but not even in rumor would Xavier become the fifth member of this couple.

"I beg your pardon, dear lady, but I think I hear our hostess calling my name." He dutifully dragged his eyes up and down her form and was rewarded with an impish smile. Fair enough. He'd been forgiven for the earlier awkwardness.

His guests might be easily led, but they were equally ready to be convinced. *Show us what to think of you*, they bleated. *We'll follow.*

So he showed them the same thing he always had: a willingness to titillate, to smooth over rough-edged interactions. But this time, there was a purpose to it. He was Lord Xavier, only kinder. Less dismissive, and a little better. Good enough, he hoped, to restore their faith in him.

What he'd do with that faith, he'd no idea. Of all the gifts Louisa had given him, only her belief that he could be *more* lingered still.

He veered in the direction of Mrs. Tindall, gave that good soul a pat on the arm, and then—having fulfilled his duty to the observant Lady Weatherby—he made his way to a divan at the far end of the room and sank onto it with a sigh.

This part of the room was much dimmer. It took him a second to notice Signora Frittarelli at the opposite end of the lengthy seat, almost hidden in shadow. Evidently she'd used a nearby lamp to ignite one of her fragrant little cigarillos, then had extinguished the light.

Belatedly, Xavier asked, "May I join you?"

She shrugged within her claret-colored velvet, then tugged a slim gold case from the valley of her generous bosom. "You want some smoke?" She extended the case to him.

"No. Thank you."

This was a surer sign than any that Xavier had altered: he hadn't flirted, hadn't taken a cigarillo from the gold case, warm from *la signora*'s bosom. As far as he knew, she hadn't come to anyone's bed since the house party began; she was ripe for the plucking, if he wanted her.

But he didn't.

She nodded and blew a ring of clove-infused smoke from her painted lips. "You are *triste*." She mimed crying, hands waggling before her face.

"Careful, careful." Xavier snatched the cigarillo before she singed her coiled hair. He handed it back to her as soon as her gestures calmed.

"*Sad* is the word you mean, but I assure you I am not." He tried to think of something else to say, but his wit seemed to have deserted him along with Louisa.

"*Ciò che un bel bugiardo,*" she muttered. *What a beautiful liar.*

"I am not that, either." He drummed his fingers on his knee. "Well, not beautiful."

"Ah. You have some good *linguaggio*." She smiled. In Italian, she added, "You fool these others, but you cannot fool me. I know poor acting when I see it. It is my livelihood."

She reached across the length of the divan and gave his knee a comforting little pat, then sat back as though nothing had passed.

Xavier was too surprised to be insulted.

So there were two women who'd seen through his act: a scholarly innocent, and a seductive performer.

Maybe his mask wasn't as good as he'd thought it. Or

maybe he didn't care so much about keeping it affixed at all times.

To one so steeped in notoriety as *la signora*, his own trespasses would seem as nothing. "May I trust you with a confidence?"

She studied him under heavy lids, her face sleepy and lush under her weight of dark hair. "Yes. You give me *invito* to your house. I give you my ears."

He nodded his thanks. He'd once wanted much more than that from the prima donna—or if not precisely wanted, felt obligated to pursue. But the offer of listening ears now seemed the better gift.

He studied the giggling guests, sitting on one another's laps, tumbling to the floor, grasping and groping. Bathed in the crystalline light of the great chandelier, they seemed a species entirely apart.

"I've made a mistake," he began. His fingers fumbled over the cloth-covered buttons on his coat sleeve, twisting them until the threads strained tight. "But there's nothing else I could have done."

He had hoped that saying the words would help to roll away the weight on his shoulders. But if anything, it seemed heavier.

"Then why you are sad?" She held her cigarillo lightly, letting the smoke trail away to nothing, and studied him.

"Because. It was a mistake. *Errore*," he added impatiently.

She frowned. "Yes. I know this word. But if you can do nothing to change this mistake, why feel sad?"

Snap. Thread popped under his twisting fingers, and a black button fell loose into his hand.

Well, it wasn't the worst damage he'd done today.

He slipped the button into his waistcoat pocket, alongside his quizzing glass. Then he laced his fingers and considered his reply.

"Because my best wasn't enough. Not today. Not for . . ."

"I know who," said *la signora*, and again she reached across the long cushioned seat to give him a friendly little pat. "It will be well. Women forgive the mistakes."

"Men don't," Xavier muttered. "Not even their own."

In truth, he wasn't sad, but angry. Angry with himself. He had created a private disgrace for Louisa so she could avoid a public one, which seemed to loom despite his efforts. He'd made himself vulnerable. Not only to Lockwood, but to everyone who expected both more and less of him than he would wish. He had bowed to them all, let them mold his behavior.

And for what? So he'd be marked the winner in a betting book. So he could preserve a shaky reputation that was built on sand and smoke.

He'd thought he would have nothing without it, but he'd been wrong. Only now that he'd forced Louisa from his house did he feel true loss.

"*Cazzo*," replied the singer. *Cock*.

She jabbed her cigarillo at Xavier, and ash sprinkled the dark upholstery of the divan. "You think with your *cazzo*, like all men. You want the biggest *cazzo*, the biggest sadness, the biggest mistake. If you do wrong, you want that you do the wrongest ever. You think you are most terrible and no one could forgive."

She sat back and put her tiny cigar to her lips again.

Xavier stared at the bright ember, unsettled by her words, until she spoke again.

"What if," she said more quietly, as the tumult of the game continued across the room, "you not be a *cazzo*? What if you ask your *bella* to forgive?"

She cast around for a word, then shrugged and continued

in Italian, "It is harder to ask for forgiveness than to assume you cannot be forgiven. But that is the only way to have a hope of making things right."

But Lockwood said he would violate her . . .

No. That would not be. Xavier had been led by fear. It had been easier to slice away the whole tangle than to fight his way through the problems—to disarm his cousin, to ensure that Louisa had . . . well, whatever it was she wanted.

She had thrown away the mistletoe berry. Yet she'd still given him her trust, hadn't she? He might still be able to set things right. At the very least, he could find a way to wash the mud of rumor from her name.

He gave *la signora* a nod of understanding, and she smiled, looking both shy and sweet. It was a smile that made Xavier wish that earls and opera singers might be friends, somehow.

In quiet, accented Italian, he answered her. "Why do you not join the others in their game?"

She blew another smoke ring, then stubbed out her cigarillo on the lid of her gold case. "For the same reason you do not. My *caro* is not here. I must act the part of scandal, but my heart is not in it."

Her eyes met his, then dropped. She busied herself with the clasp on her cigarette case, letting this sink in.

Xavier had heard that she was the well-paid mistress of a royal duke, though the affair was meant to be as clandestine as it was notorious. *Caro*, she called her protector. *Beloved.* It seemed the secret liaison had captured *la signora's* heart as well as her pocketbook.

A royal duke could never marry a foreign-born, Catholic performer who'd been known to conduct affairs with any number of men in the past. She faced nothing but hopelessness in love.

"I am sorry," he said.

She shrugged, but Xavier could tell the carelessness was an act. "It is the part I choose," she said. "I do my best with it."

"You do admirably well," Xavier said.

He let himself sag against the upholstered back of the long divan. The rosewood frame underlying the overstuffed cushion braced him, kept him up straight.

He'd had enough of Petrarch and Dante: poetry had not served him well. It had made him sentimental and far too yielding.

As long as he was consulting a variety of Italians, he'd mull over the advice from the opera singer. But he'd also keep Machiavelli's words in mind: "Among other evils which being unarmed brings you, it causes you to be despised."

He was not unarmed now. With Louisa safely away, he could go on the offensive. He could put rumor to work for him, put together some sort of plan instead of drifting among the whims of others.

And then he could take *la signora*'s advice, and seek the solace of undeserved pardon.

"Have you heard," he asked her, "of the betting book at White's?"

Chapter 24

Containing a Great Many Resolutions

December 31, 1818

Resolutions of the Hon. Louisa Oliver,
Spinster, Bluestocking, Eccentric,
for the Year 1819

~~*Find a husband*~~
~~*Find some fascinating new books*~~
Find a bucket of cold water in which to douse my head.

Louisa's hand hovered over the sheet of foolscap. How should she continue? There were so many things she wanted that her head felt over-full.

But her hand wouldn't write them down.

The desire for kisses and books seemed long ago. Everything she wrote now seemed a habit, not a true yearning of her heart. In the day since she'd left Clifton Hall, her carefully catalogued self had been scattered like paper in the wind, and she had no inkling how to collect it again.

After slamming the trunk lid on her creased garments,

Louisa and Lady Irving had driven for hours through a chilly rain over pitted roads. They had reached Nicholls, the country estate of Viscount Matheson, late in the evening. Here lived Louisa's stepsister, Julia—one of her dearest friends in the world—and Julia's husband, James.

James, who had once asked Louisa to marry him. James, who thought his old friend Xavier had betrayed him once upon a time.

Louisa had never intended to return here to live; nor would she. But she couldn't go anywhere else with a trunkful of damaged clothing, and after the bumpy, nerve-testing carriage ride, she and Lady Irving had been too exhausted to repack and travel on to the countess's home in London.

So here she was, as though the house party had never happened. Sitting at the little walnut writing desk in her familiar cream-and-green bedchamber, waiting to catalogue her life.

How she'd hoped she was done with waiting.

The quill trembled in her hand, and she wiped it and set it down.

A knock sounded at the door. Louisa didn't want company, but a distraction from her disappointment would be welcome.

"Come in," she said, drawing a blank sheet of paper across her stubbornly incomplete list.

A rounded belly entered the room, followed by the rest of Julia. The young viscountess was as slight as Louisa was tall, and the weight of her unborn child coupled with her untidy fair hair made her look like a kitchen maid smuggling a melon.

She heaved herself onto the bed and regarded Louisa with suspicion. "I wasn't expecting your return for several more days, which means something must have happened.

And you've been hiding inside your bedchamber like a buzzard with a carcass—"

"Charming," Louisa muttered.

"Which means," Julia continued, "that the mysterious *something* that happened must have been momentous. And now you've had a night to think about whether it was wonderful or dreadful. So which is it?"

"This thing that you are fabricating, that you've compared to a carcass?"

"Yes." Julia pulled a face. "Stop stalling or I'll have you pitched out a window."

"Impending motherhood has done wonders for your temper," Louisa commented. Her fingers played over the blank sheet of paper that covered her non-list of non-resolutions.

The full truth was too embarrassing. She had already been shamed enough in the eyes of the people who loved her. Why should Julia—married, a mother, loved and wanted—know that Louisa had been cast aside once more?

She decided on a partial truth. She pasted a secretive smile on her face and rose from the chair to join Julia on the spring-green counterpane. The ropes under the mattress creaked as she settled onto her back.

"As a matter of fact, the carcass-thing is more in the realm of wonderful, and it's for you and James. Lord Xavier sincerely regrets his falling-out with James. I believe he never intended to do anything wrong, to hurt any of us."

Julia plumped backward next to Louisa. "Is that all you came to say? That wasn't worth driving over soupy roads for. You could have simply sent a letter. As a matter of fact, Xavier did that this morning."

Louisa jolted. "He—what?"

Julia looked innocent. "I'm sure you heard me correctly.

Oof. Is there any chance this child will outgrow me before he's born?"

"Julia. The letter." Louisa poked her in the arm. "Explain."

"Oh." Julia blinked, then studied the canopy of the bed. "Yes. It came in the morning post. A very nice letter covering everything that happened at the time you broke your engagement. 'Carelessness, all an accident, never meant to hurt, deepest regrets,' and so on. James forgave him at once and is currently trying to compose a reply that will communicate his clemency without damaging his manly pride."

Louisa felt like a poked soufflé. "I see. Well, good. That's very good. I'm glad."

"Hmm." Julia was still determinedly studying the canopy. "So. That's the only reason you returned in a tizzy with your clothes all damaged?"

"What other reason could there be?"

Julia hoisted herself onto one elbow and peered down at Louisa. "Excellent dodge, my dear sister. But I think a man is involved."

"Nonsense."

"Is it?" Julia patted down the side of her dress, searching for a pocket, then pulled out a folded paper. "Is this nonsense, then? This letter for you that came from Clifton Hall, along with the letter for James?"

Louisa's fingers went cold as she made a grab for the paper. "Likely it is. But I'll never know until you show me."

Julia held out the paper, watching. When Louisa snapped it up, the viscountess's piquant face crumpled.

"It's true, then? You and Xavier? I shouldn't be disappointed. I know I shouldn't. James is all ready to forgive him, and I . . ." Julia closed her eyes for a long moment.

"Well. Couldn't you have picked anyone else in the world? Even a pickpocket would be better. Or a Frenchman."

Louisa had to smile at that. "Julia, you of all people ought to know, it's not always possible to choose whom one"—she pressed her lips together before the treacherous word could escape, and settled for the lukewarm—"cares for."

Julia shoved her bulky body up to a seated position. "I know. I know, I know, I know." Her shoulders sagged, and of old habit, Louisa patted her on the back. "I just want to believe he deserves you," she finished in a small voice.

"I want to believe that, too," Louisa agreed. "But I won't without evidence. Never you fear about that."

Julia slid to the floor and lumbered toward the door of the bedchamber. She turned, her fingers on the door handle, and smiled. "Read your letter. Sort the evidence. I know you'll render a fair verdict, whether he deserves one or not."

She paused, then added, "You're not going to stay, are you." There was no need for a question.

No need for an answer, either. Julia's wide eyes and rueful mouth showed that she already knew the truth.

Ever since their childhood, Louisa had tried to protect Julia. But it had been a long while since Julia needed any such help. Vivacious and stubborn, her stepsister had built her own life.

There was nothing for Louisa here. Not anymore.

She sat up, the letter crackling in her fist. "No. I can't. I'm sorry, Julia."

Julia gnawed on her lower lip, then nodded. "I thought so. Truthfully, I wasn't sure you'd ever come back from the house party. It was time, wasn't it? For something new, I mean. I could tell you'd been ready for a while."

Louisa could only stare. It seemed her sister had been noticing the change in her before she'd seen it in herself.

"I'm selfishly disappointed, but selflessly happy." Julia grinned. She placed a hand at the small of her back for support. "I'm glad you came back, if only for the turn of the year."

"What better way to ensure a new start?" Louisa smiled, but the expression faded as soon as the door closed behind Julia.

Actually, she was talking utter rubbish. Returning to the home of one's pregnant sister and one's former betrothed was hardly the way to jump into a new life. But since Louisa had no idea which direction to go, returning to a familiar path had one small advantage: she knew she wouldn't be alone.

She collapsed back onto the bed, cracked the seal on her letter, then unfolded it. A ten-pound note fluttered out, landing across her face as lightly as a feather.

The accompanying letter was as brief as her own had been.

It was not a fiction.

She stared at the words, as though the sight of them would help their meaning assemble in her brain.

The first words that came to mind were: *Damn you, Alex.* Because of course it was a fiction. His whole *life* was a fiction.

And that made her annoyed—no, *angry*. Because he had trapped himself in a thankless role. He, who read Dante and was interested in ciphers, who had a sly sense of humor and was embarrassed by his weak eyes.

He denied all of that. And so he denied her regard, or the possibility of anything real between them. With his ten pounds, he denied even her gesture of understanding.

We made a lovely novel, she'd written. Those words were intended to convey much: regret, pleasure, the willingness to let it recede into a fond memory.

He wouldn't let that stand. He denied that, too; that what had happened between them was a fiction. Yet he'd sent her away like a disgraced servant, so it could not possibly be real.

And so it was . . . nothing.

She should have known that was all it could ever be. She *had* known. She'd simply wanted that not to be the case, because—well, because she had come to love him. Alex. The man he tried so valiantly to hide.

And that didn't matter one bit. For all her *noticing*, she'd missed the essential in a storm of sweet inconsequentialities: he lacked the courage or the desire to change his reputation. It was only a matter of time before he became the man that, for now, he only pretended to be.

The idea was nearly unbearable, that he would lose himself under the weight of meaningless expectations. But what could she do? Add to them? She crushed the note in her fist and wished she could toss it aside, like a mistletoe berry. But the time for pretending she didn't care—that she could use Alex for pleasure and sport—was long past. In the essentials, she had never changed: she was still quiet, wary, hungry for love.

Lord Xavier had taught her something after all. It didn't matter how she felt. She'd show a confident mask to the world, unhurt and untouched—and eventually, she, too, would become the type of person she now only pretended to be.

Chapter 25

Containing the Aggravation of Shakespearean Insight

"Shall I bring up more champagne, my lord?"

Xavier considered his butler's words, then the complete chaos of the drawing room. His guests were already more than kite-high.

"No, Wheeling," he decided. "If they drink any more, they'll be sick on the carpets, and the maids will all give notice. But there is something else I require."

Once he gave his order, he allowed the butler to depart, then surveyed the damage.

Lord Weatherwax was humming to himself in a chair by the fire, waving around the snifter that seemed a permanent extension of his hand.

Jane was following Kirkpatrick around like a puppy, yapping about mistletoe, holding a sprig in one hand. As though one hundred sixty-one kisses hadn't been enough. Kirkpatrick, for his part, was trying valiantly to look like a reputable version of Byron, hair tumbled just so over his brow. Somehow—Xavier thought he could guess how—a button of the baron's waistcoat had come undone, which spoiled the dignified effect he was going for.

Xavier squelched a smile, though Kirkpatrick's Byronic act was amusing. A cover for the man's insecurities—but then, didn't everyone wear a mask?

Which reminded him: it was time to sport Expression Number Three, Amused Tolerance, and catch the eye of *la signora*. With a complicit nod, she slipped from the room.

Not slipped. Thundered. She aimed to be noticed, trailing her flowered shawl in Lockwood's champagne, squeezing past Lady Alleyneham's chair with a loud *scusi*, and fumbling with the door handle for several seconds before letting herself out into the corridor.

Xavier smothered another smile and waited until the ormolu clock on the mantel had ticked away one minute. Then, with a similar lack of grace, he excused himself from the room.

When he shut the door behind him, Signora Frittarelli was struggling to light one of her sweet-scented cigarillos. Even so, her full mouth was pursed with self-satisfied pleasure.

"You are a fine actress," Xavier told her.

She waved off the compliment. "*Venti minuti*? It is enough?"

"It's all we can spare." Xavier stepped closer, taking her tinderbox and thumbing the small metal wheel. When it cast a spark, he held it at arm's length and ignited her cigarillo.

"*Grazie*," they both said at once.

And headed in opposite directions.

Xavier had no idea where the singer went during their small allotment of time. He went upstairs to his bedchamber, grabbed his quizzing glass and a book, and slung himself onto his massive four-poster bed, booted feet hanging off the end.

He'd chosen Machiavelli tonight. He was still laying his traps, weaving his protective webs, and he thought the old medieval plotter would help him.

This supposed interlude with the opera singer was part of his strategy. The partygoers were meant to notice Xavier cavorting about, unconcerned by the departure of Miss Oliver. *His cousin was wrong*, they were to say. *She couldn't have meant anything to him. Pity. It would have made an interesting bit of tittle-tattle.*

If he and *la signora* played their parts well, Louisa would vanish from the minds of his gossipy guests, just as she had from their presence. She'd be safe then, in the return of her anonymity. Lockwood would leave her alone. Everything would be just as it had been before the house party began.

The thought should have been bracing. But instead of taking in the printed words of Machiavelli, his mind drifted to Shakespeare.

Not to Ariel's song this time, though the memory of his mouth drifting over Louisa's skin flickered and vanished with a swift pang of longing.

No. This time, he thought of *Othello*'s Iago.

Who steals my purse, steals trash . . .
But he that filches from me my good name robs me of
     that which not enriches him and makes me poor
     indeed.

Iago was the largest hypocrite imaginable. Everything he said was a lie; every flex of his features a Numbered Expression.

Surely he had hoped for something more, though;

hoped that, through his lies and manipulations, he could win renown for himself. If so, he had failed. By the end of the play, he had destroyed the lives of several honorable people.

Including his own wife.

Xavier's mind galloped away from that idea. The champagne he'd drunk tasted sour in his mouth. He slammed his unread volume shut and sat up, then squinted at the mantel clock. Only five minutes to go before he and *la signora* were meant to return, mussed and panting, to the drawing room.

He would end the year with a lie, just as he had ended so many others. But Louisa was right about his false front of a reputation: he had nothing with which to replace it.

At least, not yet.

As Xavier slunk down the stairs from his bedchamber, he teased open the knots of his cravat and looped it sloppily around his neck. He encountered Signora Frittarelli in the corridor outside the drawing room, from which the din of tipsy song was leaking. The singer was pulling hairpins from her dark hair, letting it fall in long waves down her back.

Xavier wished pointlessly that he'd taken down Louisa's hair and touched its glossy strands. His fingers ached for the missed opportunity.

"You look . . . *spaventoso*," his partner in deception commented.

"Frightful? Thank you. If it weren't impolite, I'd say the same of you."

With a satisfied nod, she accepted this comment and held out a fistful of hairpins. He extended a hand to accept them, then stuffed them into a pocket. She looked him up and down, then reached forth to flick open a few buttons on his waistcoat.

He felt not a single stirring except that of amusement.

"*Molto meglio*," she announced. "You say that how in English?"

"*Much better*," Xavier said. "Though you could also say *much worse*."

"Yes." She grinned. "I go in first."

She eased open the drawing room door and slipped inside. Raucous song grew louder, then faded again as the door swung shut. Xavier counted off a minute, then followed her.

Sound crashed over him in a wave as soon as he stepped through the doorway. Lockwood, full of champagne and self-satisfaction, was standing atop that Chippendale chair he seemed determined to destroy, conducting the other guests in a near-shouted version of "Heart of Oak."

Come, cheer up, my lads, 'tis to glory we steer,
To add something more to this wonderful year . . .

The lyrics were not inapt, but Xavier caught his cousin's eye and shook his head. His hand made an unmistakable gesture: *climb down*. Lockwood's eyes flicked over Xavier's disarranged clothes, then widened.

As though hiding his disarray, Xavier stepped behind a massive vase atop an occasional table. All part of the act.

He was hidden better than he'd realized. Almost at once, Xavier overheard his name beneath the billowing song.

"Really," Lady Weatherby was saying to Mr. Simpkins, "isn't it a little tactless for our host to take up with someone new so quickly?"

"Quite right, m'dear," said Simpkins. From the corner of his eye, Xavier saw that man's fingertips pinch at the lady's nipple. "Ought to mourn one reputation before destroying another, what?"

"Ah. Well, that singer doesn't have much of a reputation to worry about, either, does she?"

"Likely she was always the one for him," Simpkins said. His other hand slid over the curve of the lady's bottom. "Got a prime pair of bubbies on her, doesn't she? Why bother with a skinny little virgin when one can go for a sure thing?"

"You like a sure thing, do you?" Lady Weatherby's own hands began to roam, and the conversation turned both personal and filthy.

Xavier stood, half-hidden and wholly unnoticed behind the vase, awash in contradictory thoughts.

First—he was being criticized by two of the most sexually amoral people he'd ever met.

Second—though they'd hardly spoken well of Louisa, they'd entertained the idea that she was innocent of scandal.

This was exactly as he'd hoped. He'd never redeem Louisa's reputation without throwing away his own. Which made it less likely that he could ever have her, but . . . she could have someone else, someday. She could walk away from him, untouched.

Was this what a noble act felt like? He hated it. It felt as though his heart was afire and his body ice, and there was no poetry in the world that could say what he felt, because the inside of his head was like a writhing mass of cobras.

Yes. He hated it.

Yet he would not undo it for the world, because Louisa was worth all this shuddering agony of feeling. His *cara*, whom he could never publicly claim.

Before he could explore that realization further, Lockwood had jumped down from the chair that had been his stage, still waving a hand over his head to the rhythm of the song. At once, Mrs. Protheroe hitched up her skirts and climbed up in his place.

Lockwood battled his way to Xavier's side and leaned an elbow on the occasional table, setting the huge vase to teetering. "So, Coz. You look rather unruly."

Looked? That was nothing compared to how he felt. But Xavier stuffed all that oh-so unruly emotion down. "Do I? Should've been more careful."

He hadn't mustered the correct custard-bland tone, but under the din of cockeyed song, it hardly mattered.

"I hadn't expected this of you, Coz," Lockwood said. "Are you—have you—" He drew closer, almost nose to nose, and his face went blurry.

"When I am involved, the answer to both those questions can generally be assumed to be yes." Xavier's neck felt vulnerable within his sloppy, loose cravat, as though he'd bared his throat to an enemy.

Hell. He needed to see Lockwood's face. He needed to know how this plan was going over. He tugged his quizzing glass from his waistcoat pocket, and *la signora*'s hairpins pattered onto the floor in a rain of naughty little hints.

Damn. He'd forgotten he was holding those for her. He caught her eye across the room, and she gave him a dramatic pout before flouncing into the mass of singing guests.

This could be part of the plan, too.

When Xavier returned his gaze to Lockwood, this time through the clarity of his convex lens, he saw that the marquess looked confused.

Very well. Confusion was acceptable; Xavier could hardly expect a more decisive response. Lockwood had won his idiotic wager on Louisa, but his main joy, Xavier thought, had been in spoiling the pleasures of his cousin. If Xavier now had a new pleasure, Lockwood's threats against Louisa were toothless.

This was how Xavier hoped the marquess's thoughts were grinding along. "You look befuddled, Lockwood. Something troubling you?"

He twisted the knife a little, making his face all concern. "Not getting anywhere with Mrs. Protheroe, are you? Shame, that. She looks fetching." He nodded toward the blond widow atop the chair, all bright hair and loud laughter and prominent bosom.

Lockwood ground his teeth. "As a matter of fact, Coz, I've been getting exactly what I want. This wager of ours—" He cut himself off.

"Is at an end," Xavier finished, stuffing his glass back into his waistcoat.

Wheeling padded over to him then, an open bottle of what appeared to be brandy in his hands. "The vintage you requested, my lord."

"Grande Champagne?" Lockwood sounded interested.

"No no. Nothing so distinctive as that. Wheeling, locate some of Lord Lockwood's favorite vintage, would you?" The butler bowed, and Xavier added, "And—let's have someone clean up all these hairpins. Yes?"

Wheeling never smiled; his station wouldn't permit such familiarity. But in the way his gaze traveled to the floor, then back to a scrupulously correct point just below Xavier's eyes—there seemed to be a squeeze of humor in the pinch of his lips. "It will be done, my lord."

Lockwood's nostrils flared, but he padded away after the butler in search of his costly favorite liquor, leaving Xavier with his new bottle.

He sniffed at it: nearly odorless. Good. It was exactly what he'd requested.

Xavier had once told Lady Irving that he had a brandy the exact shade of brewed tea. This appeared in the decanters throughout the house so that the guests could imbibe to their heart's content.

For his part, he would drink a brewed tea the precise shade of brandy.

It was easier to enter into the spirit of a raucous affair when one was half-soused all the time. But he *wasn't* in the spirit of it, and so it was easier to pretend with a clear head.

He poured himself some of the false brandy and stashed the bottle in the window seat. From here, he could scan the whole room. This odd conglomeration of proper and bawdy guests were ringing in the New Year as his guests always had—toasting one another's every word, ripping down mistletoe to kiss one another. Squealing and falling across each other's laps.

It seemed that when the year came to an end, the polite world was just as ready to drench itself in drink and flirtation as were the more dissipated members of society. Even the cautious Lady Alleyneham had relaxed for this occasion, downing flute after flute of champagne, allowing her daughters to drape themselves on various gentlemen.

And why not? Everyone was drinking, everyone was joyful. It was all in good fun. It was a New Year and a new beginning.

It was the house party he'd have had if Louisa had never been there at all.

Atop the poor beleaguered Chippendale chair, Mrs. Protheroe had tugged up her skirt and tugged down her garter as she continued the song. Things would only get worse from this point. Or better. It was all in how one chose to look at it.

He leaned against the wall and shut his eyes.

* * *

While his guests slept off the effects of their celebration the following morning, Xavier began the year at the polished mahogany desk in his study.

He had a few resolutions for the year, and there was no reason why he couldn't begin them today.

First, he would master the account books. Second, he'd speak to his steward about them. He was determined to understand every detail of how, precisely, his earldom stayed in funds.

Chatterton was sure to talk his ear off. Both ears. It would be a painful experience.

Xavier cast a longing look at the decanter on his study's sideboard.

No. He rubbed a hand over his chin. It was clean-shaven. He was not bleary-eyed. He couldn't remember the last time he'd seen the sun on New Year's Day. It was . . . novel.

No one else would know he had awoken. But *he* knew it. And that seemed like the essential beginning. When he was alone, he didn't have to pretend. When he was alone, he could admit the truth: that he cared about a number of things he never had before.

He cared about the half-curious, half-resentful glares his tenants had shot him at church. He cared about the account books that held the details of his earldom. He cared about that encoded ledger that had fired Lockwood with imagination, venom, and vengeance.

He cared, too, that all the best bits of himself had been as carefully catalogued as a shelf of incunables, exotic and original—and that he'd trundled his cataloguer away several days before, with only a sentence of explanation to reveal his heart to her.

A heart he'd once claimed he didn't possess.

How he wished he could pretend none of this was true,

after all. It had been so much easier being Lord Xavier, though he'd been a fake of a rake, nothing but a shell.

The carved back of the seraglio chair pushed at him, and he realized he had slumped. No. There would be no slumping this morning. He had sent Louisa away for her own good, and his skeleton could no more abdicate its duty now than the rest of him could. Body and soul, he must go on as though he was perfectly fine.

He straightened his back; shuffled through his papers for a blank sheet; drew inkwell and quill toward himself.

Onward. Third resolution: he would find out the truth about that encoded history Lockwood was so enamored with. Xavier's butler, Wheeling, had served the earldom for decades. A few questions in Wheeling's ear would be an excellent place to begin.

And finally, Xavier resolved to pluck out Lockwood's claws. Family was family, but honor was honor, and *tit* was the correct response to *tat*. Lockwood could not be permitted to victimize the innocent for his amusement.

A smile crept across his face. Signora Frittarelli had been most illuminating on the subject of rumor, scandal, and the betting book at White's. Spending time in a royal duke's bed apparently allowed her access to many secrets.

Lockwood had much to hide, and more to lose than Xavier had ever suspected.

A cramp was developing between his shoulder blades, and he rose from the fussy, cushiony, undeniably too-small seraglio chair he'd been using as a substitute for the horrible Norman throne. Clasping his hands behind his back, he rolled his shoulders. Tension popped and released down the length of his spine.

One more resolution. He'd get a chair he liked for his study.

Chapter 26

Containing a Most Unexpected Guest

The two weeks had passed; Xavier had long since lost the wager to Lockwood. But the marquess hadn't found the triumph he'd expected, and Xavier hadn't found the shame.

He had decided to extend the house party a few more days, through Twelfth Night. A certain young lady had once reminded him that Christmas didn't end until then. And he couldn't yet let go of Christmas and all the gifts it had brought, even though he had already let go of Louisa.

After her departure, he'd had the library restored to order. On seeing the clean carpet, the well-ordered shelves in all their *potential*, he regretted the step.

The days since New Year's had passed in a shallow riot of teasing and flirtation among his guests. He and *la signora* had slipped away each day, all the better to convince the others that neither of them was pining for an unsuitable person. The deception probably wasn't necessary, though. His guests had ceased to look to him for their amusements; the planned activities of the first week had given way to a languid hedonism. Innocent for some; decidedly the opposite for others.

It was all the same to him. Xavier had learned to expect positively everything at his house parties. They involved all manner of ridiculous misbehavior, yet he never blanched. After the gossip and pretense of New Year's Eve, when he'd faced his heart, then denied it, Xavier thought he was immune to anything his guests—or he—might do.

But when, on the evening of January the fourth, 1819, Wheeling announced to the party in the drawing room the return of Lady Irving . . .

Xavier felt a bit light in the head. Just a bit. And his hand shook as he laid down his hand of whist.

Well. Anyone would shake when faced with Lady Irving's gimlet eye. Especially when that eye was framed by a scarlet turban with peach-dyed plumes and a sun-yellow gown of painted silk.

Xavier excused himself from the card table, at which he was partnering Signora Frittarelli. With a wave of his hand, he caught Lockwood's attention. The marquess sauntered over with a leer to take his place and, no doubt, pocket the pile of silver Xavier had amassed over the last hour of play.

Never mind that game; what game was Louisa's aunt playing? Xavier crossed the room toward her, bowed over the countess's hand, and escorted her to a chair near the fireplace. "Lady Irving. You do me too much honor."

"I certainly do." She settled into the chair, then nodded at the facing chair in which Mrs. Tindall dozed, mouth agape. "The party's hostess is keeping a close watch on things, as usual?"

"As you see." He strained to hear any click of the door behind him; hoped to catch the breeze of a door opening to admit the countess's niece.

"Pay attention, you young rogue." The countess looked

stern, and Xavier dragged his awareness away from the doorway, back to the stubborn oval face of the middle-aged woman seated before him. Who looked as though she'd like to take a hammer and tongs to him.

"I assure you, you have my full attention."

She sighed. "No, I don't. What you want to know is: yes. Louisa returned with me. She's been shown to her bed-chamber. And you—don't even *think* of trying to see her there."

She was older than he, and she was annoyed. Therefore he would refrain from pointing out that, as this was his house, he could visit any room he wished.

Also, she had snapped a hand around his wrist and was physically preventing him from leaving.

"Please release my wrist, dear lady. You are wounding my dignity." Expression Number Two: Haughty Certainty.

She drummed a slippered foot on a footstool. "Sit down, Xavier, if you can pull that poker out of your arse long enough to bend at the middle."

"How repugnant." He sat at the edge of the footstool. "You seem to have something to impart to me. Are you ready to tell it, or shall I steel myself for more personal insults first?"

Every word was a mine, charged and dangerous. He had to get this exchange exactly right—to show Lady Irving that he welcomed her, but he wouldn't be trampled. And that he was worthy of her return. Of Louisa's attention. And forgiveness?

He was still reeling.

There was no hope of getting it right. In desperation, he dragged his hand through his hair, catching the gesture too late. He batted at his head, trying to press his spiky hair back into place and save his dignity.

Unaccountably, the countess's mouth softened. "No

need for more insults. We've returned because you have some explaining to do. Explaining that can't be done in a letter."

Her eyes were as clear as amber, and as hard. But not unforgiving, if he was reading them correctly.

He dropped his Numbered Expression. "You are right. I need to speak with Louisa."

She shook her head slowly. The plumes on her turban bobbed with every tiny movement. "Not yet. You'll speak with me first."

Xavier shot a glance over his shoulder. The drawing room door remained shut, and Mrs. Tindall was still asleep. "Am I to be drawn and quartered, or merely guillotined?"

Lady Irving's mouth pulled tight. "I'm still deciding that."

She steepled her hands, tapping her forefingers against her chin. "I thought you a master of society when we arrived, you know. Deliberate in your every action. Sure of everything you did, and sure of its effect."

Xavier sensed the shadow of the axe about to fall. "There must be a second part to your remark."

"Yes. I was wrong about you. You're a young man, and that means you do stupid things."

Xavier's jaw went slack.

"Don't get all missish, you rapscallion. There's a germ of praise in there. I believe I judged your behavior too harshly. I thought you'd been cruel, but I now believe you were merely stupid."

When her mouth curved at one side, his foolish silence broke. "You have my thanks for this candid assessment."

"Thanking me for an insult? That almost makes up for the pain of travel over these abysmal winter roads."

Her tiny smile grew, then was squelched. "Believe it or not, Xavier, it was your letter to Matheson that saved you.

A man without hope of redemption doesn't admit his faults so readily."

"My letter. To Matheson."

His hands wanted to drag through his hair again, to grab something he understood. No one was meant to know of his letter of apology but Matheson himself. Apology made a man seem weak in the eyes of strangers.

Yet to those he cared for, an apology could strengthen ties.

Except he *hadn't* apologized to Louisa, and he had a sick, plunging feeling that was no more of a secret from the formidable countess than his letter to Matheson had been.

"Yes," she answered. "Your letter. It proved you a human being, not just a fluff-headed, careless rake. But it didn't go far enough. You left someone out of your apology."

He folded his hands and leaned forward on his elbows. But there was no way to hide from the words battering him like hailstones.

"I said all I was able." He studied his interlaced fingers with great attention. His nails and cuticles were a bit ragged; he'd been picking at them over the past few days. He relaced his fingers, folding them inward so he wouldn't have to look at the evidence of his own agitation.

"Did you, now. You said all you were able. You did the best you could. An earl who holds the hearts of the polite world must denounce a respectable young lady to her aunt? He must allow rumor to spread about her, so that he can— what? What was it all for?"

Xavier focused rigidly on his hands. His knuckles were chapped. Likely from shuffling through papers with his steward for the last few days.

His papers. *His responsibilities*. This gave him the slap he needed to reply.

He raised his head, meeting Lady Irving's eyes. "It was

for her. I meant well, though I was, as you say, somewhat stupid."

He unfolded himself so that he sat straight upon the tottery footstool. "You'll find that no scandal has been attached to her name." A bitter smile bent his mouth. "I can't say the same for myself, but what does one more rumor matter to Lord Xavier's reputation?"

The countess studied him for a long moment, and Xavier recognized her niece's careful deliberation in the set of her jaw, the narrowing of her eyes. The recognition was like a stab, and he turned his head away to catch his breath.

"Do you know," the countess said, "I've never seen Louisa so calm and quiet as she's been since we left."

"So she's feeling well, then," Xavier said dully.

"Not at all, you ninny." Lady Irving sniffed. "She's always been quiet in crowds, but she's full of spirit around her family. Now she's simply—oh, it's hard to explain. Simply existing, I suppose."

He knew that feeling. He looked at the countess for more explanation, his mask fallen.

"You understand, then." She nodded. "She hasn't been interested in food, or conversation, or books. That's what truly startled me. And when I asked her whether she was worrying over you, she said it had nothing to do with you at all."

Xavier felt as though stones were being stacked on his chest.

"You look a little green," commented Lady Irving. "Not been drinking too much, have you?"

"No."

"Don't look so glum. Surely you understand? She's fretting her heart out over you."

A stone lifted, but Xavier didn't trust the reprieve. "She said it had nothing to do with me."

The countess rolled her eyes. "Gadzooks, boy. I thought you knew a thing or two about women. If she didn't care deeply, she'd have admitted that she was ashamed or angry about the way you sent her away. But she *does* care, and so she won't admit anything at all."

"That makes no sense." Xavier rubbed at the bridge of his nose, trying to banish a headache. "Well, maybe it does."

Hiding one's deepest emotions under a thick layer of unconcern—the idea was not unfamiliar.

That had always been the trouble since he'd met Louisa. Peeling back the layer of unconcern was incredibly painful, but only without it could he be trusted and known.

And he wanted to be. In the last few days, he'd taken stock of many things. Within Lord Xavier, he was Alex, and he'd never let that go.

"I need to speak with her," he said again.

The countess shook her head. "Not tonight. You'll see her when she's ready, and not a moment before. No, don't puff up like that. I know perfectly well this is your house, but if you want to prove you've got manners, you'll need to use them. I've got both eyes on you."

"Then you won't have them on your niece," Xavier muttered.

"I'll notice well enough if you go near her before she wishes."

"I won't hurt her," Xavier said, but he knew that they both saw this for the untruth it was. He already *had* hurt her. And how could he convince her to forgive him? How could he be certain he wouldn't hurt her again, for that matter?

He couldn't simply smother her with promises. Promises could be broken, much more easily than a code.

A *code*. That was what he needed. Louisa's puzzle-loving mind would be unable to resist teasing it out. And once she'd invested a little time, she might be willing to give him more.

"I have an idea," he said to Lady Irving.

"That makes one of us," she said. "Good luck, you young rapscallion. If you hurt her again, I'll have your manhood."

"You are as charming as ever," he commented.

"That makes one of us," she repeated. Rising from her chair, she swanned across the drawing room to inveigle her way into a rubber of whist.

This left Xavier behind; alone.

But unlike the last time—when he'd watched Lockwood march up the steps of the ruined cellar at Finchley, taking Xavier's self-possession with him—he now had an idea of how to change the situation for the better. And it depended on Louisa not reacting in the common way.

That, he thought, he could rely on.

Chapter 27

Containing the Essential Code

Since she'd tossed her heart to a man with no use for it, Louisa saw no reason to dress for dinner with special care.

Her aunt disagreed, and had coaxed her into an evening gown they hadn't managed to ruin. A wintry froth of ivory muslin, overlaid with silver net and tiny crystals.

"There's no need for me to look so elegant tonight, Aunt," Louisa said as her lady's maid wove glass beads through her hair under the countess's supervision.

"That is utter rot," said Lady Irving. "Everyone's talking about how the earl is carrying on with that opera singer. Also rot, my girl, and you don't want anyone to think you're the slightest bit concerned. You want to look dazzling."

Was that what she wanted? Louisa hardly knew. This rumor about the opera singer—it didn't matter if it was true or not. It proved that Alex was letting rumor eat him alive. If she saw him again, and the man she loved was already gone, that would be worse than if she'd never known him at all.

Underneath her beaded, silken armor, she was dreadfully afraid. Why had she returned?

Because she didn't want either Alex or Lockwood to think she'd been defeated. And because she did not want to be.

So she acted as though she was brimful of bravery. With her aunt, she entered the drawing room before dinner, her smile as crystalline as the beads on her gown. The conversation of the other guests buzzed faintly in her ears.

She greeted Jane with unfeigned happiness; then came the gauntlet of reacquainting with the other guests. Shaking hands all around, complimenting gowns, waving off comments concerning her sudden departure. A family situation with her sister—expecting, you know—had called them away.

This cheerful chatter was easier than she'd expected. Every smile she won was a victory; not over the guests, but over herself. No one looked beyond the crystal beads.

As long as she didn't see Alex, she could hold herself together. As long as she didn't meet his eye, she'd be fine.

Naturally, he entered the drawing room at that moment, all blacks and grays and blade-sharp handsomeness. Yearning stabbed through her, so suddenly that she was unprepared with her polite mask, and her expression must have shown him all her naked desire, her regret.

And what did he do with this knowledge?

He smiled at her, as though everything was right in the world. And then he turned away again.

She wasn't sure whether she loved him more, or whether she hated him for that.

After dinner, Lady Irving settled herself in a chair near the drawing room fireplace.

Not that she was getting old. It was January, damn it; anyone's bones would ache.

Jane Tindall, the earl's bold little cousin, had found a bean in her Twelfth Day cake, which made her queen for the evening. That silly fop Freddie Pellington was the king. They had put their heads together with Xavier as soon as everyone flocked into the drawing room. Something afoot, apparently. Lady Irving hoped it would be enough to distract Louisa. Xavier had promised he'd a plan in mind.

With a clap of hands, Xavier called for the attention of the party.

"Let *me* talk, Xavier," the Tindall girl said. She wore a gilt-paper crown and a rebellious expression. "You didn't find a bean. You ought to go sit down with the rest of the groundlings."

Their host folded his arms and stared at his cousin.

"Dash it," said Freddie Pellington. "No need to keep everyone in suspense and whatnot. Going to play a game of charades. Er, we all are, or most of us are, if you like. Plenty of roles to go around. Special type of charades."

Lady Irving disliked babblers. And her ankles ached. "Special type of charades? What rot are you talking?"

"In the usual fashion, the actors would perform a syllable at a time," Xavier began, but Miss Tindall interrupted.

"Tonight we'll act each letter separately. A tableau for each letter of the secret word. It won't be a very long word, or we'd be playing for days."

"Nothing wrong with prolonging a pleasurable sport." The oily voice of Lord Lockwood.

Lady Irving craned her neck to see what the marquess was going on about. At the far end of the room, Lockwood lounged on the arm of a long, silk-covered divan, looming over Signora Frittarelli. The singer seemed unbothered by this attention; she simply sat, lush as a cherry in a dark red gown of cotton velvet. Every few seconds, she blew smoke into Lockwood's face.

Good for her.

"In fact," the marquess was now saying, "let's put a wager on the game. First to guess the secret word wins the prize. Xavier, what do you say?"

Lady Irving noted that Xavier shot a glance at Louisa before answering. "As I suggested the secret word, there's no sense in wagering."

"Wager on who will guess it first, then," Lockwood pressed. The prima donna blew a particularly large cloud of ash into his face, and he had to stifle a cough.

Xavier shook his head. "I don't care to wager."

The room went silent.

"Honestly," Lady Irving muttered. Not even Lord Xavier took every wager.

Come to think of it, maybe he did. She looked sharply at the earl. He appeared calm as he stared his cousin the marquess in the eye. Who would blink first?

Another cloud of smoke enveloped Lockwood's head. *Blink.*

"But you always care to wager," Lockwood choked out. "Come, let's put a tenner on it."

"I don't care to wager," Xavier repeated. "Not this time. Find your amusement somewhere else."

The room remained silent. Lockwood broke it with a feeble "But . . ."

Lady Irving had age and gender on her side. Therefore, she felt free to snort her derision at Lockwood. "Quiet, you. Let's get on with the game."

Besides turning a bit purple around the edges, there wasn't a thing Lockwood could do by way of reply.

"Anyone who wants to act, come up here." Miss Tindall waved her arms.

As several guests joined her, Louisa perched on the arm of Lady Irving's chair.

"Turn the chair so I can see everything, girl," the countess addressed her. "But make sure I stay by the fire. Damned cold in here."

"It doesn't seem cold to me," Louisa said as she tugged at the chair.

"That's because you're secretly lusting after the earl. It's heating your blood."

"Nonsense, Aunt Estella. I find the earl merely tolerable."

Her blushing cheeks told a different story. Lady Irving decided to allow her that fiction.

She was accustomed to watching over her nieces—first Julia, now Louisa—with fierce loyalty. With her own elderly lecher of a husband, she'd had the worst of the institution of marriage; she was determined her nieces would have the best.

Was Xavier the best? She hadn't decided yet. If he kept looking at Louisa as though she were a Twelfth Day cake he wanted to nibble up, then . . . possibly.

Jane Tindall had finished waving her arms about. "We will be ready with the first clue in a few minutes," she called. The actors left the room, trailed by Pellington, who arranged a large folding screen in front of the door.

"Our host mentioned a code," Louisa said. "I've never played charades in this way before, but it seems intriguing."

"Only the game?"

Louisa stared at the folding screen. "I'm only talking about the game right now."

"Clever girl." Lady Irving shifted her feet to catch more warmth. "Lying is vulgar. Omission is good *ton*."

After a few minutes had passed, they saw the top edge of the door click open behind the painted screen; a soft thunder of footsteps, clanking objects, and hushed voices followed.

Xavier emerged from behind the screen first. Not acting in the tableaux, then.

"Our word tonight is four letters. Presenting the first letter," he intoned in a theatrical voice, then pulled the folding screen aside to reveal the actors.

Lord Lockwood, covered by a pink shawl, was down on all fours. He crawled about, snarling, bumping against a precarious mound of chairs over which had been thrown a tapestry showing a castle and moat. Lady Audrina Bradleigh—one of Sylvia Alleyneham's flock of daughters—stood next to the tower of chairs, a sheet draped across her body and a crossbow in one hand.

"They must have raided the hunting lodge," Louisa murmured.

At the right of the tableau, four men wore pieces of a suit of armor and brandished pistols, muskets, and an old spear.

"They did indeed raid the hunting lodge," Lady Irving agreed.

That quiet Mr. Channing stood in front of the others, shaking his weapon more vigorously, his hair powdered white with flour. Jane Tindall, wearing a man's waistcoat over her frock, walked past the men, holding a bow strung with a quill, which she threw at the crawling Lord Lockwood. Lockwood clutched the spot where the quill had struck him and rolled onto his back, twitching, tongue lolling out of his mouth. The four men surrounded him and mimed hacking at him with their weapons until he lay still.

Xavier drew the screen back across the scene. "End of the first tableau."

He bowed and walked behind the screen, and the door

opened and let out the same bustling and clanking assortment that had come in shortly before.

Interesting, the countess thought.

Louisa seemed to think so, too. Her stubborn quiet had completely dissolved. "They killed Lockwood," she observed.

"That's a good start to any game," Lady Irving said.

Sylvia Alleyneham was fluttering around the room. "What could it be? Something from the Bible? The Tower of Babel?"

"Who was Miss Tindall, then?" asked Lord Kirkpatrick. "An avenging angel? A goddess? A maid from some legend?"

"If Jane heard him talking like that," Louisa murmured, "she'd be leaping all over him again."

Lady Irving suppressed another snort. In the general way of things, snorting was vulgar. "Have you any idea, my girl?"

Louisa shook her head, glass beads twinkling in her hair. "I know I've heard some tale in which a woman slays an animal. I can't quite think of it."

Lord Weatherwax roused himself from the depths of his chair. "Port for anyone? Or sherry for the ladies?" He rang for a servant, and soon a footman was circulating with glasses of wine. The guests began to sip at them, still guessing.

"Something from the Crusades," suggested that hussy of a widow, Lillian Protheroe.

"This game is a bore," pouted Sylvia's other daughter, Charissa.

"A boar!" Louisa called. "That's it exactly."

All eyes turned to her. She kept her chin up and explained, "It's Atalanta slaying the Calydonian boar. It's a story from classical mythology. Lord Lockwood was the boar, sent by Artemis—"

"That was my daughter," interrupted Sylvia. "My daughter was Artemis, wasn't she?"

"Yes," Louisa continued. "She sent the boar to destroy a city that dishonored her, and there was a great hunt to kill it. The father of the hero Odysseus was one of the hunters, but the female hunter, Atalanta, drew first blood."

She accepted a glass of sherry from a footman and took a sip, seeming not to notice the effect of her words on the room.

But Lady Irving noticed: they were stunned, and pleasantly so. Everyone was watching Louisa as though she'd tossed guineas at them.

"Smile, girl," the countess hissed at her niece.

"What a wit, Miss Oliver," said Lord Weatherwax in his slightly too-loud voice. "Bravo to you. Or rather, brava."

This broke the odd silence, and the group began to talk and chuckle again.

"What's the letter, then?" This from Sylvia's daughter Charissa. "Is it B for the boar? Or A for . . . er, whatever the huntress's name was?"

"It could be either one," Louisa said. "We'll figure it out once we see the other clues."

With that, they heard the actors trooping back into the room behind the screen.

Xavier appeared first. "Presenting the second letter." He drew the screen aside again.

A bearskin had been tacked to one of the drawing room doors and sprinkled with what appeared to be saffron.

"That'll be expensive," Lady Irving said. Louisa shushed her, but the countess forgave her niece this disrespect. Louisa tended to get irritable when she was gnawing on a puzzle.

This time, Lady Audrina wore a silk-lined cloak and held a large pepper grinder in her arms. Four men sat on chairs, each rowing a broom like an oar. Jane Tindall, now wearing a green hooded cloak, jumped from behind the edge of the screen and thrust a lit taper at them.

Lady Audrina shook the pepper grinder over Jane, and Jane blew out the taper and collapsed. Channing seized the bearskin from the door, then took Lady Audrina's hand and helped her onto his chair.

Xavier drew the screen back across the actors. "End of the second tableau."

Before he followed the actors out of the room, he glanced at Louisa again. Remarkable eyes he had, Lady Irving noted. Gray as slate. When those eyes fixed on a woman—well. She was done with all that nonsense. But as one corner of the earl's mouth curled into a subtle smile, she could almost wish she were young again.

Louisa's cheeks had gone pink again by the time Xavier departed. "It really is warm in here, isn't it?"

"No," said Lady Irving. "Must be your imagination heating you up. Did you figure out the tableau?"

Louisa frowned.

"Frowning is vulgar, my girl."

"So is public chastisement," Louisa muttered. "And yes, I figured it out," she added more loudly. "It was Medea."

"Well spotted," called Lord Kirkpatrick. "She slew the dragon so that Jason could take the Golden Fleece. Like an avenging angel!"

Ninny. "Someone needs a new figure of speech," said Lady Irving.

"That was a Golden Fleece?" Mrs. Protheroe laughed. "That poor bearskin will never be the same again."

Sylvia Alleyneham asked, "So what is the letter? M for Medea?"

Louisa shrugged. "Or J for Jason, or A for Argonauts."

The actors paraded back into the room then, preventing further reply.

The third tableau was easy to guess, even for Lady Irving, who'd never fancied herself a scholar. Lockwood wore pieces of the beleaguered suit of armor and held a large pillow. The other actors stood in a line in front of the extended screen, and Lockwood mowed them all down with his pillow. He then slammed the pillow into the screen, knocking it over, and stood triumphantly with his foot on the body of Mr. Channing.

The dead bodies all rose, righted the screen, and filed out behind it.

"That one is obviously Troy," said Lord Weatherwax as soon as the actors had left.

Lady Irving turned to stare at the old drunkard; around the room, fabrics rustled as everyone else did the same.

Weatherwax drained his goblet. "Well, I mean to say, it was obvious. Walls falling down, you know." He smothered a hiccup. "Never would have seen Lockwood as Aeneas, myself. Not exactly the hero type."

Louisa snorted.

"Snorting is vulgar," Lady Irving reminded her below the growing hubbub. Nearly everyone was speculating about the secret word now that there was only one tableau left.

"B-A-T?" called Sylvia Alleyneham. "He could be talking of bats?"

"Or a bath," said Louisa. "Though I can't imagine why." She went pink again, which no doubt meant she was imagining Lord Xavier in the bath.

"Hmmm." Lady Irving gave her the Skeptical Eyebrow as the actors returned for the last time.

In the final tableau, Lady Audrina wore the leaves of a hothouse plant pinned across her gown. Again, a wreath sat upon her head, and she held hands with Mr. Channing, who looked uncomfortable with leaves pinned across his pantaloons. Freddie Pellington stood on a chair, holding a broken branch from a miniature orange tree in each hand.

Lockwood crouched behind him in a dark cloak, peering out every few seconds and putting out his tongue. He reached under his cloak and drew out an apple, setting it on one of Pellington's arms. Then he tapped Lady Audrina on the shoulder and knocked the apple neatly into her outstretched hand.

"That's our last tableau. Does anyone have a guess?" Xavier asked.

There was a good-humored gleam in his eye. And Louisa was leaning forward like she could eat him up with a spoon.

Hmph, thought Lady Irving. The earl was staring at Louisa's bosom now. Didn't look so smile-faced all of a sudden. If he wasn't careful, everyone would notice that he was watching her as if she were the only woman in the world.

Everyone *should* notice. She, Estella, Lady Irving, had never seen that look on his face before. And she'd kept a close eye on a series of rakes, ever since she'd first overseen Louisa's debut.

But the flurry of activity among the actors—not the smoldering looks their host was flinging about—had caught everyone else's attention. Pellington stepped down from the chair, and Channing began unpinning the leaves from his pantaloons at once.

"These are dashed heavy, I say," Pellington said, setting the branches down. "Anyone want an orange? Probably killed the tree, and whatnot."

"It's the garden of Eden!" Honestly. A woman of Sylvia Alleyneham's age should have more dignity than to squirm about like a puppy.

"Yes, but what is the secret word?" Lady Irving barked. "I had B-A-T before this, and now what? B-A-T-G spells nothing. Is the answer Adam? Or the serpent? B-A-T-S?"

"The second letter has to be A," agreed Lord Kirkpatrick. "That's the only way to get a word that makes sense."

Xavier's smile widened. "The answer is not *bats*, but I can't give you any clues."

At Lady Irving's side, Louisa was lacing and unlacing her fingers. "The first clue—what could it be? There's B or C for the boar, and A for Artemis or Atalanta. What else was in the scene?"

"I've no inkling, my girl. You're on your own with that guess." Lady Irving flexed her ankles again. "How about another log on the fire, Xavier?"

A wood fire for Twelfth Night. Positively sumptuous. Louisa could do worse than marry him. If Lady Irving didn't mistake the matter, there was something suspicious about this whole game. Positively designed to capture Louisa's attention, it was.

Which meant there was no reason on earth the solution should be *bats*, or *bath,* or anything nondescript like that.

"Keep thinking, my girl," she urged Louisa in a low voice. "Xavier looks too smug, so we must be wandering far from the truth. Who else was in the hunt for that boar? That flour-headed fellow."

"Channing's role?" Louisa bent her head, though her eyes never left the tall form of Lord Xavier. "He was Laertes, I think. The father of Odysseus."

Xavier must have overheard. His head turned; he caught Louisa's eye.

And then he nodded. "Miss Oliver has come the closest with her guess. The first letter is O. The first clue represents Odysseus, since his father helped slay the boar."

Two dozen guests stared at him blankly. "So the word is . . ." Lady Irving prompted.

"*Oats*," replied Lord Xavier, the wicked smile gone from his face.

Jane Tindall made a sound of protest, and Xavier stepped backward onto her slipper.

The earl lifted his brows, his hands, his shoulders. The perfect gesture of innocent supplication. "What else could it be? I am taking an increasing interest in the farming capabilities of my estate."

"Are you *serious*?" This from Lockwood, who'd played the serpent with such glee. "Damned dull of you, Coz."

"Language!" called Sylvia and Mrs. Protheroe at once.

"*Cazzo*," said the reclining opera singer, speaking for nearly the first time since the game had begun. From the divan, she blew a cloud of smoke in Lockwood's direction.

"That's right. Farming," Xavier said. "A new year, a new direction. Now. Shan't we applaud our wonderful players? And have more cake. More brandy. More—well, whatever seizes your fancy."

He gave the room a very bright smile, then tugged Miss Tindall and Freddie Pellington aside and began speaking to them in a quick, low patter of words.

There most certainly was something odd going on. Louisa would figure it out with that big brain of hers. For her own part, Lady Irving would distract the remainder of the guests so Louisa could think. "Whatever seizes our fancy, eh? Well, if any of you are willing to dip into your pockets, I wouldn't mind a game of whist before we turn in."

"Ten pounds a rubber?" Lockwood had turned his squint on Lady Irving.

"Chicken stakes," she replied. "Come up with some real money."

With swift efficiency, she organized three tables, three

quartets. She lingered behind, never joining a rubber, so she could slip back to Louisa once the games had begun.

Her niece was still perched on the arm of the chair, her beaded gown glimmering like a snowflake.

"What's that young rogue talking about?" Lady Irving nodded at Lord Xavier, whose mysterious conversation seemed to be winding down.

"I've no idea. Aunt, it doesn't make sense. Oats? Odysseus wasn't on the hunt for the boar."

"Well, it wasn't his father. Xavier put paid to that idea right enough."

Louisa sat up so quickly that she teetered on the chair arm. "What? What is it?"

Louisa stood and gripped the back of the chair. "It *was* his father. Don't you see? Xavier looked so smug until I guessed Laertes, and then—then he ended the game."

"So the answer is—what? Honestly, girl. I shouldn't have to ask this question more than once in an evening."

Louisa's voice sounded toneless. "Laertes. Which tells us he's taking a classical focus. Ovid, then, for the second tableau. Ovid wrote a famous version of Medea, though it's been lost to the ages."

"Well, then. It could be an M for Medea."

Louisa shook her head. "No, because of what comes next. Virgil wrote about the sacking of Troy."

Lady Irving understood in a flash. "And Eden for the final clue." She sank again into her chair, her troublesome ankles unable to hold her.

Love.

He'd professed his love through a code, and left it for Louisa to decipher.

Damnation. He wasn't a ninny, after all.

Chapter 28

Containing Another Dreadful Imitation of a Stag

"Oats, indeed. Utter tosh. Everyone ought to have recognized that at once."

Lady Irving sniffed her disbelief from the depths of her armchair, yet a prickle of uncertainty raced between Louisa's shoulder blades.

She might be wrong in her answer. Oats sounded like the sort of thing Alex *would* be interested in. Though it had been Lord Xavier at his Lord Xavier-est who'd organized the game.

Her aunt beckoned their host to her chair, a martial set to her jaw. "You. Rapscallion. Over here."

Apparently not even a laughing earl could gainsay this summons. He strode to the countess's side and bowed. "My name is pronounced *zay-vee-er*, dear lady. But I presume you had something more in mind than a refresher in elocution?"

Lady Irving shot an arm out and grabbed his neckcloth. She worked her beringed fingers into the starched linen folds and yanked his face down to the level of hers. "We know the secret word, and it wasn't *oats*."

He made a choking sound. "Please, dear lady. Have a care for my *trone d'amour.*"

She released him with a shove, and Alex straightened, rubbing at his jaw and stretching his neck. This cavalcade of fidgets was sufficient to cloak any change in his expression, Louisa realized.

But then his eyes caught hers, and he dropped his hand to his side. "I should like very much to speak with your niece." The words were for Lady Irving, but his gaze remained fixed on Louisa's face.

"Does my niece wish to speak with this man?" Lady Irving turned to Louisa, her lips pursed.

Bless Aunt Estella. Louisa gave her hand a quick squeeze. "I suppose I could stomach the idea of speaking to him for a bit."

The countess snorted. "I suppose you could, at that." She removed her turban, fluffed her hair and replaced the headgear. The fine lines around her mouth, her eyes, looked more pronounced as she concentrated on this ritual.

Finally, she composed herself again and nodded. "I'll give you an hour alone, and I'll create such a diversion that no one notices your absence. *But*"—she raised a forefinger, staring Alex in the face, then Louisa—"you two had better come to some sort of understanding. No more of this shilly-shallying about."

"I'm more than ready for an understanding," Alex said.

Dreadful man. He was nothing of the sort. Hadn't he transformed love into a game?

"I have a great deal to say to the earl," Louisa said in her sweetest voice. "Though I'm not sure he'll care to hear it."

Lady Irving rolled her eyes. "Spare me the romantic patter, you two lovebirds. You obviously have much to discuss. Go on, then. Go. *One hour.*"

* * *

It was more than Alex had hoped for: an hour alone with Louisa, with her aunt's blessing. He strode down the corridor, dragging her by the arm, unwilling to waste a single precious second.

As soon as he locked the library's heavy wooden door behind them, Louisa shook herself free of his grasp. Her cheeks were flushed, and she was breathing fast with rising emotion.

"You're ready for an understanding? You—you—hid me behind an oat!"

It wasn't funny. It wasn't. He kept his face carefully sober. "Louisa, I hid *myself* behind an oat. I didn't want to confess my feelings before a crowd, no. Considering you and I have not had a single conversation of substance since you returned to my house, I had no idea how you would respond."

Just as he'd counted on her love of puzzles to help her through the game, he counted on her sense of fairness to hear him out. After a pause, she nodded, though her jaw was still set. "That makes sense."

Cool relief shot through him. But this was only the beginning. "To be honest, you're right, too. I *did* hide you. That is—I knew you would figure out the right answer, but I didn't want to make a spectacle of you by revealing it before everyone. That could have been embarrassing for us both."

"That . . . makes sense as well." Her brows were knit.

"I told Jane and Pellington the truth, so they'd be interested enough to go along with the game. But for everyone else—well, I thought it would be more shocking to speak about land management than romance. New leaf, new year, et cetera."

Her posture began to loosen. "You showed them Alex. Just a bit."

"Just a bit," he agreed. "They weren't impressed, were they?"

She gave a little shrug. "It'll do for a start."

"There's—there's something . . ." He had to clear his throat. "There's something I wish to show you, too."

He fumbled for the tail pocket of his coat and found the heavy gold circlet within.

He'd chosen this ancient ring from among the collection of jewelry belonging to the earldom. Embossed on the broad band were a tiny goddess, a stag, and a dog tearing out the poor animal's heart, a blood-red ruby. The story of Actaeon; a man unmade for love.

He held it out, tongue locked. Hoping she had the usual feminine love of shiny objects and would draw nearer.

She did. Her hand stretched out, touched the ring, and then whipped back to her side as though the gold had burned her fingertips.

"You have a ring."

"I . . . yes, I do." Didn't she understand?

She blinked at him. "It's hideous."

Before his stomach could turn more than one sickening flip, she folded his fingers over it, closing it away. "Alex. Not—not yet. There are some things we need to discuss."

"Very well. Begin."

"No. You must begin." She moved around the chaise longue, facing him across its golden width. "Please, tell me why you sent me away in such an ugly manner. You shamed me before a dear relative. Why?"

He knew he had hurt her, but hearing it from her own lips was more dreadful than he could have imagined. And there was no Numbered Expression to help him now; nothing but a slow bleed of regret through his body, clutching at his heart.

He'd once told her he didn't have one. Though he'd been teasing, he had never known what it was capable of. He hadn't known it could pound so hard as to roar in his ears; he hadn't known it could batter against his ribs and unmake him from the inside.

"I meant well," he began stupidly.

The explanation was more difficult than he'd expected. He wound up telling her about the text Lockwood had decoded; the implication about his parentage.

"Not that it could have endangered my title," he finished. "But it made me simply—well, not worth associating with anymore."

"Wasn't that for me to decide?" Her jaw was set. "Let me see if I've got this correct." She raised a forefinger. "All of your—what shall I call it? Pride? Hubris? Asinine behavior?"

He folded his arms. "You can continue with your sentence at any time."

"Fine, we'll leave it at asinine behavior. All of it was because of a few lines in that encoded book? Your pride was hurt because you thought Lockwood had a hold over you, and so you gave him even more power over you."

He dragged a hand through his hair. "His power over me never came from that book." Oh, damn. There was surely a right way to say this, and he was not going to be able to think of it. "Muffin," he said desperately, "his power over me was because of you."

She flapped her hand at him. "Yes, yes, the wager. I know. It didn't bother me, truly. I could tell you had something more within you than a rotten core."

"Much obliged, I'm sure." He sketched her a little bow. "But you misunderstand me. Lockwood, for all his faults, is a fairly perceptive fellow. And once he realized striking at my reputation would no longer be the greatest blow imaginable, he set out to discover what would. And he soon found it. You."

"You are saying that Lockwood tried to hurt you by hurting me in some way?"

"It would have been most painful to me." Somehow, he managed a light tone.

"More so to me, I've no doubt." She slid her hand across the back of the chaise, then moved idly around the room. To the table where they'd first sat and formed an alliance. To the shelf where he'd laid a volume of Dante he was embarrassed to admit he treasured.

"I'm sorry I made that wager," he blurted. "Well, partially sorry. If I hadn't made it, you wouldn't have come to the house party."

"True." She bit her lip. "Alex, I don't mind that you wagered on me. As you say, we'd never have come to this point if you had not. What I mind is that you let yourself be manipulated into it. Why did you ever allow a nonentity like Lockwood to badger you so?"

The final question was unspoken, but Alex heard it all the same. *Will it happen again?*

There was the crux of it.

He gripped the ring harder, letting the warm circlet imprint his skin. "Because I let everyone badger me."

It was nothing to be proud of. "Louisa, might I sit?"

She nodded, and he sank onto the edge of the chaise. She remained standing. Watching. Listening, thank God.

So he explained the truth he'd come to terms with. "I was orphaned as an infant—I don't tell you that for sympathy, but so you understand that I've raised myself, for better or worse. I had all the money in the world, plus a title. There was no tutor I couldn't manipulate, no friend I couldn't impress."

Tighter, he clutched the ring. He studied the roughened back of his hand. "I got in some . . . habits, let's say. I was always the one with money, or influence, or outrageous ideas. But that meant I could never *stop* having those things. Do you see?"

The cushion of the chaise sank; she'd seated herself at the other end. "You were trapped."

He nodded. "Dante doesn't interest the *ton*. Nor human frailty such as illness, nor simply a desire for quiet."

"Oh, I'm aware of that," she said drily.

He looked up. She was smiling at him, rueful and sweet. "I've lived that story, too. But do finish. Please."

Grimly, he did so. "That's it, in essentials. I agreed to Lockwood's wager because I always agreed. Because if I didn't pretend all the time—if I wasn't exactly what the scandal sheets wanted for their columns, or I didn't keep filling the betting book at White's—then no one would give a damn about me."

She was quiet for a long moment. "And what about all your women? The affairs—what purpose did they serve?"

Her smile was gone now; her eyes deep and bruised.

Aha. Sometimes she *did* react in the common way. She was worried, even jealous.

He scooted closer to her and pulled her feet into his lap. With his empty hand, he tugged off her ivory kid slippers, one after the other. "I don't think you realize how much of my life has been a lie, especially where women are concerned."

"Admitting deceit? That's an unconventional way to convince me of your trustworthiness." She stroked the velvet upholstery, her hand sliding back and forth, her eyes carefully averted.

And he realized she wasn't jealous. She was afraid.

Afraid she wouldn't be enough, maybe; that he'd lived a worthless life for so long, nothing could be worthwhile to him. He'd once been afraid of that, too, in the deepest depths of his jaded pretense.

His heart squeezed, painful and tight, as though embracing her. But all he could do was explain. He toyed with her stocking-clad toes, grateful for the distraction of this small intimacy. Grateful that she permitted it.

"Louisa. Look, I'm not untouched, but . . . I've been untouched for a long while. Rumor feeds itself, and it's simpler not to interfere with its appetites."

He shut his eyes. "Yet I let things get out of hand. My reputation was a midden, a heap of trash where everyone threw unwanted rumors and unattributed scandals. Was? It still is."

He wished she would pull him to her, wrap her arms around him and tell him, *Don't be ridiculous. It's all in the past. It doesn't matter.*

But that wasn't true. It *wasn't* in the past, because he still struggled with the consequences. And that meant she would, too. Even now she struggled, and she seemed untouchably distant all the while his fingers played over the silken toes of her stockings.

So he met her eyes and continued. "Not long ago I realized I'd lost control of it. My behavior will never be interpreted as I mean it to. I can never achieve anything respectable, no matter how much I want it."

"Well, it's certainly not going to be easy." Her voice was brisk. "You made the polite world fall in love with a mask. So why *should* they love you for taking that away?"

He froze.

She finished her speech. "I've little use for Lord Xavier,

but I'm rather fond of Alex. I believe he could achieve anything he sets his will to."

He pushed her feet from his lap. "The irony is dreadful— that the man everyone else loved is the man that drives you away from me."

"I'm not driven away," she insisted. "I only want to know whether Alex will stay around."

"Yes." He drew in a breath with an effort so great that it seemed the air was solid. "But so will the rest, Louisa. I can't leave the past behind so easily. It's all part of me. This need to be needed. How can I begin anew?"

He'd thought it would seem shameful, to admit this fear. But it was like puncturing a hot-air balloon; the puffery was gone at once, as soon as he said the words. "I *want* to begin anew. In some ways, I already have."

But it would take a long time to finish the job. For so long, he'd coasted through life. Now it was time for the uphill trudge.

"I can help with that," she said. "I'll wager my reputation against yours."

He groaned. "No more wagers, please."

"But you've already made this one. Why, you were so confident in my reputation as a proper, quiet bluestocking that you and Lockwood wagered on it. Aren't you as confident now?"

He regarded her warily. "I know you better now. I know it's not true."

"Not many others do. If the *ton* thinks of me at all, it thinks me everything dull and silent. So forgettable that I survived a family scandal with my reputation intact, because— well, who cared for it?"

"I care for it."

She stretched out her hand, found his, and gripped it. "I know you do. I also know that if we wager your reputation against mine, I will win. There's nothing so dull in the eyes of the gossips as a happily married man. Your rakish reputation won't last a season, as long as you don't feed it." She smiled. "And if I win, we both win. So it's not really a wager at all, is it?"

He was still stuck on something she'd said. "Not to be tedious about the matter, but you seemed to be saying that I'd be a happily married man. Are you going to—do you mean you will . . ."

It was dreadfully difficult to ask a question when the answer meant everything.

Her fingers trailed over the width of the velvet between them. "You are like your library, you know."

"Enlighten me. Is it my gilt-tooled binding?"

"You're not far off." She leaned closer, closer, mere inches away, and her features went hazy. But he knew them so well, he could have shut his eyes and still seen them clearly. "I see great potential. More than anyone has ever suspected."

"Careful, now. I might think you find me tolerable."

"You are intolerable," she murmured, raking her nails from his shoulder to his neck, scraping them through his close-clipped hair. "But I find you essential, nonetheless."

She had tugged his head close and whispered her lips over his before he understood her intention. And then—she plucked the ring from his folded hand and slid it onto her finger.

She drew back to the end of the chaise. Arm outstretched, she turned her hand to and fro, catching the light on the winking ruby heart of the stag.

"It *is* a hideous ring," she decided. "Yet I love it. Can you guess why?"

He shook his head, wordless. Still disbelieving.

"Because it has lasted. It's been treasured through the

ages. Not because of the way it looks, but because of what it represents. Devotion. Ingenuity. The pursuit of one's ambition." She smiled, that sweet, bright crescent-moon that had captured his notice from the first. "Also, it refers to literature, which is always to be desired."

There seemed to be a lump in his throat. "And what of he who gave it to you?"

She pursed her lips, all mischief. "Always to be desired."

She wore his ring; she smiled at him. After everything he'd said, everything he'd done and failed to do.

At last, he felt the purity of forgiveness—from her, and from himself.

Then she drew close to him again, a breath apart, and her features went indistinct. "Always," she murmured. "Alex, we are sitting on a perfectly good chaise. Might I touch you a bit?"

"That would be acceptable." He tried to remember where he'd laid his dignity.

"And you would touch me, too?"

"Ah. Yes. I could oblige you in that matter."

She laughed, a sweet vibration against the skin of his neck. "How biddable you are. I think I'll like marriage."

He drew in a deep breath, cradling her against his body. How well they fit together. Her head was nestled in the hollow of his shoulder; her lips moved against his skin. She was easy to reach, to kiss, to settle closely against his form.

"I can't promise to be biddable." A smile stretched his face. No, a *grin*. "But I will promise to do my utmost to make sure you like marriage."

"Fair enough," she said. "I'll do the same."

Her hot tongue touched the hollow behind his jaw, and in a tangle of limbs and garments, they sank once again onto the fortunate gold-velvet chaise.

Chapter 29

Containing Lord Xavier's Final Absolution

She didn't mean to. She truly did not. But Louisa started *thinking* again as soon as her shoulders hit the reclined back of the chaise, as soon as Alex curved his body against hers.

"We only have an hour. How much time is left to it?"

His hand slid beneath her waist, drew her closer. "Enough. Wheeling hasn't rung the gong."

The gong. As if Wheeling would truly sound it, and Alex and Louisa were meant to emerge, rumpled and giggling, to the applause of the other guests.

Ridiculous as it was, the idea made her smile. What a blessing it would be, to cast off all masks and show the world, *yes, we want each other. No, we are not who you thought*.

He rested his forehead against her hair. "I like these beads. Very fancy. Let me get a better look." The hand not currently holding her waist began to work at the glass beads wound through her hair.

"I'll never get my hair pinned back up." Not much of

a protest. As he cradled her, only a breath away, it was difficult to think why his hands mustn't tug pins from her hair, trail over her scalp, let the long curls tumble around her shoulders, over her bodice.

"I've been wanting to take your hair down and run my fingers through it," he murmured. "I wondered what it would feel like."

"It feels like hair. Just like yours."

"Ha. Not like mine, I assure you." Those fingers. They combed through her long hair, brushing her neck, shoulders, the tops of her breasts.

He wound strands around his fingers and held them to the firelight. "Your hair is a promise."

"What sort of promise?" Never could she let a question pass, even when she wanted to grab at his hands and start putting them all over her body.

There must have been a treacherous quaver in her voice, because he smiled. "Well, if I've removed your hairpins . . ." He released her hair from his upheld hand, letting the strands float free to tickle her skin. "Perhaps you'll let me remove something else."

"Indeed, yes." She thought for a moment. "You may start with your coat."

He paused, fingers still extended. And then he laughed.

A real laugh, still so rare that she felt she'd won a prize every time she heard it. The sound was low and rusty, shaking his body, shaking her along with him. Both arms wrapped around her, crushing the air from her lungs; then he released her and sat up.

"I didn't promise to be biddable, if you'll recall. But in this case, I'll oblige."

Rising to his feet, he began shrugging out of his coat. The garment was well-tailored, very snug, and his shoulders moved around quite a lot as he freed himself. Broad shoulders, flexing; the fabric sliding down his arms. Back-lit as he was by the fire, she could trace the shape of his arms through the thin linen of his shirtsleeves.

He tossed the coat onto a nearby chair, then tapped his chin with a forefinger. "What should come next?"

She swallowed heavily. "Your boots."

"A valiant effort at distraction, my dear. But it's your turn."

"Nonsense. You've already taken my shoes. And my beads, and my hairpins."

"You're right. We appear to be at an impasse."

"Then I suggest a compromise." Her stockinged toes clenched. "I could remove a garment of yours. Then you needn't surrender your pride completely."

He gave a soft sigh, the dark fringe of his lashes shadowing his cheeks. "I already have."

He sank onto the chaise again and laid a hand on her waist. The sweet intimacy of the gesture stole Louisa's breath; he lifted his hand at once, then looked at it as though he wasn't sure where to put it.

"You can touch me," she reassured him. His hand returned to her waist, but his brow was furrowed.

"Teasing is all well and good," he said. "But. You know. There are beds for this sort of thing. And if we're to be married, we could wait until we can use a bed."

He was offering to stop. To coil up her hair and shrug back into his coat. To walk her out of the room, rumpled but respectable, wearing his ring.

The decision was entrusted to her, and she considered it carefully. All along, she'd kept up barriers to protect her heart. She'd thrown away the mistletoe berry; she'd brought up other women, or his reputation, every time their intimacy grew too much to bear.

But he had trusted her, long before she gave him the

same gift. Now that she knew the depth of fear Alex had lived with for years—that no one would want to know him, or care for him, just as he was—why, he was a part of her. She *knew* him, through and through. His masks overlaid his surface, but they could never touch his heart.

And she had already given him hers. So what need was there to protect it anymore?

"Everything you say is perfectly accurate," Louisa said. "But that doesn't mean you're right."

He darted her a sidelong glance. His hand on her waist twitched.

"I trust you," she said. "All of you. Everything you are. And if you want to do something irrevocable this time, then . . . that would be all right."

"It would be *all right*? Would it be *tolerable*?"

He wasn't going to make it easy. Or perhaps he just wanted to be sure of her.

"It's what I want," she said. "If you're worrying about me, you needn't. If you think I need a bed, I don't. Besides, doesn't this seem more fitting? The library? This chaise?"

"You always did think this library had potential." He shook his head. "I never expected it to be this type."

Tighter, his hand gripped her. She covered it with her own. "Alex. I'm not sure whether I mentioned that I love you."

"I figured it out," he said. "I've gotten practice with decoding ciphers lately."

He drew in a breath so deep, it seemed to buoy his whole body. She drank in every sharp line of his face, the cool gray of his eyes that looked at her so warmly.

Then, with a shift and a slide, he was lying next to her, propped on one elbow. "You're very persuasive."

"You were willing to be persuaded, I think." She laid her hand over Alex's heart, sliding her fingertips over the eggshell satin of his waistcoat.

And then she started flicking open the buttons.

He smiled down at her, his eyes squinting in a valiant effort to bring everything into focus. So proud, so vulnerable, so . . . *delicious*.

"Close your eyes," she suggested. "And I'll close mine, too, and we'll do it all by touch."

He smiled, then obeyed. "I'm not being biddable. It just strikes me as a good idea."

"Very logical of you."

She couldn't resist studying him for a long moment: the half-moon shadows of his dark lashes, the faint blue circles beneath his eyes. The stubble that darkened his lean cheeks, the angle of his chin. He looked as though he'd been tired for a few days; worried, too. Yet he shut his eyes, left himself defenseless. In his vulnerability, she loved him more.

"You're not playing a prank on me, I hope," he said, eyes still shut. "You won't march out of here and leave me alone?"

"What a dreadful idea," she said. "I should never get my fill of you that way."

His eyes snapped open as he made a strange choking sound. "Oh, you'll get your fill of me."

Her cheeks reddened. He could see the change in color, she guessed, for his mouth kicked up on one side. "Close your eyes, my dear bluestocking."

This time, she obeyed.

Ah. She was glad she had, for her skin awoke when her sight was gone. His arms slid around her, a comfort, an embrace; then he guided her fingertips to the knots of his neckcloth, the heavy satin of the waistcoat she'd already unbuttoned, the fine linen length of his shirt. Layer after layer gave way under her fumbling touches; layer after layer of her own clothing followed his to the floor, loosened by his careful hands. She heard his boots thump to the floor—one, then two.

And then he leaned over her, his mouth a heated promise. They were skin against skin, the hairs of his chest tickling against her bare breasts, the lean muscled length of his legs stretched along her softer flesh.

Sliding his hand over her breast like the most indecent garment imaginable, he played his fingers over her skin. His fingers rolled over her nipple, trailed over its tip, circled and plucked. The slight roughness of his fingertips—quill-callused, winter-worn—abraded her in the lightest, sweetest way. Pleasure shot through her, made her wet.

He smelled *good*, clean and warm and smoky-sweet from his vetiver oil. She could have kissed him for days, holding his face steady with her ring-weighted hand. Her other hand went exploring; her nails grazed the muscled lines of his arms, the lean planes of his sides, the coarse dusting of hair on his chest. Down, down, she trailed her hands, wondering at the warmth of his skin, the shiver of his muscles beneath her touch.

Aha. There were his trousers, low on his hips. Which meant . . . *there*. She pressed and stroked and tormented until he gasped.

"Conducting research?" His voice sounded tight.

"Exactly." Even with her eyes closed, she made quick work of the buttons on the fall of his trousers. Before she could do more than brush against hot skin, he touched her wrist.

"Wait. I need a turn," he said.

She had no urge to protest, for his strong fingers stroked her breasts, trailed down her sides, followed the curve of her hips.

Parted her legs.

She squeezed her eyes shut and tried to surrender to

sensation. *Don't think don't worry it'll be fine the past is the past and we're alone and—*

"*Oh.*" He touched her lightly, sliding over her slippery folds, and her mill wheel of thoughts simply vanished like a cloud.

"Are you all right?"

"Yes." She shivered. "You could do that some more. If you want to."

"No, no. I'll do it some more if *you* want me to."

He trusted her to stop him; so he trusted her, too, to ask for what she wanted.

No more barriers. "Yes. I want more."

"Thank God," he said, and slid a finger inside of her.

She clenched her fists against the startling intimacy. Then he slid another finger within her and did something unspeakably clever, and it was her turn to gasp at the sweet shock.

With feather-light touches, he teased her, making her gasp again, bringing her to the brink of that unbearable pleasure. He held his own body carefully still; she could feel the tension in his abdomen, his corded legs. His hard shaft lay hot against her thigh, his pulse beating in a gentle throb against her sensitized skin.

"I'm ready," she said. "Do hurry up. You're making me impatient."

"I'm honored by your impatience," he said, but his laugh died when she gripped his hips and tugged him closer. He made that choking sound again, and it was her turn to laugh.

As he nudged within her, slowly, stretching, tight, she held onto that laugh, and let it carry her above the discomfort. *Trust.*

As soon as she'd made that vow to herself, the pain began to ebb, and he was fully seated within her body. With her eyes shut, she simply *felt*—felt the hard length of him within her, the long angles of his limbs entwined with hers, the sweet heat of his chest rubbing at her breasts. His cheekbone, pressing hers; his lips moving against her earlobe, murmuring words of comfort that she didn't need, but that she loved.

She wrapped her legs around his hips, drawing him deeper.

"I still don't have my fill of you," she said, for the pleasure of hearing him chuckle. For the pleasure of feeling him move within her.

And then there was nothing but pleasure itself, great washes and waves of it.

Unbelievably, Wheeling did ring the gong.

When the low sound rang down the passage, they had almost tugged their clothing back into place, and Alex was meant to be helping Louisa pin her hair back up. Startled, he bobbled the hairpins, and they pattered all over the floor.

Louisa froze. "I cannot believe it." She slid from the chaise and began gathering fallen hairpins. "Yes, actually, I can. This is surely my aunt's doing. Do you realize what sort of family you're marrying into?"

Alex crouched to help her. The little bits of curved metal had vanished against the patterned carpet, so he felt for them, laying them on the chaise. "It's my servant who rang the gong. Do you realize what sort of household you're marrying into?"

They met eyes and smiled. "I love you," he said. "I shan't need a code to tell you from now on."

"Much more efficient to say the words," she agreed. "I love you, too. Alex. Lord Xavier."

The coolness, the peace of forgiveness, washed over him

again. He laced his fingers together so he wouldn't grab for her again. Not yet. He'd done his utmost to let her have her fill of him, though he would never get his fill of her.

"Alex, look at the clock." She nodded toward the ornamental piece on the mantel. "We've been in here for well over an hour."

"So we have." He found the last of the hairpins—well, he thought it was the last—and lined it up on the chaise. "Then Wheeling must be gonging for some other cursed reason."

"That's lucky, because we can't rejoin the company like this." Louisa scooped up the hairpins. "Even with a ring." Her voice hitched, and she shot him another of those looks that was wry and shy at once.

He found his feet, pulled her into a hug and gave her a swift kiss on the lips. "We'll have to make a run for it," he decided. "Past the drawing room, up the stairs."

He unlocked the door and they were off in a flash, Louisa holding those ridiculous hairpins in one hand and smothering a laugh with the other. As they darted past the open drawing room, he glanced in and saw that the guests were dancing. Wheeling gonged again just then, and the dance fragmented into a swirl of partner-swapping.

Part of Lady Irving's plan to distract the other guests? Maybe. As they passed by quickly, tiptoe-running down the corridor, he didn't spot her.

When he next saw her, he owed her his thanks.

They reached the great staircase without being spotted, and they slowed to a walk up the wide flight. At the top of the stairs, Alex caught Louisa's hand before she could hurry to her bedchamber.

"From this point, we'll do everything respectably," he promised. "I'll write to your father for his permission."

"I think you may take it for granted. He's given my aunt

full authority to encourage, forbid, and execute suitors as she sees fit."

In that case, he owed Lady Irving his *lifelong* thanks. By giving them an hour alone, she'd essentially given her blessing to their marriage.

"I'll speak to her tomorrow," he said. "We can begin calling the banns this Sunday. Unless you'd prefer to be married by special license? Much more à la mode."

She nibbled on her lower lip. Lord, she was lovely. And he was besotted. He knew it.

"It will mean a longer wait," she decided, "but let us have your vicar call the banns. That way, your tenants will be among the first to learn of our marriage."

Ah, his tenants. In time they would come to trust him to look out for them; he was determined on that. He would start by being present in their lives. He and the new countess. A new beginning for them all.

"That's an excellent idea," he said. "I always knew you were brilliant."

"Well, I'm not going to argue with *that*." She smiled. "In return, I'll say: I know you're not being biddable. Just logical."

Which reminded him.

"Louisa, I need your logic. And your brilliance, too, if you don't mind working out one last puzzle. Will you meet me in the portrait gallery tomorrow at noon?"

Chapter 30

Containing
Lord Lockwood's Entrapment

The portrait gallery was a long, echoing chamber; a wide corridor that spanned the first story of Clifton Hall's central structure. Because of its great size, it seemed always too bright and dim at once, the light from tall windows spilling stark and cold halfway across the antique carpet. The portraits themselves hung on the shadowed opposite wall, massive in their carved gilt frames, capped by sconces. Even in daytime, the painted images were lit only by these ovals of yellowed candlelight.

Alex seldom ventured here. It had always seemed like a mausoleum in brushwork; a place for a tutor to bore him with history or chastise him for not living up to the family name.

With the information he'd gathered, he now knew exactly what that family name meant.

Ah. Louisa was approaching, calm and elegant in a leaf-green gown. On her finger was the wide gold band he'd given her. She looked delectable.

Never mind that, though. They were here to neuter Lockwood. Figuratively speaking. But it would be good enough.

Before the marquess became visible, they heard his footsteps echoing up the wide staircase, then softening on the carpet that stretched the length of the gallery.

"Ah, Coz." His voice was soft and venomous. "I came a few minutes early, and how fortunate that was. Am I interrupting a tête-à-tête? That almost makes waking up before noon worthwhile."

As he drew close, a rictus stretched across his features. Not a smile. It was tighter than that, and a little desperate around the edges.

Alex couldn't find it within himself to pity the man, even knowing what was coming. "Lockwood, about that. I know you like to be the first to know everything, but considering the hours you keep, it was impossible today."

"Shall I tell him, my love?" Louisa looked up at Alex with a limpid, sheep-eyed expression such as he doubted had ever crossed her features before.

"If you wish, turtledove." Alex gave her a soppy look. Nearby, Lockwood huffed, scuffing his boots on the carpet.

"I see I was right," he said in a harsh voice. "There is something going on between the two of you. Dear me. I hope I don't slip and tell everyone."

"Tell everyone what?" In unison, they spoke, turned their heads to Lockwood, and blinked. It was a fine performance. As fine as any Lord Xavier had carried out.

"That we're to be married?" Alex furrowed his brow. "We made the announcement to the house party at breakfast. The ladies were most vocal in their reactions. I'm surprised you slept through it."

This was perfectly true. It had been a feat of charm, persuasion, and bribery with pastries to rouse the other guests and convene them before the sun hit its height. The fervor with which the news of their betrothal had been received made the effort worthwhile. If a few of the congratulations held more surprise than warmth, well, that was to be expected. Jane's delight at welcoming Louisa into the family had been both heartfelt and genuine.

Lockwood assimilated this news, his blue eyes narrowing. "Xavier." Aha, he'd retrieved that soft voice. Apparently it was meant to be threatening. "I did tell you what would happen if you proposed to Miss Oliver."

Alex's soppy persona shattered in an instant. "So you did. But I didn't tell you what would happen if you threatened me, or my future bride."

He summoned all the gravity of Lord Xavier's wintry disdain; all the heat of his own heart. "Miss Oliver and I will be married. Therefore, if you trespass against her, you trespass against me."

He let this sink in, then went on. "I might add, Lockwood, that if you threaten a gently bred woman who is known to be betrothed to your relative, the dishonor will be yours. And it won't be only me you'll have to answer to; it will be every woman in the *ton*."

Lockwood blinked, then recovered. "A word in the right ear, then, and I can still—"

"Oh, stop, Lord Lockwood," said Louisa. "As I intended to say when you first joined us, Lord Xavier and I don't wish to be troubled by your threats. It seems you think you have two holds over him."

"Three, my pigeon," corrected Alex, again in his

lovesick-swain voice. Even as an obvious fiction, it annoyed Lockwood.

Louisa's lips twitched; *pigeon* had tested her straight-faced resolve too much. "Muffin," he corrected.

"Yes. Three. You're right," she agreed. "There are three issues at stake. First, your cousin thinks he can threaten me—well, I hope he doesn't think that anymore. Second, he thinks the encoded book implies you're not the son of the previous earl."

"A bit of a bastard, you mean? I certainly can be at times," Alex said heartily.

Louisa surreptitiously stomped on his foot. "*Third*. He believes you fear for your reputation."

"*He* is right here," said Lockwood. "And you are correct. I can still hurt you, Xavier."

Alex dropped his cheerful mien again and looked Lockwood up and down coolly. God. The man was wearing a lavender cravat again. "Likewise."

He half turned to gesture at the portrait behind him. "Recognize this fellow?"

The full-length painting showed a dark-haired gentleman in the garb of Caesar. His head was wreathed in laurel, his body sheathed in the armor of war and the draperies of peace. Not a very memorable portrait, in truth, except for the expression on its subject's face. In the yellow light of the sconce, his dark features smirked, as though he knew a joke upon the whole world.

Lockwood made an impatient slash with his hand. "It's you, of course. I fail to see the point."

"Wrong." Xavier stood aside. "It's my father. He had this painted for my mother upon the occasion of their marriage. What about this bewigged gentleman next to him? Put a peruke on me, and I could pose for this one, too. That's my grandfather. How far back do we need to go?"

Lockwood's eyes had narrowed further. Too bad for him. Nothing could block out the evidence before him.

"I think that'll do," said Louisa. "You see, Lockwood, your cousin—yes, he is indeed your cousin—busied himself with research in my absence. The longtime servants of this house remember the late earl. They knew him as dissolute, yes. But his countess? No. Any child of hers was a child of her husband's."

"The word of servants." Lockwood sneered. "It's worth nothing. I still have—"

"The book? I thought you'd say that." Alex turned his back on his grandfather's portrait. The old roué probably would have enjoyed this scene. "As it so happens, I believe a near-century of portraiture is better evidence than either the words of servants or a few lines in an old ledger. But if you don't believe me, I wonder if you recall the form of your father's handwriting. Quite a historian, wasn't he? I think I've heard you say so."

Lockwood stilled. Slowly, he turned his head to one side. "His handwriting."

"Yes. The estate records include plenty of old letters exchanged by our fathers. It's evident he wrote out that ledger," Alex said. "Most likely he encoded the book for his own amusement, to make it look like an heirloom. Hoped to tangle the line of future Xaviers, perhaps. You've given it a fair effort, I'll grant you that. But I doubt the word of a long-dead, self-interested gentleman is worth anything to society."

Lockwood didn't give up easily. Alex would grant him that, too. "What of your precious reputation, then, Coz? Only I know how much of a falsehood it is, and with—"

"Wrong." Louisa folded her arms, tall and straight as a lily. "I know it, too. I also know a bit about *your* reputation. You brought a mistress here last year, didn't you?"

The marquess backed up and leaned against the stone mullion between two of the huge windows. "That's hardly relevant."

"But you've introduced so many subjects." Her tone was honey over acid. "How are we to judge which are relevant or not?"

Lockwood shoved himself upright and began to pace. Good. They were getting to him.

"I believe you parted with Melissande on bad terms, not long ago," Alex said. "You left her short of funds, did you not? And so she's preparing her memoirs. How do you think your own reputation will fare when the polite world knows you buy ladybirds you can't afford, and you like to be hit upon the—"

"Stop!" Lockwood whirled on them. "Stop. Just . . . stop." He was breathing heavily. "I have the funds. I can pay her."

"About that." Louisa tapped her chin. "You came into some money recently, didn't you? You made a wager on me."

"As did he." Lockwood jabbed a finger at Alex.

"Not that wager." If possible, Louisa held herself straighter. She looked down her nose at Lockwood, already every inch a countess. "You placed a side bet at White's."

They had *la signora* to thank for this information. Lockwood flinched, proving its veracity.

Louisa continued, ruthlessly calm. "You bet everything you had, and much that you didn't, on being able to best Lord Xavier. That's why you were so determined to make me leave. You didn't have ten pounds riding on it; you had *everything*."

"And I won."

This, Alex was not proud of. "So you did. You used my reputation for your own gain. Well. It wasn't the first time."

He realized he'd been bottling up his breath along with his anger. He forced air in and out; felt his shoulders relax. "Lockwood, it needs to be the *last* time you do so. You won that side wager, but your behavior in doing so drew notice. It wasn't good *ton*, shall we say. The women at this party are letter-writers, and word got back to London."

"The word of women is of no concern to me," Lockwood said. Louisa's head snapped up.

Alex could have throttled him for that remark. "Lockwood. Do consider. Women talk to men. Will men of honor choose to wager with you again? Considering you won a pile off a none-too-pleased royal duke, I should say not."

He wished for the sake of their bygone friendship that the marquess would listen, yet he knew this was unlikely. "You've lined your pockets, but your own reputation is as fragile as straw. Have a care with it."

Lockwood shot him a filthy look. "You dare to lecture me? You, casting stones?"

Alex shrugged. "I'm telling you what *is*, Lockwood. You may do what you like with the information. But know this: I will never again make a wager unworthy of the people I care about. Or myself. You're on your own."

Again in unison, he and Louisa turned their backs. He offered her his arm, and together they progressed down the long portrait gallery as though they were strolling through a garden. Only Alex felt the tension in her fingers; only she felt the cords in his arm.

Lockwood, they left behind. Where the marquess chose to go from there, Alex didn't care.

When they reached the sweeping marble staircase, Louisa squeezed his arm, then released it. "I think that went fairly well," she murmured.

"Extremely, I should say. Come, we'll find somewhere else to speak." He motioned for her to follow him up the stairs. The curving flight split here, winding upward to the second story with its less elaborate rooms.

Aha. He opened a door on a small, sunny parlor with trellised wallpaper. "You might like this as your sitting room when you're countess."

Louisa put a hand to her forehead as she sank onto a pinstriped chair. "Countess. I can hardly credit it."

As he closed the door, she looked up sharply. "Wait. A sitting room here? You wish—you don't wish to live always in London?"

"Not always. I find that I like it here," he decided. "In the country. It could be nice to see it when the grass and trees are growing, don't you think? If you've no objection."

"Objection? No, indeed. I love living in the country." She shot him a wicked little smile. "Though I also think I'll enjoy London life as I never expected to."

"I shall do my best to make sure that's so," he said. "There's a library in my town house, too."

Another wicked smile. He met hers with his own, crouching to take her hands, meet her gaze at eye level.

"Do you realize," she observed, "how much research you did to protect yourself from Lockwood? Talking to the butler, and to Signora Frittarelli. Your dear housemaid Ellie deserves some compensation for all she imparted to us, too."

Always so full of thoughts. And more impressed by his

digging for information than she would be by a diamond necklace.

Her respect made him feel every inch an earl, at long last.

"Machiavelli gave me the idea," he said. "'Among other evils which being unarmed brings you, it causes you to be despised.'"

She smiled. "There's more to Machiavelli than arming oneself. 'The friendship which is gained by purchase and not through grandeur and nobility of spirit is merited but is not secured.'"

"You quote Machiavelli, too." He turned her hand and traced tiny circles on the underside of her wrist. "I should not be surprised."

"Never. And you were never unarmed, either. Do you see? You think you've bought your friends, but your social power is real. People like to follow you. Now you can decide where you want to lead them."

He had to think that one over. "You may be right. Lord Xavier might not be such a worthless fellow after all."

"I know I'm right."

He laughed. "Without constant reminders from Lockwood," he said, "Lord Xavier can begin to fade away. Someday, we won't even have to talk of him as though he's a false person."

"I'd like that," Louisa decided. "I think you would, too. Much less tiring to be only one person. But a talent for acting will never go amiss."

He pressed a kiss to the underside of her wrist; touched it with the tip of his tongue. She closed her eyes. "That talent won't go amiss, either."

He sat back on his heels. "I can show you much more than that."

Oh, what a wicked smile. "I should like to see it. Give me your finest performance."

So he did. Not because he was biddable. Simply because of love.

And when he called to her to come, shatter with him, she did so at once. For the same reason.

Epilogue

Containing a Wedding, Then a Marriage

When the banns were called for the marriage of Alexander Edgware, the ninth Earl of Xavier, to the Honorable Louisa Oliver, the *ton* indulged in much speculation.

The men of the *ton* decided that there must be something extraordinary about the young lady in question. Seven seasons' worth of the most beautiful maidens in England had been unable to entrap the earl.

The women of the *ton* thought the reverse. They, better than their husbands and fathers and lovers, remembered the quiet young woman who'd once been dragged into a scandal. She had vanished from society after that—only to turn up betrothed to Xavier. What appeal would a notorious rake hold for a shy bluestocking?

Unless . . . he wasn't. Or unless she wasn't.

The solution to this puzzle was not provided by Lord Lockwood, who returned to London shortly after Twelfth Night. Though the marquess was much-plied with invitations from the curious, he was disappointingly close-lipped about the whole affair. In fact, he was quiet about everything, attending few parties. He drank much brandy at White's. Sometimes he requested the betting book and paged through it slowly. He was thought—only in masculine circles—to have transacted some business with a former mistress.

The puzzle only grew more obscure when Xavier's wedding took place. The modish earl was married not in fashionable St. George's church in London, but in the tumbledown old country church on his property. It was rumored that some of his tenants had attended, and that a notorious opera singer had performed a soaring aria for the occasion.

By the time the London season began in the spring, rumor floated everywhere, like dandelion seed. Perhaps the bride was heavy with child. Perhaps she had a mysterious power of influence.

But Lady Alleyneham and Lady Irving, the most sociable and most forceful countesses of the polite world, took the new Lady Xavier under their wing. And society's matrons soon saw that the young countess—who was neither visibly pregnant, nor possessed of supernatural gifts—was a pleasant sort. If she was quiet, she had a lovely smile. And when one spoke to her at length, there was no denying she was a wit.

As the season stretched on, the *ton* became accustomed to seeing Xavier at the theater with his wife rather than a lightskirt. It made sense, too, that a recently wed man might choose to go home to his wife at times, rather than staying out till all hours at his club.

Over time, the betting book at White's would fill with other names. That was the way of the world. Lord Xavier's ruling years had been riotous, but he was by no means indispensable to the *beau monde*'s happiness.

To his wife, however, he was. By any and every name.

Author's Note

Regency Christmas celebrations were often very mild affairs. Most of the traditions we now associate with an old-fashioned English Christmas (Christmas trees, caroling, elaborate gift-giving) came about during the Victorian era, a few decades later. Our Regency counterparts did enjoy a good pudding, though, as well as party games and a kiss under the mistletoe.

Sharp-eyed readers will note that Twelfth Night occurs on January 5th in this book. While we sometimes celebrate it on January 6th today—counting the 12 Days of Christmas from December 26th—during the Regency, the 12 Days began on Christmas Day itself. Twelfth Night and Epiphany were distinct celebrations.

Charades in the Regency were more elaborate than the way the game is played now. Instead of a single actor miming a word at a time, a group of actors might present a tableau (scenery and all!) representing a word from a phrase or poem. In SEASON FOR SURRENDER, Xavier's accomplices play a form of charades called Nebuchadnezzar, in which one *letter* at a time is performed. Nebuchadnezzar hit its height of popularity in the early 1900s, but there's no reason a clever and half-drunk crowd couldn't have played this form of charades during the Regency.

Finally—just what is the problem with Xavier's vision? Nothing that couldn't be corrected today with a pair of reading glasses. He has *simple hyperopia*, which is a genetic form of farsightedness resulting from a too-short eyeball. A convex lens can correct this condition. Since Xavier can't bring himself to wear spectacles, we must assume he had his quizzing glass ground to suit his needs.

Did you miss SEASON FOR TEMPTATION?

Two Sisters . . .

Julia Herington is overjoyed when her stepsister, Louisa, becomes engaged—to a viscount, no less. Louisa's only hesitation is living a life under the *ton*'s critical gaze. But with his wry wit and unconventional ideas, Julia feels James is perfect for Louisa. She can only hope to find a man like him for herself. Exactly like him, in fact . . .

One Choice . . .

As the new Viscount Matheson, James wished to marry quickly and secure his title. Kind, intelligent Louisa seemed a suitable bride . . . until he met her stepsister. Julia is impetuous—and irresistible. Pledged to one sister, yet captivated by another, what is he to do? As Christmas and the whirl of the London season approach, James may be caught in a most scandalous conundrum, one that only true love, a bit of spiritous punch—and a twist of fate—will solve . . .

Available now from Kensington!